UNFINISHED
BUSINESS

A Novel by
Richard Alan Melheim

Creative Outlet

This book belongs to the category of writing often referred to as "faction." Although the main characters are a fabrication of the author, they live on the pages of world history from August 2, 1990 (the beginning of the Gulf Crisis) to November 3, 1992 (the election that determined the winner of the Gulf War). This being the case, all conversations and actions of actual public figures involved with the fictional characters in these historical events are also sheer fabrication and not intended to demean, denigrate, libel or defame anyone. They are added simply to create realism and aid in the telling of a good story.   - RAM

Library of Congress Cataloging in Publication Data

Melheim, Richard Alan
        UNFINISHED BUSINESS/by Richard Alan Melheim.
        ISBN #0-9635106-0-6
        1. Fiction. 2. Gulf War. 3. Saddam Hussein. 4. Arab (as hero)

PART I
The Shield

Chapter 1: Dark Swans

Al Jahrah Bay, Kuwait City
December 22, 1990

"This is it," whispered the Kuwaiti. "But where is our man?"

"Are you sure he *is* a man?"

Startled pigeons cooed from a nearby cage as the two shoved a rusted door open and stepped out onto the warehouse roof. A small tin coffee pot perked on a glowing blue kerosene stove in one corner. In another sat a polished M-16 propped against a plastic Christmas tree. Oversized boxer shorts flapped together with a huge woman's dress in the evening breeze.

"Coffee's on. *Wausau's* been here in the last 10 minutes... or someone has."

"Maybe we scared him off."

They searched the dusty rooftop but found no one. Francis scanned a dark horizon to take his bearings. The three story hide-out butted directly up against a wooden pier. Other than the central staircase, the only exit was an iron fire escape along the west wall. *Shobash* motioned to the ladder with his eyes. "Do you wish to split up?"

"That's OK. I'd feel more comfortable if we stuck together on this one." They were turning back to the staircase when he heard it: something like the sound of an automobile door latching in the streets below. *Shobash* squinted at the shadows. Was there a car parked out on the end of the wharf? The world was all too black to tell.

"I don't like it. Let's get out of here."

The sudden blinding flash of a white hot flare made instant daylight of the blanket that had hidden them. Francis slid to the north side of the flat roof in time to catch the silhouette of an Iraqi Army truck emptying a dozen men and three dogs onto the pier. In the fading light he could make out the shapes of two or three other vehicles with scores of soldiers piling out on the west side. Then again all was black. The streets whispered and a cautious ascent began on the fire escape as men crept in to take position.

A cheap bull horn barked a "hold fire" order, then aimed its nasal voice toward the roof as a second flare lit the night: "Good evening, Ali al Bakr. Or should I say '*Shobash' Shobash!* And also to you, Captain Francis Khalil. It would be my distinct pleasure to visit with the two of you alive tonight. If, however, you should choose..." The voice sputtered off and his threat could not be heard above the sudden frenzy of advancing dogs and men.

Khalil gripped his new friend's arm. "Any suggestions?"

"You're the Marine."

"Hey, I'm just an analyst."

"So! Analyze!"

Francis snapped up the extra M-16 to add to his arsenal. "How many clips you got for the Uzi?"

"Three."

"Damn. Anything else?"

Shobash shook his head and emptied his first cartridges onto the fire escape below. Three men fell silent while others cursed, ducking into the block door frames to return fire. It had begun.

"How about you?"

"What?"

"You got anything else?"

"A headache."

Bullets began to fly now from three sides of the street. *Shobash* winced as a hail of lead pocketed the blocks above him, covering his red checkered head dress with white chalk and plaster. Francis scuttled to the stairway door and slammed its dead bolt in place to buy time. The second flare died and was followed by a momentary moratorium.

"Any ideas?"

Fran glanced about the rooftop. "How bad is the coffee?"

The Kuwaiti smiled. "I would have liked to have known you."

Another flare ignited the sky and the Marine spotted two Iraqis setting up shop on the lower roof of a building to his right. His M-16 made quick business of them. "Nice shooting, cowboy."

"Thanks." *Shobash* raked the outer fire escape once more to stall the advance, then threw in another clip.

A sudden concussion tore the heavy center door from its hinges, propelling steel and stone across the roof. The enemy was now in the hallway one floor below. Francis and Ali could hear their wild debate as an angry officer attempted to order his men through the passage. Their willing weapons turned to give the uninvited guests a proper welcome.

"Oh, yes. Almost forgot." *Shobash* dug a smoke grenade from his pack. "I've got one of these."

"Just happened to have one..."

He crabbed over to the doorway, pulled the pin, kissed the canister "goodbye" and rolled it gently down the stairs. A choking grey cloud billowed immediately through the opening as one of the poor beggars stumbled out of the poison and onto the roof. He lay gasping for breath not five feet from Ali. The Kuwaiti paused a moment, as if contemplating a next step. His unfortunate prey raised on all fours and opened his eyes to the muzzle. *Shobash* spoke calmly to the young soldier. "This one is for an old man who once shaded me from the sun. Your people slashed his throat." He placed the Uzi to the trembling boy's forehead and squeezed off a single shot.

A righteous anger surged to join the adrenaline pulsing through the Marine's veins. "You enjoyed that!"

"Enjoyed? You don't know me well, friend. I despise it."

"But you didn't have to..."

"Whether I spoke to his face or shot him in the back, would he be any less dead?" Francis began to shake. "Hostages, my friend. We are all simply victims and hostages. Every one of us."

A fourth and a fifth flare lit the night together as the wild tracers streamed up at them like bottle rockets on the Fourth of July. Khalil rained the first M-16 down to empty and clicked a final cartridge into his own. The Kuwaiti waved a "peace" or "victory" sign at him from across the roof, then pointed to his gun.

"What?"

"Two bullets."

"What do you mean?" He thought twice before realizing what *Shobash* meant. Two. Save two bullets for the end. Francis looked at the warmed weapon in his hands and then back to the Kuwaiti. "What will they do if they capture us?"

"We are dead."

"And if we keep fighting?"

"We are dead."

"Doesn't leave us many options."

They sat together, backs to the wall, spitting cement dust and attempting to catch their breath. Francis was numb. His legs tingled and his mind flew at 1000 mph. For all his training and all his experience, the young man was still afraid. He didn't want to die. Not like this. For the third time in 28 short years, Francis held a gun toward his own temple. The next few moments froze in time and the world grew strangely still. Noise, bullets and smoke seemed to be swallowed by the very air. He said a prayer. He fingered the trigger. Then for some reason he snapped up. *Shobash* was smiling at a silver moon as it rose over the bay.

"Beautiful, no?"

Khalil didn't answer. The soft light seemed to eclipse his friend's face.

"Do you have a woman? A wife perhaps?"

Francis thought it odd to be asked such a question at a time like this. He wondered a moment more, then nodded. "I... uh... I think I still do."

"You think so?" *Shobash* began to laugh. "In my country a man usually knows such things."

"No, I..." Francis shrugged his shoulders. Maybe it wasn't such a bad image with which to end one's life. "Yes. I do. I do. And you?"

"Oh, yes, my friend. Yes. And she is as beautiful and as dangerous as this night."

Francis smiled at a thought: "I suppose we could use these pigeons here to send a message to our women for help."

Ali grinned back. "They would certainly come to our rescue faster than you Americans have."

The Marine let out a genuine laugh and pushed his partner's face away. "I would have liked to have known you, too."

The smoke wore off in the stairway below and another volley of bullets began to shower through the opening. "I believe this is it, my friend." Ali placed his Uzi into the American's trembling hand and knelt toward the bay. "Would you care to do the honors?"

Francis stared at the foreign object, then down toward his new friend. The blue-white moonlight shimmered for a moment, then disappeared behind a cloud. A lone gull cried out. "I don't think I can..." Francis began.

"Good night, my friend."

"I don't..."

"*Shobash,* my friend. In a moment we shall both fly..."

Two heads locked up simultaneously in one thought. Ali rose and they ran together to the back side of the roof to stare out at the black waters. The warehouse, built on a pier's edge, had only the one-lane wooden road separating it from the bay.

"Did you ever see *Butch Cassidy and the Sundance...*" Francis began. "No, I suppose not."

"You think it gets deep right away?" Francis didn't answer. The resistance fighter appeared more nervous about the water than about the bullets whizzing past his head. "It looks to me as there are some rocks down there."

"Yeah. And there's lead up here."

Shobash hesitated again. "But do you think there might be rocks..."

"One way to find out." Francis climbed onto the ledge. Ali still hesitated. "What's wrong?"

"I don't swim."

"That makes us even." Francis beamed his boyish smile. "I don't fly."

A sixth flare hit the tormented sky. Orders were given. And moments later, just as the enemy stormed over the top of an empty fortress, the shadows of two dark swans were swallowed by the night.

Chapter 2: Raoul Wallenberg
Somewhere over Eastern Iraq
August 7, 1990

A light *recon* plane floated silently through night skies, invisible to the sleeping sands below. Over the headset a young voice crackled his wake-up call: "We're here. 30,000 feet and targeting *Zulu Charlie Zulu*. Are you sure you're up to this, captain?"

"How high did you say we were?" asked the dark-eyed Marine.

"High enough, sir," returned the voice. "High enough that they don't know we're here. Not yet, anyway. You'll have to 'Peter Pan' it on your own to about 1000 if you want to get under their radar. That gives you roughly eight seconds to pull the cord and open before you hit. That's it. Eight seconds."

"I suppose we all gotta go some time," joked the soldier.

"Yes, sir."

They stalled. The pilot turned to his comrade with an honest salute. The Marine nodded in silence, clipped a leather briefcase to his chest, inhaled and stepped out to join the night.

In the first days of the Iraqi invasion it was not all clear just what the aggression would mean. The people of Kuwait City huddled in their homes in total disbelief. Some went to work but did little more than talk and speculate. Others shopped. Children attended schools, instructed to go on as if not much had happened.

The invaders left most civilians alone initially. Some walked into stores, gathered items and left without paying. Frightened shop owners rarely objected. There were scattered reports of brutality and abuse at check points. Rumors of looting and isolated cases of rape spread - mostly among the servant class of Pakistanis, Filipinos, and Indians. (Those who had little money and less voice.)

By the second week a gnawing dread crept in and Westerners realized that it would be in their best interest to leave the country. Suspicion and panic seized the day as internationals disappeared without telling friends where they were going. Questions filled the air and haunted sleep. The word *"detainee"* was heard for the first time and the world wondered what it would mean.

Baghdad's rules and directives changed daily. At first all foreigners were free to go, but simply had to be processed. A few days later Westerners were instructed to proceed to the *El Rashid* Hotel for registration. No one took Iraq up on that. The government issued offers allowing women and children to go if they would leave their men behind as "guests" of Saddam Hussein. International airliners were chartered and worked around the clock to manage the exodus. Within a week the foreign planes were grounded and only Iraqi planes were permitted to lift anyone out.

As the fabric of society began to unravel, a flood of refugees streamed toward the Jordanian border: Westerners by the hundreds, Egyptians by the thousands, Asians by the tens of thousands. Most foreign nationals were in Kuwait on work permits. They had ventured to this oil rich sheikdom goaded by the promise of hard work and easy money with which to support families half a world away. Now, trapped in the desert with nowhere to go and no one to hear their cries, they found themselves at the mercy of the international community.

A few Westerners made it out in the initial days, begging, borrowing and bribing their way to freedom with tales of life in the new "Province 19." One young man escaped by offering a thirsty Iraqi soldier a can of Pepsi.

Within days, new orders came denying all male Westerners the right to passage. Many traveled to the border only to be turned back at the last moment or pulled from their cars, arrested and whisked away. One American was shot while attempting to escape. Czechs, Poles and bus-loads of Russians who wanted out could leave easily. But Westerners remained behind, expecting the worst.

In the basement of the Pentagon, a young Middle East specialist watched as a smiling caravan of East Germans passed into Jordan on CNN. And that image sparked the idea which ultimately brought Marine Captain Francis Khalil to make his jump.

"Raoul Wallenberg."

"What are you talking about?" asked the major as he stuffed his black leather portfolio with too many papers and tried to force it shut once more.

"Raoul Wallenberg," Francis smiled. "You remember the Swedish diplomat who saved hundreds of Jews from the SS by giving them counterfeit passports?"

"No." The major clicked his green desk lamp off and devoured the last of a stale cream cheese bagel.

"He'd show up at train stations and deportation centers and remove people right out from under the Nazi's noses. Bought or forged documents for them claiming they were Swedish citizens. Saved a lot of people."

"What are you getting at?"

"What would you think about having the boys downstairs make us some passports? They could be Canadian or East European. We talk to a few Ambassadors who are doing a half-decent job of getting their own folks out of Kuwait and request that they bring some of ours with them."

The major raised an eyebrow in amusement and gulped down what was left of a cold and awful cup of coffee. "Might work. I'll bring it to my staff meeting tomorrow." He rose. "Is that all?"

"No, sir. I'd like you to suggest one more thing." Francis handed his superior a written request.

"And that is?" The major reopened the overpacked briefcase chained to his wrist and crammed his young friend's paper in with the others.

"I'd like you to volunteer my name for the mission."

He searched the captain's eyes. The man was serious. Dead serious.

"I'd suggest we leave this one to the CIA. You're an analyst, not a spook. Besides, how are you going to pass for Swedish?"

"I am half Norwegian."

"And half Syrian."

"Lebanese."

"Whatever. Besides, you look too Arab."

"A little Lady Clairol and I'll look more Swedish than Bjorn Borg."

"Who?"

"Never mind. What do you say?"

The major's furrowed forehead creased all the more. "It would be like jumping into the mouth of a volcano, Khalil."

"What do you say?"

The old soldier rubbed his tired eyes.

"I speak flawless Arabic. Been over there before. Know the layout. I can take care of myself on the ground. What more could they ask for?"

"Brains?"

"Come on. What do you say?"

The major crumpled his Styrofoam cup into a wad and turned to leave. "Sir?"

Without looking, he tossed it in the general direction of a dented waste basket by the door. "Shoot. I missed."

"Sir?"

The wrinkled old basement warrior who found Francis his first Pentagon assignment made the mistake of glancing back. The moment the captain caught his eye, it was all over.

"I suppose..."

"Sir?"

If Khalil wanted it, he could have it. "I suppose I could chase that rabbit a couple a yards into the bush and see what comes out."

"Excuse me, sir?"

"Done." The Old Man ambled out, scratching dandruff and shaking his head. A moment later his basset hound face popped back into the doorway. "What... uh, whatever happened to this Wallenstein, anyway?"

"Wallenberg."

"Whatever. What happened to the man?"

The captain's eyes fell to a pile of papers on his desk, then inched slowly up to meet his mentor's question. "The Russians... the Russians grabbed him and he was never heard from again." He smiled.

The major frowned. "It's your neck, Khalil."

"My neck."

The captain saluted. The major wandered back down the hall, shaking his head and wondering how that all had happened.

The dust of suffering rose in blankets as an endless human wave rolled on beneath the desert sun. A desperate column, choked and breathless, had made this trek to the Jordanian border only to be halted without reason, hope or shelter. Old men fainted and children cried for water in their mother's arms. Women pleaded with soldiers to let them cross, only to be taunted or taken for pleasure behind the nearest truck or wall. Despair engulfed the sands as death waited its due on a massive scale. Fear and exhaustion gripped each face. There was nothing but hopelessness as far as the eye could see.

In the midst of it all one dark figure moved among dark figures, staring intently into passing eyes for shades of blue or green or grey; listening carefully to voices for a tell-tale accent or the slip of a Western tongue. The interloper scoured his tattered masses for signs of Western dress or custom. He watched and smiled as a bus of Poles and six car loads of Russians passed through the make-shift desert check point without a hitch. "Not all that glitters is golden," he thought to himself. A line from *The Hobbit*. Not all the Poles were Poles. Only half of the Russians were Russian. Lech and Mikhail would each get a warm personal thank-you from George and Barbara tonight. It had been quite a day. He had done well.

The shadow watched as his last group passed the arbitrary desert checkpoint into safety, then turned to go. Suddenly he froze in place. Through the crowd pushed a brusque Iraqi officer, making his way directly toward him. The man brandished an automatic pistol in the air and behind him followed two others toting AK-47s. The Marine waited in silence where he stood. Not a breath, not a flinch.

The hunter bore a classic Saddam mustache, (it seemed like they all had one) and was neatly groomed. His uniform, impeccably pressed, was that of a Republican Guard officer. This man, too, was a captain. This man, too, had a job to do and probably knew how to do it well. The moment their eyes met, the Iraqi snarled to flush the fight or flight from his quarry's face. Seeing neither, he stepped away, only to swirl back and plunge the small machine pistol to within an inch of the Westerner's heart.

"You are an American."

"¿Que?"

"You are American. Name please."

The hunted held on to a blank and unimpressed stare.

"Name please. Passport please." This one even smelled nice.

Fran whipped out his little blue folder.

"Name?"

"¿Nombre? Raoul Wallenberg," Khalil smiled.

The Iraqi took his passport and studied the photo carefully, holding it away, then directly upon his victim's face. He repeated the process twice more without saying a word.

"Ral Walberg. Sweden?"

The captain thought on his feet. "Si. Hay estudiado a la universidad aqui en Iraq." Spanish was the best he could do on the spur of the moment. A group of Filipino women walking past stared at him oddly and whispered to each other as he spoke. The rugged American nodded toward them, eyes imploring their silence.

His accuser glanced quizzically up and down his muscular frame, then scowled. "You are American."

Francis whispered a prayer, wondering if he had, perchance, run into the only border guard in the Iraqi army who knew Spanish from Swedish.

"Por favor, queremos que volver a me country ahora." He flinched inside as the word 'country' slipped out, but the soldiers didn't seem to notice.

The captain held the captain's passport to his face once again, then ordered his guards to wait before turning and disappearing into the crowd. The two AK-47s. remained by his side and he settled down in their shade for the duration. The elder of the men sported a surprisingly gentle smile as he rolled a wad of hashish in his palms. The younger, not much more than 16, fingered the trigger of his weapon nervously. The boy was trying hard to play the part of a cold killer, though his baby face had yet to shave. Khalil offered his temporary jailers a piece of chewing gum. "Freedent." They declined at first, then glanced about cautiously. He told the toothless one it wouldn't stick to his dental work and laughed. Finally they accepted.

The old one smiled. "Tusen tack." Then he winked.

Khalil waited in their shade, wondering what it could have meant. 'Tusen tack' was Swedish. Real Swedish. What did the old guard know that Francis didn't? And what would he say when the officer returned?

Gaunt specters of a thousand souls passed by on their road to nowhere. Asians and Southeast Asians were on the march again - refugees who had made this trek before to avoid the horror of wars not long forgotten. Indians and workers from Bangladesh, worn and parched, pushed on carrying suitcases and boxes above their heads. Refugees and refugees' refugees who knew no end to the suffering drifted by. Young brown women in *saris*, eyes empty and afraid, clutched infants to their shriveled breasts. A girl of about 13 stopped to beg from the detainee and his keepers. Her baby, too weak and dehydrated to even cry, couldn't have been more than a few hours old. Beautiful dark eyes bled sorrow as she pleaded with them to take her body in exchange for a drop of water for the dying child. The guards tired quickly and threatened her off with their rifles.

Twenty minutes passed. The old soldier offered Khalil a drag of his hash. The young spy obliged. *"Muchas gracias."*

Sixteen truckloads of Egyptians rolled past, sending a choking cloud of red dust to rise like a river through the sea of zombies. The caravan approached, waved and passed on through final checkpoints without so much as slowing down. The watcher made mental notes of this. Egyptians could pass. Egyptians could pass freely. There would soon be Egyptians who weren't Egyptians in those trucks if he ever got out of this alive.

A MiG-22 buzzed the ocean of desperate faces as if to warn them to stay in line. A cart filled with Asian children stopped as it tried to pass and was forced back. Papers were evidently not in order. Two Swiss or Austrian women, possibly directors of the orphanage, attempted to bribe their tormentors for passage. One handed the scowling gate-keepers a crate of oranges, then a six-pack of cheap imported beer. When this didn't work, the other pulled out a fistful of Kuwaiti *dinars*. The soldiers' eyes widened, unaware that the currency had become obsolete overnight. They took the money and again turned the women back. The elder governess spat on the ground and cursed the soldiers in Arabic, opening two bags to reveal piles more of the currency. Duly impressed, the soldiers bargained and haggled, finally agreeing that the children could pass if the women remained. The fools took the worthless *dinars* greedily and laughed. Children were kissed and embraced one by one and, at last, sent on their way. After following them safely to the other side with their tired eyes, the two brave women melted back and vanished into the column of hopelessness.

An hour passed. The desert heat was a blast furnace, sucking all moisture and life dry. A devil wind blew up miniature tornados not a block away. Small tails of dust twisted about and carried garbage and papers into the sky. Women grasped their babies close to cover tiny faces from the sandblasting sting. As if thirst wasn't enough!

Twenty minutes more into the wait the Iraqi officer stepped out of the crowd. "You are Swedish?"

"*Ya.*"

He shook his head in partial disbelief and demanded Khalil's hands. The young Marine offered them, palms up, for inspection. The man eyed his calluses carefully, as if searching for some hidden clue. Finally, he threw the passport back in Fran's face and waved him on.

"*Tacksa mycket,*" Francis whispered to the old guard. That was all the real Swedish he knew. Thanks much.

"*De nada,*" smiled the old AK-47 through a half-toothed grin.

"*De nada.*"

Chapter 3: The Last Steps
Kuwait City
August 14, 1990

Nadia Boussar had always known wealth and prestige. Prepped at the finest schools the West had to offer, this young Vassar *Phi Beta Kappa* was American in all but name and ancestors. Nadia was unique among the working rich in Kuwait: a woman who neither spoke how women were supposed to speak, wore what women were expected to wear nor accepted what women were destined to be and do.

Ali al Bakr was raised in an apolitical family. His father, a self-made man, had risen from poverty to a position of stature in Kuwait City without forgetting his roots. Through a shrewd business sense and more that a brush of luck, Abu al Bakr had become a reasonably wealthy merchant and a friend of both the royal family and the official opposition in Kuwait. Abu didn't much care who ruled the country, as long as he could make a profit. And he expected his three sons to feel the same.

As for Saddam Hussein's claim on the land, the Bakrs didn't agree, but they understood it. In travels abroad they had come to know all too well how the bulk of the Arab world looked upon their country. The poor and downtrodden generally viewed Kuwait as decadent, insolent and pro-Western. To the masses, these Kuwaitis in their Mercedes deserved what-ever ill fate befell them.

Ali and Nadia fell in love on the day they met, but were careful to arrange their marriage according to Islamic custom so as not to upset the young man's more conservative family. They went through all proper channels, although Ali had a most difficult time waiting to consummate their vows. As modern as Nadia was in all other respects, she had managed to save her sacred virginity for the wedding night. (To do anything less would bring great humiliation upon a future husband.) Everything was planned, everything in order when, two weeks before their life began, it all but ended as the locusts of August darkened the sky to devour their dreams.

Abu al Bakr ordered his sons to close the family shop minutes after the invasion reports buzzed in the streets and were verified. They opened again for two hours the next day, just long enough for a squad of Iraqi thieves to enter and make off with a case of $8500 Rolexes. The looters ran, but not before hanging a 6 foot portrait of the Father-Leader in the shop's main window. When he saw the picture and heard the story, Abu declared that enough was enough. It was over. Ali and brothers Amad and Salaam were instructed to hide their most expensive pieces of the jewelry in a silken pillow case under the storage room floor. Only when all was secure would they discuss their escape.

A few days later those same soldiers returned to the shop with a stolen truck. In 35 minutes the entire place had been gutted. Everything from the irreplaceable Persian carpets to the carbon paper in their trash cans was loaded and driven away. Then they came back and took the trash cans. Abu al Bakr was a proud man, but not so proud as to be foolish. On the night of the ransacking he announced that it was time to go. The Bakrs would drive to Jordan at first light. With relatives in Saudi Arabia and business contacts who owned villas in Spain, Abu felt confident that they could remain comfortably on holiday until times allowed for a safe return.

That night Baghdad proclaimed all borders open for any Kuwaiti wishing to leave the province. Ali violated curfew to reach Nadia and convince her of the escape. They violated more than curfew together in the bedroom of her uncle's vacant home that night.

Salaam was packing the family car when the two appeared at dawn ready to go. He winked when he saw the glint in his brother's eye. The family had dressed in their most modest clothing and was well into a ritual of goodbyes with the servants when Abu and his eldest son Amad began their shouting match. Amad had taken his suitcase from the trunk and announced his intention to stay when Abu stopped him and ushered his grandchildren back into the car.

"No!"

"You are my first-born son. You will obey my command."

"No, Father. I cannot jeopardize..."

Abu's fierce eyes met with an unusual defiance. He was not used to challenges from anyone - let alone his sons. "You will come with us as I have planned. You and your wife and daughters."

"I will not travel with Haifa in this condition. I am her husband. I must make that decision."

"And I am your father."

"The trip is not safe. We will join you when the baby is here."

"We are a family. All will be well. We must not allow ourselves to be separated. I have decided..."

"I said 'no'."

The thick-headed old patriarch knew his son had reason to wait, but Abu didn't wish to risk the separation of his family, either. He had seen it happen before. First one would leave, then another, then another. And soon he would be an old man alone with photographs and phone calls. Father wouldn't have it. The family would stay one.

"You will do as I say."

"With all respect, father, I cannot and I will not." Amad jerked the suitcase from his father's hand.

"Against my wishes..."

"Father!"

"...you will not go...."

"I know something that has remained in my heart alone."

"...against my wishes..."

"Against your wishes we had those tests done at the hospital..."

"Tests? What tests?"

"...and we know now what mother had first suspected to be true."

"You will do as I say!"

"We know the child to be healthy..."

"You will do as..."

"And we know it to be... a son!"

Abu stumbled into his own silence. Three daughters and as many miscarriages had denied Amad an heir and Abu a grandson. And over the years, father had waited almost as impatiently as his own son for that day.

"A son."

The child of his dreams was now ripe within Haifa's womb. He would see it to breath before he would ever put his wife in a car and drive out into the desert's uncertainty.

"A son." Abu said no more. He understood.

Amad ordered his children out of the car once again. Grandmother cried her objections. The rest of the family prayed a blessing and wished Amad, Haifa and their three daughters well before climbing into the old Volvo. (Father didn't want to drive the good car and appear too affluent.) Abu gave his Palestinian gardener three month's wages and the promise of a long-awaited raise if all was well with home and shop when they returned. Then they were off.

The exodus that followed was in huge contrast to the plight of the thousands and millions of foreign workers seen by the world only two weeks earlier. This group of refugees didn't walk - they drove Porsches and Ferraris - waiting neatly in line one after another to get through. The Bakrs made it into the anonymity of the huge caravan without incident. Radio broadcasts continued to quote sources very high in the Iraqi government promising all citizens of Kuwait safe passage.

They drove on without speaking. Ali stroked Nadia's soft hand beneath his duffel bag and drank in memories of that night. They had run like jackals through the empty streets, hearts pounding and minds racing. Ali was surprised and delighted when she suggested they stop to bathe at the home of her father's brother. He knew full well that her uncle's family was already safely out of the country. Something about the danger and that forbidden moment had flamed the passion within her. Ali had had other women before. But no one who said she loved him had ever loved him like this.

They entered the house through the servant's quarters with a hidden key. Ali checked the bottom floor to assure that they were alone. When he returned, Nadia was calling from the top of the stairs. She stood naked, glistening in the candlelight. Jet black hair flowed long upon the satin neck and quivering chest which rose and fell in shallow breath. He reached to touch her. She held back his hand for a moment, then drew it in to bury it between her breasts. He leaned in to kiss her. She placed a single finger to his lips and paused, then backed him to the wall in a delighted silence to unbutton him. And there, before taking him inside, they made their trembling vows of love before Allah and the night. In her mind, she said, they were now married. And she gave herself to him with a fervent fury twice that night, then took him once more before the sun would rise to call them to face the morning.

That was last night. Ali was praying there would be 10,000 more as they approached the first checkpoint and were relieved of passports and purses. A stark reality hit. "This is not good," Ali whispered. "We will never be able to establish ourselves in Saudi Arabia or anywhere without passports. No one will trust us. They will think we are informers working for Saddam."

"It is merely an inconvenience," remarked the businessman Abu. "If this is what we must put up with to get out, then so be it. We will obtain new papers upon our return."

A ragged warrior approached and scowled through the closed windows at the second checkpoint. The desert sun was already baking dust and sweat into clay upon the poor man's face and hands though it was not yet 10 o'clock. Nadia smiled at him and nodded. Surprised at her confidence, the soldier cursed their air conditioning and waved them on. Ali's mother winked at her son, impressed with the young woman's poise under pressure.

At a third stop they were stripped of all suitcases and valuables. But they drove on in relief, knowing that Abu had hidden ample Western currency beyond notice in a compartment under his wife's seat. Ali and Nadia now held each other's eyes and clasped hands in full view of their family to muster courage and forget their fears. She was so beautiful... so utterly beautiful and warm. She was the woman of his dreams. And the only thing in the world that mattered to him now was their future.

Inching toward the final checkpoint, the muffled silence was pierced by a scream of what sounded like a hired mourner railing at death. Ali strained through glaring glass to watch as a squad of Iraqis pulled a young man from his car not 20 meters ahead. A middle-aged woman crawled the burning sands, cursing the soldiers and imploring them to release her boy. She clawed and spat, clucking her tongue in shame and sobbing that this was her only son. Islamic law forbade them from taking him. "I am a widow! I am a widow!" she continued to cry. The soldiers hesitated until their sergeant approached and kicked the woman's grip loose. He ordered his men to throw her into her own car and marched the boy off. This was two vehicles ahead of them. They moved closer, still closer.

A golden Mercedes on their bumper passed without incident, filling all with a false hope that lasted only seconds. Then, within the sight and smell of freedom, they stopped and the men were ordered out of the car.

"We're going to Saudi Arabia," said a surprisingly polite Abu. "We have no quarrel with you."

"Where is your passport?"

Father remained calm. "The soldiers behind us took it. Speak with them."

"We must have your papers." The officer had made this statement 4000 times that morning. He was not impressed. "No males of military age are allowed to leave the province without proper credentials."

Nadia gripped Ali's knuckles white. Salaam, always hot-headed, was obviously annoyed by the man's arrogance. He shot back. "He told you, someone already took them."

The officer leered in at the boy. "You! How old is this one?"

Ali's mother scowled. "You have no quarrel with any of us. You've already taken everything we have. Is that not enough? In the name of Allah, let us pass."

"Out of the car!" As his voice crescendoed, seven rifles slapped into place and seven barrels aimed directly at Abu through the closed window. "Out of the car!"

Nadia's veil of composure disintegrated. "No! We are to be married. Have mercy!"

Lustful eyes fixed hungrily upon the beautiful young woman.

"If you don't come with us, you are all under arrest. All male citizens of the Province between the ages of 17 and 35 are to report for military service."

"We have no quarrel..." began Ali.

The officer lunged through the window, groping for Nadia's arm. "If you are not man enough to join us, maybe your women would like to come out and play."

Ali broke the invader's grip by slamming the car door open and stepped immediately out. He had heard rumors of what Iraqi soldiers were doing to women at the border. "Leave her out of this. I will go with you."

Nadia screamed as Abu tried to restrain her.

"You also!" barked the officer to Salaam.

"This one is not yet 16. You have no reason to take him," lied Ali.

"Where are his papers?"

"As we already told you, your people have taken everything!"

"He has no papers and he looks 17. He must come with us."

Salaam cracked the door and slid out before his mother could say a word. He was trying so hard to be a man. Ali glanced back. Nadia was nearly biting her lower lip through. "I'll be OK. Don't worry about me. I'll be here when you come back to a free Kuwait."

"No!" she lunged again, this time sinking nails into Ali's arm and refusing to let go. "Please! Please, we are to be married!"

"Drive on," bellowed the soldier, pounding the car with his rifle. "You are free to go! Drive on!"

"No, please. In the name of Allah, I beg of you!"

Ali held her for one last moment with his eyes. "I'll be here when you return. Whatever happens, I will live for that day when..."

They raised their weapons. "Drive on!"

The car lurched forward, breaking Nadia's grip. Ali could see the agony in those perfect eyes through the back window. In one last moment he mouthed his 'I love you'. She was so utterly beautiful. So fine.

Within the hour a transport lorry and 60 new 'conscripts' had driven off into the desert heat to join the Iraqi Army.

Three hours further into the journey their truck stopped at the office of an abandoned oil refinery. Long lines of men, mostly Kuwaitis, waited to be processed. One by one they were ushered into the front of a main building. One by one they stepped out the back side where Ali could see the sheep being separated from the goats. One group of men huddled around a water truck in the shade of some desert palms. The others sat baking in the sun behind two strands of concertina wire to the right. There were 35 - 40 by the water tank, but more than 200 behind the wire.

"Stay with me!" Ali ordered his brother. "Do what I do and say what I say."

It took half an hour in line for Ali's group to finally make it into the shade of the barracks. Here they sat on green wooden benches to play the waiting game again. A large fan blew intermittent relief across the room.

"What are they going to do with us?" asked Salaam.

"I don't know. I think that they'll try to put us in the army. But we will never fight for an occupied Kuwait. According to BBC, the Americans may intervene. And the last thing we want is to be wearing Iraqi uniforms when this happens."

"But what will they do with us if we refuse to serve?"

Ali nodded toward the men behind the wire. "We will be in good company. They will probably take us to a re-education camp of some sort, I suppose. But by then the United States will have come and we'll all be free."

"Ha! The United States? Why would the United States come for us?"

"We are their friends."

Salaam's skeptical adolescent sneer told Ali that the boy did not accept his answer.

He changed his tack. "I don't know. Maybe because we have oil. Whatever the case, they are already in Saudi Arabia with 20,000 Marines."

"Americans?"

"Americans."

"Why?"

"You ask too many questions." The brothers waited as the room emptied one man at a time. Ali heard no sounds of beating or anger beyond the walls and assured his brother that this meant they were in no immediate danger. Salaam looked so young. He was still so much a boy.

"Why did you not remain in the car?" Asked Ali. "You should not have joined me so eagerly."

Salaam feigned a nonchalant bravado. "Someone had to look after you. You are such a child." The two laughed.

An enormous guard with a high forehead and rotten teeth demanded their silence. They complied. Later, while walking past the two, he noticed their resemblance. "You are brothers?"

"Yes."

"No." Ali and Salaam answered at the same moment. "We are all brothers."

The man chuckled and motioned Ali to rise. "Then you, brother, will come first."

Behind the door was a conference room with bright blue carpet and a wall full of oil charts. Behind a large teak table sat the civilian Baath Party member with a small ledger for recording names. The wicked little man had one question and wanted but one answer: "Will you swear an oath to our Father-Leader and serve the forces of the new 19th Republic?"

"I take an oath to no one but Allah!"

"Very well." He pulled out Ali's left hand and forced it down onto a large stamp pad of blood-red ink. "Next."

Salaam rose in anger as his brother was shoved back through the waiting room door by two soldiers. The elder tried to shout out "Don't do it!" but a cold steel rifle knocked him to his knees before any words could leave his lips. The huge Iraqi sergeant stood over him sneering. "You'll pay for your insolence!" Ali spat half a tooth to the floor and cursed before he was struck again and all went black.

He woke in the center of the wired compound as a merciless sun glared down upon him: his jaw swollen and his neck stiff. Sensing a momentary relief, he opened his eyes. An old Bedouin, well into his sixties, was attempting to grace him with the little shade he could create in the noontime sun. Ali cleared a parched throat and attempted to speak: "Sit, brother. Save your strength."

"That is all right, my friend." The kind old voice was familiar to Ali, though he could not place it. "With what we have ahead, you need shade more than I need strength, I suspect."

Ali strained to see the man silhouetted in the blinding light. But with head still spinning, he could only make out a shadow and soon he dizzied and drifted away again. This time when he awoke, he sat up and asked about his brother. No one had seen him. Ali shaded his eyes and searched the area by the lorry. His heart sank. Both the truck and the men who had gathered about it were gone. Al Bakr scanned the silent and sorry masses around him looking for the old angel who had given him shade. No one knew anything of the Bedouin, either. Those who dared to speak said only that no old men were in this encampment. It was as if he had never been.

At about 7 p.m. orders came and the entire group rose to march three abreast into the biting desert wind. There was a high knoll ahead on the path. Three hundred men were ordered to stop and strip. Seventeen guards held machine guns on them and two dogs patrolled the perimeters. The sergeant pulled out a few to gather clothes and bundle them onto two nearby flat-beds. The man next to Ali was chosen as was the boy behind. Al Bakr began to recite Koran out loud. A rifle knocked him to his knees and another laid him flat upon the searing sands once more. He writhed like a snake on a skillet, convulsing inside and out.

"Ten men!" came the cry. The first 10 walked reluctantly behind the dune.

"Ten more!" came the order a few minutes later. These hesitated but were pushed on and disappeared over the top. The remaining group squatted in rows in the low desert sunlight.

Ali looked up. The old Bedouin who had shaded him before was standing there again. "Are they going to kill us?" Ali whispered.

"Don't talk. Pray, pilgrim, pray." The voice was strangely peaceful.

"Do I know you?" Ali's head was still swimming in an explosion of color.

The old man smiled. "You may."

"I'm certain I've heard your voice before."

The smile took him away for a moment, but he didn't know where. Others around them began to whimper in disbelief. A boy in front was shaking so that he lost his bowels.

"There are only 17 or 18 of them and two dogs," came a murmur from behind. "If we wanted, we could overpower them all."

"Ten more!" The line of naked sheep marched another step toward uncertainty.

"I hear no guns. Maybe they are giving us uniforms. Perhaps they'll turn us into soldiers to fight the Americans. We can revolt as soon as we have guns."

"Fool! They'll never give us guns," cursed a proud middle-aged man standing next to the Bedouin. Ali looked twice before recognizing him as an Al Sabah. This one was a second cousin of the Crown Prince. How strange it was to Ali that nakedness made all class of men look the same.

"They'll use us at the front for a human shield or send us running like Iranians at the American tanks," muttered Al Sabah through clenched teeth.

A man with a mullah's beard cried out loud: "They could never kill us like this. It is against the Koran."

"Silence!" shouted the guard. "Silence or you die."

"Ten more!" came the order. Ali's group was next. His thoughts turned once again to Nadia and the night. It had only taken him 14 hours to travel from heaven to hell. She was so gentle. So kind. He prayed only that he would be allowed to see her again in whatever world awaited on the other side.

Ali's mind riveted onto the moment their eyes first met. She was at prayer in her family's garden the hour the Al Bakrs had come to discuss business with her father. Ali was returning from the car with some charts when he walked through a wrong door. A right door. Nadia looked up from her prayer shawl as he entered. She was not the least bit afraid. He excused himself, but couldn't take his eyes from her. She smiled - more embarrassed for him than for herself - and asked what he wanted. Had she not been in prayer, he might have dared to say. It filled him with such hope to find an educated woman with a sense of humor. He remembered the hour that Abu had made the arrangements with Nadia's father for the marriage. Those were the most joyous heartbeats of his life!

Now, for the gift of a moment, Ali was back in time. He saw her smile. He breathed in her fragrance. He drank from the dark depths of her eyes. He could almost taste her - that angel from a sensuous heaven. Once again he retraced their night, their vows and the impassioned wrestling as one. Now he felt her gripping his arm. Now he saw her tears from the car and heard that frantic voice: "I love you, Ali. I will always love you."

"She is beautiful, isn't she pilgrim." It was the old man. Ali fixed his stare deep within the Bedouin's burning gaze. How could he know?

"Ten more," came the cry.

"May Allah have mercy. May Allah have mercy on our souls," Ali whispered.

"And on theirs," smiled his ancient friend as they rose and walked together to the other side.

Chapter 4: Battle Plan
The Oval Office
August 17, 1990

"We hit them fast, hard and heavy concentrating first on three primary targets: command and control; the Iraqi air defense system; and the Osiris Nuclear Facility. When these objectives have been achieved, we go for supply routes, Republican Guard positions, and Saddam, himself, if you feel it's warranted."

The president was reading ahead in the report, nodding in agreement. General Colin Powell unfolded a wooden pointer and continued: "Reliable estimates suggest that we can take out their air defense system in 30 minutes and the bulk of their air force within 48 hours of initiation. With communications to Baghdad cut, our counter-intelligence people believe they can issue a 'sit tight' order to Iraqi air commanders, making it sound like it is coming from Saddam, himself. That order, combined with the shock value of a massive bombing campaign, should keep their pilots in the bunkers during this initial phase. Those who do manage to take to the skies won't find an airstrip to return to by the time the smoke clears. British Tornados are pretrained and ready for that job. AWACs and the combined air power of the U.S., Britain, Italy and hopefully France will continue hitting targets, doing bomb damage reassessment and hitting them again and again until such time as we feel confident that we're ready for the ground campaign. After a reasonably clean first strike against his air power, our satellite eyes will allow us to remove 70% of Saddam's chemical capabilities and SCUDs."

"This will happen..."

"Very early on."

"We're talking days?"

"Hours."

The president nodded and smiled.

"With air cover obliterated and surface-to-air defense blinded, this phase becomes no more dangerous than a high altitude target practice. We expect the psychological effects of the constant bombardment to be devastating on an enemy who can't hit back. If, as time wears on, Saddam and his generals are unable to either give orders or receive accurate reports, his field commanders will become rapidly isolated and morale will nosedive. Further, if supplies are cut, if they run out of food and water and if the Republican Guard is kept sufficiently at bay so as not to be breathing down their necks, we believe that the half-million Iraqis on the front will surrender in droves. Without firing a shot."

The president cleared his throat. "A lot of 'ifs' there general."

Powell nodded.

"How are their supply lines right now?"

"They didn't have adequate supplies when they invaded Kuwait in the first place. Schwarzkopf, himself, has seen them begging for food from the Saudis. He was standing in an observation tower just the other day and looked down at a group of soldiers asking for handouts. When he didn't recognize their uniforms, the Saudi officer escorting him had to explain who they were! We'll have to be ready to absorb a huge prisoner base."

"You're sure of this?"

"Yes, sir. Reasonably sure."

"We have to be sure."

"With all due respect, sir, in war you can never be sure. We'll do our homework, control every detail we can possibly control. But once the bullets start flying and the 'Dogs of War' are..."

"And a best case scenario?" Powell didn't need to finish his sentence. The president knew where he was going.

The National Security Adviser handed all of the president's men manila envelopes containing two single sheets and began to read: "Best case? With Saddam *incommunicado* , a relentless bombing and a military leadership in disarray, they turn around and go home without firing a shot. That's the best case. In this scene we don't even have to invade Kuwait. Our Arab allies enter and mop up. We stay out except for air support. The Emir is back on his throne. He sets up a people's parliament so that we see democracy on the horizon. The oil fields are intact and they quickly resume production. The Saudis give us two bases on the Gulf where we can park a few thousand tanks and a rapid deployment carrier strike force. Saddam is overthrown by his own generals - people we can deal with. A new government in Iraq resumes trade with our blessing and the stock market jumps 1,000 points the next morning."

Quayle thought out loud: "This takes us out of the recession and you into the history books with a guaranteed second term."

"I like the way you write history." The president's smile panned the room but stopped at his general's smirk. "I don't suppose we can count on it. 'Dogs of War', and all..."

Powell shook his head.

"Suppose not. And a worst case scenario?" Bush pulled a second sheet from his envelope.

"Worst case: Saddam survives our initial wave of attacks. His foot soldiers fight like the Afghans. SCUDs wash half of Israel in a chemical fire. Some of his bombers scramble past our AWACs and plaster Saudi oil fields. Or worse - they manage to get to our carriers bottlenecked in the Gulf and the press calls it Pearl Harbor II. Thousands of Iraqis with confiscated Kuwaiti passports stage an assassination attempt on the royal Saudi family and incite the Shiites of the world against the 'infidels' on their soil. Suicide truck bombings hit our bases and back line installations making Lebanon look like a Sunday School picnic. The American public, sickened by hundreds or thousands of body bags coming home on the nightly news, turns against you. Reserve troops of hairdressers, hockey coaches and other weekend warriors snap under pressure and go AWOL. Israel takes it's fate into it's own hands and bombs Iraq."

The adviser looked up from his reading. "This, by the way, is the greatest danger we face. Israel must be kept completely out of this." Everyone nodded in agreement.

He continued. "Israeli Palestinians are herded up and dumped across the Jordanian border or barbed wired into Israeli ghettos reminiscent of Warsaw. The U.N. calls for a censure of Israel and demands sanctions or blockades. We veto Security Council measures and are perceived worldwide as following a double standard. Saddam sweeps into Jordan himself, deposing King Hussein and arming the 60% Palestinian population to push the Jews into the sea. Abu Nidal and Abu Abbas bring the war back to Sioux City, Iowa, with inland bombings of our passenger jets. U.S. diplomats all over the Arab world are expelled or assassinated. Energy prices soar. The stock market crashes. The global economy collapses. Thatcher is drummed out of office. And, in the U.S. Congress, you are impeached for entering a war without constitutional sanction."

The president curled his lips and tapped a red pen on the desk for 20 seconds. He paused again at each set of eyes in the room. "And a scenario in the middle?"

The adviser thought for a moment. "We'd have to be ready for anything. Anything in between."

"Anything in between," echoed the president.

Powell nodded. "I believe it was Eisenhower who said..."

"... the only sure thing about a war is that it will surprise you." George Bush didn't need a lesson on military history. He turned to his Secretary of State. "What do you think, Jim?"

Baker cleared his throat and set the papers into his briefcase: "It seems to me that prudence would dictate a closer check of the world pulse."

The vice president jumped in. "Congress is going to expect that we give sanctions an opportunity to..."

Secretary of State Jim Baker scoffed at the notion. "Sanctions won't do a damn thing unless we're willing to wait a lot longer than we can afford to wait. We can't sustain the kind of buildup we're talking about here for more than eight months. A year at the max. For one thing, we can't afford it. For another, we can't give a Democratic Congress and an anti-war movement that much time to ferment. We'll have an untenable situation on our hands."

"The world is going to demand that we give sanctions a shot..."

Baker interrupted again. "Expecting Saddam Hussein to simply pick up his toys and go home is completely unrealistic. Besides, sanctions don't address the true source of this problem: Hussein himself. If we allow this guy to pull out with a slap on the wrist, he's still left holding his nuclear program - not to mention chemicals and nerve agents."

"Is there any possible way we can take him out without digging him out?" No one answered the president's question. Then the silence did. "If that's the case, this is going to involve time, a huge amount of money..."

Baker knew what else it was going to take. The eyes of the room shifted to him. "...and a massive PR effort both here and abroad."

The president's national security adviser spoke: "If we attack Iraq without a carefully orchestrated alliance - including legitimate leadership from the international Arab community - it will be 20 years before an American citizen will be able to walk the streets of any Arab capital in the world without looking over his shoulder."

"You're speaking about an alliance of..."

"Saudi Arabia, Egypt, Morocco, Algeria..." The national security adviser started the list.

The secretary of state finished it. "I hate to say it, sir, but Syria will have to be in our court on this. At least she can't be against us."

The vice president shook his head. "We can't talk to Hafez Assad. The American public wouldn't stomach the hypocrisy. Look at the *Pan Am* bombing; the occupation of Lebanon; Abu Nidal. Syria is still at the top of our list of terrorist nations. We can't talk to them. "

"Baker can't." It was the first time that the CIA representative spoke. "We'd have to do this low level."

The president was looking out the Oval Office window at the late summer colors and hadn't heard the last comments. He glanced up, face drawn and eyes vacant. "Excuse me?"

"Low level," Baker nodded. "One of my assistants..."

The CIA man objected. "I was thinking of a much lower level than that. One of my agents could..."

"We don't send CIA to do the State Department's work," Baker objected. "Assad won't talk to CIA."

"And just who would Assad talk to?"

Powell raised a finger. "I may have the man we're looking for. Someone with a possible 'in.' "

"Who's that?"

"Name is Khalil. Marine Captain Francis Khalil."

"Is he..."

"Arab?" Powell shook his head. "American."

"Arab American."

The general smiled at his president. "American of Arab ancestry."

Bush shifted in his chair. "Who is he?"

"He's one of the analysts - Pentagon analysts - who's been writing our daily situation briefings on the Mideast."

The vice president looked to his chief: "The 'Raoul Wallenberg' fellow who brought over three dozen of our folks out of Kuwait last week? Russian and Polish passports?"

Bush nodded as if he remembered. "And what makes you think Assad would talk to this Khalil fellow?"

"He's smart. Savvy. Speaks the language like a native. Top it off, in his spare time he's writing his master's thesis on Hafez Assad and the occupation of Lebanon."

"This is State's job," Baker objected again.

"Preliminary contact wouldn't have to be from State." The president re-entered the discussion. "If this falls through and Syria makes it known to the world that we came a'courting, it could blow up in our faces. If, indeed, we are to make any deals with Syria - and I say 'if' - we'd have to be sure that they were sewn up - deal in hand- before anyone got wind of it."

Powell concurred: "We may only get one shot with Syria. It had better be our best. Captain Khalil's ancestry may intrigue Assad enough to get us a foot in the door. He could find out quickly and quietly if Assad is interested in talking. And if he is, State can take it from there."

"Khalil, huh?"

"Marine Captain Francis Khalil."

"Can he be trusted?"

"He's a Marine."

"Can he be trusted?"

"He's a Marine."

Bush glanced at his watch. "How soon could he leave if we decided to go with this?"

"Sir," Powell's smile broadened, "he's a Marine."

The president shoved his leather chair back to the wall and stood. "I'll take it under advisement. Thank you gentlemen. That will be all." On his way out, the commander in chief pulled his favorite general aside and waited until everyone was out of earshot. "Colin?"

"Yes, Mr. President?"

"What time do we tee off?"

Chapter 5: Interruptus
Washington, D.C.
August 18, 1990

"You're going where?"

Francis didn't like to talk when they were making love. Kathryn did.

"Away."

"Where?"

"Away. You know... I... I can't say."

"Can't say. Can't say." The way she whispered under her breath, Francis couldn't tell if she was questioning or cursing.

"Can we... not... talk... about..."

"Damn you." She slid off of him and pulled the covers tight about her neck. "Damn you, Khalil."

"What?"

"What is it about you..."

"What?"

"...that wants to make me..." She looked up. "What is it about you that wants to make me a widow?"

"Kathryn!"

"You're going back, aren't you?"

"I'm not going back to Iraq."

"Kuwait, then."

"I'm not going into Kuwait."

"You told me that you had a desk job..."

"I did. I do."

"...nice safe desk job."

"I said 'I'm not going to Iraq.' "

"Why couldn't you have just been a truck driver or a veterinarian? Now that would have been nice. Predictable."

Francis attempted to loosen the lock on Kathryn's covers and get back to where they had left off. He might as well not have tried. "I told you, I'm not going back to Iraq."

"Or a mortician. Say, there you go! Decent hours. Nine to five. A few weekends maybe..." She paused as her suspicions suddenly solidified. "Back to Iraq? I knew it! You did go! Last week when you said..."

"I didn't say that."

"Fran, you could have been killed."

"I'm here, aren't I?" He reached to touch her shoulder. She slapped his hand roughly away.

"And I'm supposed to just smile at my third graders, correct their papers and sit around this apartment every night from now until whenever waiting to see if your face shows up on the news? Another attaché who is missing and presumed dead?"

Francis quit trying. He drew back upon his own side of the bed and turned, face to the wall. "Forget it."

It always frustrated Kathryn when her husband would stop talking. Most nights she let it go, but tonight she couldn't. "Francis!"

He didn't respond.

"Francis?"

He wouldn't or couldn't respond.

"So that's 'it' then? That's all you're going to say? Case closed." She waited. And waited. And waited. " I'm just supposed to shut up about it?" There was no response. "Evidently." Finally the young bride let out an exasperated scream. "Francis Christopher Michael Khalil! I love you but you're driving me nuts here!"

"Syria."

"How am I supposed to react..."

"Syria."

"...knowing that you're flying into a war zone. You could be killed or tortured..."

"Syria."

"...come back in a body bag or not come back at..."

"Syria."

She finally heard him. The wheels began to turn. "Syria? We're not at war with... why would... are you..." She sighed. "Francis, if anybody's going to kill you, promise you'll let it be me."

The focus of the moment was suddenly shattered by the sound of breaking glass. Reflexes thrust the Marine's hand into the nightstand drawer for his revolver. Instinct threw him to the floor. He rolled to the window, cocked the pistol and peered into the night. It took him only a moment to realize what was happening in the street one floor below.

"Damn! Not again!"

"What?"

Francis bolted through the patio door and back in an instant to grab for his shorts.

"What? What is it?"

A second leg snagged in his boxers and Fran fell face-first against the stucco wall. A shot rang out and was followed by a blinding flash. Kathryn screamed. Francis stumbled to the floor, groping for his robe.

"Who's out there?"

"Not again." The soldier sounded more annoyed than angry. "Not my baby. Not again." He slammed open the second lock, hopped the railing and disappeared into the shadows.

Kathryn looked out the window and immediately knew. If it hadn't been so dark and he hadn't been so mad, Francis would have seen his young bride's near smile when he returned a few minutes later. "We gotta get out of this neighborhood."

"The Jag?"

"The Jag. My car."

"The stereo?"

Francis sucked on his newly bloodied lip. "Why don't I just leave it open? At least then they wouldn't keep breaking the window."

He turned the apartment lights on and off in one fluid motion. It only took him that long to spot the gun on the floor and the exploded picture tube of their new wide-screen TV. The second best sharpshooter at boot camp collapsed back into bed with a new headache. He buried his face in the Damask pillow case. The car, the gun and the Sony could wait. "We gotta get out of this neighborhood."

It started slowly. Kathryn tried to hold back, but knew it was no use. Within half a minute she was shaking. She held her breath, hoping he wouldn't notice, but he did. Turning over, he placed a gentle hand on her soft shoulder again. This time she didn't push away. "I'm sorry. I'm sorry. Don't cry."

She could hold it no longer. Kathryn turned to her husband tearless as the laughter took on a life of its own. "Maybe... we should all move to.... to Iraq or Kuwait. Get out of this dangerous place!"

Francis didn't think it was all that funny at first. But the infectious joy of the moment wore him down. Between frantic gasps and breathless bursts of laughter, Kathryn somehow managed to convey how ridiculous he had looked while stumbling about, half in and half out of his shorts.

Later that night, between frantic gasps and breathless bursts of another kind, Kathryn managed to convey even more.

Chapter 6: Assad's Conditions

Damascus, Syria
August 19, 1990

A huge sign lit the mountainside above the city and flashed its message for all to see: "Congratulations to the people." Street lights and bright banners hung from every lamp post and bill board, celebrating the victory of the party. A five-story portrait of the president adorned the Municipal Building downtown. It could have been any other capital in the Arab World. But it was not. It was Damascus.

Another flight and another dusty airport had brought the emissary to the estate of Hafez al Assad. Syrian security was tighter than Baghdad's. Khalil was forced to strip and was searched twice in succession. Teeth, navel and both sets of cheeks were checked and rechecked before he was allowed to walk the gauntlet of metal detectors to enter the presidential chamber. Assad was no different than Hussein as far as Francis was concerned. Both were Baath extremists. Both harbored and funded known terrorists. Both hated Israel. Both had invaded a neighbor and left a strong army there to "defend" its people. Both murdered their own when political expediency demanded. Saddam had his Kurds in the north and Shiites in the south; Assad had his own Kurds and the Shiite massacre at Hamma.

The difference at this particular moment in history was that Syria happened to hate Iraq. And that difference made all the difference in the world.

With the exception of the strip search, Khalil received a red-carpet welcome in Damascus. Assad was prepared for his guest. He had read the Marine's vita. He knew that the American was but two generations away from his Lebanese ancestors. And he liked the man the moment before he met him.

"Fascinating," remarked the president. "An Arab in the American military intelligence coming to see me! And you still have family in the Lebanon?"

Khalil waved the interpreter away and answered in flawless Arabic. "You've done your homework."

The dictator smiled in startled surprise.

"I have some great-uncles and cousins there, but we haven't kept in contact since Lebanon became part of 'greater Syria.'"

Assad's grin broadened. The American had a wit to go along with his dialect. Whether this Khalil was a clever spy or an honest emissary, he would be a delightful break to the boredom of dictatorial politics and its endless army of "yes men." The captain's story had been collaborated by Syrian intelligence prior to his arrival. (That didn't mean it was true.) The American reportedly grew up in eastern Montana's cattle country where his immigrant grandparents homesteaded and become wealthy ranchers.

The host was fascinated by images of the American West and used this occasion to probe about cowboys, gunfights and John Wayne. Khalil did his best to oblige, knowing that pleasure came first in this culture and that no real business could be transacted until and unless a relationship was first established. Something about his guest's charm and careful use of language allowed the Syrian to drop his natural defenses. It wasn't long before the two were speaking like men from the same world.

They sat in the shade of a marble portico and bantered for hours, sipping cool fruit alcohol and dining on salty Russian caviar. Finally, the American began his pitch: "I have come on behalf of the president of the United States to ask you an important question."

Assad made the motion of aiming a pistol at Khalil's head. "Shoot." He pulled the imaginary trigger and blew the smoke away.

"I know that Syria has had its - should we say - difficulties with Iraq. It cannot be pleasant living in the neighborhood with a madman like Hussein." Assad's lip curled up momentarily at the sound of the word 'madman.' "Our president would like to clear up any present negative atmosphere that exists between the United States and Syria and discuss possible security cooperation agreements that would be in our mutual interest should any armed conflict in the region arise."

Assad was caught off guard. Not by the idea, itself, but by the fact that it was coming from an American. He lit a cigarette, pretending not to be as interested as he was. "You are asking what? An agreement with the Americans?"

"I am offering you a chance to be on the side that will ultimately win. I offer you the elimination of an old nemesis, the dismantling of a menacing army on your doorstep, and the hand of friendship from the most powerful nation in the world."

"And the price?" Assad was long enough in politics to know that nothing came free.

"The price is far less at this moment in history than it will ever be again."

"Which means..."

"The Chinese have a symbol for the word 'crisis'. Actually, two symbols go together to make the one word. They are the symbol for 'danger' and the symbol for the word 'opportunity'. You, of all people, are aware that there are moments in history when danger and opportunity go hand in hand. If, for instance, the United States had not acted unilaterally to drop the first 20,000 Marines into Saudi Arabia at the moment Saddam crossed into Kuwait..." Khalil shrugged his shoulders as if to say 'who knows?'.

Assad nodded. "He could have continued on to Riyadh, to the Emirates..."

"And to the position of undisputed power broker of the Middle East."

The strongman wasn't totally sold. "Perhaps."

"Defender of the Palestinians - that's what he's calling himself. Spokesman for the Arab cause. The new Nebuchadnezzar." Assad bristled at those words as his guest continued. "We were fortunate at this moment that our president had the insight and power to rush those first Marines into place."

"A speed bump." Assad smiled.

"Yes, that's what they called themselves. A speed bump. A trip wire."

"They couldn't have stopped Saddam had they wanted to."

"Ah, but you see, that's exactly what they did. And without firing a shot. If we had waited, it could have cost us - cost the world - a great deal more. We risked much. But with it came the opportunity."

It was Assad this time who shrugged his shoulders. Khalil continued. "Now, at this new moment, our President is asking if you wish to be part of both the danger and the opportunity: to share in the risk in order to share in the gain. If we are wise, we will take advantage of this moment together. We can take Saddam out, dismantle his nuclear and chemical capabilities, disarm his million man army, and create a post-Hussein Iraq with more manageable leaders existing in a region where Syria retains a primary role and influence."

A waiter brought them each a cognac. Assad raised his glass in a mock toast. "And the price? You are speaking of what? Help with intelligence? A mute voice on the Palestinian issue? Peace with Israel? These I cannot give."

"I ask you only for something I know you can give."

"The price for Syria, then?"

"Syrian troops along side the Saudis defending the sacred soil of Islam."

Assad laughed. "Sacred soil of Islam, is it! Since when does America care about sacred Islamic anything? And you say 'along side Saudi troops'? Saudi Arabia has no troops. It has rich flyboy princes with expensive toys. But it has no troops. It buys American mercenaries to guard its 'sacred Islamic soil'. Or should I say 'sacred Islamic oil'? You are speaking of Syrian troops standing along the 'line in the sand' shoulder to shoulder with Americans? Impossible! We use your face on dummies for bayonet practice. Sacred soil of Islam?" Assad was now mildly amused. "Sacred oil of Islam."

Khalil kept an irrepressible grin on his face throughout the entire tirade. "War makes strange bedfellows. You must admit, it is a rather interesting image. Wouldn't you say? Syrian and American troops together? Controversial, yes. But then, you've never been afraid to take a controversial position before."

Francis had researched the Syrian well enough to know his greatest fears came not from present enemies but from future historians. He had chosen his words well before the meeting: "Destiny knocks but once for each man. Maybe twice. When the knock is heard, greatness comes to those willing to seize the day. The rest are left on the garbage heap of history. Forgotten."

The Syrian strongman swished the amber fluid gently about in his crystal snifter to catch the fading sunset.

"Timing, Mr. President. Timing and courage are the keys."

Assad didn't need a lesson on timing. He was a master at it in Lebanon. He downed his drink and motioned for another. "If there is a price for me, there is also a price for you."

"And that is?"

"You know what I need to hear."

Khalil knew, but didn't mention the word first.

"Linkage."

"Linkage."

"The Palestinian issue..."

The captain set his drink down and stood. "As the State Department has told you, we will discuss the possibility of linkage with you privately. But publicly we'll have to insist that these two items are totally unrelated."

"And when this is all over Israel will be forced to deal with the Palestinian issue?"

Khalil looked Assad in the eye. "I give you my word. We will do everything in our power to get Israel to sit down at the table..."

"With the PLO."

"With Palestinians present and..."

"With the PLO."

"... Palestinians and Syrians also to discuss a comprehensive peace."

"And the Golan Heights?"

Khalil shrugged his shoulders: "Who knows where this all might lead?"

Assad walked to an antique cart covered with pastries and spoke in French to the waiter. He chose a cherry and date tart and spoke without turning back. "I like you. But I don't trust you." A murderer's smile melted into a searching, calculated stare.

"I trust you, but I don't like you." The American riveted his eyes back onto those of his host. A strange contest of wills held for a moment before Assad's smile returned.

"Syrian troops will ally with Americans on the day your Mr. Bush enters Damascus to ask for them personally and shakes my hand."

Francis laughed aloud. "You are not only a magnificent host, you are also a magnificent comedian."

"As I say, Syrian troops..."

"Impossible. He'd never come. Impossible."

It was Assad's turn to grin. "You have to admit, it does make for a rather interesting image, does it not?"

"Indeed."

"See what you can arrange, cowboy. See what you can arrange."

Khalil knew what the answer in Washington would be. An American president pressing the flesh with the terrorist Assad? It was impossible.

It just might work.

Chapter 7: Sea of Corpses
Al Jahrah, Kuwait
August 20, 1990

An old man in a red-checkered headdress smoked a water pipe in the first floor doorway. A 13 year-old girl in Levis sat on the roof petting a purring kitten with one hand and clutching a rifle that weighed more than she did in the other. A middle-aged matron strained the bacon from a pot of *Campbell's Bean and Bacon* soup as it simmered on the Coleman stove in the hall. And in the back room of the former Exxon Annex guest cottage, eleven hardened survivors sipped Iranian tea and leaned in to hear the strained whisper of their newest arrival.

"We came in over the dune to the midst of hell. There was a momentary pause in our step when we saw it. It was as if the 10 of us had been simultaneously hit by the blast of an opened furnace. We stood for but a moment facing the sea of corpses. There were pits dug neatly in rows. Shallow pits with hundreds, no, thousands of naked men lying face down in their own blood and vomit. The guards pushed us on.

"Four others - only four - stood waiting for us. These were not men, but machines. Cold, mindless machines. Two carried Chinese rifles, two held the long razor-sharp machete knives. Their bloodied hands were blistered raw by the work of the day. We walked down into the garbage pit of bodies piled three deep and nine abreast in rows of shallow graves. I cried out inside, not believing what my eyes held as true. These were my brothers... my fathers... my own.

"Kneel dogs," the officer barked. He was no older than my brother. Maybe 17. We fell to our knees as if preparing for evening prayers. The sun blinded our hopeless eyes. In front of us lay the freshly slaughtered three deep... their blood glistening in the amber evening sun. Each fell neatly on top of the other, naked with hands bound from behind. Each bore one clean razor slash from ear to ear. We were not even worth the price of a bullet to the Iraqi pigs.

"The man on my left stood in defiance to face his tormentor. 'I am Shia,' he said. 'I will not die like this. If I am to die, I demand the dignity of facing the Holy City.' The officer stepped toward him without blinking, placed his gun squarely in the man's back and grinned. 'Which way do you want your entrails to face?' Before the defiant one could answer, the infidel emptied his chamber, blowing the beggar's stomach and bowels into the pit.

"What happened next was almost surreal. I shall never forget it. For a moment - one brief moment - the man remained standing as if unaware that he had been shot. Then slowly he turned to his executioner, eyes gripping him in a curse of death. This look, this ghost, will haunt him for eternity. I know it. I know it. His jaw dropped, as if to say something. A dark blood oozed through his teeth before the legs collapsed from under him. He fell perfectly into place in the pit.

"With that, two men on the far end and one from the middle broke and ran. The soldiers yelled at first... something stupid like 'stop or I'll shoot.' I knew this was my only chance and I dove into the trench, pulled the carcass of the disemboweled man over me. His eyes... his eyes were still open in the curse. I wormed my neck under his chest to be covered with blood. The moist... the warmth swept over me. His heart continued to pump. I could feel it slowly, slowly beating down to nothing. It stopped. I heard the bursts of gunfire and the gasps of the living. But I lay motionless, praying and frozen in fear.

"The old Bedouin who had shaded me now knelt and continued his quiet prayers. I didn't look but I could hear his voice. 'May Allah, the merciful protect this one, that the story of our degradation at the hands of these faithless may one day be sung from the mountains to fan the flames of vengeance and bring our murderers to justice."

"I don't know what happened next. No, I do. I do. I could hear it. They cut their throats. The bastards cut their bloody throats. Each lay sucking for breath and gasping as the blood slowly seeped into their lungs. They stirred and twitched about me like so many fish being pulled from the sea. Then one by one they moved no more. My body cramped and I tried to hold back from the earthquake within. My back and leg muscles tightened. I could hardly breathe but I knew that my only hope was to remain completely still and pray they hadn't counted bodies. At one point a shadow covered me and I thought I had been discovered. I wanted to run. But just as I was about to give up, a splash of warmth hit my neck and face. The soldier was urinating on the corpse of the Shia who had defied him. Urinating on the dead! I pledged at this moment that I, myself, would kill him. Him or a hundred in his honor.

"No other groups came after ours. The devil's work was done for that day. I thought they'd be back to bury us, but no one came. No one. The sun set. I remember the cold. The cold and the flies. I waited without movement, listening for the slightest hint that we were being watched. It was the bleakest of moonless nights; there were no sounds. No sounds but the flies. And then from a trench two or three rows away I heard a faint cry. 'Help me. In the name of Allah, help me.' A raspy voice was pleading. 'I'm dying. Help me.'

"I told the fool to be silent. That his tormentors would surely hear him if he did not cease. But the more I rebuked him, the louder his cries. 'Help me. You must help me. I can't breathe!' He was sucking air as if his throat had been only partially cut. I cursed him. 'I say, be still. If they hear you, you will be dead. We will all be dead.' He continued to plead all the louder. 'Where are you? Where are you and why won't you help me?' I knew that if I did not go to him, the soldiers would come back and we would both be exposed. Deep within I knew that I could not stay there much longer, anyway. I slid out from under my disemboweled savior and looked up. My shoulders and arms were knotted and cramped. The ropes that dug into my wrists had loosened slightly, but I still could not manage to work them free. I stumbled twice and fell head-first back onto the slippery corpses before managing to crawl out of the trench. The cold wind bit my naked skin.

"He continued crying, 'Where are you?'

"I saw a hand reach up from a trench 30 meters away and slid into the channel to crawl over the butchered bodies and reach him. This one, too, was Shia. I could tell from his beard. A man in his fifties, I'd say. He had lost a lot of blood. His nose was broken and there were burns across his face and back. His neck also had been slashed, but not as deeply. He said that he had passed out and couldn't remember a thing.

"This one had the strength to untie me, but as we rose to go he fainted and collapsed again. I knew that we had to leave if we were to survive, so I carried him to the top of the hill. From there I could see the spot where we had surrendered our clothes. It looked as if they had dropped some of the lesser rags, so I left the wounded man and went down to find something to wear and to use as bandages. There were pants. Pants and a tight-fitting shirt forgotten along the trail. I put them on. In the distance I heard laughter and music coming from the building where we had been questioned. I thought of my brother Salaam and of the prisoners who had been separated from us. I knew it was foolish, but I had to see if they were still there. I slid from shadow to shadow down the hill until I could make out the compound. My eyes stretched to see if anyone was in the detainee area. Nothing was moving. It appeared that no one was there. One guard, a small man and alone, was dozing against a jeep on the perimeter. I crept in from behind, close enough to hear his breath. I have never killed anyone before - had never - and I don't know what happened. How it happened. I must have broken his neck with my bare hands. Then I took his clothes and his keys. The jeep was on an incline so I put it in neutral and rolled it down the hill about three hundred meters into the *wadi* before starting it. Then I drove back through the ditch without headlights to find my wounded friend.

"I have clothes. Clothes and food. We'll go back into the city and hide with my eldest brother, Amad. We'll be safe with him. He has English friends. Connections." But I spoke to one who could not answer. And I held him... cried until his spirit departed. Departed. And then I cried no more.

"That was the night my heart joined the resistance."

Ali finished the dark tale and sat stirring his tea. The initial disbelief had transformed into horror in every face in the room, save one. The skeptic, a businessman in his forties wearing a Western suit, smiled unconvinced then looked about. "Yes. Well. We shall see."

Ali was confused. "Am I in, or out?"

The man picked up a Polaroid camera and loaded the film. "We shall check your story with our sources to determine whether we trust you or shoot you." He aimed the camera. "Smile."

"But I tell you the truth!"

"That, my friend, will be determined soon enough. First, we will check this photo out with your alleged brother, Amad and his wife, Azza."

"Haifa. Her name is Haifa al Bakr. She is soon to have a baby. A son."

"Yes. Well. We shall see. What was your address again?"

"110 Marga Trifa."

"Marga Trifa Street." He jotted a note to himself in his Franklin Day Planner. "Then we will visit the home of your fiancee Nadia Toussar..."

"Boussar. Nadia Boussar. But her family may have already escaped."

"Yes. Well. For your sake let us hope they have not. Finally, if you pass these first tests, we will determine your true allegiance through a series of other means."

"What other means?"

"Other means." The man put the cap back on his pen and smiled. "You could be a spy. An infiltrator. We must be extremely careful, you understand. And if we are forced to kill you, it won't be anything personal."

The man motioned to a boy who looked to be his son. The lad produced a roll of duct tape and proceeded to adhere Ali to his chair. "Sorry about the tape. We had hoped to procure some cuffs by now. But one must make due."

Before they could wrap his mouth, Ali managed a request. "Could I trouble you for one small favor?"

"Perhaps."

"My brother. Salaam. He was with me and I don't know what happened to him. He is only 16. The age of your boy. Could your people keep their ears open? Possibly?"

The man could only laugh. "Our ears are always open, my friend. And our eyes never close. You would do well to remember this, should you become one of us." He nodded to the boy. "Tape him."

Chapter 8: The Unlikely Hero
Kuwait City
August 21, 1990

Ed Lippencott was an unlikely hero. He was an insurance man - just an insurance man. Nothing more and nothing less.

His big break in life came on the day when he received the promotion to cover the entire Middle East territory. Ed didn't like the idea of leaving the home office in Wausau, but this opportunity was the rendezvous with destiny he had been waiting for all of his life. And he knew that he could not afford to let a chance like this pass him by. Businesses worldwide needed insurance. Rain or shine, recession or depression, feast, famine or war, businesses needed insurance. And Ed Lippencott was the man for the Mideast. (At least that's what his regional manager told him in the pep talk before he departed for his new territory.)

Timing had never been Ed's hallmark. He had only been on the job for three weeks when the tanks rolled in. He was visiting a fruit warehouse on that morning, about to close on one of the most lucrative deals of his own personal career when the world collapsed. And suddenly Ed found himself in the center of Kuwait City with an expired rent-a-car, no hotel reservation, surrounded by 150,000 Iraqi troops.

Ed loved fruit. He honestly loved fruit. He once told a blind date that he thought he could live the rest of his life on fruit alone. (She was duly impressed.) And so it came as no terrible disappointment when he found himself hiding in a cold storage building with crates and crates of South Pacific fruit on that first day of the invasion of Kuwait. Ed figured that he must have been the luckiest man alive. After all, if you have to be someplace during a desert war, it might as well be in a cold storage warehouse surrounded by 15 tons of fresh bananas, limes and oranges.

Lippencott was not a man predisposed to violence. He prided himself on keeping the Golden Rule and was even considered a bit of an arbitrator in office squabbles and family disputes. And so it came to him as no small surprise when he killed his first Iraqi soldiers and stuffed them into the walk-in freezer. He hadn't meant to do it. It just was one of those things.

Ed was in hiding, minding his own business, reading the *Kiplinger Washington Letter* over a pineapple shake when he heard the cooler doors open. He crept as slowly as one could to pack a 260 lb. frame into the crates behind him. At first there were no sounds. But gradually Ed was aware of a light set of footsteps sliding across the floor. Peering through a crack in the boxes just long enough to see what was what, Lippencott made out the figure of an Iraqi soldier, short and thin, opening a wooden barrel on the other side of the room. Spying the man's rifle on the floor, Ed mustered the courage to step out and object.

"Excuse me, sir, but this fruit belongs to a client of mine and you have no legal right to rummage through it like that..." Before he could relate the fact that theft and related crimes are what push the rates of insurance up for everyone, the startled sentry dove for his rifle and attempted to empty six lbs. of hot Iraqi lead into Wausau's answer to the Middle East. Ed didn't oblige. He dove behind a nearby dumpster faster than he had ducked out of Cincinnati when he learned that Mary Ellen Knapke wanted to marry him.

"Don't shoot! Don't shoot! I've got a rider on my policy that excludes acts of war!"

Either the soldier didn't understand English or he didn't understand insurance. The little man clicked in another cartridge and squeezed off a few more rounds at his over-sized target. Ed was exasperated. The Iraqis hadn't always wanted to do business with him, but not a one of them had ever tried to kill him before. (Not that he knew of, anyway.) A dreadful silence followed. The insurance rep squinted and crouched, breathing heavily through his overweight frame, wondering what he might do. The diminutive fellow would certainly be no match for Ed if he could only get the gun away. He had at least 150 lbs. on the man. (Albeit, not all muscle. But weight was weight.) Lippencott slithered like a pig-stuffed boa into a bunch of bananas and watched as his life flash before his eyes. Was the soldier going to move in and finish him off? Would he ever live to see his pension fund? Ed popped a Maalox and paused to reassess the situation.

Fumbling through his pockets for the Swiss Army knife he kept near for just such occasions, Ed came upon an envelope. Cholesterated veins tightened and an erratic, overworked heart froze as he pulled out the terrible discovery. His life insurance policy - a classic double indemnity and million dollar contract - was overdue. And the premium check had been sitting signed, sealed and undelivered in his upper coat pocket for the two weeks of the occupation. How stupid he had been! In a split-second Lippencott was filled with the greatest motivation of his entire lusterless life.

The big man leaned a bit too heavily on the throttle of a nearby forklift and the killing machine took on a life all it's own. When the metal monster finally stopped, his unfortunate trespasser was impaled against the warehouse wall and Ed had a decision to make: stash the body or high-tail it to another hiding spot. He chose the former and dragged the poor beggar into a walk-in freezer.

For a week things were relatively calm and Ed had no other company but the fruit flies. On the eighth day, however, the Wausau Wonder found himself defending his client's territory once more. This time, when he managed to lock three snoopy soldiers and their little dog in the walk-in freezer with the stiff comrade, something clicked. The rush Ed felt was tremendous! His transformation had begun.

Turning the thermostat wide open, Lippencott didn't look back in until the pounding had stopped and he was sure they were frozen solid. (Ed never liked dogs, anyway.) The man now possessed a expanding arsenal to bolster his growing confidence. Along with the cache of arms came a treasure-trove of Iraqi occupation maps, military codes and one ultra-sophisticated long-range radio transmitter. Ed began to fashion himself somewhat of a cross between Sylvester Stallone and James Bond as he modeled his new hardware in the bathroom mirror and tinkered with the radio.

The fear of being caught, however, finally caught up with him. With all that rotting fruit and a growing number of bodies in the deep freeze, Ed found himself robbed of the 12 hours of sleep a body in sales needs to maintain a cheery disposition. A week later with two additional notches on the freezer door, Lippencott knew that the time had come to make a decision. When the count finally hit nine, Wausau's answerman to the Middle East packed his radio and a large lunch. He asked the frozen corpses for forgiveness one by one, saluted and reluctantly deserted his post. It made him extremely sad to go, though. He didn't know what to do next or where he'd ever find such a great hiding place. For, next to a good actuarial discussion, Ed liked fruit.

He really liked fruit.

Chapter 9: Shatt-al-Arab
Baghdad, Iraq
August 22, 1990

Without a major open border, the blockade had the potential to bite. Oil and much-needed petrodollars had been shut off through Turkey. Trucks in Jordan couldn't begin to keep up with demand. The only possible direction to turn was north. And that meant rapprochement with the mullahs: a deal with the devil to stave off hell.

The advisers who first suggested going to Iran did so under fear of death. They believed Iraq could outlast the alliance, or rather the United States, if she could only find a large enough window to open for fresh air. The Americans made a lot of noise, but they tired fast and didn't have the stomach for either a long war or an even longer wait. Storehouses in Iraq were full. The land was productive and the people were used to rationing. But a prolonged siege could threaten the party's security. In order to hedge their bets, Saddam's inner circle needed Iran. Jordan wasn't enough. The little King could too easily be cowed into closing down his small lifeline. If, indeed, a war was to break out, the Iraqis could not fight on four fronts. History had taught them that much. And so Saddam's advisers came early on that late summers' day suggesting an Iranian option and hoping they'd live to see the next morning.

The Father-Leader scowled as he read their reports. His henchmen waited. They had prepared their scenarios as carefully and realistically as possible. If worse came to worse, this is what Iraq would be facing. Saddam had to know.

He read on, lighting cigarette after cigarette, then finally looking up. "It could be this bad?"

The boldest of the advisers nodded. Saddam didn't like negative news or opinions first thing in the morning. Yet, he was a pragmatist.

"Well then, see what you can do. If we give them back their prisoners, what then?" Iraq had over 15,000 Iranian POWs left over from a former war. Many of them had been held for seven years or more. Some had been teenagers when they were captured and now faced life in their mid-twenties. These Iranians were a trump card to Saddam. He would hold them until the right hand called them to be played. Now was the time. The cards were calling.

"The prisoners, Excellency, would be a..." a general began. He stopped mid-sentence when the Father-Leader glared up at him.

"A what?"

"The prisoners would be a..." he hesitated again. "...a start with Iran."

"A start? Only a start? What more could they possibly want?" Saddam knew the answer to his own question. The true prize of the war was the Shatt-al-Arab waterway: Iraq's trophy from the Iranian conflict and their only access to the Gulf.

One man dared speak the word they were all thinking. "Just a thought, Excellency. But we might buy an ally, or at least disarm a possible adversary if we were to give them back Al Arab." He flinched.

Saddam was unusually quiet. How could he explain this to the hundreds and thousands of crippled and maimed soldiers who littered his country? How could he explain this to the millions of civilians who had lost loved-ones in the debilitating war? How could he dare suggest that eight long years of sacrifice - a sacrifice which had sent his economy into a total shambles and set Iraq back a generation - had come and gone for naught?

How could he explain it? He didn't have to. He was Saddam Hussein. And this was a life-or-death matter. He would deal with anyone he wished in any way he chose. He would rewrite history, politics, rhetoric and attitudes with a single stroke of the pen. No one would question him. He would make a deal with his competitors, his arch-enemies or the devil, himself, if it meant holding on to power.

"It was just a thought, Excellency," whispered the adviser, clearing his throat. "Something we might... we might... consider."

Saddam eyed a fly on the ceiling as if it were a surveillance camera, then looked sharply back. "We might."

The advisers couldn't believe their ears. They pushed one step further. "If it is your wish, we will explore it." There was silence.

Saddam sighed. "It is." That was all he said.

Six days later U.S. spy satellites spotted the first Iranian supply trucks roll across the plains at Basara and turn north.

Chapter 10: Evil Incarnate

The Pentagon
August 23, 1990

Francis tore the report from his typewriter and clumsily ran it through the paper shredder. He dropped to the floor for 10 quick fingertip pushups before slapping his own face and returning to his antique hunt-and-peck machine for a ninth start.

The major stopped to look over his shoulder. "What's up?"

"I keep running into a mental block."

"Whatcha doin'?"

"Writing a report."

"Who for?"

"For whom."

"What are you, my mother? Who for?"

"For the president. He wants to know if Saddam Hussein is mad?"

"Mad about what?"

"Mad. You know, crazy. Insane."

"Oh." The major glanced down at the mess on his own desk, then back up at Khalil, raising a bushy eyebrow. "Why aren't you using the comput... what's he asking you for?"

Francis ignored that crack and slouched down to the typewriter to try once again. The Old Man continued to peer over his protege's shoulder. "How about this one: 'There's a fine line between madness and genius.' "

"Thanks, but it's a bit cliche for my taste. Besides, that line has already been quoted and requoted enough concerning Hussein. I've got to be more original."

"Suit yourself," he replied, propping his 15 1/2 D Florsheims on top of Khalil's desk and folding his arms behind his head to lean back.

Francis stared blankly at the white sheet before him and scratched his chin. Finally he frowned and began to type: *"There's a fine line between madness and genius."* A fine line. Indeed.

"Was Napoleon mad? Not when he was blowing across Europe like a storm. Not when he was conquering the finest of the world's mighty. Not while he was winning.

"Was Hitler mad? Not when he was rolling over Poland's cavalry with his tanks. Not when he marched into the Sudetenland. Not when he bypassed the invincible Maginot Line and took France without a fight. Not when he had brought the civilized English to their darkest hour. Evil, yes. But mad? No. He wasn't judged mad until he bogged down in Russia. Not until he lost in North Africa. Not until the Red Army and Patton were closing in on his beloved Berlin. Hitler was not judged mad until he lost. Up until then he was a genius."

The Major was breathing down his neck. "You're writing like you speak."

"What?" Francis looked up.

"You're not writing in complete sentences. You can get away with that in public speaking, but not when you write."

"Whose report is this, anyway?"

Francis ripped the paper from its carriage and started an eleventh time. *"Is Saddam Hussein mad? The Western world and its army of reporters likes to think so. It makes for good copy. It makes for good Pentagon PR. It makes the $26 billion price tag, the $9 billion forgiveness of Egypt's debt and the dozens of American lives already lost in training and transport exercises more palatable to the American public.*

"But is Saddam Hussein really mad? Shrewd, cunning, merciless, deadly, power driven - yes. But mad?"

The Major was playing now with a paper clip and a large rubber band. "What's he asking you for?" He shot the clip across the room in Fran's general direction.

Khalil glanced up, slightly annoyed. "Who?"

"Why's the president asking you?"

He sighed, shrugged his shoulders and flashed a boyish smile. "I think he kinda likes me."

"He doesn't even know you." The Major paused and squinted, aiming another rubber band. "He doesn't, does he?"

"What?"

"Know you?"

Francis frowned and continued, typing faster now as the ideas began to flow: *"If he is mad, this 'madman' has quietly built a million-man army, equipped it with the most sophisticated weapons on the world market and financed it all with our money. This 'madman' has marched into his neighbor's home, taken a sleeping NATO and US intelligence community by surprise and now suddenly controls 20% of the West's lifeblood. This 'madman' has weighed his risks and quietly built himself a human shield of hostages on a scale that the world has never seen. This 'madman' has cleverly trapped 10,000 Soviet citizens in Iraq and presently holds 150 Soviet advisers to contracts that will keep them working for him well into the next new year. This 'madman' has come but one order away from controlling nearly half of the world's known oil reserves. Those who wish to dismiss him or relegate him to the level of just another insane Third World despot are sadly mistaken.*

"For this 'madman' is not a mad man. He knows exactly what he is doing, what his odds are and what he must do to accomplish his goals. He has taken the most brilliant calculated military risk since December 7, 1941 - a gamble that came with a huge upside potential. By taking this risk, Saddam Hussein has written his name into the history books and has positioned himself to overthrow, overhaul and unite the entire Arab world. The beaten and repressed masses are sick and tired of the West's blindness to their grievances. These 200 million Arabs are fed up with being treated like an underclass of human. They have had it with our duplicity, empty promises, humiliation and indifference. And, in spite of the fact that Saddam Hussein al Takriti is a brutal murderer, there are millions who see this man as the first true hope for dignity since Nasser; the first possibility of a future since the initial hours of the Yom Kippur war; and the best chance to make the West pay attention since the assassination of Anwar Sadat."

Fran frowned at his last paragraph. He clicked it out of the typewriter and reluctantly handed it across the desk to his mentor. "Do you think this sounds too pro-Arab? If it comes off as partisan, the 'powers that be' will dismiss me as a fanatic and not give me another chance."

The major appeared pleased to be asked his opinion. "What am I, your mother or your English teacher?" He cocked his head up, held the report at arms' length and mouthed the words as he read.

"You need glasses."

"My eyes are fine. It's just that my arms are too short."

Khalil offered a courtesy laugh as the consultant's fee and waited for the Old Man's review. "So, what do you think? Too pro-Arab?"

The major's mouth contorted in deep thought. "Oh... I'd say... I'd say..."

"You'd say what?"

"I'd say... I'd say it looks all right."

Francis cut the last paragraph anyway and started a new tack.

"Hussein will stop at nothing in order to hold on to power. In 1980 he personally presided over a firing squad that executed 20 of his closest aides for disloyalty. In 1981 he mass-produced a pamphlet written by his favorite uncle entitled 'Three Whom God Should have not created: Persians, Jews and Flies' to justify the Iranian war. In 1982 he arrested an adviser for questioning the wisdom of his invasion of Iran. When the man's wife pleaded for his release, Saddam returned the body in a black bag chopped to bits. All throughout his reign he has routinely rounded up opponents, trumped up charges and executed them. Over the years he has quietly ordered the mass deportation, torture and near genocide of his

Kurds. In 1988, he rained poison gas on them to punish them for supporting Iran."

Khalil's mind flashed to the infamous video images of bloated Kurdish babies covered with flies, lying in silence on the stone streets and green fields of his memory. The vivid picture had become part of America's collective portrait of Saddam. It stood as a lucid reminder of just who and what this man was. Hussein had turned every Kurdish village within 100 miles of the Iranian border into a ghost town to suit his needs. He probably wouldn't flinch at doing the same to Kuwait if it came to that.

Fran resumed: *"Meanwhile in Iraq, he is revered as a god. He has flooded the air waves, billboards and street lights with his image. He has stamped his own name on the bricks of the newly restored Babylon. He has proclaimed himself 'father-leader' of the nation and is chanted in nursery rhymes, praised in poetry. With the invasion of Kuwait he claimed for himself near messianic glory by writing: 'A newborn child was born of a legitimate father and an immaculate mother. Greetings to the makers of the second of August, whose efforts God has blessed.'*

"No, this is not a madman. Neither is he a genius. He is simply ambitious, simply daring, simply ruthless and simply evil. He is a diabolical man, a gambler and a very dangerous adversary. But Saddam Hussein is not mad."

Francis sat back, pleased with what he had written. The major was fiddling with the antenna of his miniature black and white TV on the shelf and had just pulled in NBC. "Hey kid, take a look at this!"

Francis turned in time to see a shot of Saddam posing with British hostage children. He was patting a trembling little boy on the head and smiling a Darth Vader smile. "Turn it up."

The major hit the volume as Hussein spoke through an interpreter: "Are you getting your milk, Stewart?"

The Old Man laughed. "Who does this guy's PR anyway?"

"I think it's the same people who put Dukakis in the tank." Francis slid back to his station.

"Note: With the memory of the Marine barracks in Beirut fresh on our minds and bills from the S&L scandal coming due, the American public is in no mood to fund or fight a major Mideast war. We need much more than a simple 'madman' for an enemy if we are to convince Congress and the American public to spend a dime on any of this.

"Today, a month into the invasion, Saddam Hussein may have inadvertently given us the diabolical combination we needed in a marketable enemy. The video footage of him patting hostage children on the head should be played for all it is worth. We haven't had a PR image like this for an enemy since the days of the Ayatollah. We must do what we can to insure that Saddam's mismanaged attempt at this propaganda coup here backfires miserably and that through it he appears less like the benevolent despot patting heads and more like Satan, himself, kidnapping children before the eyes of the world. Take this combination of evil and madness intertwined, combine it with the very real nuclear scare , and we may finally have the enemy we need to shift America's paradigm. Madness and evil together in the

hands of a nuclear power - this image more than any other stands a fighting chance of reversing public opinion."

Francis rolled the opus from his machine, kissed it like it was his sister and handed it off to the major. "See what you think this time."

His mentor read it twice before venturing a review.

"Well?"

"Well what?"

"Well, what do you think of it?"

The major stood plucking his eyebrows and re-reading the report. "I think... I think it will pass. I especially like the line about genius and madness being a fine line. That's brilliant." He handed the report back to Fran, picked up a crossword puzzle and headed off for the bathroom. "Business, you know." A moment later Khalil heard the crusty old voice echoing down the hall. "Oh, you be sure and quote me as your source when you type it over. And don't misspell my name this time. Got two ee's at the end."

Five days later Francis was watering his dead hibiscus when the major picked up a ringing desk phone and stood to immediate attention. "It's for you. It's him!"

"Him who?"

"You know. Him!" He covered the receiver and belted out a rendition of 'Hail to the Chief' that would have made Roseanne Barr cringe. "Can we put this on the speaker?"

Fran smiled a 'no way' and took the phone. "Yes, sir. The president? Yes. I can hold." He grinned from ear to ear and 'shooed' the major to his own side of the room. "Yes, sir. The report? Yes sir. Thank you sir." The Old Man was edging in toward him again. "Do you mind?"

The major held his heart and slunk away like an over-kicked dog.

"No, sir. Not you. No.... Excuse me? Yes, Mr. President. I'd beg to differ with him on that one. This man is a minor league tyrant trying to play in the major leagues. He is willing to sacrifice anything - 300,000 Iraqis and a decade of his country's future - if it means he can keep on playing. But he isn't fool enough to sacrifice his own life. I believe that's where he'll draw the line, sir."

Francis smirked at the eavesdropping major and waved him off again. "Me? You're asking me?" Fran straightened up and stuck his tongue out at the Old Man. "Well, for starters a madman wouldn't necessarily care for his own safety. A sane man would. Saddam Hussein is sane enough to be paranoid. Changes body guards every day. Has his own personal chair brought wherever he goes so that no one can slip a poison tack on it. The only shot we have of removing him from Kuwait short of full scale war is to threaten his life personally. Yes sir. I know we have laws prohibiting assassinations of foreign..."

He paused, listening to the president's sermon for a full minute without getting a word in. Then he stuck to his guns. "Excuse me? No sir, it would have to be more than a simple bluff. Absolutely. The Arab world is accustomed to his threats and hollow rhetoric. That's the way he does business. This being the case, if we are to make an impression on the man, we'll have to let it slip through a very high and credible source that the focused goal of our entire armed campaign is to terminate Saddam Hussein, himself. No sir. Not simply his regime but his own life. Yes sir. However it is done, he'll have to believe this is more than a bluff. Sir? Yes sir, we would want to make it appear that the news got out without our wanting it to get out. A leak from the very top. He's not going to move a camel back to Baghdad unless he's convinced that we are no longer going to play by our own rules. Find a way to get this across, and you may save the world a war."

The Marine listened without responding and the Major thought he caught a hint of surprise in his voice. "Me? Why, yes, Mr. President. I'd be honored." He listened again then added a simple 'thank you, sir' before hanging up.

"Well? Well?" The major's head nodded faster than a rear window dog on a rough road. "Well?"

"Well what?"

"What did he say? What is he going to have you do?"

"Who?"

The major took a back-handed swing, missing his tormentor's nose by a hair. "Mother Teresa, who else? The president, for God sakes!"

"I might have to make a trip or two for him again."

"You?"

"Yup."

"Why you?"

Francis leaned over his desk toward the Old Man with a false humility. "I think he kinda likes me."

Chapter 11: Casualties of War
The Oval Office
September 15, 1990

General Mike Dugan had marched to the apex of a brilliant career. Two wars, a chest full of medals and 32 years of exemplary service had brought him to the position of chief of staff of the entire United States Air Force. For three months he held the job that he had dreamed about since officer training school. He was finally at the right place in the right time: in the vortex of power at the prime moment of his nation's need. After a distinguished career in Vietnam, he thought he had seen everything. And, in truth, he was ready for everything a war could toss at him. Everything except what he was to face in the Oval Office that day.

The president wanted to see him an hour prior to the scheduled meeting of the Joint Chiefs. It was something important. Urgent.

"Mike, come in. Come in." The commander in chief was finishing a call as he motioned his star General to approach. Cheney and Sununu stood as he entered. The fact that those two were there wasn't a good sign. The businessman and the bureaucrat didn't sit well with this career officer. They shook hands cordially and invisibly shook heads. Bush was finishing a call: "And how much did the Emir promise? 2.5 billion? I hope that's just through the end of the year. Good. Good. And the Saudis? Remind whoever you talk to that a few extra billion doesn't mean much in the context of a battle for survival. I'm told that an oil-price increase of $10 a barrel translates into a $36 billion annual windfall to Saudi Arabia. We expect them to be willing to 'recycle' it and defray our costs."

He motioned General Dugan to sit and held his hand over the receiver. "This will take a few more minutes."

The general nodded.

"And how did Brady do with the Japanese? What? And they call that 'doing their best?' $1.3 is nothing. They can certainly give us in-kind services like equipment and troop transportation. No. No. They were squabbling over sending 20 doctors! Tell them that they can get around the constitutional constraints by assisting countries hurt by the embargo. That's what the Germans finally agreed to. No, not much more. Bonn is still pouting over our refusal to chip in on their scheme to bail out Eastern Europe. Back to Japan, tell the Foreign Minister that if they're not willing to do more, we'll just have to start charging them for our boys stationed over there. We should be doing that anyway."

An aide offered the general a Diet Coke. He asked for a 7-Up instead.

"No. We can make it look like anything we want, but the fact is we don't have any idea how high the price tag on this will ultimately be. Cost estimates the Pentagon gave me assume we stay 12 months without a shot fired. Of course not! Too many variables. Yes, Baker talked to the prime minister about that this morning. Yes. Yes. I've got Dugan here now so I have to go. Yes. Good luck on the 'United Way' campaign. OK. Goodbye."

The president tossed the phone to his aide and thrust out an aggressive hand to the general. "Mike, I'm so glad you could make it over on such short notice."

"When duty calls, I'm here. Sounds like the Japanese want to golf at our club but don't want to pay the greens fees?"

The president laughed and placed his hand on Dugan's shoulder. "I'll have to remember that one." The two sat. "Mike, I have an assignment for you. Something only you can do for me."

"I am at your service, Mr. President." He sat but remained at attention. The commander in chief reached for his reading glasses and glanced at a single sheet sitting atop his tidy desk. Something was coming.

"I'm a soldier, Mike. I served in time of war. I was a pilot. Even shot down."

Dugan knew the story well. "Yes sir, I have always admired your record." This didn't look good. Sununu was smiling.

"I was an officer. I cared for my men and I know you care for yours. There isn't anything a good officer wouldn't do for his men."

He knew this was it. He had spoken his mind one too many times.

"Whatever we end up calling this action in Kuwait publicly, this is war. You and I know that. There's no nice word for it: altercation, police action, conflict. Our nation is at a time of war... of great need. And I'm going to call on you to serve it as a patriot."

The president turned his swivel chair to the bay window and looked out onto the garden. "We're both soldiers, Mike. We know the horrors of war. We know the capability of the Soviet SAMs that encircle Baghdad and what they could do to our planes... our boys. We know the Iraqi bravado of executing downed pilots on the spot as war criminals."

"What are you getting at, sir?"

Bush turned back to look the man square in the eye. "I'm not ordering you, but I'm asking you to consider something. I know that duty, honor and country mean everything to you. I only want to know one thing: would you be willing to put your active service on the line and go out in a blaze of glory if that meant possibly saving the lives of your men and thousands, perhaps millions of others?"

There was a long and heavy silence. The general didn't quite understand. He knew he soon would all too well.

Bush nodded to Cheney. "Had the president not been an old military and CIA man himself, he wouldn't have listened twice to the plan. But this idea intrigues us enough to justify - shall we say - a serious attempt at it."

"I don't understand." The General cleared his throat and sat erect.

"We think you can save a thousand lives," Cheney began. "No, ten thousand lives. Perhaps this entire war. It's a long shot."

"I'm listening." The guest in the leather chair straightened his tie and held his chin up ever higher.

Sununu smiled, but said nothing. The president leaned back, interlocking fingers behind his head. "I'm an old soldier. There's only one thing I relish more than a good fight and that's finding a creative way to stop one. I don't think we're going to get out of this Kuwaiti mess without at least a bloody nose. Hussein hasn't shown a single sign of flinching. He honestly believes he can outlast us. If there's even a remote possibility of shocking him into withdrawal, we've got to take it. We believe we've stumbled across a possibility that may do just that."

"And it involves me?"

Cheney spoke again. "What if he knew beyond a reasonable doubt that we had only one objective in our game plan?"

"One objective?"

Sununu leaned in. "His scalp."

"I still don't understand."

Cheney and Bush started in together: "What if he knew..." The secretary stopped mid-sentence in deference to the president. "...knew that the focus of our entire military effort would be the end of his life. If we let it slip that our first and foremost objective is to erase him from the scene so that we can deal with his generals to arrange a separate peace?"

The general didn't like the 'we let it slip' bit. "I don't follow."

Cheney took the ball. "He's already paranoid. He sleeps in a different place each night. He has killed off 30 generals and aides three or four different times in the last ten years. There have been regular attempts on his life. The man is obsessed with staying alive and appears willing to do anything to guarantee just that. What if he believes his own demise to be our number one priority? That after the first day of battle when we own the skies, chemical laden SCUDs or no chemical laden SCUDs, our primary target is going to be him."

Bush continued. "What if he knows as certain as daylight that our battle plan calls for a 'Saddam hunt'? The entire force of the American war machine will target him, personally. We will level his home, his family, his barracks. There won't be a place in Baghdad to hide. We will hit his palace, his personal bunkers, his favorite restaurant. Hell, we'll hit his mistress's house if we have to. We do know where she lives, don't we, Dick?"

"We know where she lives," Cheney smiled, "although I've never been there personally."

"And we'll keep bombing and tracking until we get him if we have to take out his entire family, top generals... aides, anyone remotely connected with him."

"And how would he (know)... that he's the target?" The general suspected an answer.

"We put the word out that we plan to stop the war the moment he is out of the picture. Once he's gone, we intend to leave the rest of the country untouched... intact and ready to resume its role as a responsible partner in the region."

"Provided they get out of Kuwait, of course."

"Of course."

Cheney looked back to the president. Sununu simply smiled. He went on: "A bit of misinformation like this could, at a minimum, create a greater paranoia on Hussein's part and siphon his defensive stance back toward Baghdad. At best, it just might force him into a diplomatic posture. I believe this is the one shot we have left at getting him to pull out."

"And how may I be of assistance." The moment the words left his lips, Dugan wished he hadn't asked the question.

Cheney responded. "Slipping this out through a double agent lacks credibility. It creates immediate suspicion. Letting Iraq break an old code might work, but there are no guarantees that Saddam will receive or believe the message. No, we need a method that doesn't look contrived but still gets us front page news. That leaves us with a hard choice."

The four men sat in silence. No one wanted to make the next move.

"Mike, that's where you come in," said the president, finally breaking the ice.

"That's where I go out," the general thought to himself, standing tall at attention. "Mr. President, I am willing to serve you in any way you see fit." He wished he hadn't said that. But he knew he must. He was a soldier. He had sworn an oath.

Sununu re-entered the conversation. "We know that you have been considering going off active duty in the next couple years."

"That was before Desert Shield came up, sir." He had to get that much out. At least that much. It was his one chance at history.

"Yes, Mike," Bush continued, "but if you'd be amenable to it, I'd like you to consider taking your retirement a little earlier than planned. In the interest of the country, I'd like you to be the man who lets this leak. You're the most credible source we have. If you come across like you're shooting off your mouth and tell the world Saddam Hussein is out number one target..."

Sununu interrupted: "It's a bit like the death penalty. Deterrence only works if a criminal knows beyond a shadow of a doubt that punishment will be swift and certain. If Hussein knows that his stay in Kuwait will unquestionably result in his own death, he may have a change of heart... a sudden interest in pulling out."

"We could possibly avert the war. Save lives. Take Saddam out of Kuwait without firing a shot. But there'll be one major casualty of this war, Mike. It will be you." The president appeared genuinely concerned. "To do this right, we'll have to make you look bad in the news for a while. You'll be relieved of your command for letting the battle plan slip. That way there'll be no question about it being misinformation. I, of course, would value your military input throughout this entire campaign. I'll certainly have you stay on as an adviser until it's done with."

"In a closet in the Pentagon or at a base in Antarctica," Dugan thought to himself.

"It would be a sacrifice. But it has to be a sacrifice from the top or Hussein won't buy it. He executes his generals when they make a mistake. If we don't at least fire ours, he won't believe it. Since the plot involves the Air Force, it would have the most immediate credibility coming from you. We feed the story to one major paper - or maybe *Time* or *Newsweek* - and let the rumors fly from there. Cheney will discipline you in front the networks for the 'total impropriety' of leaking secret battle plans to the press. You'll be publicly fired and from that moment Hussein will have to start counting the cost of remaining in Kuwait."

"You think the certainty of us going for his throat will force a retreat?"

"No guarantees. But it will certainly force him to start looking for ways to get out gracefully. It'll make him think twice about the cost of his invasion... give him a reason to change his rhetoric."

The general stood stoic and proud. "My men are willing to die if they are called upon to do so in the service of their country. I ought to be willing at least to go on pension. I am at your disposal, Mr. President."

"We aren't disposing of you, Mike. But we will be using you to get the clear message to that tyrant. And it might work. It's either this or war. You're the last trump card we have in our hand. I just wouldn't feel right about going to war without at least attempting to resolve this peacefully."

For the third time since the initial warm handshake there was a cold silence in the room. Sununu looked at Cheney who looked at the president who looked at the general who looked at the wall.

"Say the word, Mr. President. I'm at your command."

The president nodded and sized up the man. "I knew I could count on you, Mike. You will be forever a hero in my book. The intelligence people will brief you on your story and we'll get the right reporters over by tomorrow."

"Maybe we should hit the (Washington) *Post* and the *L.A. Times*. Then we won't have to wait a week for the magazines to come out," Sununu added.

The president agreed and glanced at his watch. "Is that all we need to do on this right now?" No one spoke. He rose and extended a hand. "Well, Mike, on behalf of the country I thank you. We'll bring this up with the Joint Chiefs so that they understand you aren't really talking. But other than that, no one can know. Oh, you can tell your family, but no more. And they must swear to secrecy." The president stood. "That's all from this end for now."

"Yes, sir. And let me say, it has been an honor and a privilege to have served you in this campaign. Even though it has been rather brief."

The general saluted and turned to go.

"Get yourself a haircut for the cameras. And Mike?"

Dugan paused without looking back. For honor sake, he was about to cheat himself out the fight of his life and the glory of history. His eyes clouded with more than a blur at the thought.

"You're a true soldier."

"Thank you, Mr. President."

He went to his office and started packing.

It came as quite a shock and surprise to the world to pick up the *Washington Post* and *L.A. Times* on Sept. 16 and see a member of the Joint Chiefs laying out the top secret battle plan of the United States. Everyone who understood anything believed that targeting Hussein would be a part of the overall strategy. But no one who knew anything had the guts to say such a thing out loud.

It came as no huge surprise to see Dick Cheney on the nightly news firing his general the next day. *"We never talk about targeting of individuals or targets. We never underestimate the power of the enemy. And we never demean the other forces by making it look like our branch is going to win the war without them."*

As far as the media and the American public were concerned, those were the tragic errors of the general. Dugan responded immediately with the standard intelligence-scripted apology and disappeared into oblivion.

As for the charade, it remained a tight secret. No one outside of Bush's inner circle had even a clue. Baker and Sununu, Cheney and the Chiefs, two aides and two other generals were the only ones in on it. People from the top on down looked with horror and wonder at the thought that one so powerful could err so clearly and fall so quickly.

The secret spin-off from all of this was an objective which Cheney alone had discussed with the President: Once the Pentagon saw what had happened to a general who talked, soldiers from the brass on down remained tight-lipped throughout the duration of the Gulf conflict. That didn't hurt the war effort one iota.

It wasn't 15 hours after Dugan's resignation that the plan appeared to have shaken the Iraqi leader at least somewhat. The very next day Saddam met with Yasir Arafat to suggest for the first time that he would consider a negotiated withdrawal from Kuwait. It came as no small surprise to the defunct Dugan that Saddam's statement wasn't taken seriously by the administration or even met with a response. When he attempted to question the president about it, Sununu took the call and explained that Saddam's ever-changing demands made any true negotiations out of the question. The truth was never known, but the U.S. had moved far too many men and too much foreign opinion to even consider leaving the dictator's armies in tact. No, he would not be allowed to negotiate anything. He would be taken out.

Mike Dugan spent the rest of his war out of the 'beltway' and alone with a part-time job at ABC. Bush called his ex-tactician a week after the air war began to thank him again for his sacrifice. But after that they didn't speak. Protocol, security and Sununu saw to that.

No one but a Pentagon staff analyst and his quirky major suspected a thing about the truth of the Dugan affair. The leak from the top would be written up in a book by Baker after his falling out with the president and later in Bush's own memoirs. But for the rest of the world and the rest of the war, it would stand in silence as one of the single greatest piece of psychological smoke screening that the Bush administration had pulled off. Maybe one of the best pieces in the history of the presidency.

Chapter 12: The Will of Allah
Teheran, Iran
September 16, 1990

"Iran does not do the will of Satan. Nor do we take the advice of Satan. We are subject only to the will of Allah."

An envoy was needed to test the waters. Iran had already been granted its lost Shatt-al-Arab waterway. After 8 bloody years of war, Saddam Hussein had turned and returned everything Iraq had fought so hard to win - everything except his pride. As impossible as it would have seemed only a short year earlier, the desperate man had approached his nation's worst enemy as its best hope to help him hold off the encircling wolves.

The president's men understood the risk. If anyone from the State Department were to go and be humiliated again, a huge amount of negative publicity could result. The 444 days of hostages and memories of the Iran-Contra hearings still hung too close to the surface of America's collective consciousness for this administration to be seen getting into bed with Iran. A lesser emissary would again be chosen to visit the mullahs. As the lists were scanned, it became apparent who the best choice might be. And so the seasoned young Marine was called upon again to travel into an enemy tent and quietly lay out the cards.

Francis was studying a larger than life -size painting of the late Ayatol-lah when Khameni entered the room. He held out a polite hand, but the holy man didn't reciprocate.

"Thank you for seeing me."

The Iranian feigned a half-pleasant smile and sat down behind his huge teak and silver desk. "And what does the *jinna* spy wish today?"

Francis knew the term *jinna* well. His grandfather would use it when ever a storm was brewing or a calf came stillborn. *Jinna* were the demons of the Arabian world's dark side who floated about bringing mischief into the lives of mortals.

Khalil began: "Iraq has returned the lands they took during the war."

Khameni nodded. "Did you come to tell me things I already know?"

"I imagine this 'answer to prayer' came as quite a surprise."

"You are a Christian?"

"Yes."

"Are you surprised when your prayers are answered?"

Khalil wasn't terribly interested in discussing theology at the moment, and got down to business. "We both know that Iran has no desire to see Saddam Hussein retain power."

"What is your point? I am a very busy man."

This guy was tough. Francis retained his smile and tried again. "Knowing this, it has come as no small surprise to us that you would choose to enter an agreement with your archenemy."

"You are my archenemy."

"We know that it was in your best interests to retrieve your prisoners of war and regain the Shatt-al-Arab. We applaud you for doing that peacefully..."

"Your applause means..."

"...but we are somewhat concerned and curious about your intentions with regards to the U.N. blockade... a blockade which you, yourself, have endorsed and are now violating."

"Iran does not supply Iraq. We are in complete compliance with the resolutions and the boycott."

Khalil reached into his briefcase. "I'll let you draw your own conclusions." He attempted to hand his satellite photos to Khameni.

The mullah held up one finger to halt the move. "You are calling me a liar?"

"No, Imam. I am simply stating a point. It is not in the interest of either the United States or Iran to prolong this crisis or to keep Saddam Hussein in power. We would like to see you..."

The leader stood and waved to the heavens. "Iran does not do the will of Satan. Nor do we take his advice. We are subject only to the will of Allah."

Khalil placed the satellite photos conspicuously on the desk and pulled out a letter written in *Farsi*. It was addressed to the chief of Iraq's air force. "I have come with a small request."

Khameni chuckled until he saw that the letter appeared to be penned in his own hand. "What is this treachery? I did not write this!"

"Read on. You may wish that you had." The American stood, patiently studying the judgemental eyes of the Khomeini portrait as his belligerent host read on. Through the reflection in a huge mirror next to the Ayatollah, Francis could see a broad smile beginning to spread across the face of the Iranian.

"What makes you think that Iraqi pilots would do as your letter invites? Fly to Iran and park their planes to sit out the war?"

"To sit out their own destruction? Survival is a powerful motivator, Imam. And the chief of the Iraqi air force is a wise man with no particular desire to go down with his beloved Saddam. I believe your intelligence can verify this."

"And their planes? Whose would they be when this is all over?"

"Details. None of my business, I suspect. You might return them to a peaceful neighbor when Saddam is gone."

"Sounds like a relatively inexpensive way to build an air force."

Francis shrugged his shoulders. "Details. None of my business."

"Indeed." Khameni stood and ushered Francis to the door. "As I said before, Iran does not do..."

Khalil finished the sentence for him: "...the will of Satan nor does it take the advice of Satan."

"We are subject only to the will of Allah."

Francis bowed courteously and walked backwards to the door. "Then please do pray to Allah and see if something like this wouldn't be in the Holy One's will."

Khameni shook the envoy's hand this time. "You are an interesting fellow, *jinna* spy. As for the trucks to Iraq, you can assure your people that our shipments contain food only. No. Food and humanitarian aid. That I swear."

"I take you at your word, Imam."

The cleric nodded sincerely. "We are not so foolish as to sharpen the claws of a tiger."

"I trust not." He turned to go as a bearded student appeared from no where to pull open the 18 foot solid cedar door. "And the letter?"

Khameni flashed a condescending smile. "We will let you know whether we decide to send this to the Iraqi Air Force or not."

"You needn't bother," Khalil grinned with an arrogance that unnerved his most holy host more than slightly. "We'll know."

Chapter 13: The Locusts Come
Baghdad Airport
September 17, 1990

The menacing words blared over the airport terminal speaker like one more slap in the face: *"All women and children waiting for flight 763 to Paris please be advised of a four-hour delay. We are sorry for any inconvenience. Please have your papers ready again for review."*

Karin Kensington had waited in line for the boarding through three other delays and was now numbed beyond impatience. She sat on the suitcase, frightened for herself and the children. The proud Irish woman ached to have her Stewart with them, but knew it was not to be. With three little ones tugging at her sleeves and the pressure of the world bearing down upon her shoulders, she drifted into an uneasy trance:

She was sitting out on the patio trying to balance her checkbook. Stewart was due home any minute. He had worked the late shift but promised to take her out for breakfast before hitting the sack and sending her off to shop. Her dog snoozed lazily on the floor by the wicker couch and Elvis was singing *"Heartbreak Hotel"* on the CD. The air conditioning was already cranked to the limit, although it wasn't yet nine. It was a normal day.

She remembered being startled by something that sounded like a car backfiring. There was a sharp pop, but it didn't seem at all sinister enough to move her. Karin was 21 cents off and couldn't find three checks. It bothered her to no end to be off. She wanted to have everything figured to the penny before they went to breakfast.

Karin had seen the new red Porsche in the showroom downtown and wanted to prove her financial prowess to Stewart before her planned 'coincidence' of passing the dealership on their way to the new Italian restaurant.

She had her eye on that particular car for three months and knew it couldn't last much longer at such a price. The new models were due in soon. Salesmen would be ready to deal. And so, when Stewart called and suggested she put on her best dress, she knew what it meant. He had the promotion! ARAMCO had come through like they promised when the Kensingtons had first moved in from London. "Six months, six figures," was the pledge. And now these folks had kept their word. That's what she liked about the whole lot of them. They had always been honest in their dealings. It was a red dress day. She hoped it might even be a red Porsche night.

Karin stepped into the cool, inviting shower and shaved her legs. She thought she heard him come in twice and shut the water off to listen both times, but no one was there.

She was drying her auburn hair when the first hints came that this was not just another day. Three helicopter gunships brushed in low over the town houses and hovered unusually long. She looked out the window and pondered for a moment. Karin had never seen that type of military helicopter before. The trio hung in the air for two minutes, as if unclear of where they were headed or what they were looking for. And then they were off toward the south. She thought it was the south.

Stewart was late. But that wasn't anything unusual. He was routinely late. Her husband was the last one out of the office most mornings; the last one to leave a party; the last to come to bed. He was always the last one. Too conversational. Too conscientious. But on this day it didn't matter. Being conscientious got him his masters and landed the chemical engineer job at the 'Cat Cracker'. Being conscientious had won him the raise. Being conscientious was about to cinch her the Porsche. She sat down and re-read an old issue of *Country Living* magazine and the English comic paper (with all its objectionable materials edited out).

Maria was the first to call.

"Miss Karin, you all right?"

"Of course I'm all right. Whatever do you mean?"

"Haven't you heard? There has been some kind of military action."

"Whatever do you mean?"

"I'm not sure. There are troops running all about the airport. I was just saying goodbye to 'mummy' when their plane was grounded. All the planes are grounded. We shan't be home for dinner and I'd be rather surprised if she'll be leaving at all."

"Don't be a ninny. Of course she's leaving. She has to get back to mind things at home."

"Well, the soldiers aren't letting any planes go."

"What soldiers?"

"The ones at the airport. Haven't you heard a word I've said? They're bloody swarming all over."

"Has their been a bomb scare or something?"

"I don't know."

"Well, have they evacuated anyone?"

"I don't think so."

"Maybe someone really big is due in. King Fahd or Mubarak or someone."

"I don't know. Some of them are checking people's passports and handbags. But they don't look all that jolly at the moment. I'd say we're in rather a..."

Halfway through the sentence she was cut off. The line simply went dead. Karin wondered. Karin waited.

At 11:30 she noticed the neighbor's Jeep pull in and out of the driveway. David and Carol were waiting and the children ran out of the house to jump in as soon as it honked. They were off before Karin could step out for a word with them.

At 3 p.m. she remembered hearing an air raid siren. The neighborhood was strangely silent. No one had come home from school or work in the entire development. Odd.

By 6:15 it finally occurred to her to turn on the radio. She loathed the radio and rarely played it during the day. Too much propaganda and skewed opinions for her tastes. When she finally did tune in, there was nothing but music - Iraqi march music - and a line in Arabic that kept repeating: *"Allah bless the liberators of the new 19th Province. At last, we are one again."*

Karin didn't know what it meant. But she didn't like it.

And as for Stewart, he never came home.

"Mummy! Mummy!" Little Aeric was jumping up, tugging at her lapel for attention. With the last lunge, chubby fingers caught on her good pearls, snapping the string and showering the terminal's marble floor with her 10th anniversary present. It was all too much. She started to scold the boy, then buried her face in her hands to weep.

A moment later the ugliest woman Karin had ever laid eyes upon dropped her suitcase and stooped over to gather the scattered treasure.

"Don't worry, dearie," the hoarse falsetto voice whispered. "These things happen." The stranger's lipstick was smeared and her false eyelashes were large enough to accommodate Tami Faye Baker. She wore an overbearing perfume and was squatting in a most unlady-like manner as her huge fingers fumbled to retrieve the small spheres.

Karin regained her composure and looked again. She couldn't tell, but it almost appeared as if the woman was sporting a five o'clock shadow. She bent down to thank her rescuer as the woman set the last of the pearls into Karin's open palm.

"Thank you, madam. I've tried to keep a stiff upper lip through all of this, but it's just been too much lately. What with no word from Stew... my husband." The tears began to well up again. "If I only knew where he was in all of this I'm certain that I'd be able to..." Her lip began to tremble so that she couldn't finish her words.

"There, there little missy. Don't cry. Your man will be all right. I'm sure he's doing just fine. This whole matter will be over soon and you'll have your man back. Mark my words." The stranger reached to embrace her. She sobbed for a few minutes more before realizing that the perfume wasn't perfume. It was Old Spice.

"Who are you?"

"Ed Lippenco... Ed... wina. Edwina Bond... Wausauheimer. Yes! Bond-Wausauheimer. It's one of those hyphenated names, you know. And you?"

"Kensington. Karin Kensington. My husband, Stewart works for ARAMCO and..."

"Shhhh! No details, please. You know what they say about loose lips sinking ships and all." Karin nodded, although she didn't know what on earth the woman was talking about. "The children, are they eating well?"

"Mostly rice. No dairy products at all. Very little fruit lately."

"Fruit?" Edwina's ears seemed to prick up at the mention of the word. "I've got just the thing for the little darlings." She bent over in a most appalling fashion and rummaged through her large carry-on bag. The children gathered about and were astounded as she pulled out and pre-sented them each with a perfectly ripe banana. Then she gave Karin two tangerines and a pineapple.

"Where in the world did you get these?"

"Oh, I used to work at a..." Edwina hesitated as two security guards appeared at the gate and began to request papers from those gathered. "Oh, shi..." the large woman began in a lower voice than normal. Little Aeric was looking her in the eye and she returned to her 'Julia Childs' falsetto. "Shhh... shame. Oh shame. I must be off to the lady's room. It's that time of the month, you know. Ha-ha. And supplies have been rather dreary."

"Children, what do you say to the nice lady?"

"Thank you, Edwina."

The soldiers were working their way toward their general direction as Edwina Bond-Wausauheimer dug into her purse for a mirror. She checked her make-up, popped a Maalox and rose abruptly to go. "Well, got to be off. Ta ta. And don't worry, dearie. I'm sure your 'ewartstay ensingtonkay' will do just fine." She winked her left eye and pushed the false lash back into place. "I have ways of getting messages out, you know. We'll see to it."

When the strange woman was gone, Aeric tugged his mother's arm again. "Who was that, mummy? Is she a friend of daddy's?"

"I don't know." Karin looked back just in time to see the grapefruit fall from Edwina Bond-Wausauheimer's blouse and roll across the floor. She smiled. "I dare say I don't know."

Chapter 14: The Arrangement

Sofia, Bulgaria
September 18, 1990

"You may be interested in knowing that we are making an arrangement with the Iraqis to get our people out."

The KGB was fishing. The captain knew it. At least he thought he knew it. Francis had run into this grey-eyed Russian once before and had grown to understand and even enjoy the man. Vladimir Kalinov was a professional unlike most of the party ideologues the Marine had encountered in the Soviet intelligence community. He had a dry wit, an irrepressible laugh and a mind of his own. Fran vaguely remembered the pub and the damp Brussels night just hours after news of Gorbachev's Nobel nomination broke. The two had occasion to meet and share a few jokes and more than a few brews. The Russian kept him laughing for an hour, cracking one joke after another about mutually exclusive terms like "Soviet Military Intelligence" and the "Bulgarian Ministry of Culture." They drank and talked until the bar was closing down and Kalinov remembered an appointment. Then he exited to the rest room and ducked out, leaving Khalil with a $112 bar tab.

This dreary morning they sat under the tattered yellow cloth umbrella of a sidewalk cafe. It was a meeting initiated by his counterpart's embassy. With thousands of Soviet advisers as "guests" of the Iraqi Republican Guard and tens of thousands of Soviet-made weapons aimed at allied positions, the "powers that be" thought it might be worth a cup of *cappuccino* to have the captain visit his new old friend. Heavy trucks rumbling past and jackhammers at a nearby construction site made the *Sofia Internaccionalle* a perfect spot for conversational cover.

"Before we start, I have one question," insisted Khalil. "Who's picking up the tab?"

Kalinov smiled sheepishly and brushed the comment aside with a raised hand before ordering the highest priced full breakfast on the menu and tucking a faded napkin under his collar. Khalil only wanted a hot cup of coffee.

"Let me ask you a hypothetical question" the Russian began. "What would be your government's reaction if, in order to arrange removal of our people from Iraq, we were forced to make certain 'concessions'?"

Fran shifted back in his chair trying to penetrate the Russian's eyes as he waited for his coffee to cool. "I'm not sure what you're asking here."

"For instance: if we were to arrange shipment of a few tons of needed materials and munitions through Iraq's own network past your blockade..."

"If you're planning to send Iraq supplies in violation of the U.N. boycott..."

"Hypothetically speaking."

"We, of course, would consider that a hypothetical insult and be forced to hypothetically confiscate anything you would hypothetically send. But then, of course, know that."

"But of course." The Russian shifted and commenced to devour the colorless food before him while speaking in his half-decent English. "Well then, what if I were to say we were hypothetically requesting cooperation in removal of our people from Iraq, and would hypothetically welcome any confiscation as the price of doing business with you."

Khalil wasn't exactly sure that he was hearing what was being said. Kalinov slid a copy of the *Wall Street Journal* across the table. "Have you read paper today?"

Francis wondered where in Bulgaria the Russian had found the morning *Journal*. His people couldn't get him a month-old *TV Guide* if the free world depended on it.

"I think you'll note the financial section of particular interest."

Francis quickly surveyed the cafe's patrons. There was an old Bulgarian woman warming her hands on a bowl of soup near the street entrance. Two gypsies stared hopelessly into each other's eyes at a table on the far side. A large ruddy-skinned man in a rumpled pin-striped suit sat at a corner table trying too hard not to watch them. Francis made a mental note of the bulge in the man's jacket as he opened the newspaper slowly. There, taped between an article on Michael Milken's life in a luxury prison and the mutual funds rundown was a small envelope. He closed the *Journal* immediately and slid it back toward the Russian.

"What are you up to, Vladi?"

"Let me explain." Kalinov motioned the waiter for a second order and a refill on his friend's coffee. It was steaming and thick and very, very bad.

"Ah, Bulgarian coffee," sighed Khalil in a mock seriousness, "hand-picked by Igor Valdez!" Kalinov didn't catch the humor.

The Russian waited for the attendant to finish pouring his morning caffeine fix and step out of ear shot before resuming in his slightly broken English: "This is extremely delicate operation and must be handled properly. Our number one concern is retrieval of Soviet military personnel. We must have them out before your storm..." He hesitated a moment. The waiter had moved back in to clear a nearby table and appeared to be working at too leisurely a pace. He changed his tone and topic. "Did I tell you the one about Bush, Gorbachev and Honecker? No? It seems each died and was found in waiting room in clouds. St. Peter comes and leads Reagan before judgment throne."

"You said it was Bush who died."

"Reagan, Bush, what is difference?" They laughed as three sets of eyes followed the waiter to the other side of the room. "It is my story. I continue?

Khalil nodded.

"Reagan approaches throne: 'You have robbed the people, made yourself rich off of sweat of common man, left masses hungry in streets. To hell I sentence you!' Reagan leaves room with head hanging low and stands in line for bus to hell. Next is Honecker. He is sweating and wringing hands. The Almighty looks at him and repeats: 'You have robbed the people, made rich yourself off of sweat of the common man, left masses hungry in streets. To hell I sentence you!' Honecker leaves room with head hanging low to stand behind Reagan in line. Finally is Gorbachev. He beams broad smile and walks before throne with hands in pockets. The Almighty chastises him even more severely: 'You have robbed the people, made very, very rich yourself off of sweat of common man, left masses hungry in streets. To deepest hell of hells I sentence you!' Gorbachev doesn't lower head. He smiles all the more and waltzes happily out of room with hands in pockets to make place in line behind Reagan and Honecker. 'How could you smile so?' Reagan asks Gorbachev. 'Do not you realize that you are condemned and bound for hell?' Gorbachev winks, looks around and pulls his hands out of pockets... full of rubles!"

The Russian broke into a long unrestrained laugh. Khalil didn't bother to follow suit.

"You understand, no? Gorbachev has all the people's money! You see?" He launched into his laugh again.

"It must have lost something in the translation," shrugged Khalil, glancing to see if the young waiter was smiling. He was.

Kalinov feigned an annoyed offensive. "You Americans are all alike. No sense of humor. *Saturday Night Live? David Letterman?* Now this I never understand. What is point? They use up five minutes of air space at thousands of dollars a minute on prime time American television for a sketch that has no point! No humor! I would rather spend a year in Siberian Gulag with 200 Jehovah's Witnesses than sit through five minutes of late night American tele..."

The waiter disappeared into the kitchen and Kalinov turned back to Khalil without breaking stride. "Number one concern is our military personnel. Some have unexpired contracts that Iraq is holding us to. No doubt many live and work at sites on your target list. Number two concern is technicians and their families. We want both out of harm's way when the bombing begins. Number three is certain sensitive equipment that neither your government nor mine would like to see fall into Iraqi hands."

"I'm not at all clear what you're offering or what you're asking for."

"I'm almost here. Hold pants. Now, in order to get these out, we must make, shall we say, certain promises to government of Iraq."

"You're buying their freedom with arms that will kill Americans."

"Too harsh. Is not that complex. We are not buying. Trading. Sounds like something you did only short time ago with Americans and Iran? Something you will one day do with American hostages in Lebanon?"

Khalil looked down and motioned to the newspaper. "And the envelope?"

"I was getting to that." Kalinov pulled out a cigarette and offered one to Khalil.

"No thanks. I quit."

The Russian searched his pockets and then the tables in the vicinity for a match.

"The envelope?"

"Ah, yes. The envelope." He found an old lighter in his overcoat pocket and coughed as he savored a long first drag. "You know, this is one of few ways that America is ahead of us. We Russians smoke too much."

"The envelope?"

"Did you know that more Colombians die from result of American tobacco than Americans who die from Colombian cocaine? Is true. I read it in *New England Journal of Medicine*."

"The envelope, Vladi."

"Oh yes..."

"You read the *Journal* ?"

"The envelope? Routes, dates, ship loading dockets. They are all there. Seven shipments in all. You may have five if you wish. If you were to let first and third through it would benefit our credibility greatly. We will route the materials directly through Saddam's network and chief buyers so they will all be clearly traceable for you to sting."

Khalil set the paper back down on the table and paused. The Russians were the world's finest chess players. With them, nothing that appeared so clean and clear on the surface ever ended up that way. He studied the KGB face for a missing piece or hint of hidden motives.

"We take this as personal favor from Mr. Bush to President Gorbachev. And, might I add, we do this at great internal risk. There are those in KGB who have stood with Hussein for many years and consider him ally. Not many of our own people even know of this action." He leaned over the table. "Especially Pavlov."

Prime Minister Pavlov had recently been set in place by the Soviet hard-liners to keep Gorbachev in check. Pavlov just happened to be a personal friend of Saddam Hussein. "Soviet Army Intelligence is charged with coordinating these shipments to Iraq. They are being kept totally out of knowledge of these interdiction plans. Certain elements of KGB are being left out as well. Many will know of the shipments, but only a handful at very top will have knowledge of scheduled American seizure."

The whole thing looked about as innocent to Fran as a Claymore mine. The Soviets wanted their people out. That was fairly certain. But the rest fell together all too neatly. If, indeed, Kalinov was telling the truth and giving Khalil plans that his *komissars* didn't even know about, Francis was holding a promotion in his hands. Everybody would win. Saddam's agents would think that the U.S.S.R. had acted in good faith. Hard-liners in the Russian Army and KGB would believe they'd won a policy coup by supporting their old friend Saddam against their old enemy, the U.S. American agents would show up at the last minute and shut down Iraq's entire smuggling network. And 1200 Soviet citizens would be home to Leningrad for Christmas.

If, on the other hand, Kalinov was lying, then Francis was being set up for something big. If there was a hidden agenda, the Marine would be back in the motor pool at Paris Island or in the brig at Fort Dix by New Years.

"You don't just set yourself up for altruistic reasons. What exactly do you want from me in exchange for this newspaper?"

"Nothing, my friend. Absolutely nothing." Kalinov had a smiling squint in his eye.

"I find this all just a bit too hard to believe."

"OK. OK. How about from now on you laugh at my jokes?"

The waiter returned to seat three Japanese businessmen and an overweight Bulgarian wearing a back brace. The Russian finished his coffee in 30 seconds of silence. Khalil glanced at the sports section. Daryl Strawberry was signing with the Dodgers for $20.3 million.

"We want nothing. Nothing except the approximate commencement of the 'storm' so that we might remove our people before it all begins. We don't need to know specifics. A general timetable would be ample."

Khalil made a mental note that the Russian used the term 'storm' again. He hadn't recalled using that word himself for the American campaign.

"Or so that we might inform Saddam to be ready."

Khalil glossed over the comment at first, but suddenly reared up in alarm. The Russian was smiling. "Before I was insulted when you did not laugh at my jokes. Now I am hurt."

"The comment about informing Saddam was a joke, I take it?"

"Come now, don't you trust me?"

"Reagan always used to say: 'trust but...' "

"Trust but verify. That's the only Russian you Americans know."

"That and Smirnoff," smiled Khalil, raising his cup in a mock toast.

"You want the date of the invasion?" Francis was careful to use the word 'invasion'. That's all you want?"

"Come now, we both know full well that an invasion isn't about to come along until quite some time after the air campaign begins."

"You want the date when hostilities commence?" The Russian nodded. "That is absolutely all you're asking in exchange for the Iraqi smuggling network delivered to us on a silver platter?"

Kalinov nodded 'da', then 'nyet'. "We may also need certain small friendly favors in future as well."

"Favors such as what?" Here it came.

"Oh, it is most difficult to say at this time."

"Try me."

"These favors might take shape of..." he shrugged his shoulders and paused. The bus boy was back cleaning tables again. "Such as taking *Letterman* off air. Possibly replacing with reruns of *'Lucy Show'*. Now that is humor a Russian can appreciate. Objective, not subjective." Kalinov turned and nodded to the fellow in the rumpled pin-striped suit sitting at the table in the corner. The man rose, ambled over to the waiter and spoke with him a moment. Then he opened his jacket. The boy dropped the tray and hastily left the premises.

"There is one other immediate possibility for favor. We may soon be forced to take certain steps in Baltics which will not play so well on *Nightline*. We would only request that you restrain official criticism should these events arise. Things are most tenuous... situation is most tenuous now in Soviet Union. Gorbachev finds himself walking on fine line between *glasnost* and the old guard. He could be gone any day. It may be that the Baltics will be testing ground for KGB resolve. We don't know this. We don't know what will Black Beret do if push comes to *putsch*. But if it happens..." Kalinov shrugged his shoulders and sipped his cloudy coffee.

It was starting to make some sense. There was a hidden agenda after all. Khalil studied his counterpart's face once more, wondering if this, too was smoke and mirrors for another motive. He laid the paper down once more. "I can't make any promises for the president or the State Department."

Kalinov motioned to his friend across the restaurant. Aware that he wasn't carrying a weapon, Francis tensed and searched for the nearest escape route. The large man stepped in from behind, then pulled up a chair.

"Uri Mendelev, I'd like you to greet my old friend Captain Francis Khalil, U.S. Marine Corps on special assignment." Mendelev nodded and held out a huge hand. Francis caught a hint of something in the man's eyes that he hadn't expected to see. It almost looked like humility.

He sat and Kalinov continued in a noticeably lower voice. "Uri and I both have family there. I have brother. Uri has son."

"Where?"

"Iraq. Northern Iraq or western. My younger brother is training mobile missile crews and is on contract for six more weeks. Uri's son is at listening post near Iranian border and will be there in all likelihood well into Desert's Storm. We want them out. We want them all out."

It slowly occurred to Francis that this man might finally be getting around to the truth. He searched the somber face of Kalinov's Cossack comrade. The man nodded again, slowly rubbing his stubbled chin. Fran tried to weigh all of the angles. These two men could possibly be working on their own. In that case, the report in their possession could be their death warrant. Or it could be that a small faction within the Soviet Intelligence community was attempting to pull the plug on the old guard KGB. Anything was possible. It could even be a setup or trap to compromise Francis personally. He pushed the paper back to the Russian a final time. "I have to handle this one by the book. Let me talk with some of my people. You can get back in touch with me in a few days. I believe you have my number."

"Tell you what, my friend," Kalinov rose and placed the newspaper on top of Khalil's attache case, "you take it and do whatever you will with it. I've already read sport's page. Twenty million dollars for baseball player? We are in wrong business, comrade." He grabbed his overcoat to go. "I know we can trust each other. I've read your dossier."

"Trust, but verify," answered Khalil.

The Russian laughed again and looked at his watch. "Good day, Mr. Reagan." Mendelev winked at Francis and helped his boss with the coat. They shook his hand and wandered across the muddy street.

"Trust, but verify."

The sun popped momentarily through the grey, oily morning as Francis sat trying to write the entire dialogue to memory for his report. Across the street a tour bus unloaded its cargo: a group of long-faced Bulgarian diplomats, their chests filled with metals, and their aging, red-cheeked wives (whose chests were filled with chests). Fran stretched and sipped one last dark sludge of the poor excuse for a coffee now turned cold. Tucking the newspaper under his arm, he pushed away from the table and glanced down as a small brown sheet fell to the sidewalk. He frowned.

The Russian had left him with the bill again.

Chapter 15: Israel
Tel Aviv, Israel
September 19, 1990

"Overseas collect call from Francis Khalil. Will you accept the charges?"

Kathryn screamed so loud that every teacher in the lounge heard her. "Fran! Where are you?"

"Israel. I don't think I'll be able to make it home tonight."

"You've got to."

"I don't think I can."

"You aren't in a body cast or anything, are you?"

He laughed.

She hadn't meant to be funny. "Francis, tonight's the night." There was more than an aching urgency in her voice. "If you're serious about wanting a baby, then there's this little thing called timing."

"Can't we do it tomorrow?"

"We should have made love last night."

"Well, maybe we'll just have to skip this month."

"We skipped last month. You were gone then, too. Remember?"

"Yeah. OK. I'll see what I can do."

"How many hours difference is there where you are?"

"I don't know. It's probably already tomorrow here."

"Well, get home yesterday."

"Right. I'll try."

"What are you doing in Israel, anyway? Or can't you say."

"I'm just supposed to brief someone from State. He's in a meeting right now, but maybe I can bust in or catch him on a break and take a different flight."

"See what you can do."

"I'll try."

"If you're serious about having a little Joseph or Josephine running around the apartment some day then you better do more than just try."

"If there's a way, I'll find it."

"That's my man. I'll leave the light turned on for you."

"Keep yourself turned on for me, too."

"I'm sure you'll do that when you get here."

The Marine-turned-diplomat talked himself past the guards at the Knesset conference chamber and was ushered in as Assistant Secretary of State Lawrence Eagleburger was attempting to reason with Israel's fiery prime minister. Twelve Israelis and four Americans sat eye-to-eye around the olive wood table with its Star of David inlaid in gold. Eagleburger didn't have time to acknowledge Khalil's entrance. He was mid-sentence in a hot debate: "Israel must not and will not bomb Iraq's nuclear power facilities."

Shamir remained unimpressed. "If you don't, we may be forced to."

"As we agreed in August, Israel must stay totally out of this. Your nose must be completely clean."

"We agreed to consider it for that moment. The winds have changed."

"We are counting on you..."

"And if you fail?" interrupted the obstinate little man. "Do you think we will stand idly by and allow our fate be determined by outsiders? If Hussein is permitted to possess nuclear weapons, do you think for one moment that he will refrain from using them? We will allow no such..."

"The very first wave of our bombers will erase both Saddam and his Osiris Nuclear Facility from the face of the earth."

"You Americans are so cock-sure of yourselves. We cannot afford to be. What if he withdraws from Kuwait prior to your attack? What if, at the last moment, he comes to his senses and retreats to fight another day? Another day when he possesses the bomb? The entire international community will breathe a collective sigh of relief and go home leaving us with a butcher in our back yard. Your hands will be tied by both the U.N. and the American public. I've seen the polls. Your people don't want war. We, unfortunately, do not have the luxury of time on our side. Each week that this madman is left alone is another week closer to our destruction. We cannot, will not stand for it."

Khalil knew he was out of line, but he couldn't keep silent. "Saddam will never leave Kuwait voluntarily. That scenario is highly unlikely. You don't have to worry about it. We're going to get him. The man has too much invested in this to simply pull stakes and disappear into the night. Highly unlikely."

"Who is this man?"

"Someone who knows Saddam Hussein personally." Eagleburger winked at Fran and shrugged as if to say "So, I lied. Sue me."

Shamir studied the Marine more carefully than the Iraqi captain on the border a month earlier. "Highly unlikely? Highly unlikely! You can afford to take such a gamble. We , however, have no such luxury. You are an ocean away. This is our back yard. You can afford to toy with Iraq. We can afford no second Holocaust." Shamir sneered. "Highly unlikely."

Eagleburger took back the conversation. "The United States will do whatever is necessary to protect the state of Israel. Of that you can be sure. But if Saddam Hussein gets even so much as a hint that you are preparing an attack or that you are assisting in our strikes, he'll drive a wedge so deep between us and our Arab allies..."

"Arab allies! These words are mutually exclusive to us." Shamir feigned a disgusted spit.

"... he'll drive a wedge so deep that you'll be able to tow an oil tanker through it. You'll be playing into his hands. All along he has wanted to widen this whole affair into the Arab/Israeli conflict. That's been his goal from the start. As of today we've got 22 nations assisting us in this venture. That's 22 nations! All from a UN with a history of being fantastically inept in opposing anything. This *is* the new world order, and we are not going to let you jeopardize it."

"Israel will do whatever is necessary to insure her sovereignty and protect her existence."

"Mr. Prime Minister, in all due respect, I've got one billion dollars in sophisticated weaponry in the pipeline to you. It won't make it off the loading docks if you so much as hint of a preemptive strike against Iraq. The only chance you have for additional American aid comes if you stay completely out of the news, lighten up on the *intifatah*, freeze construction of new settlements in the occupied territories and keep your boys out of Saddam's line of sight until this whole ordeal blows over. Do you understand?"

Shamir didn't answer.

"Do you understand?"

He had no more to say.

"There's too much riding on this. If so much as one Israeli mosquito breaks Iraqi air space, our whole alliance in Kuwait falls apart. The Syrians, the Egyptians, hell, even the Saudis will be forced to rethink their positions. They'll pack up and go home."

"Israel will do whatever it deems necessary..."

The veins were bulging in Eagleburger's neck and his teeth were grinding. "We have stated our position. Keep a low profile and there'll be Patriot missiles ringing Tel Aviv and Jerusalem within a week. Keep your nose clean and a billion in aid is on the way. But if you so much as sneeze in the general direction of Baghdad, there's no way we can follow through with any of it. You'll have pushed a bridge too far. You understand? And there'll be very little any of us can do to protect you." The Americans stormed out.

Shamir waited until the doors were closed, then turned to his aides with a wry smile: "Well gentlemen, I believe we have the aid package and Patriot missiles all but sewn up."

No one, not even his closest aides, could tell if the man was joking.

Much too long afterwards, a taxi pulled up to the Khalil apartment in Washington D.C. and a tired soldier dragged up the stairs to his bedroom. Fran had found a Canadian exchange student willing to take $150 over fare for a ticket that would get him home before morning. He threw his bags on the couch, brushed his teeth and slid in between the fresh satin sheets. Some things were worth going out of one's way for.

He moved up into the field of her body's warmth and placed his left hand on her thigh, moving it slowly up in a circular motion between her legs. She caught it at the last moment and held it there, then kissed his fingers one by one and gave his hand back to him.

"It's probably too late for this to work. Let's just forget it this month."

If Fran hadn't been so tired, he might have objected.

Chapter 16: 110 Marga Trifa Street
Kuwait City
September 23, 1990

"A new home. Isn't it wonderful!"
"And a room of your very own," said papa.
"Of my own!"
"Just look!"
Sa'id's family had been apprehensive about moving at first. But the more information they received, the more desirable the whole idea became. Sa'id would be teaching history in a new school. Abril would stay home with the children. And they would finally have the new home that they'd always wanted, compliments of the Baath Party.

The new 19th Province was homestead territory, rich and ripe for the pickings. Anyone who wanted a place in history and a new start was welcome to apply. (Even many who didn't want to go were welcome to be sent.) It was the need of the country, the will of the Father-Leader. It was the quickest way to secure eternal union and, thus, to insure that even an eventual American attack would not succeed.

They had packed their meager belongings and were ready on the curb at the appointed hour when the troop truck arrived. Abril was apprehensive at first. Forced relocation hadn't been in her plans. And stories of what happened to the Kurds who were forcefully relocated hung in the forefront of her mind. Sa'id assured her that this was different. A new job, a new home, a new life: these were exactly what they had been praying for. The future would begin today.

Someone had entered the house long before they arrived. Everything of value had been already spirited away. Sa'id was promised that the beds and kitchen tools would be left. (Abril was finally sold on the idea when she heard that.) But the looters had picked the place so thoroughly clean, not even nails from former pictures were left in the walls. The family did have a new home. But they would have to start from scratch with everything else.

The children's eyes bulged when they saw the size of it all. They jumped out of the truck, yelling and screaming in delight, rushing through the main floor and up the stairs. No one could believe that this was really their home.

"Who has lived here before?" the children asked. "Why would they leave such a beautiful place?" They ran out back and shrieked with delight when they beheld their new courtyard. "These people must have been rich!"

"Yes," said grandmother "everyone in Kuwait is rich. But it is money stolen from our own tables in Iraq. The children of our country have been starved by their own brothers in this small province who hoarded all their oil money for themselves throughout our war with Iran."

The couple smiled when they passed through the upstairs door and stepped into their new bedroom. It was twice the size of the entire flat they had shared with Abril's extended family throughout 14 years of marriage. She started to cry.

"It is beautiful, isn't it?" asked Sa'id.

"We have waited so long. And now this!" she sputtered.

"You should be happy. What is wrong?"

"I can't. I can't be happy knowing what it cost to be here."

"It didn't cost us a thing. This is our home now. We are here and it is ours simply because we had the intelligence and good fortune to have volunteered."

"Volunteered? Ha! Like my cousin 'volunteered' for the army! Like my family 'volunteered' to take fewer ration coupons! We volunteered nothing! We were ordered!"

"Silence. Do you wish the children to hear?" Sa'id was fearful. The walls had ears. Even children were required by law to turn their parents in if they complained about any of the new requirements.

Abril regained her composure as Sa'id opened the windows. "Come. Let us explore."

She rose slowly, shaking her head, and moved over to the closet to look behind the one door left in the house. As she did, a photograph that had been taped behind the door fell to the floor. She stooped to pick it up and began to cry once more.

"What is it? What this time?"

Abril handed Sa'id the faded photograph. It was a picture of a Kuwaiti family in western dress. They were sitting in the garden porch, hugging and smiling at the camera. A dignified looking middle-aged couple sat in the center, surrounded by three fine sons, a pregnant woman a bit older than Abril and three beautiful little girls.

"They all seemed so happy here."

"Abril, do not think of it."

"I wonder where they are. What they did with them?"

"They are probably basking on the beaches of France. Probably left for Saudi Arabia when the first tanks rolled across the border."

Abril turned the photo over. The names were written in red. "Abu, Azza, Amad, Ali, Salaam, Haifa and the darlings." She closed her eyes.

"They'll never return."

"Oh, Sa'id, how can we know that? How can you be certain that the Americans will not bomb this city and kill us all? We and our children? How can you know that these people won't come back and force us to leave? That the secret police won't find out about your uncle the thief and come in the night to take us all? How can you know.... how can we know..."

He reached to shake her, but she beat on his chest. "How can you know we'll even be alive to see our own baby born?" She tried to fight him off, but he prevailed and held her tightly until the thrashing stopped. Finally a fevered body fell limp against him and angry tears evaporated into an exhausted whimper. "How can you tell me that all will be well? How... how can you know anything?"

"I do not know, Abril. I do not know. All I know is this: we are here - 110 Marga Trifa. Our new home. We are safe..."

"For the moment."

"For the moment. That's all we have - this moment. That is all anyone has. From the king to the slave, that is all any one of us really owns - the moment. And in this moment I choose to live. I have a new home. I have my children. Our children. I have my health. And I have you. The rest I leave to Allah. It's in his hands."

"It is in Hussein's hands. Bush's hands. Nothing is in our hands except the power to take our own lives."

Sa'id raised his fist to slap her for thinking such thoughts, but couldn't strike. Instead, he drew her back into his arms to console. At that moment he felt the baby move once again. It wouldn't be long now. Maybe a month. Abril sobbed softly.

"Hush. Hush, my love." She cried as he held her for 20 minutes more, then slowly fell into a restless sleep. Sa'id glanced at the open closet and noticed another photograph taped to the door. It was a black and white engagement picture of a handsome young couple. He reached for it, but this one also fell to the floor. There were words scrawled hastily on the back in Arabic. He squinted to see without his glasses.

It read something like this: *"To my dark jewel Nadia, on our engagement. With joy in all the future will hold. All my love, Ali."*

Chapter 17: A Simple Question

National Athletic Stadium, Kuwait City
September 24, 1990

"Where are you hiding them?"

He didn't respond.

"I ask you a simple question. Where are you hiding them?"

The Inspector seemed like a gentle man. His black eyes appeared kind, almost soft as he spoke in a hushed sincerity. Surely this wasn't the butcher Amad had been warned about. This was just a regular fellow.

Amad al Bakr had been arrested off the streets of Kuwait City two nights before. He was attempting to buy food and had waited in line just a bit too long when a troop truck circled the block. If he had only gone when his friends left, he would not have been waiting there after dusk. He would be back in his uncle's house with Haifa and his daughters by now instead of sitting in the shower room at the national athletic center. He would be hungry, but he would be safe.

The make-shift jail in Kuwait City housed hundreds of his fellow countrymen. Most of them had been picked up under similar circumstances. Some had been out after dark. Some had simply been out. Others weren't carrying proper identification. Some were neighbors or relatives of known 'terrorists'. A scant few had been involved in the resistance, themselves. Others had simply been detained because they looked at an Iraqi soldier the wrong way.

The prisoners gathered nervously down on the open soccer field anticipating the future. Some sat in stands and spoke in hushed tones about their 'crimes'. Many prayed in stunned silence as they awaited their turn in the stadium showers with the one rumors called 'the Inspector'.

Amad was in deep trouble. He knew it. Stewart Kensington, a British geologist with ARAMCO and a personal friend, was being sought by the authorities. Kensington had been a guest of the Bakrs for three weeks in

June. Friends and neighbors alike knew about the Englander's stay. A delightful, outgoing chap who made friends easily and loved to talk, Kensington was wanted by the Iraqis. Everyone knew that Amad and Stewart were close. And so, on August 2 when the invasion was under way, Kensington had stopped by Amad's own home to ask for help. Amad kept the man hidden in his uncle's vacant home, and too many people knew that he had been there.

When it became clear that Stewart was no longer safe there, Amad sent him to his brother, Ali, who was now fighting with the resistance. Ali knew a friend who knew a friend who knew a way out. Neither of them heard what had become of Kensington after that. But somewhere along the line the Iraqis had stumbled upon his name in connection with the Englishman. When the edict was proclaimed that all Kuwaitis harboring foreigners would be hanged, Amad considered fleeing Kuwait again. But he could not leave now. His wife was days away from the birth of his first son. Amad knew he could be in trouble with this Kensington business. To make matters worse, there were now many in his neighborhood who knew that his own brother, Ali, had returned and was active in the underground.

They had taken his papers upon arrest and not returned them. Amad was now sure that they knew who he was. If anyone had done even the slightest piece of investigating, they would be aware of his many connections to Kensington. They would know about his brother. And they would ask questions about their whereabouts that he neither could nor would be able to answer.

The guards had been rough with him at first, stripping him, wrenching his arms behind his back and lashing them onto a broom handle. Abrasive ropes dug deep into his wrists and held his shoulders at a point almost out of joint. Pain turned to numbness as he waited naked in fear. When he finally entered the shower room, the Inspector scolded his tormentors for treating him so shamefully and demanded that they loosen him. "He has not been found guilty of any crime," said the Inspector. "Not yet. He should not be treated like a criminal. Like a dog. Not yet."

The man greeted his "guest" with a brotherly Islamic salutation and invited him to sit and be comfortable. He offered a cool drink of water. Amad gratefully obliged. The officer smiled, removed his spectacles and spoke softly, intently.

"You are a friend of Kensington."

Amad didn't know how to respond. If he said "yes," he could be indicted simply for knowing the fugitive. If he said "no" and the questioner knew it to be a lie, he could be in deeper trouble.

He tried to show no emotion. "I knew him."

"Knew him?" A small tremor rose in the man's voice. "He lived in your home." It was a prelude to an earthquake.

"My uncle's home."

"Your uncle's home?"

Amad's breath dried up within him the moment these words left his lips. The Inspector had been referring to Kensington's stay in June. Amad now may have given away the Englander's August 2 location. "I offered him the hospitality which the Koran beseeches us to give the wanderer."

The Inquisitor stared past his eyes into his mind. "And when he arrived at your doorstep on the morning of the liberation of Province 19? What did you offer him then?"

"I offered him..." What should he say?

"Yes?"

"I offered him..." What could he say? "...shelter..."

"Shelter..." The man's evil eye twitched for but a moment.

"The shelter of my uncle's home until he felt he needed it no longer."

The man looked sharply at Amad at first, then gentled his posture. A transparent smile spread over his face as he stood. "I have just one question for you, my brother. One simple question." Lighting a cigarette, he began to pace. "Our beloved homeland has come to the moment of its destiny. The Arab nation stands on the verge of a unity - a unity of which our parents could only dare dream. But the birth of this new age is being held back by the menace of imperialism. We must shield our future from this threat. We must shield our homeland from the rape of the infidel. We must shield our women and children from the war which would eat their flesh, devour their dreams. There is only one way to do this, my brother. Only one way. We must have shields of flesh." He slowed to a quiet forcefulness which riveted itself deep into Amad's very soul. "Kensington and eight others have managed to elude the efforts of our people in your neighborhood. And the question to you is a simple one: Where are you hiding them?"

Amad spoke with all the sincerity a frightened man could muster. "I am sorry, sir. But I don't know where any foreigners are."

The man bent over and opened a maroon leather case at his feet. "A shame you can't remember. Maybe this will help."

The guards retied Amad's arms to the chair.

"Extend your fingers forward," requested the man.

"Why? What are you going to do to me?"

They set two wooden hand-shaped boards on the table in front of Amad and clamped each finger into a small stirrup in the contraption.

"What is this for?"

"My brother, it is for the salvation of the Arab world."

The soldiers secured his legs to the sides of the chair and tied his head back against a post with his own belt to immobilize him.

"Where are they?"

"Are you going to kill me?"

"Oh, no, brother. I will let you live. But if refuse to tell me what I want to know, you will only wish that I had killed you. Where are they?"

"What are you doing with that?"

"I have ways of keeping you alive a long, long while, while only killing one small piece of you at a time. Now, where is Kensington?"

"I told you I don't know."

The demon took a sharp steel object from his case and squeezed it like a vice grip gently over Amad's right index finger. Without a word, he scraped it back and yanked. A hot and piercing fire raced from Amad's hand to his shoulder and he seized up in the chair. The device was removed from his finger. He stared in horror at the bloodied stump, exposed to the bone. The nail had been torn out at the root.

Amad wanted to scream and shake his hand, but he couldn't move a finger. Tensing, he tried to stifle the pain and breathe out a shallow, controlled plea. "By the mercy of Allah! What are you doing?"

"The question. I return to the question. Where are they?" His tormentor calmly placed the wicked little machine onto Amad's middle finger.

"I told you, I do not know."

It flashed again without warning and turned a second finger into a bloodied stump. He inhaled a shallow cry. Water welled in his eyes. "Please, I beg of you. I tell you the truth."

The Inspector connected the devil tool to his ring finger. "Where are they?"

"For mercy sake, do not do this to me! I don't know where he has gone."

A trembling man bit through his lower lip. The fire shot again. This time the pain overwhelmed him and he began to faint. The master called his dogs, who picked Amad up, chair and all, and set him into the shower chamber. They turned it to cold. Ice cold. The royal emblem of a lion in the floor tiles bled, turning from white to a beautiful amber. They held Amad's face in the stream of water and forced his mouth open. He gulped for air as the freezing waters clogged in his throat and entered his windpipe.

They kicked his chair over. A crimson sheet covered his left eye as they turned the water off and went away. Amad lay shivering, naked on the floor and bound to his chair. The nerves of his right hand were raw, pulsing. He shook uncontrollably as the swelling in his forehead grew and cold welts rose on his skin. He could barely breathe. They would be back. That much he knew. He cried to Allah for mercy.

An hour passed. Muscles tightened. He flailed about like a fish in the bottom of a boat, but the chair and the hemp chains held him immobile. The numbness which tingled in his hand crept slowly to cover his entire right side, denying the pain and the cold their full power for a short time.

Then they returned.

The Inspector was conciliatory and almost sincere: "It is most regrettable that this has had to happen. Here, let me help you up." He slapped Amad's face lightly to assure his victim's attention. "I just have one question for you." The device was clamped onto his left index finger. "Where are they?"

"Can't you see, I do not know where Kensington is!"

A flash of steel and a scream brought his next nail to the floor. "I can't tell you something I do not know. Don't you see? I can't tell you something I do not know!"

The man was unmoved. "Let me ask you another way." He covered the middle finger as his unfortunate guest struggled for freedom. "Where are they?"

Amad cried in anticipation of what was to happen next, but faded to a whimper when the insidious deed was actually done. This time it didn't come off so easily. The man had to take a knife and pop it away. By now the pain was so great that Amad couldn't stop his words.

"Kensington was at my home but I told him to go back to his own place. His own people. I told him it was too dangerous for him to stay there. I told him. I told him."

"And so, where are they?"

"I do not know. Please! Don't do this to me. I swear I do not know."

He tore out another.

"Let me put it another way? They are where?"

"I don't know! By the Prophet, I do not know."

This time he ripped the right thumb open. Then the left. Then the ring finger. Then his little finger. With each pause the Inspector asked the identical question. With each pause Amad pleaded and begged for mercy. He could not tell on his friend. And he would not tell on his brother.

His mind wandered: *"Ali al Bakr. Ali al Bakr. Get that name out of your head. Ali al Bakr. Al Jahrah. If you so much as whisper it aloud you will be dead. They will know he is your brother. They will believe you are with the resistance. Ali al Bakr. Al Jahrah. You will be dead."*

The expressionless Satan returned with his miniature guillotine and went back about the sinister business of destroying a man's nerves. Amad passed out again. The Inspector pulled his limp head up by the hair. It fell back like a broken doll. He slapped Amad conscious and asked once again. "One last time. Where are they?"

Amad's head snapped down again. He tried to whisper something under his breath, but couldn't talk. Not a sound. Amad found himself on the spinning floor of the showers again. This time the frozen stream seemed almost inviting as he prayed to the gracious waters to numb the pain. The faint had saved his last two nails. Laughing soldiers cursed and reversed the nozzles. Now steam poured out into the room. He lay, groping and twitching as the waters scalded tender skin. The guards kicked at his kidneys through the chair back and then put the boot to his face and ears. Their Satanic laugh echoed through shattered eardrums as Amad spit blood and writhed upon the slippery floor.

The waters were turned abruptly back to ice and again they held his lacerated face under the spray. They kicked his chair over and set him up twice, three times, four. He returned to the floor and they continued to batter his face with their black boots. A warm discharge oozed from both ears before he faded from reality once again.

Amad came to an eternity later in a pool of blood and vomit. He was coughing up his own excrement, but couldn't remember them forcing him to eat it. The loss of blood and the stun of the cold had together stolen much of his pain away. He found himself crumpled on the floor of a cramped cell. The ropes were gone and his nakedness was covered by a rotted woolen blanket. Dozens of children - mostly adolescents - huddled in horror around him and spoke quietly with each other about the fate of their comrades.

"They've taken us three or four at a time and none has returned," whispered a girl of 12.

"I don't know where any foreigners are," murmured another. "But I heard that you must tell them something about a collaborator even if it is a lie or they will rape and murder you."

He faded out again and woke to a bright light. "This is your last chance. Why do you make me do this to you? Why can't you simply tell me what I need to hear so that you can go back to your children? Your son."

"My children? My son? My son is not yet born..."

A dark smile spread over the Inspector's face as he left the room.

"No. No, not my children!" Through the wall he could hear the tortured cries of a little one being beaten. It sounded like his own Hala, but the ringing in his ears made it impossible to know for certain. "Where is he?" demanded the Inspector again and again. "Who? Who do you want?" cried the little voice between blows.

"Please, not my Hala! I tell you whatever you want! Please! Not my Hala." No one came to the door. The demon heard his offer. He knew that he heard. But no one came to the door. And the beating went on until the child's cry ceased.

Another beating began. This time, he recognized the voice. It was his Bani. He was certain of it. He screamed again to let her go. "I'll tell you. I'll tell you everything. Everyone I know who has contact with the Englishman! I'll tell you dates and times and people! Come back! Come back, I say!"

The cries turned to whimpers as the blows increased but no one came to the door. Then her cries also were no more. At first he prayed that she hadn't died. Then, that she had.

A third little one was beaten. Still, no one came to his door. This one was too young to even talk. She could only scream. Little Azza. Precious Azza. Oh, God, no.

Finally, the Inspector returned.

"Where were you! I told you I would give you names. You heard me! I know you heard me!"

The Inspector managed an indifferent grin and spoke in a business-like fashion. "I had work to do and couldn't be interrupted."

He spit in his tormentor's face. "I will see you rot in hell!"

"You will see nothing," cried the Inspector as he dug the right eye of his bloodied project out with a sharp knife. Amad thrashed his head back in pain.

It was strange at first - so strange. The fire was only momentary. A world turned red, then grey, then black. A thousand shades of purple and green swirled in his forehead, followed by the dots. Tiny dots pulsing and growing, changing from red to green to red. He was aware for a moment that his eye was bouncing against his own cheek. Then with a flash of light everything changed to a dull yellow. He could still see! Even hanging out of its socket, his eye could still see! Both eyes.

Two guards forced his head up and held it until the Inspector could clip the eye clean with a scissors. He stepped back and lit another cigarette.

"All right now. We are finished with these little games. Shall we have some names? Who are the enemies of the people?"

The bloodied stump cried out: "Saddam Hussein! Tariq Aziz!" Before he could shout another name, a wooden club cleaned his mouth of teeth. They seized his head once more and the Inspector pried open his good eye. He tried to hold it shut and could smell his own burning flesh. The white hot star of a cigarette burned through his eyelid. This time when the beating continued, a blessed unconsciousness came quickly. It didn't take much now. He had lost enough blood.

A tortured mind stole him away to nowhere for a time, and a time, and a time that was no time. A black-red smudge fell from the sky and Amad could hear a man being tortured below. The poor beggar was screaming a name he could not make out. He choked and cried for help, bellowing his hoarse and eerie plea. Then he looked down, as if floating from the ceiling while the soldiers threw cold water on the poor man. He was wired with stripped extension chords wound about his genitals, ears and feet. Around his neck, tied with its own umbilical chord, was an unwashed newborn child. A male.

Amad prayed for release. "Please! Someone help this poor soul! Someone! Someone stop them! In the name of Allah the merciful, do not torture this man!" But no one listened. They continued to wrack the broken body with an ever increasing voltage and alternate their torture with buckets of ice water. The man screamed and screamed until he woke up. A hideous laugh echoed the halls of the stadium. With it, the hounds of hell shook the hope of every prisoner, penetrating even the unconscious in that purgatory to jar them awake. The laugh continued until Amad realized that there was no man.

He was the man.

Then all was silent.

After a momentary escape, the pain returned. He awoke to another strange but sensuous dream. A woman in a paisley dress, dark and battered, was fondling his genitals. She held them, caressing gently. Her soft brown hair fell over his chest and on to his waist. She was stroking his penis, softly blowing cool air over him, kissing his navel and moving lower. He faded in this dream and saw his own hands, whole and clean. Then again all was black.

Amad looked once more. Light filtered down from broken windows into his hell. He inhaled a shallow breath as again the dull ache returned to skeletal fingertips. Now the wounds had been washed and bandaged. A high-pitched ringing sounded through both ears. An erratic heart throbbed in his throat. He could smell cooked flesh: his own. Still tied to the chair, still naked, he could not move. She was there again, licking and sucking gently. In a clouded horror he laughed, this time only to himself. It wasn't a dream.

The Inspector stepped from the shadows. "Shall we have names, then?"

"I do not know anyone." He wasn't sure he had spoken. "Anything."

He motioned the woman. She pulled harder. Sucked harder.

"Who is your brother? Is he Ali al Bakr?"

The Inspector waited impatiently.

"Is he *Shobash* ?"

She was biting him now. Rough. Painful.

"Where is this man you speak of?" shouted the Inspector, now holding a large scalpel in his hand. The woman's tongue brought him to a peak.

"Where is he?"

He pushed her face away and held the knife to his testicles as he began to ejaculate. In the most quiet and calm voice a demon ever uttered, he asked once again. There was no reply, only a faint, incredulous whimper. Like an expert tanner, the man pealed his scrotum away with the knife, pulled out and clipped each testicle. There was little blood. Amad looked down in astonishment. So little blood.

"Has your brother been hiding them?"

No answer. His inquisitor bore down against the chair and carved off the tip of his penis.

"Who is this man *Shobash?* "

Then the root.

He prayed to die and tried to swallow his tongue. The Inspector dug it out of his mouth in a blind rage, but this time he was not so careful with the knife. At that moment Allah was gracious. Amad gulped the gushing blood as it spilled warmth down into his trachea. And before the Inspector could do a thing to stop him, he had inhaled as much as he could manage into his lungs.

He held it there.

And in a moment he was free.

Chapter 18: Free Kurdistan
Washington, D.C.
October 1, 1990

The region of the Kurds was a fierce land and the home of a strength born in struggle. Nomads had inhabited the mountains of what was now the Iranian, Iraqi and Turkish borders for centuries. In that time they had seen maps drawn and redrawn without giving so much as a nod to those who pretended to rule. These people were their own people. They respected no boundaries, paid no tribute and accepted no outsider's law. They would neither be tamed nor subjugated, and for this fierce independence the Kurds had paid an enormous price throughout the generations.

The Peacock Throne had attempted a silent genocide of its own during the reign of the late Shah. Iranian tanks rolled into Kurdish towns routinely to intimidate, harass and shoot at anything that moved. The world hadn't noticed then. America's intelligence community knew what was happening, but the Shah was a staunch ally and nothing was said.

Saddam Hussein had ravaged his own Kurds in the days when he was a major client of Western grain and arms. But again, no one spoke up. He burned their crops, leveled their villages, poisoned wells and fields and forcefully relocated hundreds of thousands of Kurds with little international objection. It wasn't until he shelled them with poison gas during the Iranian war that the world sat up to take note. The shock value of those images - bloated babies rotting in their mothers' arms - managed to horrify the world for a short time. Outrage was expressed, but nothing much done.

The Syrians and the Turks were not much better. The sad truth: Kurds were both unreachable and expendable. No one could do much. No one would do much.

Before the Shah and Saddam Hussein there were other massacres. And before the others there were others. The Kurds were victims of history and geography as much as anything else. But this proud people didn't want pity.

All they wanted was to be left alone. For that to happen, they needed guns. And for guns to happen, they needed a supplier.

Even as the American military buildup continued its remarkable speed in the Gulf, the president was impatiently groping for some measurable covert success to prove to the congressional leadership that he was making headway. George Bush was not about to become a Lyndon Johnson, tied up in details, choosing targets and directing the war machine. (LBJ had once bragged that there wasn't an outhouse blown up in North Vietnam without his prior approval.) But this president, a man who once directed the CIA, was becoming anxious. He was itching to see something happen behind the scenes. Clandestine measures were the only matters which he could control directly without going to and through the scrutiny of the media, the approval of arguing allies, and, to quote Spiro Agnew, the 'nattering nabobs of negativism' in the press.

Frustrated by the CIA's lack of operatives on the ground, Bush invited his young captain to the Oval Office on that first crisp morning in October. Khalil's quiet successes were one bright spot in the long dark days of America's buildup. Operation 'Wallenberg', the courting of Hafez Assad, the arrangement with the Russian Kalinov to thwart Iraq's smuggling ring, and his recent trip to visit the Iranians had all been done without a headline. A track record like this, built up in only two months, had turned Captain Francis Khalil into something of a hot property at the Oval Office. And the president was anxious to hear anything his rising star had to suggest.

"An alliance with the Kurds?" echoed an interested voice on the phone. "We've discussed it. But who do we deal with? They aren't even a nation. My sources say that the Kurds have been decimated. Shattered and scattered. They don't have the leadership or the power to move against anyone."

"Beg your pardon, sir," challenged the unusually cocky captain. "But those sources are the same people who told you on August 1 that Saddam wouldn't attack Kuwait. Some of the same people who convinced Reagan that the Afghan resistance would retake Kabul two weeks after the Russians pulled out. The same people who said..."

The president smiled with his voice. "OK, OK, hot shot. Come on over. I've got 10 minutes to hear what you have to say and then I have the Japanese Foreign Minister for lunch."

"Serve him well-done, sir," joked the captain.

"What's that?"

"I'll be right up."

The major straightened Fran's tie and shook his head at the same time. He wished his junior well before slapping his face and pushing him out the door. The Old Man was more than a tad jealous; more than a tad proud. "You know what to do if a terrorist tosses a hand grenade through the window while you're there, don't you son?"

"Yes, sir." Khalil saluted and made for the door. "Throw Quayle on it."

He shouted as Francis disappeared down the hallway. "Give my regards to Barbara, would you?"

"You know her?"

"Yeah. We went to different high schools together."

Scowcroft and Cheney were there when he arrived. Bush was at his desk on the phone and waved him in. "Look," said the president to the voice on the other line, "tell the Admiral that Barbara could row faster than that. And tell the Ambassador that if his boys won't fit in under our supreme allied commander, they might as well pack it up and go back to Paris!"

He hung up in disgust, but changed temperament the moment he spotted Fran's sheepish smile.

"So this is the young Marine I've heard so much about! Good to have you with us, captain. It's a pleasure to finally meet you." The president's shake was strong, but his hands were colder than what Fran had expected. "I've only got five minutes, but I am interested." He motioned to his other guests. "Now tell Brent and Dick what you think we could do to turn the remaining Kurds into a thorn in Saddam's hide."

"I'll be brief with my brief." Bush chuckled but the others didn't think it was all that funny. "I've studied the situation and believe there is an opportunity here that we're wasting."

"The Kurds don't take orders from anyone," objected Scowcroft.

"Kind of like the French," added Francis, nodding to the phone. "But that hasn't stopped us from trying to work with them." Even the president's aids thought that was funny. "They have something we need and we've got something they want. That's the stuff deals are made of."

"What do they have that we need?" asked Sununu, entering the room.

"Position. The ability to tie up key Iraqi divisions. Hatred for Saddam Hussein. Three rather important ingredients in any insurrection, wouldn't you say?"

"And all they want from us is weapons?" Scowcroft was unimpressed.

"Weapons, money and a promise."

"And what promise, praytell, is that?"

Khalil straightened up and handed each man a copy of his report. "This ought to explain things very clearly."

Bush raised an eyebrow immediately. "An independent Kurdistan?"

"Yes, sir."

Scowcroft shook his head and threw the paper back onto the president's desk without reading further. "We have no authority to promise anything of the sort. It would take U.N. action and that would destroy the covert nature of the whole proposal."

Sununu was stepping out of the office to speak with someone in the hall: "We don't have to deliver. We just have to promise it."

Cheney sided with Scowcroft. "It's beyond our reach."

Bush removed his glasses and rubbed his temples. His hands seemed to be shaking slightly. "If we're going to promise anything, we'll have to be in a position to fulfill that promise. If they're ready to give their lives for the cause, we can't renege. We'll have to come through. And I honestly don't believe we can do that. Guns and the money we can arrange. But as for this independent Kurdistan..."

The captain glanced at his nay-sayers and then spoke directly to his commander in chief: "Forgive me for disagreeing, sir, but you'd be building a two-legged stool with only guns and money. The third leg - the promise - is essential in any dealings with the Kurds. That promise is the only glue that will hold them together long enough to make 'em into an effective fighting force against Saddam Hussein. It's the catalyst. Remember the problems we had with the Contras? If all you give them is guns and money, all you have is hired mercenaries."

"These aren't the Contras," objected Scowcroft.

"You're right there. These folks are more like the Afghans. People of honor with their backs against the wall. And motivated? They've had generations to be motivated. It's in their genes. Give them guns and money, and every little faction will use it to build its own position. Give them the promise of an independent state and you stand a decent chance of initiating and uniting an army of honest-to-goodness freedom fighters."

"The promise will do that much?"

"You give them your personal word that when the smoke clears the United States will do everything in its power to create a homeland. That will be enough."

"That and the guns and money."

Cheney turned the Khalil. "Turkey and Syria won't go for this. They've got their own Kurds to contend with."

"I believe they can be brought aboard."

"How?"

"Would you rather have a strong Saddam or a weak Kurdistan as a neighbor."

Scowcroft continued shaking his head. "We've yet to decide whether we even want a strong Iraq in place after this."

Khalil was unclear about that statement. "What do you mean?"

"To counter Iran. Chopping up Iraq could lead to a destabilization of the entire region. We've yet to decide if we're going to leave Saddam in place after we..."

Sununu entered and shook his head to stop the national security adviser mid-sentence. Francis didn't realize until much later what Scowcroft had slipped and how it would affect the world. Bush picked up the report in front of him. "One hundred miles along the Iranian border? Couldn't we just negotiate some kind of security zone in that area for them?"

Francis shook his head. "Policed by whom? The Republican Guard? No, one hundred miles of sovereignty where they can be left alone to live their own way. They were promised that much by the British earlier this century, but cheated out of it."

Scowcroft objected again. "You're asking us to arbitrarily and unilaterally redraw the map of the Middle East. We can't do that."

"I'm asking you to promise you'll try."

The captain looked to the president. The president looked to the captain, then to the map in his hands. A shaky grin spread over his face. "OK, Captain Marvel. We'll consider it."

"And sir..."

The commander in chief raised an eyebrow.

"I'd like to..."

"Personally oversee this mission?"

Khalil was pleased that the president knew him well enough to finish his sentence. "Yes, sir. If you believe I'm the man for the job."

"Thank you, captain. We'll take it under advisement. That will be all."

Francis saluted and walked out into the fresh Washington air to meet his young bride for lunch.

Chapter 19: Another Ollie
The Oval Office
October 2, 1990

"We can't have another loose Oliver North parading around here and running Rambo missions from the basement of the White House!" Baker was livid. "Have you any idea what the media would do with this?"

Cheney remained calm and businessman-like. "He is not in the basement of the White House. He's at the Pentagon. He's not an Oliver North. He's directly supervised by an orderly chain of command. And he's doing nothing illegal. He's carrying out communications missions and keeping a very low profile."

"If this gets out, you can forget another term." Baker gritted his teeth. The president sat motionless, his chin resting on his right fist.

General Powell ended the silence. "A few good contacts on the ground are worth a thousand eyes in the sky. Our listening posts in Turkey have been invaluable. The satellite we put up in November should be even better in terms of raw data. It'll be able to read the want ads from the Baghdad phone book if we want it to. But all this hardware put together can't interpret a thing about Saddam's intentions. Hardware can't incite a revolt. If we want to encourage the Kurds in the north and the Shiites in the south to tie Saddam up, then we've got to put people on the ground. People on the ground. And young Khalil here is the best we have at the moment."

Bush panned the room. "What do the rest of you think?"

"My only concern is... well, clearance." It was Scowcroft. "Are you sure we can trust him?"

"What do you mean by that? He's a Marine," objected Powell.

"He's also an Arab." Sununu continued his objections: "I can see the headlines: Ollie and Ali."

"What kind of racist remark is that?" Powell was furious. "He's an American!"

"He's not an Arab, he's a Catholic." The vice president caught himself the moment the words left his lips. He had meant to say "he's not a Moslem, he's a Catholic."

Now Cheney took the defensive. "His allegiance is completely to the United States and to this president."

"I just want us to be sure." Sununu was a bit more subdued than usual. "Please don't begrudge me for being careful. We all know how much could be riding on this."

"He's just an analyst," Baker objected.

Powell, now at the edge of his anger and the end of his chair, spoke in a terse clarity: "He's a Marine. He's been on the ground before. He's fluent in Arabic. He's smart. Tough. Knows the region and understands the conditions. Who else do we have with qualifications like that?"

Cheney chimed in: "Hell, he's been writing our situation reports on this whole thing for us since before it started. We trusted him then."

Powell took it back: "He's also got a better chance than anyone else we have on the ground over there right now." No one said a word. He looked around the room. "This is all because he's an Arab, isn't it? Isn't it?"

Bush gazed over the papers on his desk for a moment. The secretary of defense softened his voice to break the tension. "We were talking about Kurdish aid long before Mr. Khalil waltzed over here and offered us more than talk. Our sources tell us that the Kurds have seen our people - men, women and children - used as human shields at power stations and hydro electric plants over there. If we can make contact here, we might find ourselves with a highly motivated ally and get some more of our folks out at the same time. I'm inclined to go with our boy again. Give him a team..."

Quayle didn't agree and interrupted his boss to get the objection on the record. "Excuse me, Mr. President, but we can't promise an independent Kurdistan. The Turks will go through the roof. They have enough problems with their own Kurds. Not to mention Syria, Iran..."

Sununu chimed in. "We can promise anything. We just can't deliver it."

Bush asked his personal secretary to leave the last comment out of the transcripts for the presidential library. "Let's keep our options open. Internal Security has given Khalil a clean bill of health on both scans, as has the CIA. As long as he's producing, I say we get beyond our petty suspicions. If Colin and Dick have faith in him, I say we explore it. That's all."

"But carving up Iraq, that's not in the plan..."

The president raised a finger to his mouth. The tapes were running. "I said that will be all."

Bureaucrats nodded. A general saluted. And the image men of Pennsylvania Avenue held their breath. Washington would sleep yet one more night in the dark as a young Marine kissed his wife 'goodbye' and stepped aboard the waiting plane at Andrews.

Captain Khalil had another jump to make.

Chapter 20 : The Hawk & The Dove
A Washington Restaurant
October 2, 1990

The Hawk & The Dove had been their favorite place for lunch since the day Kathryn arrived in Washington. Filled with college students, congressional staffers and more than its share of gossip, there was always something happening or someone to see at this restaurant. Today was no exception: Senator Danforth was treating his office to a birthday lunch for a prized secretary. Rumor had it that Jesse Jackson and an entourage from the former Rainbow Coalition were on their way. Somebody big from the Smithsonian was retiring in the back room. And at a table by the front window, a young bride of six months was waiting for her Marine captain and their promised anniversary lunch. As usual, he was late.

Kathryn read the menu and graded a pile of third grade English papers to fill the time. When Francis said noon, she routinely spotted him until 12:30. But any time after that threw her off. She had places to go, too. At 45 minutes, Kathryn was just starting to pack her papers when her soldier came waltzing apologetically into the bar. He promptly produced a clump of fresh cut flowers and a bouquet of excuses. She was used to it by now.

"Let me guess. You had to walk Mrs. Bush's dog and couldn't call to warn me you'd be late."

"Worse. I had to walk Mrs. Bush."

He pecked her on the cheek and pulled up a chair. Kathryn wanted to hit him only slightly less than she wanted to eat. She didn't have the time to do both. Her favorite, New England clam chowder, was the daily special. "I can always beat on you after our anniversary date tonight."

Francis tried to quickly change the subject. "Remember our first date here?"

Kathryn remembered. She had just arrived in town and the young journalism grad was supposed to be meeting a new roommate - another student doing the same summer internship with her at the *Washington Post*.

The people at the paper had set up the meeting, telling her to look for someone carrying fresh flowers. She asked the host if anyone in the place met the description.

"That would be table 13."

"My lucky number." She glanced at the name "Francis K." on the waiting list and was promptly taken to the only empty table in the place. The flowers were there, but the patron was evidently in the wash room. She ordered a light lunch and began eating before the tall, dark-eyed stranger stopped to stare.

"Do you mind." Kathryn didn't care to have anyone watching her eat, no matter how good looking he was.

"I'm sorry, but I believe this is my table."

"I'm afraid you'll have to sit somewhere else. I'm meeting my room-mate here."

"But this is my table." Francis reached for the flowers.

"I'm sorry, but these belong to my roommate."

"Your roommate?"

"Yes, my new roommate, Francis."

He smiled sheepishly. "Your new roommate, Francis..."

"Yes. We are to be sharing an apartment here in the city. Now, would you please leave before I have you thrown out."

Instead of leaving, Khalil slid in to the booth to look at a menu.

"What are you doing?"

"So, is this 'Francis' of yours good looking?"

"Why should I tell you anything?"

"Does 'Francis' come here often?"

"As a matter of fact, she does. Now would you please..."

"She does? Oh. I don't think I've seen her before. I come here a lot, too."

Kathryn motioned to the waiter.

"What is it, ma'am?"

"Would you kindly escort this annoying man from the premises or call the police or something?"

The host looked back and forth at the two of them, thoroughly confused. "But I thought you said you were joining Francis for lunch?"

"I am. And this obnoxious..." As she spoke, a thin platinum blonde with an obvious overbite entered the restaurant carrying a huge bouquet of flowers. "Obnoxious..." She looked at the soldier and groaned. "I suppose... I suppose you're Francis K?"

He flashed his trademark mischievous smile that simultaneously unnerved and endeared. "Marine Lieutenant Francis Khalil at your service, ma'am."

Her eyes fell to the table. "The flowers..."

"I was taking them to my brother."

"Oh." Kathryn was more than embarrassed, but she didn't want to leave. "You don't know anyone with a room for rent here in town, do you?" She watched as her new roommate peered in from the lobby.

Francis considered telling the beautiful intruder that his housemates just moved, but couldn't quite figure how to get rid of them on such short notice. "No. But I do know of a place that might be opening up... soon. It's near where I live. Quite near, actually."

"It is? Oh." Kathryn was drawn to his smiling eyes. "I stayed at a hotel last night and can't afford to do that much longer. Actually, I was supposed to meet someone here today about a room, but she hasn't shown." She couldn't bring herself to get up. "Is he in the hospital or something?"

"Who?"

"Your brother."

"Excuse me?"

"The flowers..."

"The flowers. Oh. No, he's over at Arlington."

Kathryn didn't know what the Marine meant. "Must like flowers, huh?"

"No, he never did like flowers but I bring them anyway."

The waiter approached. "Excuse me. I believe there's a woman in the lobby from the *Washington Post* looking for a Ms. Kathryn Marie Carlson. Are you..."

Kathryn's reluctance registered just enough for Francis to notice. "My roommate? Wonderful. I guess I won't be out on the streets after all." She rose and picked up her coat. "I'm sorry about commandeering your table sergeant..."

"Lieutenant. Lieutenant Francis Khalil, ma'am." Francis made a mental note of the fact that the woman worked at the *Post*. "I hope to run into you again."

She picked up her purse and dropped a $20 on the table with the bill. "Well, gotta go."

Francis grasped for anything that would prolong her stay. "You're a reporter?"

Kathryn nodded. "Actually, I'm a teacher but I have this opportunity at the *Post* and I can't let it pass by. You know how it is with opportunities. Why?"

He seemed a little let down and shrugged his shoulders. "The *Post*. I suppose that makes you a Democrat. Too bad."

What did he mean by that? Kathryn was disappointed by his disappointment. "And you're a soldier?"

He stood to see her off. "A Marine."

"...and a Republican?"

"I am."

"Too bad." She smiled and walked away. "I suppose that makes you an idiot."

Four rocky years, two broken engagements and a cathedral wedding had come and gone since that day. Kathryn went back to teaching and Francis transferred to a job at the Pentagon (thanks to a certain major friend of his father). The 'hawk and the dove' remained too much alike on the stubbornness scale and too different on the outlook scale for anything but a roller coaster relationship. Their first six months found them floating from frustration to ecstasy with little middle ground. When they were able to crowd out time, politics and telephones, love was tender and intense. But a dozen times in half as many months, 'Mr. and Ms.' had found themselves lying back to angry back in their cold bed, silently wondering if this marriage would last a year. To complicate matters, Kathryn wanted children. Now. Her mother was battling a degenerate heart disease and the doctors only gave her a couple of years at the most. Kathryn, an only child, wanted nothing more than to place the gift of a grandchild in her mother's arms before she died.

Tonight they were scheduled to visit the Kennedy Center for the Russian ballet. Kathryn had been dreaming about this event since she heard it was coming to town. Fran joked about not wanting to sit around for three hours watching grown men jump around in tights, but he knew what it meant to his bride. He had traded a pair of choice Redskins tickets for tenth-row ballet seats and popped them into Kathryn's lunch box to be discovered a month ago. Noon today was intended as a prelude to a wonderful evening: lunch, the ballet and love. But now, as usual, Francis had come with the good and bad news. He had to reschedule.

"Sorry."

"Sorry? What do you mean, 'sorry'? I've been looking forward to this for weeks! We've got great seats and everything. Francis..."

"Look, I said I'm sorry..."

"But you just got back."

"I know. I know. It will only be for a while."

"What do you mean by 'a while'?"

"Just a while."

"Well, OK. The ballet is going to be here for two weeks. Maybe we can exchange our tickets for next Saturday or..."

"I'm afraid it's going to be a little longer 'while' than that."

"Francis!" Kathryn couldn't decide if she was more angry or upset.

"I'm sorry. It's just that I've made an impression with some of the top brass and I can't let them down now."

"Can't they get someone else to do it? It's our anniversary."

"You know how I feel about this. It's the break I've been..."

"And just how do you feel about me? Am I a priority?"

"You know that you are, Kathryn. But this is the one break I've been waiting for."

"Yes, and this is the one ballet I've been waiting for. After next week it's history. We'd have to go to Cleveland to see it."

"I hardly put these two opportunities on the same level. This is my career."

"Yes, and this is supposed to be our life."

"Supposed to be?" Francis was as angry at himself for not explaining clearly as he was at her for not understanding. "Let me start over: This is not one concert, this is our future. Our life. They value me. Me! My skills and opinion. I speak the language. I understand the culture. They trust me. And if I do well here, we could be set. Another promotion and we get out of the apartment. Out of the neighborhood. We could buy that little house in Georgetown that you have your heart set on."

"That I have my heart set on? I thought it was 'we'!"

"We. We have our hearts set on..." He reached his hand toward her under the lace table cloth and she slapped it immediately away, shaking the table and sending his water glass directly into his lap.

The waiter came immediately to their rescue with a towel but Francis waved him away. "Thanks, Emillio. That's OK." He picked up a red cloth napkin and held it toward Kathryn. "Would you care to do the honors?"

She flashed a cold "you wish." They sat in silence, Kathryn picking at her pasta and Fran's mind spinning for a way out of this one. He tried to be funny. "I suppose I could have let Emillio mop it up."

"As far as I'm concerned, Emillio can 'do the honors' for you from now on."

"I don't know. I don't know." Francis leaned in to his bride, glanced around and spoke under his breath. "Our apartment is awful small. It would be a lot easier for Emillio to move in with us if we had that little house in Georgetown."

Kathryn wanted to stay mad but couldn't. She glared at him once. Stared at him twice. Then, fighting a smile, grabbed the napkin and slid it under the table. "Damn you, Khalil."

Francis looked about, a little more than embarrassed. "That's OK. You don't have to... uh..."

"Bush really likes you, huh?" A zipper unzipped.

"Kathryn!" He wiggled back in the booth.

"I suppose you're one of the few he trusts who can travel without my old friends at the *Post* noticing anyone's gone."

"Kathryn. Not here." He tried to push her hands away. She was enjoying making him uncomfortable.

"Maybe you're expendable."

Emillio stepped up to the table. "Anything I can help you with."

They looked at each other and broke into a laugh that brought the eyes of the entire crowd to their table. "Uh, no. That's all right. We can handle it."

Kathryn smiled and let go. "I can handle it." The waiter left.

"I don't believe the president thinks I'm expendable."

"Maybe I do." Kathryn was only half joking. She pushed her chowder away and sighed. "So, what am I supposed to do with the tickets?"

"Why don't you call your sister to come down and see it. She appreciates this kind of stuff even more than I do."

"She's tied up with her fashion show. And besides..." Kathryn slowly caught his last phrase. "This kind of stuff, is it? I thought you wanted to go with me!"

"I'm sorry. I do. I didn't mean it that way. How about my mother?"

The young bride tried to glare again, but couldn't.

"On second thought, how about someone at the school?" Kathryn had recently finished her masters in education and was now working at one of the private schools that catered to the children of Washington's elite. "There's bound to be someone there who'd love to go."

"Most of my friends there have to go to bed by nine o'clock or they get grounded."

Fran tried to come up with a jealous frown. "You seeing a younger man?"

"Every day at recess." She batted her lashes. "I'd rather have you, but I guess I'll just have to settle."

"That's what I like to hear." Francis flashed a grin and got serious. "I'll make it all up to you. I promise."

"When?"

"When this whole Iraqi thing settles down."

"Oh, that's a real comfort. And when is that going to be? You might as well have said 'when Israel pulls out of the West Bank' or 'when Gorbachev lands a column in the *New York Times*.' "

"Come on. Let's go home. I gotta pack." They rose to leave. "Maybe Emillio is free."

The soldier and the teacher parted that night without totally resolving the disappointment. Francis had a plane to catch. Kathryn couldn't find a friend in Washington over nine years old who was both free and willing to take in the ballet at such short notice. She scalped the tickets at half price, bought a gallon of Rocky Road and stayed home to watch *'thirtysomething'* with the cat.

Maybe she'd see the ballet in Cleveland.

Chapter 21: Ali's Revenge
Kuwait City
October 3, 1990

It was somewhere a world away in a distant dream that Ali had viewed this street before: a lost and haunting memory of beauty, order and sanity. He hadn't set foot in his old neighborhood since that uncertain dawn when his family loaded up the old Volvo and drove to the border. It had been the last morning of joy he had known. Slipping over to Nadia's home after sunset, he had stolen his fiance away from her family. Her mother and sisters cried softly as they said their goodbyes. Nadia's father simply nodded and turned a face to the wall, as if to say *"she is your responsibility now."* The memories seemed like scenes from a forgotten movie: their night of passion; the drive to the border; the hours of waiting, only to be pulled out of the car at the last checkpoint; the separation from his brother, Salaam; the march to the other side of the sand dune; the old Bedouin angel who had shaded him; and his narrow escape from death. The final vision of Nadia's sorry eyes saturated his every waking moment at first. But this, too, had dimmed and blurred, and finally faded into the caverns of his subconscious as an image that couldn't quite be trusted as true.

She lay often by his side in that moment between slumber and sleep. He would reach instinctively out to the twilight and, in an instant of both heaven and hell, could almost embrace her essence before it vaporized into emptiness.

Al Jahrah had midwifed Ali for those first days of his rebirth. The resistance cell was hiding hundreds of deserters and over 70 Westerners in warehouses, homes and burned-out business just west of Kuwait City. They would slip fugitives out a handful at a time in exchange for weapons, food and hard currency. With a healthy smuggling operation, a sizable stash of weapons and decent radio connections to both American and British intelligence, *Al Jahrah* brought hope to thousands of remaining Kuwaitis as they waited for the invasion that never seemed to come.

Ali's quick mind and natural ability with electronic equipment won him an immediate position in the underground. A month of truck bombings, drive-by shootings and abductions won him credibility. But it was his manipulation of a bribed Iraqi general and later the cunning deception that set the hated man up to be executed by his own people which won Ali the respect of his comrades and the title *Shobash*. (Kurdish for "good night.")

The brutality of the invaders left visible scars on the streets and on Ali's back. But the random and capricious nature of death in Kuwait left an even more permanent brand on the young man's soul. Prior to August 2, Ali Jalib Hassan al Bakr had never entertained a political urge in his life. The re-occurring nightmare of lying naked, cold and still in the trench of the freshly slaughtered changed all that. Al Bakr had been born a child of the privileged few in the Arab world. That was a world away and a lifetime ago. Upon arising from the grave, he had been reborn a man of the oppressed. Once he had cared for many things: his education, his career, his fiance. Now he cared for only one thing: the freedom of Kuwait. And, as he once read in a forgotten book, "there is nothing more dangerous than a man who cares for only one thing."

Following Ali's successful fire-bombing of a troop truck from an overhead bridge in Kuwait City, the Iraqis quit playing games. Their reprisal was immediate. Within the hour over 200 women, children and old men from the adjacent neighborhoods were gathered and locked into the water department warehouse. Soldiers spread fuel oil around the building and burned it to the ground. The few children who managed to break out of a back window were shot in place. *Al Jahrah*, taken totally off guard by the incident, was forced to put all lethal tactics on hold and change agendas to setting the stage for the allied invasion.

Twice, while delivering Westerners to Navy SEALs in the harbor at *Ash Shuwaykh*, Ali found himself with an opportunity to escape. On the first occasion a black face had asked in jerky Arabic if he wanted a ride to Saudi Arabia. He simply shook his head and pretended not to understand the question. The second time, while helping a sick Scottish businessman onto an American landing craft, a huge arm reached out and started to pull him into the boat. He was lost in it all for a moment. It was as if Allah, himself, was raising him up from hell. But at the last moment something stirred within and he stiffened, broke free and slid back into the ebony waters.

"I have a job to do. Sorry." That was all he could think to say. He waved the perplexed sailor on and sat down by the shore to weep.

Weeks, then months passed without news of the promised invasion. Rumors flared everywhere, only to be extinguished by the cold reality of the BBC. The dismantling of the capital city grew more methodical as time dragged tediously on and the death grip tightened. Marauding trucks of enemy soldiers made travel during the day impossible. Helicopters nailed a coffin lid over the city from sunset to sunrise, making night movement extremely dangerous.

The news of the 'resettlement plan' for Kuwait hit Ali like a cold slap in the face. It suddenly dawned on *Al Jahrah* that Saddam's offer to let Kuwaitis leave, his policy of terror and the subsequent emptying of Kuwait City were all part of a master strategy. The Iraqis were hoping to repopulate their new conquest with loyal settlers and, thus, to solidify control. Saddam would give away land, homes, jobs and positions to the poor of Iraq. They, in turn, becoming the new landed gentry would owe him their gratitude and allegiance. Then would the assimilation of Province 19 be irreversibly complete; the name *'Al Kuwayt'* erased forever from the world's maps and memory.

Ali had purposefully stayed out of his old neighborhood, and for good reason. Once the fame of *Shobash* spread, he became a marked man. Anyone seeing him was required under pain of death to report it. He knew that his former street, as deserted as it seemed, would be a tomb for everyone who saw him if he were to venture back. When news of the first settlers arrived, Ali considered going home. But when news of his brother's disappearance came, Ali had no choice. He had to know for himself. His brother was worth any risk.

Two treasures had been left behind which now called out to the night for his return. Hidden in the floor of Abu Bakr's shop was a silken pillow case filled with the best of his father's merchandise. If the stash was still there, *Al Jahrah* could be funded for another year. Even more valuable than the gold, however, was the second treasure: an engagement photograph of Nadia taped behind the door of Ali's own forgotten closet. He had no choice. He would rescue the photo before someone else got there. Before it was too late.

The eyes of a deserted street turned aside and even the dogs refused to bark as a dusty ghost from the past slid from shadow to shadow and entered his father's shop. No helicopters were flying tonight, in honor of the Sabbath or the fuel shortage. Inside the once proud store, shattered window glass and ceiling plaster lay in piles like hardened dung. Dirt and sand had blown into every crack and crevasse. A few spent shell casings were scattered here and there about the floor, remnants of an earlier resistance execution. All of the cases, shelves and lighting fixtures were gone. Electric wires had been cut and yanked from the walls. The handsome door to the back room had been removed and its hinges unscrewed from the frame. Even the stool in the bathroom had been an intended victim of the looters. When it cracked in the loosening process, however, they settled for the padded lid and left the broken porcelain in place.

The searcher edged cautiously into the back room to find his floor half dug away. Apparently someone with suspicions about the secret stash had been scared off before finding the exact spot of the treasure. It was probably his father's Indian gardener. The little man was standing behind Abu when he ordered his sons to go to the store and hide the best of their wares under the back floor. "Allah is merciful" *Shobash* thought to himself as he quietly pried three floorboards from their place and smiled at the familiar silken case that appeared. This would buy more than a month of food, ammunition and overlooking glances. The hunt had been half successful. But the greater treasure awaited.

Shobash listened carefully to the night before slipping out into the alley and down the trash-filled path. Across the street from his house, so close but yet so far away, he stopped to meet his brother's memory. Young Salaam always used this corner when he was angry with father. He would stand near enough to be heard and shout a vow never to return home again. Holding court on the corner and cursing Abu's old fashioned ways, more than once he threatened to join the Socialists. Brother Amad would come to stand on the other side of the street and argue politics with Salaam, unwilling to cross for fear of symbolically siding with the boy. The scene would end with Ali and his mother coming out to give some vague promise that things would change. The stubborn adolescent would ask what was for dinner. And again the world would be at peace. (At least until the next time.)

So lost was Ali in memories of his brothers that he almost did not see the truck lights bearing down upon him. He managed to drop flat into the shadows only moments before he would have been spotted. An anxious heart raced as Ali laid the silken case carefully at his feet and kicked it under a pile of rubbish. The truck stopped between him and his destination and three drunken soldiers emerged for a moment to relieve themselves by the roadside. *Shobash* clutched the Uzi under his coat and tried to stay one with the shadows around him. A voice mumbled something about 'citizen patrol' being an impediment to black market business dealings. Another man, completely inebriated, laughed at his friends and told them they needed to learn how to mix business and pleasure more productively. The third soldier, too inebriated to speak, simply staggered in and out of the truck without belching a word.

The trio stood with backs to Ali and rifles out of reach against the truck. Had he wished, he could have taken them all out in one quick raking of his pistol. He weighed the joy it would bring him against the result: being forced to leave without his photo of Nadia. The Uzi was raised. It cried out to be fed. A finger itched to move. But gradually the desire for blood was overwhelmed by the siren song of an enchanted photograph hanging behind his closet door. These three weren't worth it. He would take out three Iraqis another day in their honor and call it even. For now, he had an appointment to keep.

Looking beyond the moment and the three urinating dogs, Ali gazed to a window across the street. A tingling warmth spread down his spine and settled in the pit of his stomach. For there, in what had once been his own bedroom window, a candle shone and a pallid figure stepped in, then out of the moonlight. The spectral image peered at the soldiers, closed the shades and vanished as quickly as it had appeared.

Someone was living in Ali's house! But who? Certainly not Amad. After his older brother had contacted Ali to hide Stewart Kensington, Amad had taken his family into hiding with another resistance cell. That was the last he'd heard of him. It was safest for everyone that way. Could it be that Amad and Haifa had returned? It would have been as dangerous as it was foolish. But if the elder Bakr was again living in his house, who was this old woman? A nursemaid for a new son? If Amad had not returned, who then was this intruder? A Baathist party official? An Iraqi settler? Whoever it happened to be, if it was not Amad, this unfortunate soul was about to meet up with the most feared and frustrated man in all of Kuwait. And *Shobash* was in no mood for talk.

The truck's starter ground five times before turning over. Finally it caught and the soldiers pulled off, leaving Ali with his anger and his Uzi. He wasted no time. Bursting into the living room, he cocked the weapon and cursed. Three frightened children shrieked and huddled together in a circle of fear.

"Who are you!" the eldest objected. "What are you doing in our house?"

"Your house! You have trespassed in my house and will pay for this!" Ali suddenly realized that he was speaking only to children. "Where is the man here?"

An elderly woman stepped out into the light of the upstairs doorway. "Who are you?" she demanded. This was the figure from the window. "Who are you and what do you want?"

"I am your worst nightmare, Iraqi whore sow!" Ali's words spit hatred with every syllable. " I am *Shobash*, the ghost of this house and I've come to take your man with me to hell! Where is he?"

"Please!" cried the old woman, throwing herself between Ali and the children. "Please, we have no quarrel with you. Leave us."

Ali shoved her to the floor and grasped the eldest male child by the hair. "This is my home! The home of Abu al Bakr! Of Ali and Salaam! Of Amad and his children. You have no right to be here. How dare you violate me like this! I will protect what is mine. Now, get your collaborating father out here so that you may watch him die like I have watched my people die these last months. Where is he?"

"He has gone to Gahra Hospital to bring a doctor!" The youngest girl, not more than 6 years old, clawed at the intruder to release her brother. "He has no quarrel with you. Why must you hurt him so?"

"Silence!" Ali cast the boy to the floor and slammed his fist into the wall inches from the little girl's face. Plaster mixed with flesh on the course block; red on white, white on red. Pain shot up Ali's arm, but the madness held all feeling away from his consciousness. "You live in my house, you die in my house! You will all pay the price for taking what is not yours."

A sharp and tortured cry cut through the air from the room beyond the doorway where the old woman had first appeared. Ali spun instinctively and fired a burst of shells into the wall. The children screamed as he jumped up to meet the call. He took the stairs in three bounds and tore the heavy blanket which covered the portal to the ground.

Demon eyes seethed into the darkness and were met by a delirious voice: "Is that you, Sa'id? Did you bring the doctor? Are there any drugs? Please, please give me some drugs. It is time and something is wrong. Oooh!" She screamed again, panting like a rabid dog. "Something... something... something is terribly... terribly wrong!" Shrill cries turned into low murmuring gasps, then trickled to guttural whimpers. She was lying on the table, legs spread wide and bleeding. Ali looked away in an instinctive humility until her staccato cry pierced the armor of his hatred. With bearings jarred, he looked to the woman twice before it slowly it dawned on him that she was giving birth. He was confused. At that moment Ali thought he heard a voice whispering: "It's Haifa, pilgrim. Haifa."

"Haifa?" In an instant all was transformed. The woman before him was no longer an interloper screaming out in pain. She was Haifa - Amad's Haifa - his brother's wife. The children were now his nieces. And Ali's only nephew was screaming for life on the other side of a collapsing wall.

For the next blurred minutes an inexplicable wave of clarity gripped Ali's focus. Propping a canteen under his chin, he emptied its contents onto the woman's forehead while simultaneously washing his hands. He laid the Uzi at his feet and instructed the fevered woman to take shallow breaths and to not push. A gush of water and blood splattered onto his feet to wet the floor below. A tiny leg protruded, but no other appendage was in sight. Ali placed his rough forearm between her pelvic bone and navel, and with the other hand reached to lock fingers around a second little foot, waiting for the next waves to begin.

They came thirty seconds later. "Now! Push! Push, Haifa! Push!" He pulled with one hand and forced his entire weight down upon her diaphragm in a flushing motion with the other. The woman screamed, thrust a tremendous inner convulsion and began to laugh hysterically.

Ali caught the slippery prize by a tiny arm, inches from the floor. The afterbirth oozed out with a second push and the black-red blood of new life washed the tiles and painted the walls. Lost in that moment of wonder, Ali hadn't seen the children enter the room. Nor had he noticed an awe-struck father join the relieved old woman who now stood behind him. When he finally did look up, eyes blurred with tears, Ali was speechless.

He offered Sa'id his new son. The father held him awkwardly for a moment as the old woman cut the chord, then laid the wrinkled miracle at his mother's breast.

No one noticed Ali kneel to retrieve his weapon or lay the satin pillow case on a broken chair by the door before silently slipping away. It was five minutes before another word was uttered. Finally Sa'id turned to the old woman: "Who was he?"

"He said his name was *Shobash*," answered the brave little girl.

"*Shobash*? That means 'good night.' This shall be your new brother's name. *Shobash*." Sa'id looked down on the tranquility of the nursing child and thanked Allah for the gift of that dark angel.

"*Shobash*. And why was he here?"

"He came to kill you."

Chapter 22: Peshmerga
Mosul, Northern Iraq
October 5, 1990

He evidently arrived at a bad time. After meeting his contacts on the ground an hour outside of *Mosul*, he was blindfolded, tied and left in a truck for the night. "No one can speak to you now," came a young raspy voice through the canvas. The accent was distinctly British. "*Peshmerga* are rather busy tonight and cannot come out and play. It is too dangerous."

Peshmerga was the name the Kurdish resistance fighters gave themselves. It meant "those prepared to die."

"Nice reception," Francis thought as he shivered the cold night away tied up in the truck. His blindfold was removed for an hour at dawn and he was allowed to stretch before they bound him back up into the lorry and moved out across the Tigris traveling due east. The driver was an old Kurd with a snarling grin and thick glasses. His keeper was a dirt-faced boy with short, cropped black hair, opaque sun glasses and a baggy shirt.

"Why the ropes and blindfold?" he asked the boy.

"You might be an Iraqi spy."

"If I am an Iraqi spy, why don't you just take me out and shoot me?"

The boy was silent for a long while, as if considering Khalil's fate. "Because you might not be?"

They drove on, stopping and starting at irregular intervals and eating only once that day. It was a dish tasting so raw and warm that Francis was almost grateful he couldn't see it. Some time the next morning their truck lurched to a halt and Fran was yanked out into the sunlight of another village. The men of *Shaqlawa* told Khalil's chauffeurs that they would be happy to take this stranger off their hands. The American was quickly shuttled back into their truck and on they drove. Francis could hear mortar rounds popping and scattered machine gun fire in the distance. In the third town, *Mamazelka*, they waited for only five minutes before being told that no one there wanted to speak with them. The elders of the village doubted that anyone anywhere would. Again they drove on.

"You speak beautiful English," said the Marine to his young jailer.

"My French is even better."

"Where did you learn to speak it?"

"French?"

"No, English."

The boy let out a hearty laugh. "England, of course. Where else would one learn to speak English?"

"How about America?"

"Americans don't speak English."

"They don't?"

"They speak..." He paused, searching for the right word. "They speak..."

"Americans speak a form of English."

The boy sighed heavily. "Yes, I suppose. And a very dreadful form, at that."

The truck worked its way on up an increasingly more treacherous road. "I guess we don't need this anymore," said the young Kurd after Francis hit the side of the wall for the third time. The boy removed Fran's blindfold and untied him. Slightly effeminate in looks but all boy in actions, the young warrior appeared to be about 15. He had fine features and was not yet in need of a shave. If one scrubbed away the dirt and removed the dark glasses, one might even say the boy was handsome.

"Aren't you afraid I might try to escape?"

The fair-faced *peshmerga* shrugged his shoulders and looked out to the countryside. "Escape? To where?" Khalil scanned the horizon. The terrain had changed considerably. Instead of a plain, they were now facing the valley of a high mountain pass. Defoliated scrub trees dotted the grey rock cliffs. Francis knew something was wrong with the picture, but couldn't quite place it. He studied the trees - skeletal wooden hands reaching to a merciless heavens for pardon. He scoured the path of a small stream which ran through the plateau of stone 100 yards below. Finally it dawned on him what was missing: green. The color green. The entire landscape was painted in shades of grey and brown. Not one leaf, not one blade of grass, not so much as a tuft of moss could be seen in the whole poisoned pass.

"Where are we? Iran? Turkey? Possibly Iraq?" Khalil posed the question.

"It is best if you do not know." The truck stopped and Fran's host jumped out and scampered to the top of a nearby ridge. He motioned for his guest to join him. "You see those blocks over there?" The young man pointed down the path. One hundred and fifty feet below another boy squatted with a galvanized bucket, collecting murky water from a foul ditch. Francis nodded. "That used to be my father's home. The Iraqi army blew it up in 1988. It was a grand house. Seven rooms. The biggest in the village. You see that over there?" Farther down the hillside a twisted column of cement stood like a defiant middle finger against the sky. The Kurd spoke with a definite pride. "That is my mosque." Francis stared at the pile of rock and rubble until he could envision the bare outline of a demolished foundation.

The American listened as an entire village was spread out before his imagination. Here and there he could see faint traces of what used to be foundations. A bakery. A newspaper office. A gunsmith's. All of them were bulldozed or shelled into oblivion by a government determined to completely clear the region of its unwanted inhabitants. "four thousand villages such as this were systematically destroyed. The fields and streams were poisoned. Even the cemeteries were erased from our hillsides. All of this while the world closed its eyes and you Americans slept with the demon Hussein." As the young man spoke, a small caravan could be seen winding its way up the twisted trail below.

"We leave the truck now. It is time to ride. You do know how to ride, don't you?"

Khalil nodded. "I grew up in Montana."

The Kurd looked at him with an unknowing stare. "What means that?"

"I know how to ride."

The leader of the horses was a glaze-eyed old warrior with a red turban and a Kalishnikov rifle. Behind this thin and wiry *peshmerga* trudged 17 heavily laden pack mules and six riders on ponies. Each toted an antique weapon straight out of '*The Charge of the Light Brigade.*' They passed by like ghosts without so much as acknowledging the foreigner's existence until, at the last moment, a rear guard cut two ponies loose and the captain and his guide mounted. Without so much as a whip stroke, the small horses bolted up the path toward a high mountain pass.

"What's your name?" Khalil asked his young friend.

"The horse's name in *El-Baruq*. That's all you need to know."

Fran knew enough about Islam to recognize *El-Baruq* as Mohammed's legendary horse who could jump to Jerusalem in one bound.

"So, we're going to Jerusalem?"

The young man smiled, only slightly impressed.

A half hour later Francis tried again. "How about your name?"

"How about it?"

"How about telling me your name?"

"Why do you want to know?"

"Maybe I'll write a book about you."

The young man laughed this time but said nothing for five minutes more. Finally he spoke. "Adanon."

"Adanon who?"

"Just Adanon. That's enough for you. Any more is too dangerous. And your name?"

"Dan Quayle."

His companion didn't react this time. Maybe he didn't get it. They traveled on, continuing the ascent. The path gradually seemed to disappear and their small horses worked all the harder to negotiate the steep and rocky gorge.

"You call this a road?"

"What do you call it in English?"

"I can't see so much as a goat trail here."

"The animals can." Adanon whipped his horse and passed Francis. "I guess that makes a Kurdish donkey smarter than an American vice president."

It took Francis a while to realize that Adanon understood his earlier Dan Quayle joke.

Beast and burden continued their grueling climb for three hours before the gnarled old mule driver raised his bony two-fingered hand to indicate a break. He stepped up to Khalil's horse and shouted in the animal's face: *"Man kastam!"*

"What was that?" asked the captain.

"It would appear that he spoke to your horse."

"I know that! What did he say?"

"He told your horse that he's tired!"

"Man kastam." Fran could relate.

Seven strangers dismounted, nodding and laughing. Francis gazed down across the rugged terrain unable to even see the path they had just taken. Suddenly a shot rang out from the eastern ridge. The American's pony reared up and bolted away with rider still in saddle. Twenty seconds later Fran's face was cut by a branch he couldn't manage to evade. A moment after that he parted company with his mount and flew into the near-freezing waters of a mountain stream.

Seven pack drivers and 17 mules watched him go down and cheered. They cheered again when he stood and bowed. The pony continued on below the ridge for a minute, then stopped cold. Francis climbed out of the gully and began picking gravel from his hands and knees. He looked up. The squidgey-nosed old idol masquerading as company commander laughed and called down to him. *"Ma mirem opteni?"*

"He wants to know if we go to swim?" shouted Adanon.

"Arb sardas?"

"He asks if the water is cold."

Francis collapsed on the ancient rocks to catch his breath and count his bones. The frightened pony gradually wandered back to stand almost apologetically by its master. Fishing a leather pouch from his own saddle pack, Adanon climbed down to attend to his friend's wounds.

"All I have is some salve and gauze. But you are welcome to it."

Khalil looked at the meager medical kit the Kurd carried. He squeezed out a couple drops of the iodine for the deepest cut in his hand and threw the tube back to the boy. "Save it for someone who needs it. I'll just wash up."

"Isn't that what you just did?" Adanon laughed and tucked the package away, then bent down upon his haunches to survey the mountain ahead. He was a beautiful boy, grinning from ear to ear, but definitely in need of a bath.

The Kurd's stare asked a question Fran couldn't interpret. "What?"

Adanon shrugged his shoulders.

"What? What?"

"I thought you said you knew how to ride."

"I do. I did."

"I think you fly better than you ride."

Francis was beginning to like the kid.

They rested for 15 minutes more while the *peshmerga* recinched their loads and scoured the horizon for the source of the stray shot.

"What were you doing in England, anyway?"

Adanon didn't respond.

"Were you there with an exchange program of some sort?"

Adanon shrugged his shoulders.

"How many miles to our destination?"

"You sure ask a lot of questions for an American. You say you're from Montana?"

"Eastern Montana. Why?"

"You have traveled long distances there by horse?"

"Yes. When I was a boy. It's quite flat there."

"I have a cousin in Minot, Dakota."

"North Dakota."

"Yes. North Dakota. It is right next to Montana. Maybe you know him."

Khalil didn't know anyone in Minot, North Dakota. "It's a big state. I really haven't been back much since I joined the service."

"He left in the '70s when this campaign of genocide began. The Lutheran World Relief settled him." Adanon lit a cigarette and offered Francis the first puff. "I have a handmade quilt from 'Ladies Aid', Minot, Dakota. Very pretty. You wish to buy?"

Francis assured Adanon that he wasn't in the market for a quilt, but that he would try to contact the boy's relatives the very next time he went through Minot. As they were speaking, the old *peshmerga* returned and spoke directly to Khalil's horse once more.

"*Zur boshum!*"

Adanon interpreted. "He says to the horse: 'Very good.'"

"Very good? For what? For throwing me in the river? Thanks a lot!"

"*Chone? Schma kastaste?*"

"He says to the horse: 'How are you? You are tired?'"

"He's tired? What about me?" The captain pointed at his own chest and aimed an annoyed statement at the old man. *"Man kastam!"*

Adanon was duly impressed. "You learn quickly."

"In my business you have to."

They mounted for the last leg of the journey. "And what business is that? Exactly which kind of a spy are you?" asked Adanon.

"I'm not a spy. I'm an emissary from the American government with a message for your leaders. What kind of a spy are you?"

"I'm not a spy, either." Adanon whipped his horse and yelled back at the American. "I'm a dentist."

The caravan arrived at a village tucked into the mountainside as the chill of twilight was beginning to set in their bones. A crowd of peasants raced toward them from Stone Age huts, startling Francis with their shrill cries and clicking tongues. Young and old gathered round about to unload the grateful ponies of their communal cargo. Teary-eyed women beat breasts and hugged sons and husbands as if they had returned from the grave. (Francis surmised that some of them may have done just that.) A small man with brass wire-rimmed reading glasses and cotton white hair stood on the other side of the square watching the festivities with particular interest.

"Who's that?" asked Fran.

"He's the one you really want to speak with."

"Ask him to come over."

"Sabcoem! Bia!" Adanon waved at the man.

The dentist conversed with the proud elder for a few moments, then returned. "He wants to know which president you are working for: Nixon or Ford?"

Francis knew his history and what the remark meant. In the '70s, both administrations had prompted the Kurds to rise up against Iraqi regimes at a time when Baghdad was badgering the Shah. The U.S. hoped such a diversion would force Iraq to shift attention homeward and, thus, take pressure off its Iranian friends. When the Shah said he no longer needed assistance, the U.S. turned its back, kicking the props out from under its promise to the Kurds. Soon afterwards, Saddam embarked on a demolition and relocation program against the rebellious people as a punishment.

"Tell him that I don't work for men who give their word and break it. I work for honorable men."

This time the caravan driver joined Adanon to speak with the village chief. They returned again, wagging their heads. "He says there is no one in this village who will speak with an infidel. Sorry."

Francis threw his hands up in frustration. "What are we supposed to do now?"

"We?" The young man started to laugh. "This is where I stop. I tried to get you an appointment in three towns. I told Salah Kadir that I could take you this far. And here is where you are. Now I've got a cold supper, a warm bath and a hot lover waiting for me at home. Goodbye, Mr. Quayle." He turned to go.

"Adanon? Adanon!" Khalil was quick. "But what if I need a dentist?"

"You have to learn to pull your own teeth in this part of the world." Half-way down to the village square, Adanon turned back once more. "Don't call me. I'm not in the book."

It didn't happen all at once. The air grew heavy and almost still as the world ground slowly to a halt. The young interpreter's laugh continued on. But everything else - time, motion and breath, itself - seemed to freeze in place for the moment. And then over the mountain blew the sound of a million locusts. It was an unmistakable drone to the Marine: helicopters. Soviet-built Hind helicopters.

First fire hit the center of the village, knocking half of the pack animals and three riders to the bloody earth. Explosions and trails of bullets rose from stone streets as women and children ran for cover. Handguns and rifles materialized from out of nowhere to answer the attack from rooftops and hillside shelters. There were three choppers in all, but there might as well have been a thousand. The Kurds were no match for something they could not chase.

Death rained from the skies for seven eternal minutes. Rockets blasted homes to rubble. A machine gun nest near the main road was torn to pieces as its frantic ants swarmed to unload the jammed ammo clip. The Iraqis knew their maneuvers well. Ducking and weaving through smoke-filled skies, they quickly ate the life out of every crevasse that dared defy them with return fire. They dug and dug at each source of resistance until most *peshmerga* were silenced.

The analyst and the dentist dove for cover behind a large rock near the place they had spoken to the elder. Adanon pulled a .45 from his hidden shoulder harness and watched the horror show, jumping out infrequently to take a wild shot here and another there.

Francis looked up to see the gnarled old mule driver bolt fearlessly through the fire and dive into the smoldering machine gun nest. He pushed bodies aside, then quickly moved the gun into place, attempting to reload. The droning birds hung with bellies wide open to the antique British fire-spitter. Francis made his move. Darting through rising smoke toward the jammed weapon, he landed headfirst in the sand-bagged entrenchment.

The glaze in the ancient *peshmerga's* eyes seemed to miraculously clear as he pulled frantically at the ammo belt. Locked into place too quickly, a bullet had apparently lodged in the firing chamber and had frozen the entire mechanism. Khalil slid a knife from the boot of a nearby corpse and cut into the tip of the soft lead bullet. It sprung immediately out and the belt was free.

The death machine directly above them shifted its tail in the wind and Francis could make out the yellow-toothed grin of the attacker. Spinning the bulky weapon into place with the aid of the old man, they raised their sights and unloaded 10 lbs. of British lead into the deathbird's fuselage. A sputter, a clunk and a small internal explosion sent the Hind slowly reeling into the flaming hell of the village square below. It lit down almost peacefully before two pilots emerged dragging their wounded comrade. From nowhere and everywhere came the small arms fire that dropped them all to a cobblestone grave. The second Hind returned and hovered momentarily over this execution sight, firing blindly into the acrid smoke.

Khalil's new friend pulled him down and the two sprawled motionless on a pile of corpses, feigning death as the tornado wind paused over them. They sprung back into place to renew fire the moment it passed, bullets tearing through the vulnerable backside of the armored bird. It suddenly turned and whirred out of control toward the outskirts of the village, blue smoke pouring from both sides. It disappeared. A moment later the black-orange fireball silhouetted the village against the mountainside and sneezed a yellow dust from every rooftop.

A final enemy hung above them as if making a judgement call, then dipped and flew directly into the valley to make its escape. *Peshmerga* continued firing on into the night sky to celebrate their victory. And for one silent moment, a burning world stood strangely still. Smoke. Oil. Fire. Blood. Death. Silence. Victory.

It was almost beautiful.

Adanon rose from behind the hiding rock and made his way over to the two unlikely comrades who had downed the deathbirds.

"*Shuma marde kobbie hasta,*" smiled the old man, kissing Fran repeatedly on both cheeks, then on the mouth.

"He says you're a good man. For an infidel."

"Thanks," answered the captain. "*Shuma marde kobbie hasta!*" Tell him he is, too."

The Kurdish alliance had begun.

Chapter 23: Kafsh Dacana
Diyana, Iraq
October 8, 1990

The time for prayer was over. It was time to talk of war.

"*Kafsh dacana!*" shouted Adanon to Francis. "*Kafsh dacana!*" Put on your shoes.

The captain didn't need to convince his new-found friends that Soviet helicopters were difficult to destroy with small arms. The *peshmerga* knew it was in their best interest to get their hands on some Stinger missiles. They were well aware of how the Afghans changed the tide of their war using Stingers. Within a few months of the first delivery, the *muhajadin* were taking out an average of one of the invincible monsters a day. Soviet air force morale deteriorated so quickly that transport pilots wouldn't leave the hangers to resupply their own units, even when they were hopelessly pinned down. They simply refused to fly.

Khalil's new friend Schwan, the spectacled *muktar* of the high mountain village, couldn't promise anything. But he thought he might at least get the American a hearing among the elders of the area's scattered resistance. The next morning he and Adanon left to talk to some people who could talk to some people. Within three days they had gathered a loose confederation of Kurdish chieftains to listen to a man they normally would have just as soon murdered in his sleep. They came from the Revolutions' Banner, the Patriotic Union of Kurdistan (PUK) and the Toylar Party, as well as from a number of smaller factions that made up the ever changing face of the Kurdistan Front. These *peshmerga* were weary, scarred and wary of most outsiders. But they agreed to listen to what the American had to say. Maybe then they'd cut his throat.

They entered the village of *Diyana* on a moonless night: Adanon,

Schwan, Francis and the toothless old mule driver who accompanied them to keep an eye on his animals. The cool evening breeze smelled of hashish and spice and goats. Huddling women warmed their hands by a dozen dung fires and eyed them suspiciously as they marched through the town. Tiny silent faces peaked secretly at the intruders through tent flaps and cardboard windows of make-shift shacks. Arriving late, the four took their places in a dimly lit rock building with a canvas top. It was the only home left standing in the once thriving bazaar section of town. Around them waited the most embittered and embattled collection of warriors Francis had ever seen. Defiant. Angry. Scarred. Worn, yet strangely unworn by the wear.

Schwan greeted the group in the name of Allah and explained why the meeting had been called. Then he motioned to Khalil. Eyes, fierce like knives, cut deep into his soul. He had only seen this look once before: in his imagination. The major had told him of a night long ago in the hills overlooking Kabul when he couldn't deliver promised arms to the Afghan resistance. For a moment Francis was transported in time to the major's side, and the two of them wondered if they would leave the room alive.

The captain stood and cleared his throat to speak, but an old friend's two-fingered hand held him back. *"Sabcoem! Rockde kordon."*

"What did he say?" Francis whispered to Adanon.

"He says it is time to eat. We eat first, then we talk."

Fran wondered for more than a moment about what these people might dig up to eat. Literally. Most of the valley fields had been poisoned or scorched by the Iraqi air force. And flocks appeared virtually nonexistent. These were the Kurds who wouldn't be moved - the brave or stubborn fools who chose to question Saddam's relocation to concentration camps in the south and were answered with gas attacks. These were the living in the land of the dead. What could they possibly find to serve a guest?

The meal prepared was a feast by siege standards. There was a lentil and herb soup with heavy bread and a heady cheese. There was a cabbage dish which tasted rotten to Francis but was the hit of the party for the visiting dignitaries. They drank an unstrained goat milk with the scum still floating about in it. The main course was a roast ginger lamb (which was actually quite tasty). Fran did his best to honor his hosts by choking every last bite down. By now he was hungry.

When the dining concluded, the Marine and his interpreter were ushered to the center of the chamber. Schwan gave some sort of invocation to Allah, introduced his American again, and told the story of how Khalil had helped down the Iraqi helicopters. Finally turning to Francis with a nod, he reclined. Adanon stood by his friend's side to color the foreigner's words for their ears.

What the captain had to say surprised the elders. He could see it in their eyes. Instead of simply offering Stingers, TOWs and a few other goodies, this man was proposing something much greater: "A dream, gentlemen. A dream that only the boldest of you have dared to open your eyes and see. Not simply an unstable autonomous region, but a new sovereign nation. A free Kurdistan one hundred fifty miles long inside what is now Iraq, stretching from *Zakho* in the north past *Shaqlawa* in the west. When the American/Allied invasion of Kuwait is accomplished and Saddam Hussein is no longer a power, you will be free to realize this dream. The U.S. will supply the weapons to take and hold your land, to protect and maintain your villages and countryside. All we asked is this: that your leadership re-initiates the civil war against Saddam in earnest before the war to free Kuwait gets underway; that you harass divisions in northern Iraq and keep them tied up for the duration of the Kuwaiti conflict; and that you locate and free any Western hostages you may find who are being held at facilities within your reach."

Khalil finished his speech and sat. A shroud of silence enveloped the night. Spiders traced silk in the moonlight above. A dog barked in the distance. No one smiled. No one moved. No one breathed.

Suddenly, the oldest man there pulled his knife from a hidden harness and slammed it into the table, inches from the American's hand. Francis didn't flinch. The *peshmerga* muttered two words which Khalil didn't recognize at first. *"Kirkuk. Sulaimanyia."*

"What is he saying? What does this mean? "

Schwan nodded to the dentist. Adanon whispered into the American's ear. "These are major Kurdish cities in the south. 150 miles may not be enough."

"Tell him that he can have as much as he can take."

Adanon passed the message on. The chieftain continued to glare.

"Tell him I should be pleased to be his first official guest in his new palace in *Kirkuk* next year..."

He still wasn't impressed.

"...at Saddam's former summer chateau."

The frown began to melt. The old warrior picked up his knife and stuck it into a pomegranate. Flipping it into the air, he sliced it into complete fourths before it hit the ground. "Iraq!" he grinned, pointing to the divided fruit on the floor. *"Boshum. Zur boshum."* The captain remembered these as the mule driver's words when he, himself, had been thrown into the creek. "Good. Very good."

The elder pulled out two alien objects: a pack of Kent cigarettes and a silver lighter. Somehow, these were the last things Francis expected to see. He lit up and offered one to Schwan and the captain. They obliged. Ghostly spirits of smoke rose and danced in ribbons intertwined above their heads. It was almost unreal. Almost spiritual.

Schwan spoke for a good 20 minutes more about the torment and horror his people had faced for 800 years. The old voice was filled with a holy hatred. He used the word 'genocide' three times in English, no doubt for Khalil's sake. Pulling his headpiece back he gestured to his own gruesome scar roughly stitched from ear to ear. He cursed the Iraqis. He cursed the dead Shah. He cursed the infidels - present company accepted, of course. He called on Allah to bless the captain for his efforts, if such a plan would result in their freedom. Then he called on Allah to curse the American's loins should his word not hold true.

Adanon glanced at Francis and started to laugh, but caught himself so as not to defile the solemnness of the moment.

Two other characters had lines in this drama. An angry young man, clearly more sanctimonious than the rest, spoke against taking any money or arms from an infidel. It would be dirty money and couldn't be used. Another, one whom Adanon described as a socialist, pointed out that even Mohammed used un-believers to help him win his battles. Then he offered a comment which made the whole group laugh.

"What did he say, Adanon?"

"He said, 'He's an infidel, but at least this man isn't a Jew!' "

Adanon registered a momentary horror when Francis didn't respond. "You... you aren't a Jew, are you?" He was relieved to no end when Fran pulled out a silver crucifix from beneath his shirt and assured them of his Catholicity.

The generals and chiefs argued for an hour more on how best to join forces to midwife the dream. They squabbled a while longer about just who would take orders from whom. As the night wore to morning, the old warriors begrudgingly agreed to settle the debate another day. They said their *shobashes*. Then, realizing it was already morning, added a few *shoba bahairs* and went their separate ways.

The gutsy spook captain who no one would ever know had pulled it off. With a handshake and a promise destined to be broken, a secret war was underway.

The clandestine Kurdish alliance was not without its difficulties, however. Rival chieftains regularly took pot shots at each other when tempers flared. Individual factions were so fiercely independent that coordinating major attacks and dividing the spoils was next to impossible. Weapons were dropped and many disappeared, only to turn up in black markets from Cairo to Kashmir.

In spite of the differences, these Kurds did make some headway. In the weeks that followed, a great deal of damage was inflicted on material and psychological targets in northern Iraq. A handful of hostages were quietly removed through escape routes in Turkey. Homes of Iraqi officials were shelled and left smoldering, oil equipment and pipelines were sabotaged, and supply caravans were unable to travel without heavily armed escorts. The Stingers did their job and proved well worth the small investment.

The Kurds avoided military bases and electric power plants as much as possible. Bases were too well fortified to justify the casualties. (No one wanted to fight on Iraq's terms.) As for power plants, a few choice ones were left untouched. Schwan and three other chieftains had each received a promised Sony Trinatron color TV from Francis with the first shipment of TOWs. When it was all over, they fully expected to watch CNN and *Dynasty* from their village chateaux in a free Kurdistan. And they couldn't very well do that without electricity.

These Kurds would pay a heavy price for letting themselves be seduced into rebellion, however. Two million of them would one day camp as refugees on the very same bleak mountainsides which Khalil had traveled. Thousands more would watch in disbelief as American troops stood down and allowed them to be butchered by the Iraqi air force. Only four of the elder statesmen who witnessed the promise of that night would live through the next six months. Together they would make a blood oath to skin the infidel alive if ever he stepped foot in their country again.

And the young Marine captain who had made this promise would sleep forever with his betrayal and images of the toothless old mule skinner waiting for him each night to close his eyes.

Chapter 24: Stayin' Alive
Cairo, Egypt
October 10, 1990

"Liberated Kuwait will rise from the shadow of the Constitution of 1962 to solidify democracy and deepen popular participation. This was, and remains, a goal we all strive to realize and struggle to achieve."
  -Crown Prince Sheik Saad Abdullah Salem Sabah to the U.N.

It was the set from *Saturday Night Fever*, only with an Eastern flair. A glittering globe spun from the ceiling, bouncing flickers of blue and white light across the floor. Dancers discoed to the Bee Gees' *Stayin' Alive* and *Disco Duck*. Young men with golden chains stood on the sidelines sipping vodka and beer. Loose women, over-painted and under-dressed, blushed and twittered when asked to dance, then acquiesced to begin their nightly ritual. But this wasn't 1975, it was 1990. And it wasn't New York. This was Cairo.

A room full of red-checkered headdresses told the story. These were the Kuwaitis fortunate enough to escape Iraq's invasion. Some had been away on vacation when the tanks rolled in. Others were abroad on business. Still others had bought, bribed and prayed their way out of the country in those first days. Yet however grim or glorious the past had been, it mattered little now. These young princes were all on a stipend holiday. And they drank and danced their Arabian nights away, in no particular hurry to return.

This Kuwaiti jet set was neither interested in training for an invasion nor in working to fund an army. They were in Egypt to sit out the war. Night after night they cruised the bars, dropping half an average Egyptian's annual salary on drinks and girls. They were enjoying their stay and weren't overly concerned if the mercenary Americans got around to fulfilling their 'contractual duties' right away or not. Some were actually hoping it didn't happen too soon. Cairo's night life beat anything Kuwait City had to offer.

Nadia hadn't intended to go to the disco. She was more interested in politics than play. Aside from that, the 'homeboys' were an embarrassment to her. They all thought that they were acting so *chic*. So modern. She had been in America long enough to know that disco was a generation out of date and a joke to anyone who knew anything.

The young woman had spent her first weeks in exile working at a Cairo newspaper and listening to the BBC. She managed to land a paying job tutoring English at the American University where her uncle taught. Her own family escaped from Kuwait a few weeks after she got out and was reunited with her through the efforts of the American Red Cross. Nadia managed to keep in touch weekly by phone with her fiance's family, the Bakrs. Together they searched for news of Amad, Ali and Salaam with every report that leaked out from the resistance.

Life for Nadia had become a purgatory of apprehension. As she described it in her nightly journal, Ali's fate and her own future were now hanging tragically in limbo. And the lack of reliable information was driving her quietly insane.

Nadia's parents were both educated and widely traveled; modern in their ways. They knew that the world was much larger than the Persian Gulf and that philosophy was broader than even the richest precepts of Islam. They did not deem it necessary to bind their daughters to the societal restrictions which condemned so many young Kuwaiti women to lives of sanctioned mediocrity. Nadia appreciated this about them and reveled in an unusual freedom for a female in her station of life.

It was but two months into the exile that Bahrah al Sabah tried to cheer her up. Attempting to jar her focus from both war and worries, Sabah invited the beautiful young Vassar grad to see the sights of Cairo. She declined twice. Finally, at her mother's insistence, Nadia gave in. What could it hurt? Bahrah was a family friend who had done a fair amount of business with Nadia's father. Although arrogant and even rude around most other women, this filthy rich 30 year old shirt-tail cousin of the Crown Prince had always treated her with respect.

They went to see the Great Pyramid on a miserably wet day but Bahrah managed to make a decent time of it, acting the part of the perfect gentleman the entire afternoon. And, in spite of his reputation as a playboy and his knowledge of her Western ways, he didn't so much as try to hold her hand.

The next evening Bahrah picked her up to take her to a political rally. The Crown Prince had addressed the United Nations earlier that day and a group of exiles was gathering at the University to listen to the speech again and use it as pretext of an evening forum. Instead of traveling to the school, Bahrah's chauffeur made a wrong turn and pulled up at *Ishmael's*, a high priced disco in the ritzy section of the new city.

"Where are you taking me, Bahrah?" She was not pleased.

"You don't want to dance?" He seemed almost hurt. "I thought you were a politician? That's what politicians do best. Dance! They dance around issues. They dance around promises. They dance, they dance, they dance."

She managed a polite smile. "The disco never interested me after it went *out* of style in America."

He shrugged his shoulders and watched as a large woman and a slicked-back worm of a man maneuvered across the floor in a step that wouldn't have been approved by the mullahs. "First we dance, then we'll make it to the forum."

"That wasn't our agreement."

"I am sorry, but I promised some friends I'd meet them here. I, of course, cannot go back on my word. Do you want a drink?"

"Mineral water will be fine."

Bahrah overtipped the waiter and turned to his non-date: "You know, Nadia, the likelihood of Ali being alive is very slim. Very slim, indeed."

She didn't want to hear it. "I thank you for trying to cheer me up. But I'll ask you to keep your opinions to yourself."

"The situation is grim. Very grim. Since September the resistance has been squelched; declared nearly dead. No one has heard a thing from *Al Jahrah*. Since the first report that Ali was alive, we know hundreds have been arrested and executed in his operations area.

"You have had contact with *Al Jahrah* ?"

"I have sources. Ways. Friends."

"Money always has friends."

"Indeed." She had meant it as an insult. He took it as a compliment. "That is who we are here to meet tonight. I thought you might wish to speak to them. But if you would rather be going..."

"No!" She surprised herself with the forcefulness of her answer. "No... I would like to visit with them, also. Who are they?"

"I cannot guarantee anything, of course. But we might be able to spend some money and find something out."

"Who are they?"

"These fellows - I could tap them further if it pleases you."

"It would please me greatly. Who did you say they were?"

He reached for her hand to dance. She hesitated, then gave in.

"I know what this means to you."

"Bahrah, I would be forever in your debt if you could contact Ali or bring me any news of him. Any news."

"Then, it is done. If anyone can get a message in or out, it is my people." For the moment Bahrah appeared sincere.

"You would do that for me?"

"Consider it accomplished."

"Who..."

"Now, let's dance."

They set off across the floor to a pulsing beat. When the slow music began, Nadia turned to sit it out. Bahrah blocked her exit by placing his arm about her shoulder in a 'fatherly' caress. "I know that it bothers you - no - it pains you to think of Ali."

"It pains me to see these cowards spending night after night on expensive Egyptian whores and liquor when they should be buying arms and preparing to take back our homeland."

"This pains me, also." They danced on.

Nadia spoke with a transparent sarcasm: "Your second uncle, the Crown Prince - may he live forever - speaks of reinstating the constitution in Kuwait after we are freed. What treachery is this?"

"It will be studied and gradually put back into place, yes."

"And you believe him?"

"It will eventually come about. Maybe not at first. There will be a transitionary time to rebuild the country and guarantee our security of course."

"Of course."

"A time when martial law must be held in place and such luxuries as a constitution will remain suspended. But after that..."

Nadia didn't believe a word. "The Emir..."

Bahrah interrupted with his own cynical tone. "May he, also, live forever..."

She smirked. "I believe he already has." They danced on.

"Touché!"

"I'm sorry. I interrupted you."

"An apology? From Bahrah al Sabah?"

"Go on. Please, go on. I find your politics fascinating, if not seditious."

She was beginning to enjoy this. "The Emir, may he live forever, says what is expedient only to gain temporary support. You cannot tell me that, once this whole nightmare ordeal is behind us and we have returned, we will see any change. We will have to fight for freedom twice: first for the land and then for our rights."

Her royal chaperone grinned. "I thought I was dancing with a politician. No one told me I was to be dating a *muhajadin*."

Nadia flashed a curt smile. "In the first place, *we* are not dating. In the second place, *this* is a political issue, not a religious one. And in the third place..." She stopped herself, realizing that her own voice had risen above the volume of the music. They faced off as the disc jockey announced the winners of his disco contest. The floor emptied, leaving them alone in the spotlight. "In the third place, Ali is not only your friend. He is my fiance and I'd thank you to remember that."

"My dear, whatever do you mean?"

Nadia slid out from under his strong arm. The light followed her to the edge of the room. "You know exactly what I mean."

Two young Kuwaitis with gold chains and shirts unbuttoned to their navels appeared at Bahrah's side after Nadia walked out. He motioned them to a dark corner before saying a word: "See what you can find out about *Al Jahrah* and my old friend Ali al Bakr. He and his brothers had the jewelry shop we used to frequent. I believe their address is in my book. We may be able to use whatever you learn to our advantage some day soon."

They nodded and left with pockets full and a woman on either arm.

Chapter 25: Gone Fishing

Kennebunkport, Maine
October 17, 1990

Grey cold waters smashed hard upon the ragged Maine coastline. A lonely gull cried to the morning as it worked the shifting currents to stay aloft. A stiff breeze cut through yellow rain gear and salted the faces of three men as they scanned the horizon for a boat.

He would be out fishing again, as he had been on the week that it all began. He would be out fishing, trying to make the point that he wasn't about to be held hostage to the hostages. He would give the image that everything was under control whether things were unraveling or not. His advisers, divided about the wisdom of such a move, told him to sit tight in Washington. But this man wasn't the least bit worried. He knew what message he wanted to send, and how best to send it to the likes of Saddam Hussein.

He would be fishing. Vulnerable, with only a couple boats of Secret Service around him. Boats which could be easily evaded. Boats which couldn't stop a craft traveling at 75-100 knots.

Their homework had been done. This chance would be the best they would have - the only they would have. The moment of destiny was upon them.

He would be fishing.

And they would be hunting.

Chapter 26: Soviet Advisers

Near the Turkish -Iraqi Border
October 21, 1990

Peering through the infrared night scope, Khalil tensed. "Damn."

"What is it?" asked Adanon.

"The Iraqis aren't alone."

"Hostages with them?"

"Worse."

"What?" The Kurd picked up a green night scope and checked it for himself. "Damn." Soviet military advisers.

He lay back against the stone wall and wondered what to do next. The frigid mountain night was suddenly a degree or two colder. Winds whipped the sands, stinging his face and neck. Plans had been made, but the presence of Soviets at their target site altered everything, complicated everything. They would have to call off the attack.

The dentist didn't think along the same lines. "One guard by the tower. One by the gate. Maybe some more in the barracks. I can't tell. We can take them."

Francis shook his head. "Call off the raid."

"*Peshmerga* are not going to like this," whispered Adanon, rolling over to his pack and digging for the radio. "They have come too long a journey simply to turn and go home."

"Call off the raid."

A shot pierced the still night air and three sporadic bursts of submachine gun fire followed.

"What the hell are they doing?" shouted Khalil. "I said call off the raid!"

A flare hit the inky sky and lit the Iraqis in their compound as a wave of Kurdish guerrillas scaled the barbed wire perimeter.

"Too late," shouted Adanon as he hoisted a TOW onto to his shoulder and locked the night scope into place. "You coming?"

"Damn." The captain followed.

The firefight that ensued was brief and brutal. Six Kurds were killed and 13 wounded. There were 20-25 Iraqis dead - half of them still in their pajamas. The limp bodies were dragged from barracks and bunker to be laid in line for a quick photograph and a shallow grave. Nine Republican Guards, including two officers, and two Russian advisers were captured. But no Western hostages were found. Not this time.

"What are we going to do with the prisoners?" asked Francis.

Adanon and Schwan smiled at each other. "We take care of them."

"I'd like to speak with the Russians."

A gesture of the hand, a nod, and two minutes later the former Warsaw Pact advisers stood before Francis in the upper room. Pale and in shock, the trembling men were instantly relieved to see Khalil.

"American! God bless American! We want free."

Francis had expected to see the hardened Soviet shock troops of his Marine training films. But these two were little more than boys. The first, a pasty-faced kid with pimpled complexion, spoke a little English. The second, tall and lean with a black patch over his shirt pocket, spoke less. Cyrillic letters spelled out a riddle on this man's shirt: *I. A. Mendelev.* Francis remembered the bodyguard who had accompanied his old friend Vladi Kalinov to the *Sofia Internaccionalle* in September. That man who was looking for his son - his name was Mendelev. Could this be his boy? Francis needed to know more.

"Untie them."

The Kurds didn't move.

"I said untie them! I'll be taking them with me." The force of the Marine's insistence caught his hosts by surprise. They jumped to his bidding until Schwan held up a hand. At that, they stopped in their tracks.

It was a classic Kurdish stalemate. Schwan sized up the captain, who wasn't about to give in, then finally nodded to his guards. He shook his head, scowled and left the room. Francis reached for a knife to cut the Russians loose. The first ropes snapped as a single shot rang out from the yard.

"Sniper!" Khalil snatched his M-16 and dove for cover.

Adanon laughed. Another shot was heard. Then another. Fran made his way quickly to the window. There, in the center of the courtyard below surrounded by 18 Kurds, knelt the remaining six prisoners. Hands were tied behind their backs and they looked up, pleading for their lives. Three already lay face down in pools of arterial blood.

"You can't execute prisoners!" shouted Khalil. "It's against the Geneva Convention!"

Another shot was heard. This time the man wasn't dead and it took two bullets to the face to stop him from jerking about. Francis looked to his young friend. "Adanon!"

"What are we supposed to do with them? Free them so they can fight again? Send them to summer camp in America?"

Another shot was heard.

"You kill them and you're no different than they are!"

The young dentist looked at the soldier as if the concept didn't register. "Of course I am different. I am alive."

"Can't you see..."

Another shot was fired. The Russians winced with each cartridge.

Another. Khalil riveted his eyes upon Adanon and wouldn't release him. Another shot. And another. And a final one.

There was no point in arguing now.

A savory soup bubbled over the coals, creating the first appetizing scent Francis had encountered in his three weeks on the ground. A rotten-toothed grandmother offered him the metal cup. He graciously obliged. Even with the goat's eyeball still floating in it, the broth tasted as good as it smelled.

"They ought to sell this at McDonalds."

The old woman laughed, although she hadn't a clue what the stranger was saying.

Peshmerga sat around their fires, smoking hashish and trading stories. Some cleaned and oiled their newly confiscated trophies. Two scholars read from the Koran and argued over an interpretation of the Judgement Day. Another scanned an Iraqi newspaper. Another thumbed through a Dick Tracy comic book written in French. The Russians, tied securely for the night, were attempting to sleep next to the American's small fire. Francis had tried to inquire as to the background of Mendelev, but neither boy spoke enough English to understand. Schwan sat not far off, picking a haunting minor tune on a small string instrument that Francis had never seen before.

Upon eating his fill, Adanon sat down by the Marine and his Russian guests to give them a lesson in reality politics. Still stung by the executions of the night, Francis tried to ignore the young dentist as he approached.

"May I sit?"

"What?" He looked sharply up.

"May I sit down?"

"I suppose it doesn't matter what I say. You'll do what you damn well please anyway."

Adanon pulled up a saddle for a pillow and laughed.

"I don't find it funny."

"Excuse me?"

"It's not funny. Why did you do it?"

The Kurd picked up a stick and started to stir the fire.   "You

Americans - you make no sense at all. You shell the coast of Lebanon with your battleships. Throw bombs as big as Volkswagens into populated neighborhoods and scores of women and children die in their beds. But since you don't look in their eyes when you kill them, you don't call it murder. It is war. Simply war. "

"I don't think that you're in any position to judge..."

"Firebomb Noriega's barrio into oblivion in Panama City and hundreds of innocents die in 20 minutes. But since you don't see your own bloody hands on *Nightline,* you don't call that murder. You call it war. Or maybe simply 'police action.'"

"You executed defenseless people in cold blood."

"You bomb the terrorist Qaddafi's home in Libya and manage only to kill his little boy. Do you send condolences? No! This is war, not murder. Little boys die all the time from it. War."

Fran could only shake his head.

"But this animal called war is not clean, my friend. Antiseptic. No! From ship or plane or cement bunker 10,000 miles away - it doesn't matter - the innocents still bleed. The children still writhe in agony. Just because you are half a world away when you pull the trigger or press the button, this doesn't make them any less dead or you any less a barbarian. Just because you do not see them die, this does not make you any less a murderer."

The Russians eyed the American as if expecting a response. It was almost like they knew what he had said.

"We killed them. Yes. We murdered them. We are murderers - not warriors, knights or soldiers. Murderers. And what of you - you who press faceless buttons in the dark night. Are you not murderers as well? And is that not even more barbaric? More demonic? I know one thing, my friend: I want the man who kills me to look in my eyes when he pulls the trigger or sets the knife. Somehow it seems much more civilized."

Francis had no answers for the young philosopher. Only questions. He lay back to look at the stars, happy to be finally heading home in the morning.

Chapter 27: Goodbye, Adanon
Somewhere in Northern Iraq
October 26, 1990

The valley that stretched before them held a raw and harsh beauty. For Francis it tickled a memory of a spot where the Canadian Rockies met the western plains. He had traveled that North American highway ten years earlier, following the trail of his elder brother. When Joseph graduated from high school, he and a half dozen friends made the trek from eastern Montana through the wildernesses to the 49th state. Planning, training and plotting their course for nearly two years, Francis and his two best buddies started off the morning after turning in their cap and gown.

The reality of the struggle set in early with this later crew, however. The three only made it halfway before there were two. And when the grumbling started with the gravel of the Alaskan Highway, even his best friend turned back.

Francis didn't want to abandon his goal but he knew from his brother's photographs and stories that the worst still faced him ahead. He spent a night camping at the foot of a mountain much like the one he now viewed before making his decision. At the next town the determined boy put in the call to his father. Francis would finish the trek by himself if it killed him. Too many plans had been made and too big a game had been talked for a Khalil to come back home empty-handed. Failure wasn't in brother Joseph's vocabulary. It wasn't going to be Fran's, either.

"Attaboy, sport. Joe would be proud."

That was all he needed from his dad. Francis finished the trip alone and actually enjoyed the solitude of the last few hundred miles. And there, waiting for him at the other end, was Joseph, Sr. They took a picture together with the trashed bike before Francis rode it off a cliff and into the bay. The two Khalil men then spent a dream weekend salmon fishing before flying home. It was one of those rare experiences in life when fathers and sons transform from whatever they were before into friends. True friends. Equals. Francis would never forget it.

Adanon slapped his horse and rode down the ragged mountain trail to the American's side. The two gazed in wonder at the panorama spread before them. "There is a lake at the tree line below us. If you are thirsty, the water here comes directly off the mountains and is safe to drink. Not poison like the standing streams. We can camp on the far side of the lake and in the morning your 'taxi' should arrive to pick you up."

Francis couldn't find words. "I'm... I'm going to miss you, friend. These last few weeks... I think... well..."

"Yes?"

"What I mean to say is..." The young Adanon didn't look so young anymore. Through firefight and firelight Francis had come to appreciate the mysterious young dentist as a warrior, a philosopher, a healer and a friend. But Fran was never good at either expressing thanks or saying goodbye. He entertained the thought of both for a moment, then changed the subject. "I asked you before and you never did give me a straight answer. How old are you, anyway?"

"Why do you ask now?"

"Just curious."

"Twenty two."

With his perpetually dirty face, dark glasses that never came off, close cropped hair and unshaven complexion, the kid didn't look a day over 17. "How old?"

"Twenty one."

"How old?"

"Old enough to fight."

"In this part of the world that could be 13." Francis hadn't meant to insult his young friend, but it appeared he had done just that. They rode on down the mountainside for ten minutes before he brought himself to patching things up. "However old you are, my friend, you are wise beyond your years. *Shuma marde kobe hasta.* You're a good man. I will miss you."

Francis could see the tears start to well up behind dark glasses. He said no more until they found themselves by the side of the sparkling water.

"Oh, this is just too inviting. You say the water here is safe?"

"Yes. You may drink of it. It is straight from the snows."

"Drink it? I want to swim in it. I haven't had a bath in two weeks." His shirt was off before Adanon could object. "*Ma mirem opteni.* We go to swim."

"Ah, no thanks. I'll just watch."

"Come on. Strip down and hop in."

Adanon was more than a shade reluctant. "I said 'no.' Thank you."

"What's the matter? Too cold for ya?" Francis pealed off his pants and tested the water with his toes. "Ahhh. Yup, it's cold. But come on in anyway.

You need a bath yourself."

His young friend turned away when Francis slid off his shorts. "What? You've never seen a grown man naked before? You guys really are modest."

Adanon flushed when Francis walked past to take a hat from his saddle bag. "Teddy Roosevelt always used to take one of these along for a swim whenever he'd jump in a river. Just in case he ran into the ladies. Smart man, Mr. Roosevelt."

"Smart man." Adanon's shy eyes were drawn to Fran's taut figure as he returned to the water.

"Come on in. The water's fine."

"Is he a friend of yours from Dakota?"

"Roosevelt? Oh, he was from 'Dakota' for a while. But that was long before my time."

The boy looked down, then up at his friend again.

Francis turned back. "Come on. Take that baggy shirt of yours off."

"I, ah..." Adanon sighed.

"What you got to loose except six pounds of dirt?"

"I don't think..."

"Come on. Take your clothes off. We're all friends here."

Adanon sighed again, this time deeply.

"*Ma mirem opteni*. We go to swim!"

Adanon smiled nervously and shook his head.

"Come on." Francis splashed the water. "*Sabcoem! Bia!* Come on!"

The Kurd whispered under shallow breath. "OK, Mr. Francis Khalil. All friends here. *Ma mirem opteni*. "

Before Adanon's toe hit the water, Francis was grasping for his hat. Adanon was naked. And she was absolutely beautiful.

They swam for a time in the only green valley, the only crystal pool left to the Kurds. If one strained the imagination and blocked out the rest of the world, this ancient spot could almost have been mistaken for Eden. "You never told me you were a girl."

"A woman."

"Barely."

"Barely? Is that what you Americans call a pun?" They groaned, smiled and warmed under separate blankets by the fire. "You never asked."

"How long have you kept it a secret?"

"Three years. Enough to get some medical training and a position in the resistance."

"But how... I mean, how did you manage? Do you manage?"

"You saw my tight halter. I wear baggy tops. Try to speak little and when I do I use my lowest tone." She had a raspy, yet engaging voice. Now that Francis knew 'he' was a 'she', he enjoyed it even more. "I keep my hair short. Very short. Wear the dark glasses. Dirt on my face. It is not difficult to find dirt here."

"Why do you do it? Why would you?"

"Why? I thought you were smarter than that."

"I don't follow."

"See?"

Francis stirred the coals. "You aren't..."

"Lesbian? No. There are no lesbians in Iraq."

"No living lesbians."

"No lesbians."

"Then why the charade? Why a 'he'?"

"It is simple. I'm a 'he' because if I were a 'she' I would be mending tents and herding goats for some smelly old barbarian who would grab me every night on his way to his first wife." Francis kept stirring. "Why? Because I would never have been allowed to go to a higher school. Possibly I wouldn't be allowed to learn to even read. I would certainly not be allowed to fight with the *peshmerga* or carry a gun or ride alone with an American to get him to his helicopter. Or go swimming!" She blushed. "If I were a woman, I would be nothing. Now I am something."

Francis was beginning to understand.

"If I were a woman, I would have three children sagging my breasts by now." She inhaled proudly and threw her head back.

Francis belted out a laugh. "So instead of children sagging your breasts, you flatten them yourself?" For some reason it struck him funny.

Adanon watched him for a while, trying to stay mad. Finally she folded her arms tight and lay back on the bed roll to hide her own spreading smile. "I did a good job, didn't I?"

"You did. You do." Francis broke down again.

"What? What this time?"

"Last week, when the whole line of old men was pissing in the wind..." His infectious laugh started to work on her all over again.

"I guarded them well, did I not?" Francis laughed on, imagining the young woman as she guarded that row of elderly Kurds relieving themselves. In a moment she was laughing too, this time so hard that her sides hurt. When their heads finally cleared, Francis looked at his companion with a sudden and deepened respect. "How old are you. Really?"

"Nineteen."

"How old?"

"Nineteen."

"How old?"

"Nineteen. True. And I have had a year of dentist school. I swear it. In England."

"Did you have to stay a 'he' in England?"

"No. I was a woman there. And it was wonderful!" She stressed the *wonder*.

"And your real name? It isn't Adanon."

"No. That part is true. My first name is Adanon. Father decided I was to be a son and had picked that name before I was ever born. He was surprised, but being a stubborn man, he stuck with it."

"He couldn't have been near as surprised as I was today."

Adanon smiled, then closed her eyes.

The fire was dying and Francis set another log in the center to take the chill off the night. She woke and looked up at the diamonds of the sky, wanting in the worst way for Francis to hold her, touch her. But how to ask without asking? "And how old are you, Mr. Francis Khalil?"

"Too old for you, kid." That hurt. "And I'm married."

That hurt even more. "She is a lucky woman."

"Thank you. And the first *peshmerga* who wedges his way into your warrior heart to snatch you up will be a lucky man."

"Or the first smelly old goat herder."

"Or the first goat herder."

Adanon closed her eyes, then sat up and chuckled again.

"What?"

"The look. The look in your face when I came down to the water. I shall keep it in my heart. And I have never seen an American move so quickly."

"It was... uh... you were..."

"Do you think that I am pretty, Francis Khalil?"

"Adanon, you are beautiful." She was. She truly was.

She smiled. "Yes. I am. And you are beautiful, as well." She shook her head and pulled a stick from the coals. Her eyes were glowing with the firelight. "*Shumaha,** my captain."

"What's that mean?"

"*Shumaha*. It means... it's like... " She grasped for courage to say what she wanted to say but the English wouldn't emerge. It lodged in her throat like a dry crust the moment their eyes met. "Oh, never mind." Adanon looked down, then up, then down again before smiling sadly and reluctantly changing the subject. "Smart man, Mr. Roosevelt."

"Smart man."

The young woman fell back asleep, pained by her silence. At about a quarter to three Adanon stirred and sat up again. Francis was shivering, still tending the embers. She spoke in a trance-like voice: "We make loff?" Fran didn't know whether she was asking him to 'make love,' or simply stating that they 'made laugh.' He smiled and shook his head. Before he dared ask what she meant, the beautiful young *peshmerga* was sleeping again.

"All for the better," whispered the Marine. "Good night, Adanon. All for the best. "

Shumaha: Kurdish for "I love you."

Chapter 28: Stewart's Letter
London, England
October 31, 1990

"Ali my friend, would you possibly consider giving this letter to one of your American contacts? Karin doesn't know if I'm dead or alive. I haven't been able to contact her. And I'd be forever in your debt if... what am I saying? I'm already forever in your debt. You and your brother."

Ali took the Englishman's letter. The vivid memories of Nadia's last smile had been etched on the inside of his own eyelids. Every time he closed his eyes he saw her again. And he knew that if Stewart and Karin's love was anything like his own, this letter would mean more than life to him. "My friend, I will be honored."

Three weeks and a miracle later there was a knock at a Hampton door.

"Who is it, Maria?" Karin peered through the window of her second story flat to the street below. Her heart sank the moment she saw the young man in uniform standing at the stoop.

"You want me to get it for you?" asked the nanny.

"No. It may be best... I'd like to... I'll just go myself." She descended the stairs without a breath and stood for a moment on the nether side of fear. In a moment her whole life could be changed. If Stewart was dead, she didn't know how she could go on. That's why soldiers came to the house, wasn't it? To notify the next of kin? The Irish woman pulled the door open a crack, but left the chain in place. "What is it?"

"Are you Karin Kensington?"

"I am."

"Good news for you, mum. A letter. I believe it's from your Stewart. Stewart Kensington." He handed the tattered envelope and her life back through the door slot at the same moment.

The first page was blurred beyond legibility from what may have been salt water, may have been tears. Karin could only make out her own name and something about being "moved every few days" and "news is scarce... BBC every day." The second page was completely clear:

"Food is rice and bread. All we have to drink is chlorinated swimming pool water. I've lost 39 pounds in the hundred days. Our Kuwaiti friends are risking torture and execution for even knowing us. Many have been brutalized for harbouring Westerners. Last week an acquaintance of mine, M.C. (you'll remember him from the O'Connel party), was caught by the Iraqis in a home a block from here. It was a place where we stayed last summer. (You'll remember it as the home where Aeric lost his tooth.) I, myself, spent a week there when this ordeal began and couldn't get back to you. Anyway, when they captured him, they chose to make an example of the father and oldest son of the family who harboured him. These two were taken to the street and the wife and other children were ordered to stand in a doorway to watch. They were bound, then kicked to the ground by a dozen Iraqi soldiers taking turns. The entire neighborhood was ordered to watch. I could see it all from a hidden window.

"They continued kicking for what seemed like an hour, long after the men stopped moving - well into nightfall. Then they spun their lorries about and aimed lights so everyone could see. They kept this up, on into the night. When one soldier refused to kick any longer, his own officer whipped out a pistol and shot him in the back of the head. Others continued pummeling the corpses. Finally the woman was allowed to go to her husband and child. She held their bloodied bodies in her arms as the soldiers spat upon them. I'm told they charged her 1500 dinars for the return of the corpses before they left. M.O.C. was in the truck ten feet from them, watching this whole time. He was bound and unable to move. I could see him. I don't know where they took him after that. Please contact his wife, B.L.C. with the news. She works at Christy's in London.

"I have remained in reasonably good health thanks to the sacrifices of my friend RKABHJA. If you have any idea where his family or fiance are, please pass the message that he is alive. His younger brother is missing. Older brother was detained by the authorities and we fear the worst.

"I am maintaining a stiff upper lip through this all, but I honestly don't think we can hang on much longer. If the allies don't come soon, there will be literally nothing left to save. Every day people are taken from their homes, from the streets and never heard from again. We are praying for an invasion, even though it would mean we, ourselves, might be bombed and killed. Anything would be better than this hell. From what I've seen and what I know..."

Karin could read no longer. The letter was clear, but the clouds in her eyes would not allow it.

PART III
The Wait

Chapter 29: The Front
The Kuwait/Saudi Border
November 16, 1990

"There's someone out there. I can feel it."

Salaam al Bakr crept cautiously over to the panic-stricken sentinel as he crouched by the entrance with his unloaded AK-47.

"What is it, brother?"

"Listen."

"What do you hear?"

"Listen, al Bakr. The soft grinding noise."

Salaam heard nothing. Three months in the 4 x 7 meter bunker had taken its toll and made them all more than just a little bit crazy. Three times a week Tariq was shooting at phantoms in the night. It got so bad that they had to take his ammunition away. The others weren't much better. Bani was crying himself to sleep each night for no apparent reason. Philip couldn't sleep or keep his food down at all. Salaam al Bakr was the youngest, yet the only one among them who had managed to remain relatively unphased by their frontline captivity.

Fate and the devil had thrown the four of them together to serve as an advance team in that small outpost on the Kuwaiti border. Tariq was the only true soldier in the pathetic bunch. He had served in the marshes of Basara at the close of the war with Iran. Enlisting with a military fervor, the young Baathist's politics soured when his three year tour of duty was extended indefinitely and he found himself indentured into a lifetime career in the army.

Bani and Philip had been students at the University of Michigan five months ago. Bani's first degree was in political science and he was finishing a masters in business when he was thrown out of the country. Philip, a mechanical engineer, was working on a Ph.D. and a fiancee when the invasion canceled his plans for both. They and a few thousand other Iraqi students had tried to extend their visas and avoid deportation, but only a handful could prove they were in danger and deserved political asylum. The moment they stepped onto the tarmac in Baghdad, their entire flight was sworn into the Iraqi army and shipped to Kuwait for front-line duty.

Tariq was wringing his hands raw to keep warm as he scoured the distant dunes. The sky was alive with a billion stars and the moon was rising as an orange sliver on the horizon when Salaam awoke to relieve his companion. Had they not been in such miserable circumstances, it would have been a breathtaking and beautiful night.

"They can see us. I know this," whispered Tariq. "They have goggles that look through the darkness. They have flak jacket that are impenetrable to our bullets. They have infrared scopes on their rifles. Who knows? They may be aiming at my head at this very moment. And we? We have nothing. We are nothing."

"You don't know this," Salaam chided his night watch companion. "You have only rumors and Saudi radio propaganda."

"Propaganda," agreed Bani from his poisoned sleep.

Philip shook his head. "No. He's right. I know it to be true as well. The United States gives the very best to its troops. They will spend anything to protect even the lowliest of soldiers. They can't stomach the chance of losing their boys. Not one."

"And we? Who are we, al Bakr? I'll tell you. We are shit. Expendable shit. Cannon fodder to our 'beloved' Saddam."

"Quiet, fool!" Salaam held his hand over Tariq's mouth.

"Pawns."

"They will hear you."

"Who? The Americans? Let them hear me." He jumped out and shouted to the silent night. "Shit! We are shit!"

Salaam pulled him backwards onto the bunker floor. "Quiet!"

"Shit!"

"Fool! The Republican Guard has listening posts everywhere."

"Shit!"

Salaam slapped him full across the face.

"Shit!"

He hit him again.

"Shit!"

And again. Tariq let out an insane laugh and crept into the filthy corner like a mad dog to lick his wounds.

Philip yawned and squinted up toward the flickering kerosene lantern. "It is such a pity. This is not the way it should end. We are more afraid of our own brothers than we are of the enemy."

"Who is the enemy?" Philip and Bani began an old political debate anew. "Is it Bush? Thatcher? The American people?"

"The American people gave me my student loan and you your scholarship."

"And my fiance. Don't forget my fiance."

"Why not?" howled Tariq from his corner. "She has forgotten you!" He laughed the laugh of madness. The others ignored him.

"We have no quarrel with the Americans. The British. I have no quarrel with anyone. How is it, then, that I should sit in this hell hole aiming a rifle at them?"

"We'll have no time to quarrel when their tanks fly over that dune and crush us or throw a flame in and burn us all to a crisp."

Tariq's dark face tightened. "You'll not even have the time to stick your stinking underwear on a pole and wave it to surrender. You'll all be dead. We'll all be dead." He laughed once more.

"How can this happen? How can this happen to civilized men?"

Salaam shook his head. "Shit." It was now his turn to laugh.

The Republican Guard had placed and supplied them for the first two and one half months at their post. Two weeks ago they rolled in to lay mines in the field circling their bunker. They repeated this around hundreds of similar bunkers that lined the 200 mile border. The soldiers-turned-prisoners watched carefully - especially noting north and south escape routes. Salaam and Philip etched a secret map and felt confident they could safely exit if worse came to worse. But once the mines had been laid, each squad was moved to another hole so that not a one of them would know how to move ahead and surrender or behind and desert. With the Allies in front, the Republican Guard to the rear and a field of land mines all about them, the victims were doomed to either fight or die. There was no escape.

Food had been scant. Twice weekly a runner would step gingerly across the path from the trip-wire field to heave them their water and supplies. There was beans and rice - never any meat unless they could catch a snake or rat on their own. The only thing they had in plenty was dates. Pounds and pounds of rotting dates. And how they hated them! Their breath, their clothes, even the wind smelled like dates. Every corner of their foul cement sarcophagus reeked of the fruit. By now, even their bowel movements looked like processed dates.

Each night the ritual was the same. Tariq would hear some strange noise from the no-man's land 100 yards to the south and empty a chamber or two in the general direction. Bani and Philip would argue politics and discuss possible escapes. Tariq would accuse them of being traitors and threaten to turn them in if they weren't quiet. Salaam would watch it all while keeping mostly quiet. Each day he marked off another notch in the wooden beam that held the poured concrete slab in place over their heads. Each night he prayed for rescue to any god who might hear him.

Bani and Philip believed that Tariq was going mad. They put up with him at first, but later chose to ignore him. Salaam turned quietly 18 on the first of November without telling anyone. He didn't feel like a party. That was the first night he thought he was going insane as well. From then on Salaam regularly heard Tariq's phantom noises. He just didn't let on to anyone that he heard. On some nights it sounded like dune buggies were racing in the distance. On other nights, while alone on guard duty, he could swear that there were feet shifting about in the sands. One night he knew he saw a pair of green glowing eyes pop over a dune not 50 yards in front of him to watch. That was the night when the strangest thing of all happened. He was covering an old latrine outside the bunker when he heard a noise that begged investigation. He stepped to the back of the bunker and stared off into the night at a flickering light for five minutes. When he returned to the hole, his shovel and the feces were gone. Whoever (or whatever) was studying them had confiscated his date-laced dung! He mentioned that only to Philip. The others didn't need to know.

Rumors spread that the Americans were now grabbing whole regiments as they slept to spirit them away to Saudi Arabia for questioning. Two different food runners swore it was true. Salaam al Bakr prayed each night that this would happen to him. Other rumors suggested that Republican Guards had implanted listening devices in each bunker roof, and that they were executing soldiers who complained too often about the situation. Ten complaints and you're dead.

The Guard had been there that afternoon, forcing each conscript to sign a "loyalty pledge" and promise that he would defend his post to the death. Since Tariq was the only true soldier in that hole, he was warned that he would be held personally responsible if any of his men deserted their post. Tonight the madman was extra itchy and demanded his ammunition back to protect himself and keep the others in line.

Philip and Salaam had just traded watch and the teenager was laying out his moldy mat when they heard it: As clear as a hammer against a steel pin, the popping of a mortar echoed from the other side of the dune and whistled over their heads.

"Cover! Cover! Mortar attack!" Tariq dove to the floor as a canister exploded overhead and a shower of white paper began to rain upon their bunker. "It's starting. It's starting. Oh God, we're dead."

Tariq began to empty his rifle into the darkness. Salaam pulled the weapon from his grip and slapped him twice. The four stared out at the unexpected shower. Winds blew most of the magic little sheets away, but Philip managed to crawl out and retrieve three or four. They were simple tracts - pieces of propaganda - extorting and exhorting all who didn't wish to die on the proper techniques of "surrendering without being shot." One leaflet contained a cartoon character explaining what to do with weapons, how to hold hands in the air and what to say when approached. If they wanted to live to see their families, they were to follow the instructions implicitly. Another sheet - a pink one that dropped in with the white, told of a horrid practice American troops had been known to use in the heat of battle: The enemy often would bury dead and wounded soldiers together in mass graves. And to bar passage to heaven, a hog's carcass would be thrown into the pit just for spite.

That was enough for Bani and Philip. They knew that they'd have to get past Tariq, so they waited until he was asleep to make their move. Philip emptied Tariq's assault rifle of its clip and poured sand into the chamber. Bani begged Salaam to leave with them. They had grown quite close in their confinement those many months.

"We have studied it carefully. I have a mental map up to the spot where the date thrower approaches. We can be across the (mine) field and into no-man's land in 15 minutes. You'll be with your family in Saudi Arabia by Tuesday."

"Or I will be dead." Something didn't feel right about abandoning his post. "You go. I will watch. If you make it, I will come tomorrow night."

The three embraced and wished each other luck. Salaam followed them as far as he could with his binoculars until they disappeared into the blurred greyness of the desert night.

The sun was drawing waves across mirages by seven the next morning when Tariq stirred, screamed and kicked Salaam awake. His voice betrayed the terror of what it all could mean.

"Oh, shit! Oh, shit! Where are they? Did you see what happened to them? Shit! Where did they go?"

Salaam wiped the sleep from his eyes and feigned ignorance. "Who?"

"What do you mean 'who'? Who have we been living with all this time? They're gone. They've deserted or escaped. Or the Americans got them last night when they went to the latrine! Shit! We are dead. I am dead."

"Calm down, Tariq. Maybe they got away. They made it through the mine field. There are no bodies! Maybe they'll come back for us tonight."

"And maybe the Republican Guard has already executed them and is coming for me!"

Tariq was rapidly approaching a frenzy. Salaam reached to shake him but was quickly slapped away.

"I'm dead. I'm a dead man. Wherever they are, I can't stay here now. I must leave at once. Before they come for me." The poor deluded fellow began to sweat profusely. He tore into his Army bag looking for the pouch where he kept his lucky charm. "I must go now. I could report them and take my chances that they'd think me loyal. But no, they would never believe me and let me live. I don't have a prayer and what am I saying? No, I've got to run. Now. I've got to run."

Salaam attempted to grip him once more. "Not in broad day light. Wait until tonight. Wait 'til dark and I will go with you." Tariq wouldn't listen. He pulled the amulet and *dinars* from his bag and shoved his pistol under his belt. Without saying goodbye, he was out the front and stepping carefully toward the mine field.

Salaam watched in disbelief. "Come back, Tariq! The daylight is no time to be doing this."

"I don't have a chance. I've got to go now or they will kill me. I know what they've done to others who were responsible for their men." Tariq had stepped out a safe course 100 feet before, but it appeared to the boy that he was too far to the left this time.

"Are you sure you shouldn't be closer to the latrine path?"

The soldier was counting his steps so carefully that he hadn't taken bearings properly at the start. He looked down in horror when he saw that he was off. "Salaam!"

"Trace your steps, Tariq. Trace your steps backwards. Trace!"

He started back, but at the third step they both heard the telling click. "Salaam! I've stepped on one. Salaam! You must come and disarm it." Al Bakr froze. "Salaam! I can't dig under myself. You must come and take this from me. If I move my weight, I'll lose my leg!"

"I can't! I don't know what to do!"

"Salaam! Shit! Salaam!"

The boy aged to an old man in that instant. He watched it all as if in slow motion: the tuft of dust rising; the body lifting from the ground; the leg separating and flying end over end above its torso; and a single boot landing upright in the spot where the mine had been. Numbed and nauseated, al Bakr vomited onto the floor, then buried his face in his musty blanket. He wanted to die, to cry, to tear away his own eyes. He had let his friend die. And he hadn't lifted a finger to stop it.

Not 50 feet away, Tariq's head lay with coal black eyes still open, condemning Salaam for his sin. The boy begged forgiveness from the silent stare, but it would not absolve. Those eyes - those haunting eyes. Salaam screamed obscenities at them to close. He begged Tariq, then cursed the poor beggar's ghost. But there was no forgiveness offered. Only the stare. That accusing stare. Salaam placed the pistol into his own mouth to gently squeeze himself into the arms of Allah, but could not pull the trigger. Those eyes - they taunted and haunted and laughed at his impotent cowardice.

It took seven shots with the pistol and two with his rifle to finally close his tormentor's dreadful eyes. It took Salaam a lifetime to close his own.

Chapter 30: Italian Leather

The Pentagon
November 18, 1990

"How could they be so stupid?"

"I don't know. But this wouldn't be going any better if we had written the script ourselves."

Francis was sitting in the stall and minding his own business, not intending to eavesdrop. He was finally back at his safe nine-to-five Pentagon desk job - much to Kathryn's relief. He had descend into the bowels of the Pentagon to find a quiet place to catch up on a pile of *Newsweeks* and rid himself of a month's worth of fine dining with the Kurdish *peshmerga*. Doubled over in discomfort, Fran was studying the wall philosophy of the lower regions when it happened: two pair of shoes stepped into what the owners thought was a vacant space and two whispers hinted at something they didn't want anyone else to hear. Francis was pondering an etching on the wall which read "What is time for, but to measure the steady disintegration of life?" when the wearer of the expensive black Italian leathers stepped over to the sinks and immediately turned on every faucet to cover the conversation. The brown shoes that followed moved suspiciously from stall to stall, checking for unwanted company. The captain instinctively drew his legs up so as not be seen.

"Boss says there's no turning back now? It'll go on as planned?"

"Was there any question about it from the start?"

"What I don't get is how they've played into our hands up to this point. Is it pride or ignorance?"

"I don't know. But I think we've got 'em."

"So long as Saddam doesn't turn tail and run at the last minute."

"He won't back down. He can't. It would show weakness and his whole power structure is based on the mirage of invincibility. Let the American public think whatever it wants. Let them think that he's a reasonable man and will back down when he sees he is hopelessly outnumbered. He won't. He can't now. One sign of weakness, one hint of a chink in his armor, and his own officers will do to him what he did to the last Iraqi president. He won't back down. Pride is everything to those damn sand niggers. We've got him where we want him."

Francis wanted to step out and remove the owner of the Italian leathers from the conscious world, but something held him back.

"There are those on the Foreign Relations Committee who think otherwise. They believe that he's smart enough to know when he's outmatched. He may not come out publicly offering to withdraw, but he'll do what he has to in order to secretly sue for peace."

"We can see to it that he doesn't."

"How do you mean?"

"Unlike you folks, my people have their ways. A little misinformation here, a subtle miscommunication there. He'll hear what he wants to hear and believe what we want him to believe. Even if he tries to contact us secretly to negotiate, who is to know about it? Messages get lost. Codes are misplaced. I think we can insure that he'll be there when the bombs are scheduled to fall."

Fran made a note of the "scheduled to fall" remark and wondered just who could be doing the scheduling.

"What about the Russians' overture?"

"Too late. We've committed. They can do whatever they damn well want, but it has already been sealed. Hell, it's been sealed since 'Braintree.'"

Francis recognized 'Braintree' as a town in Massachusetts, but he didn't know of any special meetings held between the Allies there.

"I understand that the president will be writing a letter to give Saddam one last chance to duck and run. What if he goes for it?"

"When is this?"

"Next month. Once everything is in place."

"I don't think we have to worry about that. Aziz will reject anything the secretary..."

The conversation stopped as a door squeaked abruptly open and six new pairs of shoes walked in. The black Italian leathers stepped out of the room and the brown suedes walked over toward the end stall where Francis was crouching. He stepped into the booth next to Khalil to wait for the others to leave. Francis didn't breathe a molecule or flinch a muscle. His eyes drifted back to the bathroom philosopher's words: "What is time for, but to measure the steady disintegration of life?"

Fran waited until the company was long gone and the lights were long out before making his move.

The major was scanning ads for a new bass boat and didn't bother to look up when Fran re-entered the room. "How's that sour stomach?"

"Rapidly approaching tolerable."

"I've got some 'pepto' in the bottom drawer if you want it."

"Thanks. I'll be fine."

"I used to take a few extra passengers home with me, too, when I was in the field. Did I ever tell you about the parasite I had for three years?"

Francis was not terribly interested in the major's intestinal companions.

"I had an old English teacher once who told us that you can never really speak in the plural unless you have a parasite."

The captain offered the obligatory courtesy smile to get out of this conversation and sat back to think. The Old Man dug through the bottom drawer and pulled out a bottle of another kind. It certainly wasn't Pepto Bismol. "You want a shot?"

"No thanks." He poured two anyway. Fran set the glass aside and dropped to the floor for some pushups. "Brain - tree, Brain - tree, Brain - tree." Fran was thinking out loud with each inhaled and exhaled breath.

"What you got there? A new mantra?"

He hopped back up and took the drink, after all. "What does the name 'Braintree' mean to you?"

"It's a town in Massachusetts. Why?"

"Just wondering."

"You taking the Mrs. there?"

"Kathryn? No."

"Someone else's Mrs.?"

"No."

"Nice vacation spot. I spent my third honeymoon at the Motel 6 there."

"You aware of any official or unofficial meetings..."

"...or was it my sixth honeymoon at the Super 8?"

"Any meetings with Allied leaders that might have happened there while I was gone?"

"No. Were there supposed to be?"

"I don't know. I don't know. But I'd like to find out." Fran flipped the switch on his computer and started the search.

"Why's that?"

"I don't know. Call it a hunch."

"What are you talking about?"

"I'm not sure. I think I just heard something I wasn't supposed to hear."

"In the bathroom?" Francis nodded. The major picked up his bass magazine. "I've heard some pretty strange sounds down there myself at times. But none I'd care to talk about. Here, kid," said the Old Man, tossing Fran the entire bottle of Jack Daniels, "you been gone too long."

Chapter 31: Thanksgiving Day
Baghdad, Iraq
November 24, 1990

They didn't believe it. They couldn't.

Most Iraqis had been quite optimistic. The dates and oranges were plentiful. Electronic goods were restocked on shelves. Crates bearing Lebanese shipping marks arrived daily on Jordanian trucks. Food and materials from Europe passed easily through Iran to fill the bazaars. The bread lines took a little longer than normal, but most people were accustomed to it from the rationing days of the Iranian war.

Old men sat in Baghdad open-air restaurants and watched soap operas as they smoked. Young men walked the streets hawking their wares. Most citizens believed that the U.S. would never invade Iraq. They knew that Bush was a paper tiger. He would talk a hard game but never act. He had too much to risk and was too far away to be capable of following his hot words with action. When told by Western newscasters that there was a good chance the Allies would go to war, most simply replied: "Oh God, oh God." Others flashed queer disbelieving glances and shuffled quickly away. They didn't know who to believe.

"The report is late and sketchy!" snapped Saddam with a dark glare.

"I am sorry, Excellency. My wife has been ill and I was at her side most of the night. I was unable to leave her until the morning. I studied the tapes and was only able to compile a brief..."

Saddam flashed an annoyed smile and glanced about the room at his generals. "Did I ask this man for excuses? Have I ever asked this man for excuses? No. I think not. I have asked simply for a report. Thorough. Accurate. Complete. I have asked for no excuses!" A volcanic stirring held itself in check slightly below the surface. "I ask only for one thing! That is competence! That is loyalty! That is accuracy! I ask for no excuses and I'll have none!" He slammed his fist to the table.

The man recoiled in fear. Once before he had witnessed his uncle attempt to hold back anger like this. The passion built and built within until it could not be contained. And, in the explosion, a trusted adviser through the worst days of the Iranian war was assailed and assaulted before this same room of officers. The man had given Saddam an understated report of Iranian troop strength at Basara. His estimate almost cost them the city. Saddam, when stumbling upon the truth, invited his closest officers and advisers to a party. After a pleasant dinner in front of that same inner circle, the dictator rose to offer a mock toast to the man. Words began as a glowing tribute of his 'beloved' adviser's contributions to the war effort. They ended with a pistol between the eyes of his honored but sorry friend. The man begged for mercy for himself and his family. He was allowed three minutes to speak. There were as many holes in his head before his body hit the floor.

Now Saddam was angry again. And this time the focus of his rage was his own sister's son. "Excuses lose battles. Battles lose wars. Lives! Nations! Excuses lose a man's reputation. A man's soul. Now, what is this report that I've been handed? It is toilet paper. It tells me nothing a child could not see. I expect more and I will get more. I cannot protect you if you continue to perform like this. I cannot keep you close or safe if you do not perform the tasks - these simple tasks - assigned to you. We have too much to lose. You have too much to lose. Now, I want an accurate assessment of America's will to fight, and I want it now! Do you understand?"

He quivered and cleared his throat. Saddam calmed instantly and sat like a cat with a bird in its paws. For the moment he was more interested in finding a cigarette than in his own specific need to reprimand and punish.

"As the sources say, Excellency, the English Prime Minister has resigned."

Saddam nodded at his chief of staff. The officers cheered. "My observations of the most influential newspapers are documented on page 13. Each of the American networks makes it clear that Thatcher was far more abrasive an adversary than any we'll meet in the three contenders. It may be possible that Herd will keep some of the anti-Iraqi rhetoric. John Major, possibly. But as far as supporting a hot war, the staunch American lap dog is gone. None of these men will bow to Bush so easily, speak so forcefully or commit troops more readily as Margaret Thatcher."

The room erupted again with applause. Saddam played with his mustache. "We truly have reason to celebrate. The witch Thatcher is on her way to hell. And no one in her Conservative Party will be so formidable an adversary as she could have possibly been at war."

"Then you assume this will take the wind out of the American sails?"

"It will throw some question into when they will move, how they might go at it and who will stand by their side. It can only be seen as a matter of great joy."

The officers buzzed with the first honest relief the bunker had witnessed in weeks. Saddam held his hand up and the room silenced again. "What else have you gleaned from your weekly viewing?"

"Three nights ago I became aware that the American Army medical facilities are using outdated equipment. Basic materials are unloaded in Saudi ports and there they sit. They are by no mean ready to launch a campaign to take Kuwait..."

Saddam hissed.

"...to take the 19th Province in the foreseeable future. It will be months before their medical system is in place."

The Father-Leader studied the eyes of his officers. "Is this your assessment as well?"

The man on his left ventured an opinion: "As we have suggested and you have stated, America is a paper tiger. It is in their history to attack only those they can totally smother and defeat. The Panamas and Grenadas attest to this. These were small nations and close to home. In their own hemisphere. We have a million men and tens of millions who would fight in the streets and die for you. We have the entire Arab world - with the exception of a handful of imperialistic puppets - who will unite against America should they attack us."

The young man cleared his tightening throat and managed a brief smile. "And time. We have time on our side. There are, right now, 30 congressmen suing Bush to stop the war. They are threatening to impeach him."

Saddam looked at his nephew in confusion. "What is this 'impeach'?"

"To try him in the Congress for breaking the law and moving toward an undeclared war."

His Excellency laughed in amazement. "What a foolish form of government these Americans have. They question their own president on the eve of war? How would we survive if we allowed this?" He laughed again and his officers with him.

"What else? Summarize."

"There are citizens protesting in America's streets. Law makers will demand Bush ask them to declare a war. It is doubtful they will. The U.N. will send no major detachment of troops apart from the Americans to put bite in their resolutions. Israeli Palestinians are being humiliated daily and are ripe to revolt. Our major trade routes in Iran and Jordan continue to grow. Within three months we will pass the season that America can attack and we will enter the Holy Month when the winds of the desert will stall the infidels and the snake of radical Islam can be charmed to bite the House of Saud."

"Then, nephew, you believe we are secure?"

"Unless Bush can pull off a miracle in both the U.N. and the U.S. Congress..."

"Then we are secure?"

"There is even better news, Excellency. We have reason to believe that the Russian Shevardnadze, the prime minister, will also be gone before Christmas, replaced by Pavlov or another more reasonable man."

The officers looked at each other in a desperate hope. Pavlov was a man they could deal with. He was also a long-time friend of Iraq.

"When this happens, the picture will change for us all. The Soviet Union, and possibly Gorbachev himself, will modify its stance. With these two key allies gone and the Soviet government back to a rational leadership, the U.S will stand alone against us. And, although the U.N. will not withdraw its sanctions soon, we will certainly not be facing the imminent threat of war. We will have the time we need to secure the eternal union of our 19th Province."

"Anything else?" Saddam knew he was stalling.

"I do believe we will see more protests in America's streets and a growing anti-war movement. They allowed this during the Vietnam era, and it turned out to be America's downfall. You may remember..."

Saddam nodded. The young man, encouraged, spoke more boldly. "Finally, we will not see America going into war without the complete support of the Arab world. And that support is highly unlikely. With both Britain and the Soviets out of the picture, we will watch the coward Bush vacillate. Was it but two years ago when his own election detractors spoke of him as a 'wimp' - a weakling? If we can make it to Rammadan, we will see our plans for the Saudi Royal Family unfold. When the Arab World understands the true treachery of the House of Saud and witnesses its downfall, we will exit the Haj with a government that, itself, pushes the infidel Bush off its soil."

Saddam poured himself a drink. The officers waited the signal to cheer. "This is your report?"

"Yes, Excellency. That is my report."

Saddam lit a cigarette and flashed an opaque smile. "This is your report." He took a slow drag, thinking. "This is your report." He picked up the first pages of the report before him and dropped them on the floor. An eternal moment passed before ashes were flicked into the glass tray and the cigarette snuffed out. "This is... opinion. This is rubbish."

The man didn't answer. There was nothing to say.

"Your services are no longer required."

He knew what that meant.

"You are relieved. Go home to your wife..."

The entire room knew what that meant.

The man started to tremble. "But uncle..."

"Silence! Do not call me that!" The master jolted up, thrashing an open backhand at the paper and throwing the remaining pages in his victim's face. "I ask for a report, and you give me prophesy!" Clutching the man's throat, he slapped repeatedly with each syllable. "I've tried... tried... tried!

Tried to protect you! Tried! Tried! Tried!"

The quivering heap collapsed against the wall, covering his face. His tormentor scowled in derision, then returned to the table for another cigarette. An aid offered a light. Saddam's calm snapped back with a second puff. The Father-Leader spoke in a partially cloaked vindictiveness without looking back at his nephew. "Go back to your wife. You are excused."

Two rose from the table to help their former colleague to the door. Saliva bubbled from his mouth as he searched the eyes of the room in an anguished horror. Would no one speak for him? Though each had once called him friend, none could betray the slightest pity without becoming suspect.

"Sadr!" called Saddam to the man across the table, "you are not prone to speculation. Tell me what is the wisdom of your vantage point."

The clean-cut officer stood in a humble poise. "I do believe in miracles, Excellency, but we must not rest our future on them. It pays to be neither unprepared nor naive."

"Speak."

"If our entire strategy is based on stalling the Americans past March - the opportune time of attack - then I believe a carrot dangling on a stick before them might be the wisest and most auspicious move."

"I am pleased with your candor. What do you suggest?"

"We give the Americans the one thing they value most. The one pawn which will disarm them fastest and diffuse our critics."

"And that carrot is?"

"At the risk of angering you, Excellency, I believe the one most disarming move we could make at this point would be to release a certain number of their citizens gradually over the next months."

"Their citizens?" Saddam locked up, entirely surprised. "You are suggesting we throw away our 'desert shield'?"

"Yes, Excellency, I suggest we do just that. Holding these people has inflamed the international community against us. It may be the third point the U.N. has against us on paper, but it is first in their hearts. It is the only reason for the average American to vote for war. These Americans are a strange lot. They chant in their streets 'no blood for oil.' Yes, they might be willing to shed blood for blood, but not for oil. I suggest we promise the release of, say, 50, maybe 100 of our 'shields' each month during a prolonged negotiation. As long as we see they are not mobilizing toward attack readiness, we continue in good faith, stalling them past March and their optimum…"

"And when our shield is gone? What will keep them from attacking us then?"

"By then our strongest critics will have packed up and gone home. How long can they sustain this alliance without their key issue? America alone will be left. With the detainees home, the emotional momentum in America for war will vanish. These people have no feelings for Kuwait. Most of them did not know the country existed six months ago. Their feelings are not for Saudi Arabia. Yes, they care about the oil, but the common man in the streets is inflamed most by the image of those Americans being held against their will. It is the hostage situation that will make or break the will of most Americans. If we keep them, they may vote for military action. If we release them, they will demand their soldiers come home. If we give the appearance of reasonability and let them see that patience will move their citizens from harm's way, we will buy the needed time. If we can hold them off until March, they will not be able to attack until fall. And if they are held off until fall, the desert heat, the arguing of allies, the anti-war movement in the U.S. - all these will have had time to gather sufficient strength. Everything will be set for us. The balance will be in our favor."

"If we can! If we can! If this! If that! If, if, if..." Saddam was not happy with the word. "This is a gamble."

"Yes, a gamble."

"A gamble we cannot afford to lose."

"You are correct, Excellency. And yet, no other issue has united the Americans so. I believe there is no greater method of disarming them."

"What of their pride?"

"America has more pride than resolve. More pride than money. But how long can they keep this action up?"

A sudden burst of machine gun fire from down the hall cast a black pall over the room. They all knew what it meant. Saddam smiled an innocent grin. His nephew had been properly disciplined. "Go on. Speak your mind."

The new adviser cleared his throat: "Just a thought, Excellency."

"Yes, yes. And how would we go about this gradual release?"

"I beg your indulgence, Excellency. This is how I would go about it: We let enough 'detainees' go in December, January and February to keep America believing in the negotiation process. By March it will be too late. The winds and rains will bog them down. Protests at home will have time to ferment. Unrest and questioning will chip away at any alliance they have put together. Province 19 will be settled and irrevocably ours. The alliance will have splintered, the American public will be crying for their soldiers back, and the Haj will have had a chance for its royal surprise. We may have even punished Mubarak by then. An American attack will not be possible, not be plausible, for six months. By then they will be left alone. We will have won by default."

"Aziz, what do you say? You have been to America recently."

Tariq Aziz, the Iraqi foreign minister, had traveled most extensively in the West during the earlier weeks. He agreed: "There is no other issue uniting the American people, no issue they would rally around faster than their hostages." He quickly caught himself. "So-called 'hostages.' With the detainees free, support for a war is completely eroded. Congress and the people in the streets..."

"You believe that America will not shed blood for oil?"

"I believe they cannot publicly exchange blood for oil. They would need a greater excuse than this to justify their losses."

"The freedom of Kuwait?"

"Most Americans had never heard of Kuwait five months ago. And they are far too sophisticated to justify a war to free a petty sheik and his family. No, take away the detainees..."

"You believe that the judicial release of certain detainees on a regular basis will stave off the planned American attack?"

Aziz nodded. Saddam panned the room. No one but these two advisers dared to venture an opinion until he nodded his own head. The room burst forth in applause.

"Sadr!"

The outspoken officer stood at attention.

"Congratulations. You shall be my new media expert to fill the recent vacancy left by my nephew. See what you can do with this." Hussein threw him the last pages from his late nephew's report. A lucid face registered alarm and the man swallowed in a near-audible fear.

"Yes, Excellency. Thank you for the honor of your faith in me."

Saddam sucked the life out of his last cigarette and snuffed it into the glass in front of him. "We will enjoy receiving your written report and deciding on this matter tomorrow."

"Yes, Excellency. Tomorrow."

The 'tomorrow' came and the pivotal decision was made to begin a gradual release plan. The first Americans were freed and all went well for Sadr until a *New York Times* poll announced that 54% of the American public now approved of an attack on Iraq to destroy its nuclear weapons capabilities. General Sadr hadn't mentioned a word about the American nuclear position in his reports.

He was asked to name his own replacement prior to a leave of absence and convenient disappearance three weeks later.

Chapter 32: The Assessment
The Oval Office
December 1, 1990

The commander in chief managed to squeeze out a tense grin for the benefit of the congressional leadership assembled. Reaching into a top pocket for his reading glasses, he surveyed the charts. "So Dick, it's time to let these good folks in on the big picture. What are we up against?"

His secretary of defense stepped around the desk to interpret. "First of all, you must know that Iraq possesses an extremely large and integrated Soviet and French- built air force. Hardened bunkers for men, fuel, ammunition and material. A layered command and control system that we may have problems with. A ground force of varying capabilities. Some of their frontline people were waiters and accountants three months ago. We don't know how they'll fight. There is anecdotal evidence of low morale and some defections already. The Republican Guard, however, is a different story. These are the battle-hardened elite from Saddam's hometown, 150,000 strong. The Guard is at the heart of his military power and political clout. He used it to turn the tide in the Iranian war, and now again to take and hold Kuwait. We believe the Guard to be extremely loyal and dangerous. He trains them harder, pays them more and provides them with the very best equipment money can buy."

"What's the status of their air defenses?" asked Senator Nunn.

"Early warning capabilities are advanced and state-of-the-art. But they are ones we can knock out. We're shipping a computer virus over to them right now that we believe will immobilize their mainframes."

"You're certain of this?"

"Reasonably certain."

"We'll have to be more than reasonably certain if we are to risk our pilots."

Bush nodded. "We're not going to do this without air superiority, Sam.

Immediate and uncontested air superiority."

Cheney continued: "We hope to take out 30% of their air power in the first two hours. That is, if we are able to keep the element of surprise to our advantage. If they scramble to meet us in the air, it will take a couple of days to achieve total control of the skies. If they try a blitz straight at our carriers in the Gulf and even a few get through, we could be in for real trouble. Remember the damage one Exocent missile did to the Stark."

The men nodded.

"If Saddam were to send everything against us at once, it would be suicide for him. But it would be the most massive and costly event of the short war from our perspective."

"We'd rather engage his planes..."

"A few at a time." The vice president finished Nunn's sentence.

"A few at a time or not at all. Our plan is to knock his eyes out, then his ears so that Iraqi pilots can't get scramble orders from their commanders even if they're given. If they hold back, keeping some planes in hardened bunkers, we can take them out one at a time and it won't cost us nearly as much in terms of men and material."

Bush shifted in his chair and twisted a stiff neck back and forth. The tension of the last few days was wearing on him.

Nunn pressed Cheney further. "And what do your people say he'll do? With the air, I mean."

"If it was difficult before to ascertain Saddam Hussein's game plan, it is even harder now. He's not a tactician, but he does have people around him who did surprisingly well against the Iranians."

"We're not the Iranians," Bush added.

"No, we're not the Iranians. But don't forget that he has had the best of Soviet training up to this point."

"What's your bet?"

"Most of our people say that he'll throw it all at us at once. Inflict as much damage as he can as fast as he can. He needs and wants at least one grand and glorious battle to set himself into history books and Arab folklore as the one man who stood up to the West and bloodied its nose. After that, he thinks he will be able to negotiate from a position of strength. Pull partially back to the Ramalla oil fields and Bubiyan Island - the jewels he wanted in his crown in the first place - and sue for peace.

"Most of our people believe this? What about the others?"

Cheney straightened in his chair. "Some think that he'll hold back and send planes at us a few at a time. Drag it out as long as he can. He does this and the situation becomes very manageable."

The chairman of the Air Force jumped in. "That's exactly what our AWACs are set up for. It would be like swatting one mosquito at a time."

"Others think he may feign weakness at first and hold out until such time as he thinks we are getting careless. Then go for the huge counterattack

- an aerial 'Battle of the Bulge' so to speak."

"And what do you believe he'll do? One blaze of glory or an attempt to draw it out?"

The secretary looked up over the top of his glasses. "It is my opinion that we have to prepare for the worst. Expect the worst and be ready for any eventuality."

The president took a deep breath and quietly asked an aide for a glass of water and his Halcion.

"Our first targets, of course, remain the command and control structure, weapons delivery systems and his chemical, biological and nuclear production facilities. We think these will be relatively easy to take out."

Rostenkowski objected. "These are also the targets where the most Americans will be held."

"We know approximately where our people are held and are reasonably confident that our smart weapons can hit specific enough targets so as to avoid excess collateral damage."

"Collateral damage?"

"Hostage deaths," whispered Scowcroft.

"The Soviets assure us that Iraq doesn't have the capability to launch chemicals on SCUDS - that he'll have to rely mainly on air and artillery for chemical and biological munition delivery, should he choose to go that route. That puts us out of range if we can dismantle his air power soon enough."

Tom Foley spoke for the first time. "The Soviets also told us that he wasn't going into Kuwait. We can't rely on their Intelligence or their intelligence."

The men chuckled. Cheney continued: "All fixed SCUD stations can be taken out immediately. We will try our best to minimize collateral damage here but we can guarantee nothing. Mobile SCUDs can be spotted by satellite and knocked out within a week or so."

"Your advisers are sure of that?" questioned Senator Foley.

"They are unanimous in the belief that we'll have his SCUDs out by the end of the first week. Two weeks max."

"Unanimous?"

"Except for Khalil," offered Quayle.

"Who's Khalil?"

The president glared at his vice. He hadn't wanted the good captain's name mentioned to these folks.

"An analyst. Just an analyst who's been doing situation reports and psychological briefings for us. That sort of thing."

Cheney took back the reigns. "Khalil believes he'll go to the ropes and try to hold on as long as possible. Play 'cat and mouse' with his SCUDs as long as he can, pulling them out a few at a time to launch on Tel Aviv and Riyadh. Keep the terror going over the long haul. "

"Why is that?"

"Every hit he makes on Israel is another hit with the Palestinians. He may attempt to stretch this out long enough to incite the world's Moslems. This may be his one last shot at Arab unity. If even a couple SCUDs get through every day for a month, Saddam Hussein believes he'll reserve a spot in the history books for himself alongside Nasser and Saladin."

"Let's finish here with the rest of the game plan."

Cheney nodded. "Thank you, Mr. President. The other main objectives, of course, are Iraq's two nuclear facilities. These will be leveled in our first wave. Saddam has moved some of his enriched uranium and equipment from them, but we have them tracked fairly well. We believe that we can account for 85% of it. Biological warfare factories will be taken out immediately as well."

Sununu stood. "That sums up our progress to date, gentlemen. Dick will join you in the Senate conference chamber in a half hour to answer any questions you might have. Right now I'm afraid we've got some other unfinished business with the president pressing."

The group rose and each shook hands with Bush to offer best wishes and pause before the White House photographer. When the last man left, Sununu turned back and nodded to the secretary of defense.

"Mr. President, we'll have to be prepared to take the heat from some of the biological and nerve targets because of their locations."

"Where are they?"

"Some of the nerve agents are being produced in heavily populated areas. People think they are neighborhood baby milk factories. Intelligence indicates that some of these targets will cost us both Iraqi civilians and American hostage casualties. Westerners are being held in a variety of target areas. Our smart weapons, as accurate as they are in testing, have never been used in actual warfare conditions. And although we are reasonably sure that they will perform as expected, they aren't smart enough to distinguish between our people and their people.

"If hostages are held too close to target centers, there will be casualties. If we are going to go through with this, we must come to terms with it and be willing to suffer the political fallout - excuse me for the poor choice of words - the political and moral consequences of eliminating innocent civilians. We'll have to be ready with an awfully good explanation as to why we hit these knowing full well that we were bombing Americans."

The president's jaw set in a painful and determined grimace. "Something that I'll live with... we'll all have to live with for the rest of our lives." He stood and walked over to the window. "Can we get our people on the ground to remove hostages before the bombs fall?"

An aide brought the president his customary .25 milligrams of the sleeping pill, but Bush motioned him back. "Let's go for .50 tonight. I'm going to need it."

"They don't suggest going over .25..." Bush didn't need to say a word to the aide. His eyes alone sent the man back for more.

Cheney continued. "Our anti-terrorist teams are available to run 'Operation Lightening' at twenty or thirty sites simultaneously prior to actual initiation of the air campaign. Khalil's Kurds are standing by. But we are talking hundreds of targets here. There is no way we can remove them all. Even if it were to be synchronized to happen all at once, we'd still lose more soldiers and civilians than we'd save. Our computers have played this one out at every possible angle. It would be a diminishing return. You just can't beat the odds. Hostages - as much as we'd like to spare them - hostages will end up paying the price of anything we try to do to save them. If we are going to start the bombing, American and Allied civilians will be killed by American and Allied bombs."

"We are talking dozens? Hundreds?" asked the vice president.

"Hundreds. Maybe not. Maybe more. Right now they are human shields. They will be casualties of war."

Two hours later Dick Cheney stood before the cameras as calmly as a businessman addressing a Rotary luncheon: "You, the members of the press, must know that first and foremost in our minds is our concern for the hostages. We will do and are doing everything in our power to avoid loss of American life. But Saddam Hussein also must know this: That if innocent civilians continue to be held as shields in chemical, nuclear and biological production facilities, he will be held personally responsible for any that are injured should we decide - and I'm not saying we will - but should we decide to take them out."

Charlain Hunter Gault from *MacNeil/Lehrer* asked the question: "What do you mean by 'personally responsible?' Are we talking war crimes trials?"

"I'm not going to speculate on any specifics, but I wouldn't rule that out."

In a deep dream that night, the president saw himself looking out his office window. A light snow floated in to blanket the city. The crystals were large and clean, glistening in the amber streetlight as they drifted gently down. He looked again and saw that the snow flakes weren't snow flakes. Each was a parachute. Then each transformed to the face of a young man. Those who fell on the grass held together, turning the entire lawn to a fantasy white. But those unlucky enough to hit the pavement dissolved at the moment of impact. They simply vanished, gone forever. "Good night, gentlemen," he heard his own voice whisper. "Good night and pleasant dreams."

Chapter 33: Collect Call
Hampton, England
December 7, 1990

The phone rang. Karin Kensington placed the sleeping child in her crib and reached to pick up the receiver.

"Collect call, ma'am. Will you accept the charges from Edwina Wausauheimer?"

"I'm afraid I don't know any... who?"

"Overseas call from one Edwina Bond-Wausauheimer. Will you accept..."

"Yes! Oh my God, yes!"

The static on the line made it difficult to hear every word. Yet the message was totally clear: "Go to Baghdad."

"Baghdad? But how? When?"

"As soon as you can leave."

"They're not giving Brits any travel documents. I can't go."

"I think you can. There are Muslims in America who will be going over soon to bring some folks home. Get in with them."

"But I haven't the foggiest..."

"Dearie, I've contacted some people who've contacted some people. Go to the American embassy in London. I believe that you'll find your pathway cleared. Now, you must be brave, KiKi."

Karin gasped. "How did you..."

"Stiff upper lip and all. I don't dare talk any longer. Toodles." She hung up. Karin's heart was racing. No one in the world called her KiKi. No one except her husband. Edwina must have talked to Stewart.

Within three days the brave Irishwoman was in the air.

Chapter 34: Bahrah

Cairo, Egypt
December 10, 1990

Nadia was confused. She hadn't meant to fall in love with the man. But the feelings were there and they were strong. And now even she didn't know what to think.

Everything about him had repulsed her at first. Everything except his ruggedly handsome face and those dark smiling eyes. He was wealthy without having earned a penny in his life. He was arrogant and conceited but could charm water from the desert. He had his damned sexist views of where a woman should be in society. But on every available occasion this spoiled traditionalist treated her like a princess. He was sitting the war out on holiday in Egypt while his former friends and brothers languished in the hell Iraq had created of their country. But he said he was funding the resistance. He joked about her education having been a waste of time and even laughed at what he called her "Western complex." But he often asked her opinion on matters as if he actually valued what she had to say. Was he playing mind games or was he playing love games? Maybe he wasn't playing at all.

Time, insecurity and attention wore on Nadia. Bahrah's confidence, which initially repulsed her, gradually became the magnet that drew her in. The search for his friend and her fiance kept Nadia near Bahrah and planted the seeds of admiration. And his ability to say the right words of comfort at the right time slowly warmed her heart.

In three months, Nadia had ridden the roller coaster from joy to guilt and back again many times. Bahrah spared no expense to keep her off balance. One winter night he asked her to wear something warm, then flew them both to Venice for an evening on a private gondola. Another morning he called and requested that she wear something cosmopolitan. Six hours later they were in Paris at a fashion show. On her birthday they skied the Swiss Alps. On his, they dined in Rome.

The flowers and presents were nothing compared to the way he held her. When he kissed her the first time, Nadia wanted to slap him and cry out. But, to her bewilderment, she kissed him immediately back.

"We can't do this. We can't..." she objected.

"I know. I know. Ali is my friend."

All of this was tempered with bits and pieces of news smuggled out of Kuwait City through the underground. Bahrah wouldn't speak of how he received his information. He only referred in cryptic terms to the resistance he was personally funding. From what Nadia could gather, Bahrah had already spent a small fortune on bribes and intelligence to bring her word of her love. She knew nothing of how Bahrah got that information. She also knew nothing about the four cables which Ali had sent her in care of Bahrah, although he had actually lit her cigarettes with three of them.

On the 10th day of December, the security chief of the government-in-exile called Nadia with the bad news. He had heard from *Al Jahrah*. Two men from Ali's own resistance cell had escaped and were now in Cairo. And they brought word of their leader's ill fate.

She thrashed about in denial when they first spoke of how Ali al Bakr had been killed. Her fiance had died a noble death - a martyr's death. Strapping 10 lbs. of plastic explosives to his chest, he had walked into the stadium prison in Kuwait City disguised as an old woman. When he got near the office of the notorious Iraqi Inspector, he detonated his bomb, killing himself and nine of the enemy.

Nadia clutched Bahrah, unable to breathe, unable to cry. She could only gasp and quiver. The woman had known this might happen at any time, but somehow she was still not ready for it. How could anyone ever be ready for such a thing? She beat her breast, then his.

"Shush. Shush. I am so sorry, my child. He was a hero." A trickle of honest tears fell from Bahrah's eyes and joined the salty river on Nadia's face. "Our Ali was a hero and we shall never forget him." Al Sabah nodded to the two messengers to leave. His bodyguards winked and handed the men a large envelope as they made their way to the rented limo.

"My child, I am here. Do not worry. Bahrah al Sabah will hold you. Shush. Shush. We will always remember him. Our first son shall be named in his honor."

Nadia didn't object.

Chapter 35: Braintree Station
The Pentagon
December 14, 1990

The words rolled over and over verbatim in Fran's mind. He even remembered the inflections and the long, drawn out word "hell": *We've committed. They can do whatever they want, but it has already been sealed. Hell, it's been sealed since Braintree. Sealed since Braintree... sealed since Braintree...*

"You and the little woman still trying to make a baby?"

Francis wasn't listening. The major stepped into the green glow of his protege's computer.

"I asked if you and Kathryn were still trying to make a baby."

"Huh? Oh. Yeah. Well, no. We haven't exactly had a lot of luck lately."

"Ah, I wouldn't worry about it. It's just like shooting crows off a fence post with a shot gun. Keep shooting long enough in the general direction and sooner or later you're bound to hit one."

Francis still wasn't listening.

"You sure you want a kid for the right reasons, or are you just doing this to save your marriage?"

Fran glared up at the major. This time he heard.

"Just kidding around. Just joking." Fran didn't think it was all that funny. The Old Man might have hit a little too close to the truth.

"Can we change the subject?"

"Oh. Sure." The major picked up the newspaper. "Amazing things happening over there in Eastern Europe, wouldn't you say?"

"I suppose so." Fran stepped to his bookshelf, searching for a book on Massachusetts to look up 'Braintree' for the twentieth time.

"Yup. The walls have come tumbling down. I never thought I'd live to see it. Says here that the former East Germans are worried about their connection with the West bringing on a lot of crime and decadence. Did I ever tell you about the time I was over in the East? The most amazing thing. People would leave their baby buggies outside of stores with the babies right in them while they shopped inside."

Fran glared again. "Can we not talk about babies?"

"Oh. Sorry." The major tried to change his direction.

Francis found the book he was after and started flipping through the pages. "Braintree. Braintree."

"You still worked up over the conversation you over-heard in the bathroom the other day?"

"Yeah. I guess so. Whoever it was made it sound like the invasion of Kuwait was already a done deal."

"Some people believe it is."

"Evidently. But this guy sounded like he actually knew something."

"That's odd."

"What?"

"Someone in the Pentagon who actually knows something."

Fran smiled. He just couldn't get serious with this man. Maybe that was why he liked him. "Well, whatever the case, it has something to do with 'Braintree.' " The Marine flipped through the pages of the book.

"I took the train from Boston to Braintree once."

"Yes, I know. It was for your honeymoon."

"Stayed at a Motel 6."

"Super 8."

"Were you there?"

"Can we not talk about this right now? I'm trying to look something up."

"She didn't look like you. Although she had a five o'clock shadow that wouldn't quit. I've always enjoyed taking the train. Did I ever tell you about the time I took the East Berlin subway?"

Francis paid absolutely no attention. "Braintree. City SSE of Boston."

"No? I tell you, the station was cleaner than an underground ABM site. Amazing. And safe? You could let your sister ride it at midnight and not worry about a thing."

"Braintree: population 36,377."

"There isn't a subway station in the Western world as clean as East Berlin's. I tell you, there are some benefits to a police state."

"Subway station?"

"Say whatever you want about Mussolini, he made the trains run on time."

"Subway station! That's it!" Francis grabbed the major by his shoulders and kissed the top of his balding head.

"Whoa! Hands off the furniture, Sally. We barely know each other."

"Don't you see. That's it. Braintree isn't just a town in Massachusetts. It's also a 'T' station. A subway station."

"Yeah? And I'm not just a military genius, I'm also a Country and

Western singer. But what does that have to do with anything?"

"Braintree Station. It's on the Boston 'T' line."

"So?"

"What was our security password for the NSA computer system last summer when it broke down?"

"Harvard Yard. So?"

"So..."

The scales fell from the Old Man's eyes. "Oh. Oh! It's a password. An access code!"

"Bingo." Fran jumped over to the computer and started to search.

The people in Fran's department who were writing daily situation reports for the Joint Chiefs had been using Boston subway stations to access the mainframe computer system since a June 15th security scare. The pool of Pentagon analysts occasionally shared information with other agencies. Each normally worked independently, keeping their own files, managing their own security and using their own codes. But in July, when Fran was reassigned to write special briefings for the president, he was granted limited access to nearly all of the information the government had on Saddam Hussein. Although he had read through a thousand files, 'Braintree' had never been given to him as an option. It was time he accessed that new password.

Fran first opened his own reports from the summer using clearance: STRATCOM/HARVDYD-FMKALIL: 7-00-90. All his files seemed in order. Next he tried every variation of 'Braintree' he could think of: BRNTR, BRANTR, BRNTRE, BRAINTE, BRAINTR and so on. Nothing opened. He spelled it backwards and forwards and inside out. Nothing. He sat staring blankly at the green screen cursing the blinking cursor. "HARVDYD... Braintree.... Braintree Station... Station! I forgot the station!"

"You getting anything?"

"No. Not yet. I'm trying to access some of this new information but I can't seem to remember any of the old codes."

"Should have written them down."

"Gee, thanks mom."

Khalil worked on BRNTRST, BRNTRESTN, BRAINST and a dozen other combinations without success. Moments before giving up, the glow of the screen popped on and it accepted his last try. "Damn!"

"What?"

"It's working."

"So? What are you mad about now?"

"I don't know what I just entered."

The major smiled again. "Should have written it down."

Where ever the ghost screen had come from, Francis didn't know. It could have been CIA, could have been Army Intelligence or National

Security. A series of titles stared him in the face under the full heading "BRAINTREE STATION". He opened the window of the first report entitled "BCASEE" and read in stunned silence. Whoever the writer was and whatever agency had originated these reports, they had clearly gone beyond any analyst's jurisdiction. These folks were creating policy.

Classified: Presidential Briefing
BCASEE: 7-17-90

The U.S. intelligence community is split over Iraq's intentions in these late days of July. First reports have surfaced that Saddam is up to something on the Kuwaiti border. Baker has warned Shevernadze, but he brushed it off as paranoia. It has come to us through our own sources on the ground, through Moussad and through British intelligence, that Saddam is rattling his sword. We have warned the Emir and asked if he desires help. He has declined. Half of our Mideast specialists are quietly working to convince the Saudis that something is happening. The other half are immersed in preparing reaction plans for each of the possible scenarios. Up to this moment in history, the U.S. has had no viable options with regards to thwarting Iraq's nuclear capabilities. Although it appeared only yesterday that no one would have the opportunity to keep Saddam from possessing his nuclear toy, we may finally have a golden window here at this moment.

Classified: Presidential Briefing
Clearance KTO STRATCOM
BCASEE 7-24-90

Think Tank has known it for some time: There will eventually have to be a military action against Saddam Hussein. There is no arguing that. He has stepped beyond the perimeters we placed upon him and is beyond being bought out. He will have to be taken out.

This will be an expensive venture, but we calculate that it will cost less if it happens now rather than later. The reasoning is simple: No hostile force anywhere can be allowed to control (or threaten to manipulate) 46% of the First World's life-blood. No Third World despot with the potential to rally the Arab masses and overthrow the Saudi Royal Family can be allowed to remain in power. Most important, no potential adversary within a SCUDs throw of Israel will be allowed to develop and hold nuclear weapons.

The mechanisms have been put into place. The wires will now be tripped. The price must be paid - in American blood if necessary. And when the smoke finally clears, the man and his monster will be militarily castrated. This cannot become a matter for public debate. It must only a matter of how and when.

Classified: Presidential Briefing
BCASEE: 7-25-90
Glaspie has her instructions.

Francis blinked twice at the screen. Up to this point the writing appeared to be a maverick's opinion piece. With these four words everything changed. It didn't say "Glaspie should be instructed." It said "Glaspie has her instructions." April Glaspie was the U.S. Ambassador to Iraq who told Saddam that the president didn't care what he did with Kuwait.

Fran sat whispering the name "Glaspie" out loud, entranced by what he had just read.

"You found something?"

"Glaspie."

"What about Glaspie?"

The Marine looked up, unwilling to share his suspicions. "What? Oh, nothing."

"You look a little shook. Need some help?"

"Uh, no. No thank you."

"If you're in a pickle, you know where to turn, son."

"Thanks but I'm doing just fine on my own."

The Old Man was visibly hurt. "I've got some good ideas too, you know. Didn't get this job just because I knew how to make a good cup of coffee. Maybe next time you talk to the president you could mention my idea about the robot dune buggies."

Francis smiled and scratched his stubbled chin. "OK. OK, maybe I could use a little help. What do you make of this?" He punched print and turned the screen around to face the major.

"Of what?"

"Of this BCASEE stuff."

"What BKC stuff? I don't follow."

Francis spun the screen back to his side of the desk and stared at a green flashing "interrupt" sign. The ghostwriter had vanished the moment he pressed print. "Do you think... do you think you can help me retrieve something I just had up? It seems to have disappeared."

"Can't get it up, eh kid? Happens to the best of them. Although it has never happened to me, of course. Well, you've come to the right place. All you have to do is..." The major went through the usual steps to access a lost screen, but nothing seemed to work. They tried to save the reports by another name and bring them back up, but the files were either locked or frozen. And then the queerest thing happened. The screen spelled out "BCASEE ACCESSBNK - Enter code." It beeped three times, asking for a code once again. Francis tried every combination of "Braintree Station" he could think of before the computer flashed a final warning. Then came the words "station access denied" and blank screen. The Old Man had never seen that happen before on the Pentagon's luxury system. "Odd." He scratched his bald head. "Who's BKC?"

"I don't know."

"What exactly were you reading?"

"I don't know."

"You sure don't know much for a kid who thinks he knows so much." The major paused. Francis was shaking, as if chilled. "You into something over your head, boy?"

The captain shook his head "no," but his mentor knew him better than that. "You got problems, you just let the Old Man in on it."

"I'm not sure, but I think I just saw something I wasn't supposed to see."

"And it has to do with hearing something you weren't supposed to hear?"

Francis nodded.

"And both of them have to do with Ambassador April Glaspie." Fran kept nodding. "And BKC? Three letters?"

"No, capital B,C,A,S,E,E."

"B,C,A,S,E?"

"Two 'E's. Like your last name."

"Could mean anything. Braintree Case Assessment EE or..."

"BCA Secret Service Estimate something, or..."

"Bill Casey?"

Khalil was startled by the thought. "Bill Casey is dead."

"True. Someone could be using his name as their handle for the code. Or it could mean something else. Although..."

"Although what?"

"Although I always thought it was just a little too convenient that William Casey would pass on just hours before he was to testify at the Iran/ Contra hearings."

"What are you talking about?"

"Hell, if anyone in the world could fake his own death and get away with it, the director of the CIA could. And with the nature of Reagan's White House and Bush being a former CIA director himself and all... well..." The major hummed the Twilight Zone theme and wiggled his fingers in Khalil's face. Fran didn't buy it. It sounded a little too "Oliver Stone-ish" for his taste.

"It happened when you tried to print, right?"

"Yeah."

"Should have written it down."

The two worked together for more than an hour without results before the major's growling stomach called him to look at his watch. "You want to grab a bite and come back or order out?"

Fran shook his head, still locked on the screen. A moment later he slammed his fist on the desk and leaned back. "Damn!"

"What?"

"Kathryn. I have a date with her at 5:30."

"Have?" The major shoved his watch in Khalil's face. "More like had."

Francis flicked off the computer. "Gotta go."

"She gives you any problems, just send her to me. Tell her I was having troubles with my 'ex' and needed a shoulder to cry on."

"Thanks." He grabbed his jacket and jerked an informal salute. The Old Man yelled down the hallway: "I got an extra couch if you need it tonight!"

"I'm sorry."

"When I married you I thought you needed a 'low maintenance' wife. I was OK with that. But what you really need..."

"Look, I said I'm sorry."

"What you really need is a 'no maintenance' wife."

"What do you mean by that?"

"You know exactly what I mean."

"You don't understand. What I'm on to right now is really important."

"And what about me? Us? Am I..."

"You know that you're important to me."

"It sure doesn't feel like it sometimes. Camping trips to Kurdistan - without me."

"Funny."

"Exotic lunches at romantic European sidewalk cafes - without me."

"If you call Bulgaria romantic."

"I'm sure that it's all more exciting than being with some frumpy school teacher..."

"Cut it."

"Francis, I don't have to be first in your life. I just want to be in the running. You know what I mean?"

"You are."

"Tell me about it."

"You are. Really are. I promise I'll make it up to you. But right now..."

She gave him her quick and transparent "I've heard that one before" smile. "Francis, I love you but I'm beginning to dislike you. I don't need all of your life. But I want a chunk. I don't want to strangle your ambition or get in the way of your dreams. I just want to be a part of them. You know? I want you to think about me, too. My needs. I want you to remember me when..."

"I do think of you."

"I want you to want me."

"I do want you."

"No, you don't understand. I don't want to be the one who has to remind you that I'm alive. I want to be important to you because I really am important to you. Not just because I want to be. I want you to want me because you want me, not because I want you to want me."

Francis had to think about that one for a while. Right now he only wanted to make up and make out. Kathryn just wanted to make up.

She won.

Chapter 36: The Missing Peace
The Khalil Apartment
December 15, 1990   1:00 a.m.

Francis couldn't sleep. He stood in the pale blue moonlight of the bedroom window, trying to make sense of it all. The pieces just didn't fit together. Who (or what) was BCASEE? A rogue analyst? Someone with an overactive imagination? The late director of the CIA come back from the grave to direct U.S. foreign policy? And what about the July 25 report which stated that *"Glaspie has her instructions"*? July 25 was one day before the ambassador made her ill-fated visit to Saddam to inform him that the United States wasn't concerned with Iraq's border squabbles. Whatever or whoever BCASEE was, Francis couldn't let it go. It wouldn't let him go. Ms. Glaspie was a key to the riddle. He had to talk to the ambassador.

April Glaspie was a 25-year career diplomat and the first American woman to hold an ambassador post in the Middle East. She was intelligent, observant, seasoned - not the type prone to error or misjudgment. She knew when to address a situation in clear and certain terms and when to say nothing. She knew how to assert herself in tough situations and when to acquiesce. And now this woman appeared condemned by history to carry the blame for the Kuwaiti invasion. Quarantined by the State Department, sequestered from the media and under orders from the president to speak only to Congress (and then only when demanded on the hill), Ambassador Glaspie was being held in the deepest political purgatory a diplomat could face. Denied the right to answer her critics, she would be remembered as the bungler who gave Saddam Hussein the wrong signal at exactly the wrong time.

Francis rubbed his tired eyes and sat at the edge of the bed. Kathryn stirred, sneered at the red numbers glowing on her radio alarm and dropped back to her pillow. "Come to sleep, Fran. It's past midnight."

"I can't understand it. It just doesn't follow."

"What's there to understand? Glaspie made a mistake. A huge miscalculation. She was misunderstood by the Iraqis and a week later, bang! Now her censure is the price of that mistake."

"I still don't get it." He yawned and slapped his own face.

"Go to sleep, Francis. Come to sleep."

"Glaspie had the intelligence reports. She knew Saddam was mobilizing. She had regular psychological profiles on the man. She had to know that giving him the *'America isn't concerned about Arab territorial disputes'* line was like giving the coyote the key to the chicken coop. She must have known he'd go for it. She couldn't have been that stupid unless..." Francis spun around with wide open eyes. "Unless they want us to believe she was that stupid while in reality she was doing exactly what she had been told."

"What are you talking about?" Kathryn sat up in bed.

"Hold it! Oh my God. What if..." Francis began to pace about the room. "What if this was all in the plans? If we wanted Saddam to think we didn't care? What if this was the only way?"

"The only way to what?"

"If luring him into Kuwait was the only way to ultimately take Saddam's arsenal out?"

"You're saying we wanted Saddam Hussein to invade Kuwait? Right... I think you need some sleep." Kathryn pulled the covers up over her head to block out the world.

Francis tried to pry them back. "No, listen. Say the president and his inner sanctum know that Saddam is going nuclear and a nuclear Iraq can virtually dictate the price of Middle East oil. They are searching for a way to take him out, but no opportunities are presenting themselves, right?"

"I'm not listening." The young bride tried to burrow deeper but he dug her out.

"They determine that Saddam has to be eliminated before his nuclear weapons go on line, but how are they going do that?"

"Fran, I don't know and I don't care."

"The CIA is bound by law not to assassinate foreign leaders. (Not that they wouldn't arrange for it.) But a coup against Saddam is virtually impossible. He's eliminated all his opponents inside Iraq. There are no enemies in the region with both the will and the means to take him on except Israel. And even Israel couldn't get by clean this time. In '81, when they bombed Iraqi nuclear reactors at Osiris, Hussein didn't have SCUDs or chemical or biological agents sitting on the pad aimed at Tel Aviv. He didn't have a million-man army. No, Israel couldn't hit Iraq this time without initiating World War III. So that leaves us."

"And I'm leaving you. Good night." Kathryn dug herself in again.

"So that leaves us. But how do you muster American public support for a major military action half a world away with memories of the Beirut Marine barracks on our minds, the S & L scandal to pay for and Hussein as one of our biggest grain and weapons importers in the world? Impossible, right?"

"Right. Good night."

"Wrong. There is a way. One way. No one in the world could take him out. So we had to get him to take himself out."

Kathryn looked at her husband with a clear confusion. "What?"

"The only person who can take Saddam out at this point is Saddam. So we use Saddam's own greed to take him out."

"I got a class in the morning." She reburied her face in the pillow.

"Six months ago there was no way in hell the voters would put up with anything of the sort. Now: enter the dispute with Kuwait over loans and oil revenue. Suddenly here comes April Glaspie telling Saddam Hussein that we have no interests in 'inter-Arab' conflicts."

"Go to sleep."

"Doesn't that sound just a little too convenient?"

"Don't I sound just a little annoyed? Go to sleep."

"The president instructs his ambassador to pass the message on to the Iraqis: 'We don't care what you do with Kuwait.' She relays the message on July 26, knowing full well that Saddam has 100,000 troops on the border waiting for the green light. Knowing full well what is going to happen if she does. And at this point it is too much for the dictator to resist."

Kathryn sat up again. "You've used the 'green light' analogy twice in the same train of thought now. Bad choice." She dropped straight back into the pillow and held it tighter than before.

"A few days later big Iraq pounces on little Kuwait. Oil jumps $20 a barrel overnight. Gas prices at the pump go up a dime as America panics at the thought of Saddam controlling Saudi oil fields. The media plays into this with anti-Arab rhetoric and pocketbook paranoia. Saddam is set up as a madman on the cover of *Time*. The networks call him another Hitler, comparing the situation to Chamberlain appeasing the Nazi's in 1938. Fickle America shallows the whole thing and 'viola.' "

"Viola?"

"There you have it."

"There you have what?"

"Deployment." Francis slowly covered his mouth. "Oh my God. Even I got sucked in on this. I was writing their briefs for them! Even I..."

"Francis, read my lips: No new conspiracies."

"Funny." He got out of bed and started looking for his pants.

"Francis! Where are you going?" She changed tactics and reached for him. "Let's make love." He moved away.

"Think about it. How could a career diplomat bumble into such a horrendous snafu? She knew who Hussein was. She had the intelligence reports about his mobilizations on the border. She couldn't have been so stupid as to give him a green light without knowing he'd go for it."

The elementary English teacher wrote in the air with an invisible red pen: "Green light analogy tired and overused. C minus. Let's make love." She dove back under the sheets, expecting him to follow.

"So if she knew, then why..." Francis peeled off the covers from his bride. "If she knew! That is 'if' she knew." He tried to pry the pillow from her face. "What if Glaspie didn't even know?" He loosened his grip on Kathryn's pillow and covered his own mouth in amazement.

Kathryn screamed through the duck feathers. "What if Glaspie didn't know what?"

"What if she was set up, too? That would explain her quarantine from the media! They'd want to keep her quiet as long as they could. Let's say she was told by Baker that we really didn't care what Saddam did in Kuwait. If she knew we were trying to entice him to take it, she'd have to lie to Congress - not that ambassadors haven't done that before. But what if even she didn't know? She couldn't very well lie about something she didn't know, could she?"

Francis stumbled over a chair, mumbling to himself and trying to find his pants again. Kathryn reached for the radio clock. "Francis Christopher Michael Khalil. It is now one stinking o'clock in the morning. I've got to teach tomorrow and... and where do you think you're going?"

"I've got to see if I can get to Glaspie."

"What?"

"Glaspie. Glaspie is the key."

"Make love with me."

"Glaspie's the key to... say what?"

"You heard me. I want to make love. Right now." Kathryn never wanted to make love after midnight. Not after she had already been sleeping. Francis hesitated a moment, then resumed the search for his pants.

"You've got to teach tomorrow, remember."

"Francis!" He had never turned her down before. "I want to make a baby."

"You're not fertile for three more days."

"OK. I want to practice. How are we ever going to..."

"Sorry."

"...make a baby if we... how do you... how do you know I'm not fertile?"

"I've got it on my calendar." He threw her a little blue book from his jacket pocket and dug under the bed for some shoes.

"Gee, thanks for penciling me in."

"Don't mention it."

She tried to lighten things up by pulling off her T-shirt and throwing herself on the bed. "Take me!"

"Sorry. Gotta go."

"They're not going to let you see her."

"We'll see."

"They're not."

"What? Is she under house arrest?"

"Francis! It's one o'clock in the morning! Have you any idea of the kind of trouble you could be in if all this turned out to be true?"

"We'll see." He dressed quickly and vanished.

"Fran-sis Khalil! You're driving me nuts here!"

Two minutes later the Marine reappeared in her doorway.

"Came to your senses and couldn't resist, eh?" She whipped off her shirt and panties once more and threw herself back on the bed with a melodramatic: "OK, soldier! Have your way with me!"

Fran stepped in, bent over, cupped his hand over her mouth and pecked her on the forehead. "Kathy, I have to ask you a question."

She pulled him down by the collar of his flak jacket and kissed him hard on the mouth. "What is it?"

"Where... did you put..." he whispered seductively in her ear between kisses. "...my car keys?"

She hit him with the first hard object she could find.

Chapter 37: April Showers
The Home of Ambassador Glaspie
December 15, 1990   2:00 a.m.

"I'm sorry. The ambassador is asleep. She's had a rough two weeks and I will not disturb her."

Francis was surprised to see Federal agents at the door of the Glaspie residence. He knew she'd be under wraps, but didn't expect to find a home under siege. Two men sat in the car across the street, both sleeping like babies. (Snoring babies, to be exact.) One was at the front door the moment he hit the bell and two others were playing cards on the living room sofa.

"I'm with National Security and I've got to have a few words with the ambassador immediately." Khalil flashed his I.D. and thought on his feet. "We have some people in trouble in Iraq and only she can help."

"I'm sorry." The agent stepped to block the Marine's entrance. "But I'm going to have to ask you to leave. I've got my orders. You understand orders, don't you?"

Francis knew the trouble he'd be in if he stepped through that door. Crossing the threshold would be a move he could not retrieve. Career, rank, possibly his whole future would be at risk if his suspicions were true and he pressed the ambassador on them. He didn't want to do it. Yet, Fran felt he had no choice. It was as if the gods were pulling the tragic strings on his life, compelling him toward his own self-destruction. There was only one moment when he could have turned back. He held it. It held him. Then he put his foot in the doorway: "I've got orders, too. And I'm afraid I can't take 'no' for and answer."

"Ambassador Glaspie is unable to talk to anyone right now. Why don't you leave your name and number and I'll have her give you a call the first chance she gets?"

A light went on at the end of the hallway. "Who is it, Mike?"

"Someone from National Security. He says he's got a guy in trouble in the field and wants to talk to you. I told him that..."

"I can make my own decisions about who I'm going to talk to, thank you very much."

Fran stuck his head in past the Neanderthal. "Sorry to wake you, ambassador. It's urgent."

"I wasn't asleep. Who are you and what do you want?"

"My name is Captain Francis Khalil. I was in Iraq a short time ago and I stumbled across something that I believe you need to know."

The ambassador appeared much older than Khalil had remembered her. It may have simply been the lack of make-up or the fact that it was now almost 2:00 in the morning, but her eyes seemed swollen. She was wearing an old mint-green robe with a wad of Kleen-ex falling from a ratted pocket. Her hair was matted and unkempt. "I've already talked to everyone I'm supposed to talk with and said everything I have to say."

"Excuse me, ma'am, but I believe someone we both know is in trouble and may need your help."

She paused in a moment of consideration, then waved the Feds away. The reluctant agent stepped aside to let Khalil pass.

"Thank you." The captain need not have said it.

"Now, who is it that needs my assistance?"

"I'd rather we talk alone."

"Very well." She led him down a long hall of mirrors into her walnut paneled den. As they entered the room Francis noticed a trash can full of used tissues. Either she had a cold or the ambassador had been crying.

"Now, who is this mysterious person in so much trouble and how am I to help."

"The person, Ms. Ambassador, is a woman named April Glaspie."

Glaspie was suddenly very much awake. "I think you'd better leave." She rose to show him out.

Fran spoke quickly: "I believe you were set up to take the fall for the entire invasion of Kuwait. You were manipulated into telling Saddam Hussein that we wouldn't retaliate - exactly what he needed to hear in order to go through with it..."

The woman's face grew hard and wary. "What kind of game is this? What do you people want from me?" She cinched her robe tight and glanced nervously down the hall toward the Feds.

"...and as soon as Saddam took the bait, your superiors pulled out, shut you up and left you hanging in the wind looking like an incompetent."

"An interesting theory, captain." She spoke now in a low near-growl. "An interesting theory, but sheer speculation on your part. How do you know I just didn't make a mistake?"

Fran couldn't quite read her veiled shock. Was she stunned because he knew what he knew? Or was this idea - that she might have been used - something she hadn't considered? "How do I know it wasn't a mistake? A historical misjudgment on par with Chamberlain's statement to Hitler about 'peace in our time'? "

Glaspie nodded.

"How do I know? Because you're not that stupid. You're too good. You're not inept. My only question is this: did you know that you were feeding misinformation, or did you believe it to be true?"

The woman's lips drew thin and tight. "I'm afraid that I can't tell you anything relating to my testimony. I believe that you... "

"If you purposefully set the trap and were willing to go down in history as a fool for your country, well then, I commend your patriotism. I don't know if I could do that. On the other hand, if you were being used - set up to take the fall..."

The ambassador stood abruptly and cut him off. "I'm sorry captain, it's very late and I have to testify tomorrow on the hill. I'm under clear directives not to discuss this with anyone." She turned and called down the hallway. "Mike?"

"Ambassador Glaspie, I..."

"I appreciate your concern, but I don't need your speculation or pity." All five Feds were now awake and waiting in the doorway to "assist" Francis to his car. The ambassador changed her tack the moment they were within earshot. "Thanks for your concern captain. I'm sure our 'friend' will be all right on her own. She's a big girl. She can take care of herself."

The Arlington night was clear and cool. A mist crept through the streets and lingered about the lampposts. Francis sat for a moment before sliding his key into the ignition. An upstairs light flicked on and the silhouette of a woman watched him watching her. The figure didn't draw her shades until long after the Jaguar's taillights disappeared down her drive. Then she picked up the phone.

"I don't care what time it is, this is urgent!"

A few minutes later a groggy and annoyed voice picked up the line at the other end.

"Hello, this is April Glaspie. We may have a little problem."

Chapter 38: The Last Call

Georgetown Mall
December 15, 1990   3:00 a.m.

He was being followed. Francis knew that much. The black Cadillac bore classic CIA markings with its Virginia plates. But something about these trackers didn't sit right. The Company usually ran a more discrete tail than this. These spooks were just close enough to let him know they were there, just far enough back to stay out of his way. The Marine's appetite was wet and he decided to check them out.

Running a red light at the empty Georgetown Mall, Francis kicked into fifth around the block. The Cadi squealed a corner and the chase was on. Three miles and a bridge later, the Jaguar took a quick left and ducked into a blind alley. He backed out just as they sped past, and moments later the tailers had a tail. He honked. The smoked windows didn't respond. Francis pulled up on their bumper and waved before slamming his breaks and spinning down the ramp onto the highway.

"Lost 'em." He smiled to himself and turned off on 395 for a drive down the coast.

The phone rang. As standard operational procedure dictated when Francis wasn't home, Kathryn let her Lily Tomlin tape do the talking: *"Gracious good afternoon. Is this is the party to whom I am speaking? If you aren't selling something or asking for child support, please leave your name and number and we'll get back to you."*

"Kathryn, it's me." She was still mad enough at Francis that she didn't want to talk. "I'm OK, but I need time to think. I'm going to take a little drive. I'll talk to you about it in the morning."

An hour later it rang again. Kathryn, half-asleep, recognized the major's voice. "Francis, it's 4 o'clock. Give me a call when you get home." She let it go.

It rang again. "4:15. I know you're there, Khalil. Answer the phone, will ya? Answer it."

Again: "4:30. I'm telling you, son, we gotta talk. Pick up the phone."

She sat on the bedstand clutching her pillow. "5:00. Pick it up, son. Do I have to come over there and get ya? It's practically daylight."

And again: "Look, you're going to have to stay out of this. For your own good, you're going to have to forget this Glaspie business. It's none of our damn business anyway and it can only get us all into a hell of a lot of trouble. You understand?"

At 6 am the final call came. This voice was one Kathryn didn't recognize. "Captain Khalil, Langley wants to see you at 0900 packed and ready to go."

That was the last message.

Francis didn't return home that night. He picked up a hitch-hiker in Ocean City and drove down the coast.

Chapter 39: The Last Mission
The Pentagon
December 17, 1990

It was now 7:35 a.m. Monday morning. Francis had just reached into the bottom desk drawer for his chordless electric Norelco when the major came storming in. "Where the hell have you been?"

"What are you talking about?"

"I'm talking about Friday night through Monday morning!"

"I get weekends off, don't I? I thought it was in my contract."

"Don't play smartass with me! This weekend I've had more brass than and Indian import shop breathing down my neck about you waking Ambassador April Glaspie at 2:00 in the morning!"

"1:45."

"Whatever! If I don't have you over to Langely by nine bells I can forget my pension!"

"You think I'm in trouble?"

"If the CIA doesn't kill you, your wife just might. And when she's through with your carcass, I want what's left over. Where the hell did you go Sunday?"

"So you think I'm in a little trouble?"

"Blazes, soldier. If you aren't dumber than a box of rocks sometimes!"

Francis wasn't sure if the major was actually angry or if this was just his way of showing affection.

"What were you thinking?"

"OK. So I'm in a little trouble. What do you think I should do?"

The major smirked at his protégé for the longest time, then heaved a sigh. "I don't know, son. I don't know. Take a shave and splash some water on your face, I suppose. Then get your keister over to talk with the spooks. But for God sakes, get this Glaspie business out from under your craw. It can't do any of us any good at this point."

"Did you tell them anything about... about 'BCASEE' or 'Braintree'?"

The major shook his head and mimicked Sgt. Schultz from *Hogan's Heroes*: "I know nothing!" Francis bent over and removed his razor and a tooth brush from the bottom drawer, then rose to hit the bathroom. "Thank you, sir. I appreciate you worrying about me."

"You owe me a couple good nights of sleep, kid."

"I owe you a lot more than that, sir."

The major didn't know if Francis was being sincere or sarcastic. "Yeah, yeah. Now get out of here."

The captain sat in the waiting room and paged through a three year old *Field & Stream* next to what had to be a one-way floor-length mirror. At one point the CIA's director, Robert Gates, himself, walked out of the office to give his secretary a file. He nodded at the captain but didn't say hello. Finally a lesser official called over the intercom to bring Francis in.

"About this Glaspie business..." Fran began.

The agent shook his head. "I don't believe that we're here to talk about anything other than your next assignment."

"My assignment?"

"Yes, your next mission."

"I wasn't aware that I was up for another mission. My supervisor..."

"This is an urgent matter that has nothing to do with the Pentagon. We're running this one completely out of our office and would appreciate your assistance and your silence on the whole operation."

Something didn't seem kosher to Khalil, but he listened anyway.

"This is a two part job. First, we need you to establish contact with the Shiites in southern Iraq and ready them for the resistance when Desert Shield becomes Desert Storm."

"Pardon me, sir, but the Shia aren't any friend of the United States. They are completely in Iran's court. They're not going to take orders from..."

"We know it won't be easy. But we believe you are the man for the job. You've got the record. Your work with the Kurds has given us every confidence in you."

"The Shia are not the Kurds." This didn't make sense. Everyone in the CIA knew that a pact with the Shiites was impossible. Aside from that, no one in the Administration wanted to arm an ally of Iran. "Sir, I don't think..."

The man silenced him with one hand. "Our operatives will meet you in Kuwait City and help you cross from there. Your contact is the head of the *Al Jahrah* resistance cell: a man called *Shobash*."

"Good night?"

"Excuse me?"

"That's his name. Good night."

"That's his code name. We don't know his real name, but Bahrah al Sabah recommends him personally as the best man for this particular job."

Fran knew many members of the ruling family of Kuwait by name, but he hadn't come across any Bahrah. "And who is Bahrah al Sabah?"

"He's a shirt-tail relative of the ruling family. A business man who uses the family name to make and break deals. We've found him, shall we say, useful in the past with regards to making connections in Kuwait." The man handed Francis a packet. "If you're up for this, we'd want you to memorize the mission instructions before you leave here today and shred the papers. You know the procedure."

"Today?"

"Yes, you'll be leaving this morning."

"Impossible."

"We're operating under a tight time frame here."

"Couldn't this wait until after the holidays?"

"I've yet to see a war that waits for anyone's personal schedule. You'll be home in plenty of time for Christmas."

"Why the rush?"

"That's where the second piece of this pie comes in. We have a man on the ground in Kuwait City who's been there since before the whole mess started. We've got to get him out yesterday."

"What's his name?"

"We're not sure it's a he, but 'he, she or it' goes by the code name *Wausau*."

"Who is he?"

"Could be a hostage in hiding. Could be an independent mercenary of some sort getting his kicks. He has been on the outskirts of Kuwait City since the tanks rolled in on August 2."

"Working for whom?"

"That's the foggy part. We're not sure. He's been feeding us raw intelligence, bombing coordinates, hostage whereabouts and the like. Most of it has been verified. Some of it has been valuable. But he's been giving us the 'mayday' for three nights now. Says he's in trouble and that the Iraqis are closing in every time he broadcasts."

"Why don't you bring him home with the rest of the Westerners? From what I've read internally, Hussein is going to send them home for Christmas."

"Not this one, he won't. Iraq believes *Wausau* is CIA. They'll interrogate him and, from what he knows, it could be very embarrassing for us if he talks. Deadly."

"And you want me to bring him home?"

"As long as we gotta pick you up anyway, you may as well have some cargo."

"You think he'll talk?"

"He's an eccentric. We don't know what he'll do. But he knows too much. We've got to get him out." The agent shifted in his chair. "There is one other catch here."

"And that is?"

"We can't determine exactly if he is who he says he is."

"Excuse me?"

"He's either an extremely lucky idiot with a ham radio who was left behind and has somehow managed to elude the occupation army. Either that or he's..."

"He's what?"

"I'll level with you, Khalil. He could be an Iraqi spy."

"And if he is?"

"Get him out or take him out."

"By that you mean..."

"Just what I said. If he's an American, get him out. If he's a spy..."

"I'm a Marine, sir, not a hired assassin."

The spook wasn't the least bit impressed by moral platitudes. "A lot of lives are at stake here. We can't have civilians playing 007 while we're trying to get on with the final phases of the preparations. He knows too much and can't be trusted to keep his mouth shut. So you've either got to get him out or take him out. That's your second task."

"This whole thing is beginning to sound a bit too much like *'Mission Impossible'* to me."

"You want out?"

"Do I have a choice?"

The man didn't respond. He simply pointed to the door.

"I didn't say I wanted out. I just want to state for the record that the first half of this mission doesn't appear to be very well thought out. And the second..."

"We can order you to take this, but we're not going to. If you want out, say the word. You got it. But we don't have any time to waste. What's it going to be?"

Francis didn't like this. He had never taken orders from the CIA before. "I'd be home before Christmas?"

The agent nodded. "Guaranteed."

The whole thing seemed all too rushed. "I don't know."

"You've been recommended from the top on down, but I'll find someone else if your heart isn't in it."

"I was recommended by the president, himself?"

The man didn't give a "yes," didn't give a "no." Twenty seconds passed with no sound but the blue flies buzzing on the ceiling. Francis tried to read a hidden intent behind the businessman's opaque stare. He wondered for a moment if it might be a set-up. Then he thought of Kathryn and Christmas. He couldn't do this to her. President or no president, he wasn't going to miss his first Christmas with Kathryn. "Ah, I think you've got the wrong man. I'm going to have to pass on this one."

"Suit yourself, soldier." The spook rose and motioned again to the door. Francis started to salute but held back.

"Oh, and Khalil?"

"Yes, sir?"

"One more thing. There has been some woman asking for you in Turkey. I thought you might like to know. She's being held by the authorities there. One Kala Haseke."

"I'm afraid I don't know anyone by that name."

"Said she met you in Iraq. Contacted our ambassador there and asked if you could get her out. You could probably swing by Ankara on the way home. That is, if you were to go..."

"I don't know her."

"Told us to give you a code word."

Francis squinted, shaking his head. "I'm afraid I'm not interested in..."

"Adanon."

"Adanon?" He exhaled and glanced at his watch. "Adanon." 10:15. Kathryn would be on break. He'd have to call and apologize for the last two nights and find a way to make it up. She wasn't going to like him being gone right now. They had rescheduled their reservations at "The Monocle" for tonight. "OK. If I can stop in Turkey on my way back home, I'm in. I just have to call my wife and tell her I won't be home for supper. Suppers."

"Good man." The agent slid the phone to him and rose to leave. "*Shobash* will meet you at the drop site and get you to Basara. When you're done there he'll help you locate this *Wausau* fellow and take you both to the SEALs in the harbor. From there you'll go to Saudi and on through Ankara on your way to Frankfurt."

"And if *Wausau's* not who he says he is?"

"We'll leave that up to you."

Francis nodded. "When do we fly?"

"Plane's waiting."

The man stepped out of the room to let Francis use the phone. He dialed Kathryn to explain.

"Hello."

"It's me."

"Francis, where have you been? I was scared straight last night! The phone has been buzzing off the wall."

"I tried to call a half-dozen times."

"I finally disconnected it and left the house. Did you talk to Glaspie?"

"Yes."

Kathryn cursed in silence and swung at a shadow on the wall. "And?"

"The ambassador didn't crack, but I could tell I shook her. I'm on to something. I know it."

"Have you any idea of the trouble you could be in?"

"Kathryn, I'm on to something. And it won't let me go."

"Or you won't let it go." A little arm tugged on Kathryn's shoulder, asking for help. "I've got to go. We can talk about it tonight. OK? Fran?"

"You're not going to like this."

"What? What?"

"I've gotta fly."

"Francis!"

"I'm sorry, but it's an emergency."

"Sorry? Everything is an emergency with you lately."

"I've got to go back to Kuwait."

"What? Why would you go back now? You said yourself that they couldn't pay you enough to get you back there. It's too close to K-Day!"

"They need someone to talk with the Shiites."

"What Shiites?"

"Basara."

"I thought you said Kuwait."

"Kuwait and Iraq."

"You're flying into Iraq? Francis..."

"I'll be home in 72 hours. Promise."

"The Shiites are not going to get into bed with anyone from the United States. Why would they..."

"We have to try."

"I can't believe this! Tell them to get someone else."

"There's also a man on the ground in Kuwait City who we've got to grab."

"Marine?"

"No."

"If this is a CIA operation, why don't they use their own people? Besides, it's Christmas and it's time! You know? Time! If you're serious about wanting to have a baby then we've got to do it. It's time!"

"I'm sorry."

"There's this thing called making love. You remember making love, don't you?"

"I don't think..."

"You're right. You don't think. You don't. Why would you risk this? Are you doing it to punish me or to punish yourself? Maybe you don't want a baby with me. Maybe you're afraid that it would keep us together."

"You don't understand."

"Damn right, I don't understand. There's something missing here. Talk to me, Francis. What aren't you telling me?"

A frozen moment followed. Francis didn't know how to approach this. Kathryn, on the other hand, never had a problem saying what was on her mind. "Is she beautiful?"

"I've got a friend - a Kurd I fought with - who's..."

"Is she beautiful?"

"...who's in trouble and I've got to go see if there's something I can do."

"I asked you if she was beautiful?"

Francis didn't answer.

"Damn you, Khalil. Tell me something! Anything. Lie to me if you have to. Tell me it's not a woman."

"It's not a woman."

"Lie!"

"OK, it is a woman. But it's not what you think."

"Yeah? And just what do I think?"

"She's just a kid..."

"Oh, and that's supposed to make me feel a lot better?"

"I feel responsible..."

"Did you sleep with her?"

"No, I did not. I didn't even know 'she' was a 'she' until..."

"Until what? Until she took her clothes off?"

"I didn't sleep with her."

"Did you want to?"

Francis was trapped. He rubbed his eyes until the colors swirled inside his head. "I've got to do this."

"You don't have to do anything. You want to do this."

"OK! I want to do it. I want to. But that doesn't mean..."

"You do whatever you damn well please, Khalil. I just can't say where I'm gonna be when you get back. If you get back."

"And what is that supposed to mean?"

"I don't know. I honestly don't know."

Francis sighed. He didn't want to leave with this unresolved. "Kathryn, I..."

"Just what part of you is it that wants to make me a widow, Francis?" Her anger melted and her voice was now more sad than sorry. "What part of you wants to die?" She waited for an answer that didn't exist. "Fine. I've got to go. Have a nice flight. And Merry Christmas in case I don't see you."

Francis slammed the phone down but clutched the receiver tightly in his hands before picking it up again to call the major. The old crocodile was nervous about his boy working outside normal chains of command. "If anything happens to you when you're working for 'the Company,' you don't have the same kind of backup as you get with the Marines. Something happens to you with those boys and nobody hears about it. Ever."

"I guess that's the way it's gonna be."

"At least with the Marines you get a decent funeral. Picture in the paper."

"Thanks for the vote of confidence."

"You sure you want to go through with this?"

"I have a feeling that this will be my last jump for a while. Within a couple of weeks things are going to be too hot over there for anybody."

"I think I know what you mean. Well, *semper fi*, buddy."

"Yeah, *semper fi*."

Neither man wanted to hang up. The major remembered another message. "Oh, by the way, Vladimir Kalinov's in town."

"The Russian? What's he want?"

"Seems he's working for his embassy now, of all places. Came by right after you left Friday night. Said he wanted to take you out to supper."

Francis chuckled. "Yeah, I'll bet. He owes me one."

"It was the damnedest thing. I was in the commissary - did I tell you we have a new donut machine now? Makes those mini-donuts like you get at Coney Island. Now, there's a treat for ya."

"What about Kalinov?"

"Huh?"

"The Russian?"

"Yeah? Oh, yeah. Well anyway, I was working late, still trying to access the 'Braintree' files when I went down to the cafeteria for a bite. Suddenly, standing right behind me in the checkout line, I hear these guys talking Russian. Russian! In the Pentagon! Anyways, I turn around and here are these three 'diplomats' on a tour. I tell ya, it's not like the old days."

"Anyway..."

"Anyways, one of them is wearing this tag with the name Vladimir Kalinov on it. So I says to myself, I says: 'hey, how many Vladimir Kalinov's can there be in the KGB?' So I ask him. And it's him."

"It is 'he.' "

"What are you, my mother? Anyway, it's this Kalinov who knows you from Brussels or Bangladesh or somewhere. We get to talking and he says he was going to track you down. He called again this morning and left a number. Said he went after you the other night but you ditched him."

Francis remembered the little cat and mouse game he'd played early Saturday morning. "That was Kalinov? What did he want?"

"He told me to tell you thanks for delivering Mendelev's 'package' and that his own 'package' finally got to Moscow, too. Whatever that means. He says he owes you one. Was that the Russian boy you brought back from Iraq? His kid?"

There was a quiet plastic rustling, like the sound of someone somewhere picking up a receiver to listen in on their call. Francis changed the subject.

"Oh, by the way, could you do a little favor for me yet this morning?"

"What is it?"

"Could you call the florist and send Kathryn some flowers? It's our anniversary and I'm afraid I'm going to have to stand her up for the second time tonight."

"What kind of flowers?"

"I don't know. Roses or orchids I suppose. Make up something sappy like 'I'll be home for Christmas.' And could you call and cancel my reservations for tonight?"

"Where are they at?"

"It's that new Russian place, Kalinov's. Call Vladimir and tell him I'm sorry and explain exactly why I can't be there."

There was a long pause.

"He owes me a favor, right?"

"What?" The major didn't get it.

"You said Vladimir still owes me a favor, right?"

"Right. Oh, Vladimir. Right! I'll give him a call."

"And tell him exactly 'why' I can't come."

"You sure? Why should he have to know? I would think that..."

"Do what I tell you."

Francis boarded the jet at Andrews with more than a few misgivings. He didn't know why he was going.

No. He did.

Adanon.

The Capitol disappeared beneath heavy gray clouds and Francis tried to talk his racing mind into a six hour moratorium so he could get some sleep. An aid on the plane offered him some pills.

"They'll help you get to sleep faster."

"No thanks," said the captain. "Save 'em for the president."

Hours later in a dream that was no dream, an 18 year-old Francis Khalil was driving down the lonely stretch of Montana back roads that run from Savage to Wolf Point. Great streams of lightning severed the sky in a display of power unlike anything the boy had seen. A blinding rain hit with the force of hail upon his windshield, making the no-shoulder road all the more treacherous.

Yet, darker than any storm without was the one raging within. A heavy veil of depression had descended on him like a curtain: harsher than any anger, colder than any tomb.

It was graduation night and Fran was alone. Utterly and completely alone in the universe. He hadn't anticipated the meloncholy descending as the past was stolen away forever. He couldn't understand the invisible rage. But the small white crosses at each bend now called for him to let go. And each set of oncoming headlights goaded him to fly and join the night.

The pull was great. And it almost took him. But the Catholic in Fran held him in his own personal purgatory rather than releasing him to the comparative peace he thought hell must be. *Jinna* whispered and a boy concurred: "You are alone, Lui Chi. Alone with your beating heart."

Chapter 40: The Rest of the Story
After hours at the Pentagon
December 19, 1990

The Old Man signed on at the Pentagon computer with Khalil's code "Harvard Yard" and began his search in earnest. He played with every combination of "Braintree Station" he could mathematically find, trying not to spill his drink on the keyboard. Within a half hour, he found what he was looking for.

Actually, he found more than that.

Classified: Presidential Briefing
BCASEE: 7-28-90
This invasion is the opportunity we have been waiting for since the days of the Israeli bombing of Iraq's Osiris nuclear weapons facility. Although it may cost billions and place the world at the brink of war and depression, in a strange way, it is almost more than we could have hoped for. It is almost too good to be true. In these next days when the first sporadic reports of Iraq's invasion have trickled in through the intelligence network and satellite photos are on the Joint Chief's desks, the surprise and alarm will be met with a clear and somber acquiescence. Even a relief. For this is the one opportunity we have to take Hussein out. No one - not even the most daring speculators in the inner sanctum - ever dreamed that we'd have such a perfect excuse to remove both the atomic weapons and the dictator who wouldn't think twice about using them. No one could have done it to him. The dictator has set himself up for this fall, and for that our people are grateful.

Classified: Presidential Briefing
BCASEE: 8-2-90
Bush must make a slow, even-handed effort at diplomacy in the U.N. Talk of a purely 'defensive force' for Saudi Arabia is needed immediately to stall the Iraqis

long enough to get the planes, troops and M-1 tanks which are in the pipeline on the ground to do the job. Months of diplomatic measures may be needed as part of the show before the defensive posture can be allowed to appear offensive. Waiting until after the November election is preferable. The State Department must give the world the appearance of exhausting all peaceful means. Efforts at embargoes and blockades will be useful to strangle the Iraqi economy and keep Saddam from paying his bills and feeding his army during the build-up phase. But these measures won't be enough to turn him back from his new prize. There will ultimately have to be a war. Iraq can last for two years before Saddam has to fight or run. In the end, the war for a future peace will have to be fought now. This much is clear: The U.S. will eventually retake Kuwait. Iraq will be bombed back to the Middle Ages. And Saddam Hussein will be relieved of his command, his nuclear weapon's facility and possibly his life.

A little comic relief: Baker was meeting with Shevernadze minutes before the crossing and the secretary of state told the Soviet what was about to take place. Shevernadze replied that he had no reports of that nature and that he had been assured by Saddam, himself, that nothing of the sort would happen. Moments later an aid told Baker that it was underway and, when he relayed the news to Shevernadze, the embarrassed Soviet Foreign Minister had to excuse himself to call home to verify.

Classified: Presidential Briefing
BCASEE: 8-3-90
The liberating of Kuwait will happen whether or not any international sanctions are made and hold; whether or not the international community joins in the military action; whether or not anyone else helps to foot the bill. The invasion of Kuwait and its freedom is just a matter of time. Time and M-I tanks.

We suggest the Oval Office make the following early prediction: Saddam won't leave Kuwait on his own. The U.S. (and any allies we can muster) will ultimately escort him out. We also suggest a "line in the sand" rhetoric to stall Hussein from going deeper into SA. "This will not stand" must have only one meaning to the U.S. Military. Saddam Hussein's army will not stand. Iraq will eventually be leaving Kuwait. Access to cheap oil will be guaranteed. And the new Nebuchadnezzar will be gone in the post-Desert Shield world.

Classified: Presidential Briefing
BCASEE: 8-24-90
As for American hostages, they might be asked to pay the price. It is an ugly possibility and Bush may be personally repulsed by the stance he will be forced to take. But he must not be immobilized by the fate of the few when the fate of the many is held in the balance. He must not be 'Carterized' into impotency. No, the hostages must be secondary to any course of action. Saddam must never know how much they mean to the West. He must be led to believe that Bush, Thatcher, Mitterand and Kohl consider them expendable. Intelligence paints a grim picture of their fate in the

event of an Allied attack. Our crack anti-terrorist units will do everything they can to free as many as possible, but there will be no guarantees. The invasion and bombing will happen on schedule. The U.S. will make overtures and sue for peace with Saddam's successors. Large numbers of hostages will possibly come home in body bags with the 2-5,000 expected American soldiers - if they come home at all. That will be the price of freedom.

The major read on and on, wondering where this report could have originated. He sifted through a mental Rolladex trying to remember the CIA and NSA writers he had read and their styles. But this didn't sound like anyone he had met or read before. Was this BCASEE simply a renegade who wrote and was dismissed? Or was this a group who had the president's ear and were directing policy? He shuddered at the possibilities as he came to the last entries. Fran's own name was on the screen.

Classified: Presidential Briefing
BCASEE: 9-11-90
Khalil is correct. Saddam must believe he is the target. Using Dugan for the leak will solve two problems for us. It will put our man in place and also get the message across to Saddam. Our experts agree that Hussein won't turn tail and run, but he will grow more paranoid. This paranoia will play into our hands very nicely whether we decide his removal is our goal or not. As the situation plays out, we may opt to keeping a castrated Saddam rather than chance an unknown.

Classified: Presidential Briefing
BCASEE: 9-15-90
Good work on Dugan. Send someone to talk to Glaspie before she goes to the Hill.

The major turned off the screen and sat back to raise a glass towards Fran's empty chair. "*Semper fi,* buddy. *Semper fi.*" Shaking his head in disbelief, antique tri-focals slipped down his ski-slope nose and onto the keyboard below. The machine blanked out a moment and opened another file. It was an order form to the quartermaster for boots: 150,000 canvas boots. Canvas desert boots.

And it was dated 7/17/90.

Chapter 41: Kathryn's Fury
The Pentagon
December 20, 1990

"Where is he!" Kathryn was ready to tear the major's throat out with her fingernails. "Where did you send him?"

The Old Man hadn't expected to see Fran's young wife in the situation room. "How did you get in here?"

"He leaves the house in the middle of the night spouting something about April Glaspie and a conspiracy. The next morning he's gone and you tell me he can't be reached. Yesterday you say he's missing. Now you say he isn't. What's going on here? Nobody will tell me anything."

"Calm down, little missy..."

"Don't you 'little missy' me! Either I get some answers or I call my friends at CBS."

The mention of the media caught the major off guard. He poured a lukewarm cup of coffee from his thermos and tried to serve it to the seething woman. She slapped it from his hand.

"I asked you a question. I want an answer."

The major placed a finger over his lips as if to 'shush' the captain's wife. "Let's... ah... let's go to lunch."

"I don't want to go to lunch! I've had it with your patronizing attitude. I want to know what you've done with my husband! And I want to know now!"

He scrawled a note on a 3M Post-it and tried to hand it to Kathryn. She read it quickly, crumpled it and threw it in his face. "No! Here and now!"

Two MPs came in from behind to escort her out. The major pointed them instead to the conference room door. She tried to fight back, but it was no use. They "accompanied" her into the room and blocked the exit. There she sat for 15 minutes. Finally the major entered the room followed by a man in a $1,200 suit she had never met before. They sat but she remained standing.

"Mrs. Khalil," began the stranger, "we have been monitoring your husband's movements inside Kuwait and are aware of his disappearance. Due to the sensitive nature of this mission, however, we are unable to give you any specifics at this time. He may simply be lying low and staying out of sight. "

"Someone's lying, all right. But it's not Francis. Your story and the major's story don't begin to match. I want to know the truth."

"We are terribly sorry about this whole ordeal and can understand your grief..."

"Kathryn, we're doing the best we can under the circum..."

"He knew about the whole plan. He talked to Glaspie and found out..." A silent alarm spread across the unknown man's face. Kathryn knew she had made a mistake and stopped mid-sentence.

"And what exactly did he find out from Glaspie?"

She quickly played dumb. "How am I supposed to know? He leaves the house in the middle of the night and disappears for the weekend. Then he calls me and tells me he's going to Iraq to talk to the Shiites. I get a call from your baboons that he's supposed to be missing. Then he's not. Now he is again. What am I supposed to think?"

The major reached to console her. Kathryn's first instinct was to lash out, but she forced herself to accept his gesture and feigned a teary collapse. He cleared his throat: "Kathryn, Francis is my friend, too. I was the one who brought him here in the first place. Don't you think I'm concerned? We're doing everything in our power to find him and get him out. Everything. You have my word on it. My word."

Kathryn could see the major glaring at the other man through the large mirror behind her. There was something going on here that she couldn't understand.

One of the MPs brought in a sedative and a glass of water. She accepted it, sliding the pill under her tongue and pretending to swallow.

"I'm sorry. I don't know who to blame. I'm so frightened. I just want him home."

The major nodded and held her for another uncomfortable moment. "We'll... ah... I'll let you know as soon as I hear anything. I promise." He continued to provide an awkward shoulder until she stopped crying. "You want a driver?"

"No, I'll be OK."

"You sure?"

"Yes." Kathryn sniffled a while longer to make it look good, then apologized before excusing herself. She had places to go.

Before settling on a teaching certificate and an English degree, this bright young woman had done a journalism internship with Ben Bradlee at the *Washington Post*. Maybe somebody over there would listen.

The gnarled old warrior grabbed the spook by his arm as he made for the door. "You tell your boss over there that I'd better be getting some answers on this or I'll go to the networks, myself."

The man in the $1,200 suit scoffed at the bluff. "You're too close to retirement old man. I don't think you'd dare."

The major's iron grip tightened and he stared the fellow down. "Watch me, boy. You just watch me."

Chapter 42: The Haj
A Gulf Shore
December 21, 1990

They stepped silently out of the surf, two shadows in a sea of shadows. Infrared goggles made a green haze of the blackest of nights as moving shapes and figures turned into men before their very eyes. Francis stood in amazement at what he saw before him. There, stretching up and down a quarter mile of coast, two dozen Navy SEALs worked their magic: disconnecting wires, unhooking lines and disarming mines. When the Iraqis woke in three hours they would find irrefutable evidence of preparations for the Allied beach assault; an assault that was never to be. It would shake them, haunt them and send their sleeping sentries to the firing squad. For the work that had taken them three months to accomplish would have been dismantled in one night. And no one would have the slightest idea of how it had come to pass.

Fran crouched low in the knee-deep water aside a grease-faced magician, waiting for his signal. The sailor nodded to acknowledge his presence and continued on with his underwater torch, working without a sound. The escort spotted it first: a cigarette being lit in a jeep about 65 yards up the shore. The lone driver brought flame to a second, then a third smoke and puffed all three for a while. Then he threw two out in opposite directions and stood.

"That's your contact, captain. We'll meet you at the pickup point in 48 hours with or without your Mr. *Wausau*. Hope you enjoy your stay in Province 19. Don't forget to write."

Fran accepted a wet handshake and rose, anxious to finally meet the man the resistance called "good night."

It was Friday and the Moslem Sabbath had begun. The call to prayer was over and men were picking up shoes at the mosque door to return to their homes. In a corner portico of the building, a group of 35 angry young zealots waited for the Baath Party representative to resume his discussion - a sales pitch interrupted by the tower voice which had called them to prayerful submission. A pair of inconspicuous and uninvited guests listened from the rear of the crowd, trying not to appear too interested.

The official returned to face the faithful, keeping his back carefully to the wall. An Iraqi guard with a machine pistol remained alert near the side door. The man lowered his glasses and scanned from side to side. Then he offered a quasi-religious invocation and got back to business:

"Is not all Saudi soil sacred to the faithful? Does it matter whether the American and Allied troops are in the center of the Holy City or 500 miles away on an aircraft carrier? The infidel is here. He puts a rifle in the hands of his naked-legged women and calls them soldiers to insult us. He pays the Jew-dogs and Christian mercenaries in his army to hold prayer meetings in the open to defile us. He pays them! Calls them chaplains! This is a fact. They do not even deny it! We are desecrated every moment he remains."

A handsome young man with raven-black curls sitting next to the strangers scoffed under his breath. "This decadent Baathist talks to us about desecration? He desecrates our mosque with his presence now." *Shobash* and Khalil nodded in agreement.

"Our Father-Leader is no fool. As early as August when our guards began confiscating Kuwaiti passports at the border, he knew that there would come a day when these could be used for the glory of Islam. For the glory of the Arab world. That day is soon upon us."

The crowd stirred, more in suspicion than fervor.

"Picture it: The Haj. The faithful coming to Medina and Mecca. Millions of the most devout and dedicated Moslems from across the world making their once-in-a-lifetime pilgrimage to the holy shrines of Islam. It will be an explosive situation." The official's voice took on a pompous tone as he reached his hands to the heavens. "It will begin in March. Security will be tight. The Saudi Royal Family already knows they are in for trouble. But they cannot begin to imagine just what trouble they will see! American troops will be vulnerable. They will, for the most part, be confined to base. This will serve us well. With millions crossing for Haj, Saudi Arabia will be a pomegranate ripe to be plucked; a territory set for revolution and revenge. We will not be alone in this. Do not forget that the commander of Iran's own revolutionary guard has claimed the U.S. involvement in Saudi Arabia to be *Jihad*. Any Holy Warrior killed in battle against the infidel will be a martyr. We will provide the passports. We will provide the coordination. With a few thousand of you ready, everything will be in place. Like Sadat before them, the Royal Family will pay for their collusion with the Jew and the Great Satan, America."

He shifted positions and reached out his hands to the men. "And so, will you come? Tens and hundreds at first, later thousands. Each with one holy calling: to disrupt the ceremonies; to drive the Americans from our sacred soil; to destroy the puppet Saudi Family and restore the land of Mohammed to the faithful. Will you be among them?"

The Baath official ended his plea with a registration form and a card. If any of the "faithful" wished to join Saddam's plan for Haj, they could sign up now and live the next two months with a healthy stipend and a reasonably healthy whore. (Francis kept the card. It would make a great souvenir.)

When the salesman and his bodyguard were carefully out of sight, an elderly mullah spoke in a hushed tone to those who remained: "It takes a holy man to call for holy war. And Saddam Hussein al Takriti is not a holy man. We will one day give the order and you, my brothers, will be the catalyst for the Islamic world to hemorrhage from within. We may, indeed, take the pilgrimage to set up a new order of holiness in Saudi Arabia. But it won't be this year. And it won't be for the infidel Saddam Hussein. The flag of a new Islamic Republic will one day rise to guard our sacred soil and bathe these satans - Baathist and American alike - in the blood of the moon. It will arise. Of that you can be sure. And on that day, the new Islamic Republic of Arabia will become the bank that funds *jihad* throughout the next millennium and fans its purifying flames across the face of the world."

The faithful closed with a repetitious chorus of *Allah akhbars* interspersed with the usual "death to America's" before breaking up and going their separate ways.

Khalil and *Shobash* vanished together into the open bazaar, unsure of their next move. The first half of the mission would have to be put on hold. Neither believed that this was the most opportune time to discuss American partnership and covert aid with the Shiites of southern Iraq.

Chapter 43: Triple Cross
The Iraq/Kuwait Border
December 22, 1990

The return trip from Basara had been rather uneventful. That was just fine with Francis. Instead of taking the highway at *Al Zubayr*, they opted to follow the rail lines south and not chance being detained at the checkpoints on the Kuwaiti border. The night was bright, the air cool and clear. Francis hadn't remembered seeing so many stars since his boyhood days on the prairies of eastern Montana. They drove along the rutted road without words or headlights, Francis watching the driver as he watched the night. It occurred to the American that he knew very little about his host. *Shobash* was obviously a man of principle. With the daring and smarts to slip in and out of a heavily guarded Iraq, this man clearly could have escaped Kuwait at any time he chose. Instead, he opted to remain and fight. From what Khalil had been told on the submarine, *Shobash* had personally been involved in some of the most daring operations the resistance had mounted. His people had hidden, fed and smuggled over a hundred Westerners out of the country. Francis was curious. "Tell me what you've seen in these last months."

"What I've seen? What I've seen. What I've seen." For a full minute *Shobash* was lost, captured, entranced by the memories.

"I'm sorry, you don't have to tell me anything if you don't want to."

The Kuwaiti shook his head as if needing to continue. "No. No, you must know this." He sighed heavily and his eyes began to tear. "We have been raped. That is all I can say. My country has been raped."

They drove together but alone for a long while before *Shobash* could offer more. Francis waited. "Our hospitals, our schools, businesses, homes. We are violated a hundred times every day. A thousand times. They have entered and systematically ransacked our houses. Streetlights are taken from the ground to be sent back to Iraq or sold on the black market. They take tiles from the walls. Tiles from the walls! The rutting swine dig up sewer pipes from our streets with their bare hands and steal them away. I would not doubt if they are selling our excrement for cooking fires in Baghdad! It is as if a cloud of locusts has descended and eaten us alive."

"Kuwaiti women have been treated in the most of shameful ways. Kuwaiti men with any connection to the government and ruling family are disappearing by the hundreds and reappearing with fingernails torn out, burns and electrical marks, body parts missing. When the shock troops have had their fun, the mangled corpses are sent directly home and families are charged 1500 to 2000 *dinars* to receive them. A handling fee."

"Sounds like '1984' doesn't it?" *Shobash* flashed a question mark at the Marine. "It's a book." He changed the subject. "And the resistance?"

"When the reality of the invasion set in, immediately the boldest of my brothers mounted as organized a resistance as they could scrape together. You must understand, we are shop keepers and merchants, not professional soldiers. Under the circumstance we did quite well. Fire-bombings and drive-by shootings were our preferred mode of attack. One 18 year old Kuwati drove a truck filled with explosives into a building and killed 25 Iraqis. She was a cousin of my Nadia. We quickly made her a hero and martyr. But the brutality of the reprisal shook us. We became weary.

"When Iraq instituted its policy of executing hundreds of innocents with each act of so-called 'terrorism,' the heart was torn out of our rebellion. Within a few months, 75% of Kuwaitis have either fled or died trying. We have dwindled. We have starved. Each night we listen to BBC and curse you for stalling, pray you to come. We cannot understand what you Americans are waiting for. Every day's delay is another day for Saddam to increase his strangle hold here. Time is not on our side. Maybe it is on yours, but it is certainly not on ours. If you could tell me why in the bloody hell you are stalling, I'd be forever in your debt."

Francis knew why the U.S. was stalling. The politics of the situation had dictated a policy of total victory with minimal casualties. If America was going to go to war at all, she would go only after sufficient resources were amassed to smother Iraq in a matter of days. "This operation could not be done if it could not be won. The logistics of moving this many soldiers and this much material this far has, in actual terms, taken very little time."

"Talk to the dead of Kuwait about your speed." The Kuwaiti spit at the night. "Talk to your own hostages who pray for your coming. Talk to the 300 of *Mina Al Ahmadi* who were slaughtered last Thursday. Taken out into the streets and gunned down."

Francis changed the subject. "Tell me about the hostages."

"Hostages?"

"You know. The Americans."

Shobash laughed and spat again. "What a provincial view you spout! We are all hostages, my friend."

They drove on, Francis resisting the urge to question further. A few minutes passed before the mysterious philosopher continued. "Excuse me for insulting you. That 'provincial' saying is a line from my Nadia. You wanted to know of the Western hostages, I suppose?" Francis nodded. "Ah yes, the Westerners." He sighed again. "In the beginning your people were rounded up one at a time. Any man, woman or child unfortunate enough to be walking the streets of Kuwait City and later of Baghdad was fair game. After a month, the effort became more diabolical. In order to get a family's documents cleared, the men were required to sign for their women and children. Those who showed up to see families off were arrested on the spot and hauled away as they said their goodbyes. Once most of the women and children had been lifted out, the search became methodical and pervasive. The Iraqis were clever. Bank and business records were studied and traced to lead secret police and army special forces to their prey. Promises of food and threats of execution followed later. The government insisted on food stamps being redeemed in person for anyone wishing supplies.

"After the first 'detainees' were shot while trying to escape, the situation became even more brutal. We tried to help our Western friends but many of my people were executed and hung publicly when it was found that they had harbored a fugitive. We tried to hide as many as we could but it became increasingly more difficult. Whenever they were apprehended here they were immediately spirited away to Iraq for a more sinister fate."

The jeep came upon a herd of camels with a small Bedouin boy trailing along behind. *Shobash* greeting the lad and asked if he had seen any Iraqi patrols in the area. He said that some soldiers were camped at the junction about two miles up the line. The boy suggested they take a nearby oil rig road to the east. They could turn south at a lone rock outcropping to reconnect with their road. *Shobash* thanked the child and threw him a small golden object before driving off. It looked curiously like the diamond cigarette case which Francis noticed in the possession of the Baath official at the mosque earlier that day.

"What was that?"

"A gift."

Francis smiled. "You were talking about the hostages taken to Iraq."

"Oh yes. In the first weeks the 'detainees' were sent in groups of 10-35 as Iraqi 'guests' at a handful of electrical plants, factories, air fields and fuel dumps. Saddam's advisers were, at that time, envisioning 1,700 human shields to guard every major target in the country."

The jeep rolled over to the top of a mound of sand and *Shobash* slammed the brakes, stopping less than five feet from the edge of a deep ravine.

"Maybe we should drive with the lights on."

Shobash backed up without responding or turning to the lights and looked for a way around the *wadi*. "What were we saying?"

"Hostages," returned Francis.

"Hostages. Yes, hostages. We are all hostages, my friend." They drove on. "From your Kurds in *Zab al Kabir* to the walking corpses of *Al Jahrah* to the soldiers in Saddam's own army. We are all hostages of someone else's will. Hostages of fear. Hostages of duty. Even your brothers oiling their weapons in Saudi Arabia tonight, every one of them is a hostage. Every one a victim."

"How do you mean?"

"They did not ask to be here. They did not choose to be here. Someone else made that decision for them. And they will not ask to die, my friend. A handful of men at the very top will make that decision for them, too. The few sign a paper or shake a hand for the many and the bombs begin to fall. When it is all over a million lie dead, a world lies in waste and those royal few go on as if it had not happened at all. Saddam Hussein and Bush - these are the only ones who are not hostages in all of this. They have the choices. Oh yes, the Emir and a few of his cronies. They may be in exile at the moment, but they are not hostages. The rest of us are but simple pawns in their game; disposables to be used and discarded when no longer needed. Yes, we are all hostages, my friend. The one who kills and the ones who are killed - victims. I am. And so are you."

Francis hadn't asked for a political science lecture. A half-hour was spent before he ventured to ask another question.

A tense moment came when they crossed the *Wadi al Batin* and were immediately flagged down by an Iraqi colonel walking along the deserted back road. *Shobash* thought first of running the man off and slitting his throat, but changed his mind abruptly and opted for another plan when he noticed the brass on his sleeves. Instead of killing him, they would give him a ride and use his presence as passage insurance.

The Iraqi was limping and smelled of whiskey and cheap perfume. He told them a story of being separated from his unit during training exercises and said that he needed to catch a ride back to Kuwait City. *Shobash* explained that they were Palestinian oil workers as Francis flashed their perfectly prepared papers. (The people who took care of Raoul Wallenberg's documents had done it again. They knew their craft well.)

As they drove, their hitch-hiker loosened up and told them the true story. The officer had, indeed, been separated from his men but it wasn't in the line of duty. He had been to a brothel. And he wasn't limping because he had been wounded. He was sore for other reasons.

The colonel came in handy once at the border and twice within five minutes of entering Kuwait City. He must have been fairly well known, for each time they were stopped, the patrols took one look at him and waved them on without question. When they finally dropped off their fortunate passenger at his hotel, the man tried to pay them for their troubles. Francis was taking the money when *Shobash* objected. "Just give us your name and a unit number. Maybe we need a favor someday."

He scribbled his name and detachment down on the Marine's road map and invited them both in for a drink.

"Not tonight," grinned the Kuwaiti. "I, too, have a woman waiting for me this night. And you know how dangerous they can be if you keep them waiting! I would rather face *Shobash* in a dark alley than to be late for this appointment." The colonel laughed and wished them well.

They pulled out. "Why did you want his name?"

"It's good to have friends in high places." *Shobash* held the paper to the streetlight. "Maybe we will use it to pass a road block. Maybe we use it to forge some documents. Then maybe we set him up as an Israeli spy and have him shot." He laughed.

They drove down to the port at *Ash Shuwaykh* and pulled in along the pier. "This is it." The resistance fighter pointed to the four story warehouse directly in front of them and took up his weapon. "This is where we meet the second half of our challenge. My people tell me that the man *Wausau* has been transmitting from this building for six nights now. Before that his broadcasts were monitored intermittently from a number of different sites about the warehouse district. We had rumors of an American agent operating in this sector but were never able to verify them."

Shobash slid a metal door open just wide enough to slip through and motioned his guest to follow. "The Iraqis have been paranoid for some time about American spies preparing the city for the amphibious assault. We help to spread the rumors as much as we can, centering them on Kuwait City, itself, so as to tie up regiments there and keep them away from our smuggling lines. Actually, our regular contact with the Navy SEALs happens here. We smuggle Western citizens out and arms in from this very bay. No one would suspect the Americans to have the audacity to come in right under their noses. At least we hope no one would."

"Will you know this *Wausau* when you see him?" Francis was beginning to get a little nervous.

"We have heard his broadcasts and found remnants of his activities. But never have we been able to track him down. He is known only by a name. Only by a legend. Who knows, maybe he is a ghost. Maybe he doesn't exist at all."

"He exists. Or at least someone by that name does."

"A week ago we monitored him arranging his own escape with the Allies over the radio. That was the last we heard of him. We assumed he had left. But on this past Saturday night his broadcasts began anew and these were urgent. This time he didn't speak. He only tapped a Morse code indicating that he was being hunted, pleading to be brought out. He also said that he had come upon maps of all the mines in the harbor. I believe that this is what prompted your people to send you for him."

"How did you finally track him down?"

"I was contacted by members of my own government-in-exile to assist you. An old acquaintance - Bahrah al Sabah. He and his people are the ones who told me that *Wausau* is here. Otherwise we would not have been able to find him."

"You trust your people?"

"What do you mean?"

"This could be Iraqi agents using *Wausau's* legend to catch an even bigger fish. A fish like you."

He shook his head. "I trust my people." *Shobash* pulled out an Uzi from under his cloak and began the search in earnest. Climbing nine steps on four separate flights of stairs, they reached the rooftop and forced a rusted fire door open. Startled pigeons cooed from a nearby cage. A small tin coffee pot perked on a glowing blue kerosene stove and an M-16 sat propped in the corner next to a ham radio antenna. T-shirts and boxer shorts flapped together with an oversized woman's dress in the evening breeze.

"This is it," whispered the Kuwaiti. "But where is our man?"

"Are you sure he is a man?"

"Coffee's *on*. *Wausau's* been here in the last 10 minutes. Or someone has."

"Maybe we scared him off." They searched the dusty rooftop but found no one. Francis scanned a dark horizon to take his bearings.

"Do you wish to split up?"

"That's OK. I'd feel more comfortable if we stuck together on this one." They were turning back to the staircase when he heard it: something like the sound of an automobile door latching in the streets below. *Shobash* squinted at the shadows. Was there a car parked out on the end of the wharf? The world was all too black to tell.

"I don't like it. Let's get out of here."

The sudden blinding flash of a white hot flare made instant daylight of the blanket that had hidden them. Francis slid to the north side of the flat roof in time to catch the silhouette of an Iraqi Army truck emptying a dozen men and three dogs onto the pier. In the fading light he could make out the shapes of two or three other vehicles with scores of soldiers piling out on the west side. Then again all was black. The streets whispered and a cautious ascent began on the fire escape as men crept in to take position.

A cheap bull horn barked a "hold fire" order, then aimed its nasal voice toward the roof as a second flare lit the night: "Good evening, Ali al Bakr. Or should I say 'Shobash' Shobash! And also to you, Captain Francis Khalil. It would be my distinct pleasure to visit with the two of you alive tonight. If, however, you should choose..."

The voice sputtered off and his threat could not be heard above the sudden frenzy of advancing dogs and men.

PART IV
The Storm

Chapter 44: The Man from Wausau
Wausau Insurance Building, Wausau, Wisconsin
December 24, 1990

The crowd in Ed's imagination cheered and burst into a spontaneous applause, followed by a robust rendition of "For He's A Jolly Good Fellow." A fit and trim Lippencott jumped up to the podium, skipping the stairs entirely, and began his speech. The women in the office drooled in admiration. The men, and most notably his boss, nodded and applauded with a respect rarely granted anyone earning under six figures in corporate America.

"Is it wrong to miss a war?" Ed began. "I can honestly say I do. For it was there, surrounded by danger, laughing death in the face each dreary day, that I came to see the meaning of life. There are stories I long to tell but cannot for national security sake. There are people left behind who are suffering even as we celebrate, sacrificing to make the world free for you and me. Would I do it again? Risk it all again for duty, honor and company? As a wise man once said: "You only go around once in...""

Ed was practicing so intently in the rearview mirror that he didn't see the mini-van in front of him slam its brakes to let a dog pass. He swerved the best he could, but still managed to clip the rear bumper. The jolt pushed Ed's face into the steering wheel just hard enough to break his glasses but not hard enough to really hurt him.

The old Edward LaVine Lippencott would have been shaken enough by such an incident to insist on a complete emergency ward exam. (Prior to his stint in occupied Kuwait, Ed was the kind of obsessive compulsive who had his own handwriting analyzed yearly just to be sure he hadn't developed any new psychotic tendencies in the last 12 months.) The new Ed was bound and determined not to let a little thing like this get to him. After all, once you've faced the Iraqi army, what can Wisconsin traffic do to you?

Lippencott got out of the car, unaware that his nose was bleeding and more than prepared to give the other driver a piece of his mind. He looked through the steam and spray to view the accordion that used to be the front of his new Hyundai. The other vehicle, it appeared, had escaped without a scratch. "American made."

The old Ed had learned a few things in actuarial school that the new Ed was ready to put into practice. The first was to never admit guilt. The second - to immediately get the name of the other driver and his insurance company. Ed approached his adversary, ready to play tough. But the moment she rolled down her over-tinted glass, the big man's plan fell apart. The driver was an old lady. Ed couldn't be mean to an old lady.

"You... you all right?"

"What's that, sonny?"

"I asked if you were all right?"

"To hell with me! What about my car?'

"Your car's fine. Just fine. It's mine that's lying all over the pavement."

"What's that?"

"I said your car's just fine." The thin veneer of Ed's calm demeanor was beginning to wear. "May I get your name and..."

"It's fine, eh?"

"Yes, fine. Just fine. Now may I have your..."

"Good thing!" she yelled, rolling up the electric windows. "I don't have any insurance. See ya, sonny!"

She drove off.

Ed waited for the tow truck while muttering something about the "Russian Roulette" game decent, God-fearing Americans played each day driving around among the chronically under-insured. Then he walked the remaining three miles through ankle-deep slush to corporate headquarters. Lippencott was not about to miss his division's combination Christmas and "Welcome Home Ed" party.

Madge at the front desk was the first to notice him. "Ed! You've lost weight." She gave him the once-over. "But you look like shit." The former Miss Oshkosh Dairy Princess handed him a box of Kleen-ex and asked about his weight loss technique.

"You wouldn't want to try it. Trust me." He thanked her for the compliment and stepped over to the door to make his grand entrance. Streamers and presents, garlands and bows filled the brightly decorated commons. A huge "Merry Christmas" sign rotated and blinked above the crowd. People were milling about, laughing and singing as Ed wedged his way into the party.

Ed's former boss nodded as he passed, but didn't leave his conversation to say hello. Mavis Wright and Marlene something-or-other said "hi," but were on their way to the ladies' room. Bill Hutch patted him on the fanny and took the drink out of his hand. Mildred Smoeckle winked at him from across the room. If her hair hadn't stood a foot and a half above her head, Ed might have considered the woman attractive. He slipped through the crowd and headed toward the food table.

Ed was poking the pimento out of an olive with a toothpick when he saw it: An 8 1/2 x 11 magic-markered "Welcome Home Ed!" sign next to the copy machine. Straightening immediately up, he grabbed a handful of olives and a box of toothpicks to march over and stand by his monument.

Natches, the custodian, noticed it first. "Welcome home, Ed."

"Thank you. Why, thank you. It's been quite an ordeal."

"I was just reading the sign. You been gone?"

Lippencott smiled until he realized that the man was not joking. He walked on. The boss finally removed himself from his conversation and stepped up behind his boy, gripping him by the shoulder. "Ed, welcome home. We're proud of you."

"Why thank you sir. May I call you Jim?"

"Not around the office."

"Yes, sir."

"You got a minute?"

"Well, I was just..."

"Come on."

Jim took Ed aside into his own office and offered him a seat. "Ed, we here at the company are proud of you for what you've done. It must have been hell."

"Yes sir, it was. I've never had to kill a man before... not in the line of duty."

The boss looked at him for a moment in a half horror, then slapped Ed on the back and let out a huge laugh. "Not in the line of duty. Ha! That's rich. Anyway, I wanted to be the first to congratulate you on your promotion."

"Promotion, sir? Why, I'm... I'm speechless. It makes all the suffering and sacrifice, the endless nights of dep..."

"Yes, well, about the promotion."

"Yes sir?"

"It doesn't involve a raise. Not just yet. But there is great potential. Great potential."

Ed was hoping for a raise.

"We're talking virgin territory. Limitless supply of clients. No end to what the right man can do for himself in a situation like this."

"In the States?"

"Nope."

"Not the Middle East."

"The Middle East? Ha!" The boss laughed again. "What a joker."

Ed was relieved. "Sir, I was hoping to be reassigned somewhere quiet. Someplace nice and peaceful where they never make a claim. Like the

Hawaiian Islands or a retirement community on the south coast of Florida."

The boss laughed again and handed Ed his tickets and a brochure. He read the destination. "Where's this?"

"Picture it: Beautiful river valley. Peaceful little European town nestled in the trees on the coast. A place that hasn't been touched by the ravages of war in 400 years. And a country on the verge of economic boom with thousands of cottage industries ripe and ready to become major exporters. All of these waiting, just waiting for the right man, the right company to knock on their doors and sell them business insurance."

"Business insurance?"

"That's right, Ed. And that right man is you."

"Me, sir?"

"Edward R. Lippencott."

"Edward L., sir."

"The tested and true! The hero of international intrigue and insurance. The man -THE man from Wausau. You Ed. You."

"Sir, I thank you for your confidence in me, but..."

"You are the man, Ed. THE man."

"Sir, I..."

"Destiny calls."

"I'd like to think about..."

"You're our first choice. But we could always find someone else for this promotion."

Ed hesitated and weighed the price of returning the ticket in his hand against the price of taking it. "I, ah..."

"Yes?"

"I... I won't let you down, sir."

"I knew it! Ed, you're the man. THE man. You fly out tomorrow."

"Tomorrow? But it's Christma..."

"The world is at your feet, Ed. You can't leave it waiting."

"I suppose not, sir."

The boss excused himself back to the party, but turned at the door. "One more thing." He stepped to his desk and pulled a note from the 'out' box. "A woman's been calling for you."

"A woman?"

"English woman. Somehow tracked you down here and wanted to be sure we had you give her a call as soon as you got back."

Ed read the note and the number. It was Karin Kensington. "May I use your phone, sir?"

"Certainly, Ed." The boss pulled out his chair and motioned Ed to sit.

"Thank you, sir."

"Oh. And Ed?"

"Yes, sir?"

"Be sure and charge it to your own credit card. Company policy, you know."

"Thank you, sir."

He left.

The phone rang nine times. Ed didn't know what hour it was in London, but it was now going on 4 p.m. in Wisconsin. A weary little voice answered.

"Yes?"

"Karin Kensignton, please."

"She's asleep."

"Tell her Ed Lippen... Edwina Bond-Wausauheimer is calling."

The phone dropped and Ed could hear a scream on the other side. "Mummy! Mummy! It's about daddy!"

"Yes? Hello? Yes?"

"Just calling to wish you a Merry Christmas and send hopes for a grand New Year."

"Do you know anything more? About my Stewart?"

"Sorry to say I don't. But I'm sure he'll be out soon. I, myself, just made it back, as a matter of fact. They're throwing a little party for me here at the office even as we speak." Ed cracked opened the door so the sounds from the other room could filter in. "I've got to get back to my party, but I just wanted to call and wish you well."

"Thank you, Ed. It means a lot."

"This'll all be over before you know it and you'll have your man back."

"You think so?"

"I can't tell you everything I know, but I can assure you that you have every reason to hope."

"Thanks. I needed to hear that. Especially tonight."

"And KiKi?" (Karin's husband always called her KiKi.)

"Yes?"

"Keep a stiff upper lip." Ed never knew what that meant, but he had always liked the sound of it.

"How can we ever thank you?"

"Just doing my job, ma'am."

"May I... may I ask your real name? So the children can keep you in their prayers?"

"I suppose that wouldn't hurt." He straightened up. "The name is Lippencott. Edward L. Lippencott. You can call me Ed."

"And you are... an agent, Ed? Or shouldn't I ask?"

"An agent?" Ed gazed out the door at the office party and his "'Welcome Home" sign above the copy machine. His eyes fell next to the airline ticket he held in his hand. "An agent? Yes, ma'am. I'm an agent. But let's just keep that between us and the children."

"God bless you, Agent Lippencott. Ed."

"He all ready has, ma'am. He all ready has."

"I don't know what I would have done without you."

"All in the line of duty, Kiki. Well, Cheerio." Ed had always wanted to say that, too.

He paused for a moment in the boss's office looking out at the snow, proud to be associated with such a fine man as himself. Then he marched back to the party to stand by his magic-markered memorial and receive his guests.

Ed toothpicked a few more pimentos, downed an Egg Nog and popped a Maalox. Having only been home for a week, American food had yet to agree with him. The big man read the boarding times on his airline ticket once again and paged through a brochure on his new destination. The place looked so serene - river valleys and all. He had never heard of Dubrovnik before. But it sounded like a peaceful little town in Iowa. Dubrovnik. Best of all, it was a thousand miles away from the war.

Chapter 45: The President's Letter
Geneva, Switzerland
January 5, 1991

They managed a few tense smiles for the cameras before the Secret Service ushered the media out of the room. Secretary Baker handed the letter to Iraq's foreign minister. Aziz glanced it over quickly and pushed it back across the table. "I'm sorry, but I cannot deliver this."

"What are you talking about?"

"I come for a letter from one president to another. What I see here is not a letter, but threats."

"I'm afraid you don't understand the gravity of the situation. As the letter states..."

"No, I'm afraid it is you who do not understand," interrupted Aziz. "This letter contains inappropriate language for correspondence between heads of state. I will not deliver it."

The foreign minister stood abruptly and walked out.

Baker shook his head. He had come to expect surprises from Aziz, but never in a million years had he thought it would come to this. An aide picked the presidential statement from the table to tuck it away, but his boss motioned for it. Baker pushed his chair back to re-read the carefully crafted document. The aides waited behind him, stunned to silence by the suicidal nature of the Iraqi's position and the brevity of their terse exchange.

Mr. President:

We stand today at the brink of war between Iraq and the world. This is a war that began with your invasion of Kuwait; this is a war that can be ended only by Iraq's full and unconditional compliance with U.N. Security Council Resolution 678.

I am writing you now, directly, because what is at stake demands that no opportunity be lost to avoid what would be a certain calamity for the people of Iraq. I am writing, as well, because it is said by some that you do not understand just how isolated Iraq is and what Iraq faces as a result.

I am not in a position to judge whether this impression is correct; what I can do, though, is try in this letter to reinforce what Secretary of State Baker told your Foreign Minister and eliminate any uncertainty or ambiguity that might exist in your mind about where we stand and what we are prepared to do.

The international community is united in its call for Iraq to leave all of Kuwait without condition and without further delay. This is not simply the policy of the United States; it is the position of the world community as expressed in no less than 12 Security Council resolutions.

We prefer a peaceful outcome. However, anything less than full compliance with U.N. Security Council Resolution 678 and its predecessors is unacceptable.

There can be no reward for aggression. Nor will there be any negotiation. Principle cannot be compromised. However, by its full compliance, Iraq will gain the opportunity to rejoin the international community.

More immediately, the Iraqi military establishment will escape destruction. But unless you withdraw from Kuwait completely and without condition, you will lose more than Kuwait.

What is at issue here is not the future of Kuwait - it will be free, its government will be restored - but rather the future of Iraq. This choice is yours to make.

The United States will not be separated from its coalition partners. Twelve Security Council resolutions, 28 countries providing military units to enforce them, more than 100 governments complying with sanctions - all highlight the fact that it is not Iraq against the United States, but Iraq against the world.

That most Arab and Muslim countries are arrayed against you as well should reinforce what I am saying; Iraq cannot and will not be able to hold on to Kuwait or exact a price for leaving.

You may be tempted to find solace in the diversity of opinion that is American democracy. You should resist any such temptation. Diversity ought not to be confused with division. Nor should you underestimate, as others have before you, America's will.

Iraq is already feeling the effects of the sanctions mandated by the United Nations. Should war come, it will be a far greater tragedy for you and your country.

Let me state, too, that the United States will not tolerate the use of chemical or biological weapons or the destruction of Kuwait's oil fields and installations. Further, you will be held directly responsible for terrorist actions against any member of the coalition.

The American people would demand the strongest possible response. You and your country will pay a terrible price if you order unconscionable acts of this sort.

I write this letter not to threaten, but to inform. I do so with no sense of satisfaction, for the people of the United States have no quarrel with the people of Iraq.

Mr. President, U.N. Security Council Resolution 678 establishes the period before Jan. 15 of this year as a "pause of good will" so that this crisis may end without further violence.

Whether this pause is used as intended, or merely becomes a prelude to further violence, is in your hands, and yours alone. I hope you weigh your choice carefully and choose wisely, for much will depend on it.

George Bush

Baker shook his head again and turned back to his waiting entourage. "Well, gentlemen. I believe this means war."

Chapter 46: The Descent
National Athletic Stadium, Kuwait City
January 8, 1991

Francis was led blindfolded through a series of locked doors, then up a ramp and out into the light of day. The stench of death slowly melted into a stream of cool, fresh air as they pushed him onward. He could feel the ooze of blood from the cut over his eye dripping down upon his shoulder. Flies swarmed about his face and he tried helplessly to blow and shake them away without the use of his tightly chained hands. After a descent of 28 steps, the ground felt suddenly soft beneath his feet. He assumed that they were now out on the stadium field. Brightness blazed directly through the cloth that covered his eyes as they crossed the grass. Not once did the guards let up on the pressure of his aching wrists. Whispers of a thousand condemned men filtered past his ears as he counted 140 steps and started down a slippery ramp. Lights faded and the rank odor of urine and burnt flesh returned to inundate his nostrils. Francis knew where he was now. He was on his way to the Inquisition.

Down into the bowels of the stadium the new plaything was led. He stumbled on a wet staircase and fell against the stone wall, further slashing his beaten forehead. The guards pushed him on, unaware that his blindfold had slipped from his left side and he could now see. They passed by a shower room with eight stalls, each spattered with blood. An orange electrical chord with a frayed end hung in a loop from a trouble light in the center of the ceiling. They walked on through a dim locker room with a dentist's chair bolted to the floor. A beautiful dark-eyed woman in a paisley robe was mopping vomit from the floor. A door at the far end of the hall opened and three elderly mullahs were thrown into the room toward him. Francis noticed first the raw chins where beards had been freshly plucked. The victims' arms and chests were covered with small circular scabs, half the size of a penny. He thought it odd that these men had no blindfolds.

Then he looked again and realized they no longer needed them. Their blackened eye sockets had already crusted over.

The guard who held Khalil's leash greeted the mullahs in *Farsi*, the Iranian tongue. They stopped as if listening for a message from Allah, himself. Hoary heads lifted like ancient deer, searching for the source of the sound and asking who had spoken. The tormentors laughed openly at their cruel joke until noticing Khalil's loose blindfold. They cursed and cinched it tightly into place, shoving the Marine's face again into the tile in front of him. Others barked to the mullahs to squat and then paused for a smoke. The moment a match was struck Francis could sense the fear in the battered men next to him. They froze in place. Then he remembered the pattern of small burns dotting their arms and chests.

The sadists blew smoke into their prisoners' faces. Francis pulled away at first, then went limp. A strange thought almost brought him a smile: These cigarettes actually smelled better than the room around him. Why fight it? He remembered a paragraph from a book he'd once read: *"A Day in the Life of Ivan something-or-other."* It seemed that the Gulag prisoners' only joy came from their daily smoke. He drank in the sensation and for a moment forgot where he was.

A nearby door opened and Francis counted the passing steps of 10, maybe 12 children. There was not a whimper, not a cry. Only tiny shuffling feet. Another door slammed and the guards quickly stood to snuff out their cigarettes. The Iraqis pulled the victims to their feet and pushed them on in opposite directions. An order was given in Arabic that ground Khalil's racing heart to an immediate halt. He couldn't tell exactly what the officer had said, but it was either "take them out and shoot them," or "take him out and shoot him." They pushed on.

The battered American was led through three doors more. With each passage the stench grew thicker and the light grew more and more dim. Fearful images spun like a runaway reel at a cheap movie through Fran's mind's eye. He relived the jump from the warehouse roof and saw the pearl boat which first rescued, then turned him in. He relived the last grin of his friend *Shobash* and wondered how the brave man had fared. *Shobash* said he couldn't swim. A smoldering Kurdish village came to mind next and Francis watched as an Iraqi helicopter exploded into a wall of flame behind the hill. He could almost taste the yellow dust as it raised from the rooftops in honor of the victory. Now he saw Adanon, naked and grinning and beautiful, stepping down into the mountain lake. He grabbed his hat.

A cold Washington rain tapped on his face and he stood at the bottom of the steps at the Lincoln Memorial, looking up into the gentle face. He flashed across to the sea of tidy, white graves at Arlington. Now an eight year old saw his older brother's casket and heard the military band playing the Marine's Hymn. General Westmorland spoke of the tragedy of losing such a hero in Saigon when the war was supposed to be over for us. The boy flinched again with each volley of the 21-gun salute.

A tortured mind played its tricks on the exhausted soldier. Now he was looking at a Christmas album and a photo of a little girl. The child wore a darling red dress with dainty white lace across the collar. He looked again. She had Kathryn's eyes but his own smile. He heard his bride's voice fill with pride: "She looks so grown up already. Only three and yet so big." Was he was going mad or receiving a vision? Or both? He paged through the album. There were no more pictures of him.

His thoughts turned to Kathryn again. They had faced their share of problems in the handful of years they had known each other. They were so different and yet so alike. She had come close to leaving him more than once in their first year of marriage. Was it he who would leave her now? Forever? He prayed for another chance and walked on, deeper into the shadow of death.

They stopped. Keys jingled and a door was unlocked. Francis tried to ask a question but an abrupt kick forced him onto the cold floor ahead. Metal grated against metal like fingernails on a chalkboard and a door was latched. For a moment all was silent. He was alone. A flush of relief swept over him. Perhaps he wasn't to be shot. Not just yet. Perhaps he had been given the gift of an hour, a day, a lifetime - he didn't know. But he would savor the gift of that moment like no other gift he had ever received. Then he prayed.

In his first dream, Francis was walking through a maze of red doors. As he stepped into each room a small figure silhouetted against a window would turn to him and vanish. Again and again it repeated until he stood outside a black door with a red handle. He reached for the knob and threw it to the floor. The knob wasn't a knob. It was a bloody hand.

"Francis," she whispered through the half-open door.

"Adanon..." He pushed it open, leaving his own bloodied handprint at the center. She unbuttoned her shirt and let it slide to the middle of her blistered back. There were seven burns in all. They ran from her brown shoulders to below where Francis could see. "Welcome to my nightmare."

"Adanon, I..."

"Don't touch me."

"My God, what did they do to you?"

"You lied. Lied." The peshmerga turned with a full fist to his jaw, sending the Marine sprawling on the floor. She knelt with her knee between his legs. "That is for what you did to my people. And this..." she kissed him with everything she could find within her. "...this is for what you did to me."

She kissed him once again before kneeing him in the groin.

In his second dream Francis thought he was alone in his cell until someone sneezed. "Who's there? Who are you?"

"Stewart Terrance Kensington, at your service." It was an Englishman.

"British Intelligence?"

"Not quite."

"A pilot?"

"No."

"What are you in for?"

"I'm just a manager for ARAMCO. That's all. How about you? What are you in for?"

If the Brit was going to play a game, he would too. "I'm the skipper of the Exxon Valdez."

The two prisoners talked for five minutes before Kensington asked Francis if he wanted his blindfold off. The Englishman was cuffed in front so it was no problem for him to help. He used the cloth to blot up Khalil's bleeding face and rinsed it off in a sink in the corner. They talked for five minutes more before Francis realized that he wasn't dreaming.

"This is a dreary place, but we've got the only hot running water in town. They see to it that this place has plenty of it. God and a few bloody corpses are the only ones who know why."

"How long you been here?" asked Francis.

"In the stadium or in this cell?"

"Both."

Kensington strained to read the time off his watch. "I've been in captivity for three weeks but down here for about a year." He laughed. "Have you met the one they call the Inspector yet?"

Khalil shook his head.

"I only wondered because it looks like he's already played with your face."

"No. I just arrived. I haven't had the pleasure of an interrogation yet. How about you?"

"I've visited with him once or twice. For the longest time he was convinced that I was a British agent. Wanted to know who was hiding me. I'm told that if it hadn't been for my wife going directly to Baghdad, I'd be a dead man today."

"Did they beat you?"

"I must say at first I was rather roughed up. That was back when they thought I was a spy. But since my Karin convinced them I'm just an ordinary subject, they haven't laid a hand on me. I think they're afraid of roughing Western civilians up too much in case we get out."

"Apparently they don't have that same concern with Kuwaitis."

"Or Iraqis or Indians or Asians or..." Kensington stopped. He thought he heard something.

"They haven't bothered to let you go, though? Even though they have realized their mistake?"

"It may be more out of embarrassment than anything else. My guess is they don't want me going live on BBC to tell first hand tales of torture in an Iraqi prison. I imagine they are keeping me here while they try to figure out what to do with me. I'm a bit of an problem for them whether they keep me or let me go. I understand from some of my former associates that most of the Western hostages have been freed?"

"All of them."

"In time for Christmas?"

Francis nodded.

"That's nice. Nice. Then there is now nothing to keep the Allies from rolling across the sands?"

The Englishman was grasping for a thread of hope. Francis couldn't deny it to him, although he knew that an aerial bombardment would go on for some time before the 2nd Cavalry would come to anyone's rescue. "I don't think it will be long now. We should be able to expect..."

"Someone is coming." The two froze in place as a set of heavy steps plodded up the narrow hallway, stopping short of their cell by one door. Keys rattled. The unfortunate occupant stirred, then cried out for mercy. A violent struggle ensued, ending with the tell-tail sounds of a body being dragged out.

They didn't speak for 10 minutes. Finally Kensington tapped on the wall and whispered. "Did anyone see who they took?"

A hoarse voice growled back. "I think they took the Indian again."

"May God have mercy. He doesn't have a beating left in him." Kensington held his face in his hands and wept. "He was such a good chap. Such a kind man. I can't understand this. Any of this..."

"You knew him?"

"Only for these three weeks. He was in my cell when I first arrived. Strange how you can get to know someone so well and so fast when you're under the same curse."

Francis asked the Englishman how he had managed to survive. The Brit spoke for over an hour. He told of hiding at the home of his friend Amad al Bakr, of the beatings he had witnessed and the weight he had lost. He spoke of another friend, Ed Lippencott, who worked for an American insurance company and had locked nine Iraqis and their little dog in a freezer. Lippencott, it turns out, had met Kensington's wife at the airport before she left and had later somehow arranged for her to fly to Baghdad. "That man had connections. If he wasn't such a peculiar bloke, I'd swear that he worked for the CIA."

"What do you mean, 'peculiar'?"

"Odd. Funny. You know. He just wasn't your secret agent type. He was... I don't know... overweight. Overbearing. You might say he was a tad over-everything. But I honestly believe he saved my life."

"Where's Lippencott now?"

"I don't know. Maybe they got him. Maybe he got out. Maybe I'll never know."

The two talked on into the night, gleaning whatever information they could from each other. Francis told his cellmate about his capture and about the resistance fighter, *Shobash*, who had taken him into Iraq. Stewart spoke of his beloved Karin and of their children. The topic turned next to the American's family life and Fran was surprised to find himself sharing things that he had never told anyone, including himself. When sleep beckoned, neither man wanted to answer its call. Stewart was the first to drop off.

The next morning Fran awoke to the Englishman's calisthenics. "Top of the morning. 1-2-3-4. Terry Waite always used to do this... 5-6-7-8 ...to keep from going completely mad. 1-2-3-4. Routine, you know. Care to join me?"

Francis wiped the sleep from his eyes.

"...6-7-8. You think he's still alive?"

"Who?"

"Your swan-diving friend."

"Who?"

"Shobash."

"Oh. I don't know. He said he didn't swim. The water was shallow and there were a lot of rocks. I didn't see him after we hit."

"Who do you think set you up?"

"Set up? It wasn't a..." For the first instant since the fire fight on the roof Francis remembered the voice over the bull horn. The man knew their names. Both of their names. "Either some of *Shobash's* people turned on him or my own government was trying to get rid of me."

"Why would they want to kill you?"

"That's the question, isn't it." Francis was stunned numb by the possibilities. Had this hopeless mission been concocted by the CIA to get rid of him? Was there really a *"Wausau"* in trouble? Or had Francis come too close to the truth with the Glaspie business?

Footsteps echoed through the halls once again, this time coming closer and closer until they stopped in front of their own cell. A key turned the latch and the door creaked open.

"Kensington! Good news. You will be going home today. And this one," sneered a high-pitched voice from the shadows, "I believe our new arrival has an appointment. With the Inspector."

Chapter 47: The Resolution

En route to New York
January 13, 1991

"Mr. President, I think we have something here that you ought to see. Mr. President?"

The gentle drone of Air Force One and a warm cup of cocoa had conspired with the weight of the world to lull the commander in chief to the first deep sleep he'd seen in three days. Baker didn't want to wake him, but this was urgent. "Mr. President?"

The body stirred. A weary arm reached the light. "Can this wait?"

"I'm sorry sir, but I think you're going to want to see this."

"What is it?"

"The congressional resolution."

George Herbert Walker Bush put on his reading glasses, more than eager to know the final text of the resolution that would determine his place in history. Everything hinged on this one piece of paper. Everything. If the wording wasn't sufficiently vague to be interpreted as a green light, the Allied commanders would have to be put back on hold. That wouldn't do. Timing would make or break this operation. "What does it look like, Jim?" He was almost too afraid to ask. "Is this something we can live with?"

"It looks good to me," said the secretary of state. "Read for yourself."

Resolved by the Senate and House of Representatives of the United States of America in Congress assembled,

Section 1. Short title/
This joint resolution may be cited as the "Authorization for Use of Military Force Against Iraq Resolution."
Section 2. Authorization for use of United States armed forces/
(a) Authorization - The President is authorized, subject to subsection (b), to use

United States Armed Forces pursuant to United Nations Security Council Reso-
lution 678 (1990) in order to achieve implementation of Security Council Resolu-
tions 660, 661, 662, 664, 666, 667, 669, 670, 674, and 677.

(b) Requirement for determination that use of military force is necessary -
Before exercising the authority granted in subsection (a), the President shall make
available to the Speaker of the House of Representatives and the President pro
tempore of the Senate his determination that

(1) the United States has used all appropriate diplomatic and other peaceful
means to obtain compliance by Iraq with the United Nations Security Council
resolutions cited in subsection (a); and

Baker smiled at the president. "We're covered there. Our sanctions, the
slow buildup and the 'line-in-the-sand' business saw to that."

(2) that those efforts have not been and would not be successful in obtaining
such compliance.

"I imagine we'll take some heat on this one. There are more than a few
voices saying that sanctions haven't been given a chance to bite yet."

"That's subjective." Baker was confident. "A matter of interpretation.
We can argue that we are in the best position to judge."

(c) War Powers Resolution requirements.

(1) Specific statutory authorization - Consistent with section 8(a)(1) of the War
Powers Resolution, the Congress declares that this section is intended to constitute
specific statutory authorization within the meaning of section 5(b) of the War
Powers Resolution.

(2) Applicability of other requirements - Nothing in this resolution supersedes
any requirement of the War Powers Resolution.

Section 3. Reports to Congress/

At least once every 60 days, the President shall submit to the Congress a
summary on the status of efforts to obtain compliance by Iraq with the resolutions
adopted by the United Nations Security Council in response to Iraq's aggression."

"There's nothing we can't live with here." The commander in chief
smiled and handed the summary to General Powell. "What do you think?"

The Chairman of the Joint Chiefs knew what this would mean. He
answered with a restrained and somber tone. "It looks like a green light to
me, sir."

"Then," said the wartime president, folding his hands as if in prayer,
"tell Norman and his fly boys to gas up. This is it."

Chapter 48: The Bunker
Saddam's Underground Palace
January 16, 1991

"History is not kind to losers, Excellency."

The low, steady rumble of the bombardment was accentuated by an occasional flickering of the lights. Saddam sat in his cavern palace, stunned white by the fireworks in the skies half a mile above his head. He turned on CNN.

"You are a fool, Excellency."

"I am a martyr."

"Fool? Martyr? They are both dead."

The president sneered and continued to polish his silver pistol.

"No one will mourn your passing. No one. You will be drug out into the streets like Mussolini. Your carcass will rot in the sun for all to see and spit upon."

"It is not over yet."

"Yet."

"I gamble and either I win or lose. What is it to you? Either way, I go down like Saladin."

The lights flickered off with a hit directly above them and "Saladin" dove under the table for cover. He remained there as the first back-up generator kicked in.

"Saladin, Excellency? You cringe beneath the table more like Saladin's dog."

"Silence, fool."

"Saladin was known for his extraordinary tact. You are known for nothing of the sort."

"I said silence!"

"Saladin was known for his generosity and hospitality. His benevolent treatment of captives. His emotional courage."

"Was it not courage that took Kuwait?"

"Ha! To gobble up a toad? Courage? Ha!"

"Silence or you die." He aimed the pistol at his tormentor's head.

"Saladin was known for his extreme gentleness, his love for children, his chivalry to women and the weak. His total self-surrender to the sacred cause. Ha!"

"When I have rallied the Arab world..."

"Ha!"

"... from Egypt to Palestine to Arabia, then you will know and bow before me. Then we shall see who laughs!"

"You speak boldly for a man under a table. If you were a warrior, you would rise to the surface and stand in defiance. Like MacArthur. MacArthur against the Japanese at Corregidor."

Saddam rose slowly and returned to the television, switching channels restlessly and cursing the blank screen.

"They have cut out your eyes, Excellency. Your eyes and your ears. Next they will cut off the oxygen that you breathe." As if on cue, the air in the bunker grew stale and heavy. "Ah, prophesy!"

"I can outlast anything they send at me. The Germans who built this complex have assured me..."

"The Germans! Ha! The Germans are paying for the bombs above our heads as we speak!"

"I can outlast anything they send against me. It would take an atomic weapon to rut me out. And the United States wouldn't dare..."

"Fool! Have you not heard of fuel air explosives? They are the new poor man's atom bomb. They can suck the oxygen out of a mile of the city. Have you not seen..."

"They wouldn't dare."

The chandelier began to tremble above him and a fine dust filtered down. Saddam moved over to the beautiful gold-plated mirror that stretched from floor to ceiling and nervously plucked his eyebrows. His afflictor's laugh continued to echo inside his head.

"Silence!"

"Groom well, Excellency. You will wish to look handsome for your death mask!"

"Silence."

"Ah, the death mask of Saladin the Great! What a price it will bring at auction in the Baghdad bazaar!"

He whipped out his pistol and pointed it at his accuser's head. "Silence or you die!"

"Solve all with a bullet! Solve all, Excellency! That is your answer! You are a coward and you know this. Ha! You may shatter my skull, but my laugh will go on!"

"I will tolerate no such..."

"Shoot! Shoot me and see, effendi. Shoot me and hear! Ha ha ha!"
"Silence!" He didn't stop. "Silence!" He wouldn't stop. "Silence."

A shot rang out. Then five more in rapid succession. The two aides who had waited outside his door burst in. Saddam stood, holding a smoking gun in his right hand. In the other hand, he stared at the reflection in a shard of the shattered antique mirror. The lights continued to flicker. He squeezed the glass until he bled. Then he looked up, eyes glazed in confusion.
"The laugh. The laugh. It continues."
"Yes, Excellency."

There was no one else in the room.

Chapter 49: Kathryn's Shadow
Washington, D.C.
February 14, 1991

The black Cadillac parked across from school, watching her through a chain-link fence on the playground. They followed her on past the mall as she strolled with her class to the Air and Space Museum and then back. They walked through the women's department and observed as she return a Valentines Day present purchased by herself for herself. At Union Station they almost stopped her, but another woman joined Kathryn for lunch. They followed her to the headquarters of the *Washington Post*, where Kathryn stayed for almost an hour before she stormed out and bashed her purse repeatedly against the sidewalk. Then they followed her home.

She was finally alone, walking from her car to the apartment when they pulled up. Kathryn reached into her purse for the mace as a smoked glass rolled down.

"Mrs. Khalil?"

"What is it?"

"Mrs. Kathryn Khalil?"

"Yes? What do you want?"

"I believe we should talk."

"Who are you?"

"We are friends of your captain. I believe we should talk."

Chapter 50: The Briefing
The Kuwait/Saudi Border
February 25, 1991

"I know you're scared. It's good to be scared. It means you are thinking. Scared will keep you alive."

It was an ethereal, almost apocalyptic scene. The midnight sky billowed with the acrid, choking soot of 1000 oil fires. A dark crimson horizon glowed in an other-worldly light which flickered and reflected off the flapping desert camouflage. Pungent sulfur hung heavy in the air, unwashed by the biting rains. The oily drizzle rose back to the sky as steam from tanks and trucks, but clung to faces painted in dusky shades of green and black and brown. Night goggled helmets, firearms wrapped in Alligator Baggies and alien-eyed gas masks adorned the 300 men huddled around their commander. They looked more like extras in a science fiction movie than the *creme de la creme* of America's fighting force.

The general was a soldier's soldier. And on the eve of the 'mother of all battles' he was right where he belonged: standing shoulder to shoulder with the brave men and women of the 82nd Airborne who were about to turn Desert Shield into Desert Storm.

"This will be like no battle in American military experience. We've had a year to get ready for it. We've been on the ground behind the lines for months preparing, collecting data, assessing everything from soil samples to camel droppings. We know where they are, how many there are, when they eat - which isn't too often - what they eat and where they sh...". He paused as he looked square in the eye of a female correspondent sitting on the ground directly in front of him. "And where they spit."

The tension of the moment was broken and the troops let go with a relieved laugh.

"Let me stop and say one thing here. I served in Vietnam and I have an observation. I say this with a deep sense of pride at the professionalism and integrity of the American fighting soldiers on the lines: I have been aware of no terms like 'gook' or 'charlie' in this war. These are just men. Only men. Human beings. People who, for the most part, are just like you and me. Our Intelligence tells us that there is a difference, though. They don't believe in what they are doing. They don't want to fight and die for Saddam Hussein. There is no way of knowing what they'll do when they see our M1s rolling in. Preliminary reports are - we only have anecdotal evidence, let me remind you - the preliminary reports are that they will surrender in droves once you're on the move. When the Apaches appear on the horizon and these 67-ton monsters which, by the way, have a clear advantage over their T-72s, when these monsters go ahead to soften them up, we are expecting to see more white than a Kansas snowstorm. We are expecting the entire operation to take less than a week. We will be playing our game - not theirs. By our rules. With our method. Except for the Republican Guard, we can expect only limited resistance. With the Guard, we have no way of knowing. They could be a force to be reckoned with. Our carpet bombing has been chewing them up for over a month now, and we believe the bulk of them will have little desire for the fight we're about to give them."

The general knelt on one knee in the oil-soaked sand and paused for a moment. "Tonight your superiors have asked me to say a few words about combat. I can't speak in lofty or noble terms. I won't give you any illusions of grandeur or glory. Combat is unlike any hell you've faced in the training line. It is a great shock to any soldier who has never been in before. We are speaking about the face-off of 7000 tanks and 1 million men. Masses of men and materials hurled at each other in a very small area at very high speeds. It will be violent, quick and brutal. And then it will be over. This will be a massive *blitzkrieg* unlike any the world has witnessed. We have moved the largest land/sea/air force in history the longest distance in the shortest time. In the next few hours, we will be doing it again. Our goal is to smother one third of the country of Iraq with an allied blanket so thick and so quick, that Saddam will wake up in the morning completely outflanked, unable to communicate with his units and unaware of what hit him. Upon reaching the Euphrates, we will, as Colin Powell likes to say, 'cut it off and kill it.' We are hoping the element of surprise and the fact of being totally cut off and unaided will turn the trapped Iraqis to their senses and cause mass surrenders. Any pockets of major resistance will be initially bypassed, disrupted with psy-ops and given a chance to surrender. If this doesn't work we will simply starve them out.

"The first purpose will be to get the enemy out of their holes. Much of this has been done already without a shot being fired. The boycott squeezed their supplies to the limit. Until Republican Guard execution squads halted it, we were achieving our primary preliminary objective painlessly. You remember the mass surrenders earlier this winter.

"We have no question that we will prevail. We will. The only uncertainty here is 'how soon, and at what cost?' Now, I understand the greatest fear in the ranks is the use of chemical and biological agents. You're asking 'will we get slimed?' I can tell you that I honestly believe their capabilities are limited. Intelligence has been in a number of camps at every tier of their defenses and has found very little in the neighborhood of nerve agents and only a small percentage of chemical shells. Our best guess is that they are as afraid to use it as we are of receiving it. They know if they use it, the reaction will be swift and severe. I can't tell you with certainty - and we must always prepare for the worst - but I believe the use of weapons of mass destruction will be isolated and infrequent.

"Saddam's goal is clear: He wants to kill as many Americans as possible. His idea of victory is not the same as ours. He is a ruthless tyrant. He could take 100,000 casualties and still not surrender. The dictator is willing to give up Kuwait. But he wants to do it his way. If he has to turn 300,000 teenagers and old men into cannon fodder, he'll do it. If half a million families lose their sons and a country has to starve to give America a bloody nose, he'll do it. Like Nasser, he believes he can lose and still win. Not only does he win if he wins. But in many Arab eyes, if he loses and still stands he also wins. We are not going to let him do this. I repeat, we are not going to let him do this. We will stop short of nothing less than the end of the reign of terror that is Saddam Hussein."

A sudden cheer shattered the silent, unholy night and was itself silenced.

"Tonight you join the ranks of the most honored and noble club in the world: the American combat veteran. You go to meet history. May God have mercy and give us a just victory, followed by a just peace."

With that, "Stormin' Norman" stepped into his Bradley and drove off. And there for a moment, except for the light tapping of the rain, the whole world stood strangely still. The men and women of the 82nd watched tail lights fade and disappear into the night. Not so much as a word was spoken audibly. But deep within many a hard-headed leatherneck there echoed a silent prayer.

Finally, a young colonel nodded and his sergeant barked out the order: "Load 'em up and move 'em out!"

This was not a drill.

Chapter 51: *Inshallah*
Washington, Kuwait, Cairo & Riyadh
February 25, 1991

Kathryn watched the eastern sky as the first sliver of a brilliant sunrise ellipsed the horizon. A crystal-clean drizzle trickled and tickled her face and neck, kissing the Washington morning to heighten its colors. She stepped into the bathroom to wash her tear-stained eyes. The moment the water was running she heard a voice. Whether in a dream or a vision it came to her as clearly as if someone was calling her name. She paused and glanced up to the mirror. At that moment she knew Francis was coming home. She knew.

Salaam al Bakr watched as the black sinister cloud engulfed the desert sky, rolling over him from the north. A poison rain was squeezed from the skies and began to fall, stinging eyes and hands, covering the bleak country-side in a mask of death. He dug frantically into his knapsack and pulled out the only clean cloth he could find to cover his oil-stained face. Suddenly, whether in a dream or a vision, he heard his name summoned. Peering out at first, then slumping back into the bunker, he knew what it meant. She was coming for him. And at that moment he knew he was going to die. He knew.

The shimmering colors danced and whirled, bathing a glittered ceiling and polished floor in an electric glow. A deep bass reverberation pounded through Nadia's body, penetrating her very soul. Sweat trickled down a glistening brow and beaded upon her seething chest. Nadia pushed franti-cally though the crowds, ignoring the danger as she searched for a familiar face. Bahrah and his friends had run off with some cheap Egyptian whores and left her alone to face the wolves that prowled the night. How she hated him for what he had done to her! She could feel the predatory glances as she tried to suppress a creeping terror. She could read an evil intent in the coal-black eyes as they leered in at her. Nadia knew they were watching, waiting. She knew that they knew she was alone. With her back to the pulsating wall, the broken young woman prayed to disappear from the universe.

Ghastly lights flashed and spun, covering the frightened sky and grimy bunker in an eerie glow. A low, ominous rumble slammed through Salaam's soul, advancing ever louder, ever closer until it became one with his own heartbeat. Sweat like great drops of blood ran from his every pore down to the blackened earth below. He darted madly from bunker to bunker, oblivious to the mines, searching for one hole that might house a friend to die with him. But not so much as a breath remained. They had all deserted their posts or been stolen away by the demons of the night. Only he now survived to die these thousand deaths alone. Salaam felt enemy eyes crawl over him at every turn, with every step. He could see his own figure in their night sights. Fear clung to him closer than his own stench. Diving low into his grave hole to pray for mercy, he forced his back up against the cement and broke into a hideous laughter. Perhaps he was dead already and this was his hell. He prayed to disappear from the universe.

The Emir sat in Riyadh drinking his blood-red wine, picking at the $700 an ounce caviar and waiting for news. If reports were true and the bastards had, indeed, torched every well in his sheikdom, this whole ordeal would set him back months. It could take weeks to put all those fires out and return to pre-war production. The strain of this news combined with a growing *angst* over 30,000 signatures which now called out for a new parliament. Together they conspired to produce a massive and oppressive headache which the ruler feared he might never outrun. He slid into the steaming bath and laid his head against the white marble, hoping it would all fade away. By the next morning things would be more clear. He'd have to wait until then. The young girl was led in to him and he purposefully dropped the bar of soap between his legs, thinking that the amusement of this new wife might be enough to help him forget. He called her name. She held back at first, but then accepted the honor. He extended his palm and slowly, cautiously she reached to touch his hot hand. He whispered the word: "*Inshallah.*" God willing. She spoke it back and closed her eyes for the night.

Salaam squatted in his bunker drinking the brackish water from the floor, picking at the bones of a small snake and waiting for the end. If reports were true and the bastards had, indeed, torched every well in his country, the whole ordeal would be over in hours. It would take only minutes for the Americans to overrun his position and either capture him or send him to eternity. The strain of the fear multiplied his difficulty in breathing the acrid air and produced a massive headache which Salaam feared he might never escape. He slid down into the cold mud and laid his face against the concrete, hoping all would soon fade away. The boy was not the least surprised when she stood in the doorway calling out his name. He recoiled at first, but slowly accepted it. She extended a pale palm. Slowly he reached to touch her cold hand. She whispered the word: "*Inshallah.*" God willing. He whispered it back and closed his eyes forever.

Chapter 52: Sudden Death
National Athletic Stadium, Kuwait City
Feb. 25, 1991

"I understand that you're holding one of my operatives."

"And which one is that?"

"The American. He's a double agent and I want him now."

A rapid burst of gunfire in the courtyard below betrayed the sinister fate of those who were being held. Something was happening in the stadium that wasn't in the plan. Iraqi soldiers and a squad of partisans were staging mass trials and immediate executions. Prisoners who had no special status were being hauled from the cells and showers in chains to be read their death sentences. In the quarters of what was once the stadium manager, soldiers were melting identification cards on a gas stove and burning files by the shovelful.

"I'm sorry, but no one but the Inspector can authorize the release of a prisoner."

The stranger pulled out a wad of *dinars* and waved them in front of the desk clerk's nose. The man scowled up at the intruder as if insulted, then snatched the money out of his hand and stuffed it into his own shirt. He walked back to the file as something sounding like a mortar shell exploded in the center of the stadium field. The concussion shook the lights and rattled the pictures on the walls. The visitor hit the floor, but workers in the room continued with their paper party as if nothing unusual was going on.

"Are we being shelled?" he asked the clerk as he rose cautiously from the floor.

"No. We are running out of bullets. But we have plenty of explosives."

The uninvited guest looked down to the field in horror. Forty or fifty Kuwaitis were lying in a smoldering heap of blood and bone near the west entrance. Another group of more than double that size was now being shoved down onto the grass from the stands. At the east goal soldiers were removing what looked like crates of dynamite from a canvas backed truck and walking toward the cleared center line.

"I'm sorry," said the clerk, "but I'm afraid that the American's section is being cleared out at this very minute."

"We've got to get there."

"Impossible. We are too late."

The stranger shagged a white leather pouch from under his cloak and threw it at the man. The clerk glanced inside and quickly changed his mind. "But if we hurry, we might be able to catch them before they're through."

They hustled past a back door and down an iron staircase into the boiler room. Opening a metal door to what looked like a utility closet, the Iraqi handed his guest a white cloth. He questioned the clerk with his eyes, but moments later understood all too well what the cloth was for. The stench hit them like a slap to the face the moment they entered the tunnel. Human excrement and curdled blood mixed with hair matted the walls and floor to make their fast walk treacherous. Chains dangled from rusted pipes all along the ceiling where they walked. They made their way in through the dim light, stepping over electric battery chargers, jumper cables and cattle prods before coming to another door. This one opened into a steaming locker room. Three near-corpses tied to wooden chairs lay numb and lifeless on the floor beneath the scalding waters of the first shower chamber. At the sound of the door, one of the bodies twitched and turned toward them. The stranger recoiled at the grotesque, melted face which stared at him with no eyes and smelled his entrance with no nose.

They passed a second shower. A shirtless Iraqi soldier, startled by the intruders, shoved a naked woman against the wall and scrambled for his glasses to see who had approached. She fell to the floor and grabbed for her paisley dress.

Muffled shots rang out from another room. They passed an office where soldiers were sorting through cabinets of drugs and loading choice prizes into a black United Airlines duffle bag. The shots grew clearer. Entering the next hallway, the clerk shouted an order. Two guards were moving down the corridor from room to room with handguns, anxious to finish their "trials" quickly. They had made it to all but six of the 20 cells when interrupted.

"The American! Where is the American!" demanded the intruder. He ran desperately past the executioners from door to open door, pausing in each to study the broken faces for one he knew. On the floor in the second to last room, a twisted spectral shell of a man lay in a pool of arterial blood. The searcher held the stranger's battered head up but could not see his friend. He stepped toward the door, then paused and returned to look again. There was something about those eyes.

"Khalil?"

The man didn't answer.

The Russian listened to his comrade's erratic heartbeat, then studied the face once again. His battered eyes and ears were all but swollen shut. Scabs from cigarette burns circled his neck and chest and his upper leg was seeping from a bullet that had meant to kill him. The stranger tore off his own shirt and tied a tourniquet above the wound to squeeze off the crimson river. Slowly the man lifted his own head and exhaled out a single word.

"Breakfast."

"Khalil?" Vladimir Kalinov squeezed his friend's hand gently and lowered his ear to meet the pallid lips.

"Breakfast. You owe me for breakfast."

Chapter 53: Lunch at "The Monocle"
A Chic Washington Bar
March 6, 1991

"We went halfway around the world to do what is moral and just and right. We fought hard, and - with others - we won the war. We lifted the yoke of oppression and tyranny from a small country that many Americans had never heard of, and we ask nothing in return."

-President George Bush

Two men were sitting at the table behind him, drinking martinis like they were going out of style and arguing just loud enough for the Marine to hear. Francis thought he recognized the younger man's voice.

The elder, who did most of the talking, was from Senator Sam Nunn's staff: "We spend billions of dollars a year to give our president the best intelligence data of any leader in the world, and what does he do with it? He glances at it as if it were the *National Enquirer* and then makes his decisions on whim and the advice of a handful of non-elected image consultants and political advisers. Look at this: 149 Americans dead; 240 wounded; Hundreds of Allies killed; 75,000 - 100,000 Iraqis blown away. Maybe more. We'll never know. And all for what? Saddam Hussein is still in power."

"How about the principle of democracy?"

"Oh, please. Don't break my heart. This whole thing was about the price of oil. We did the same thing with Noriega. We destroy a country's economy and firebomb a barrio killing 200 innocent civilians just to nab one crook and let him sit it out in a comfortable American prison."

"You seem to forget that in both cases we freed an oppressed people from a dictator. That's what America is all about."

"The Sabahs are back on the throne in Kuwait. Our CBs are installing his a marble bathtub even as we speak, for God sakes."

"Free elections are in the works for..."

"You know as well as I do: free elections are about as likely in Kuwait as they are in Iraq right now. What are we paying our intelligence services for if they can't nab one tin-horn dictator without having to blast an entire country back into the Stone Age? At least in Panama we got our man. Here we're throwing a parade and declaring victory while Saddam sits in his bunker laughing in our face! Talk about unfinished business! A year from now, two years from now he'll be built back up and we'll have to find some excuse to go in there and do it all over again! You wait and see. This isn't over. Not by a long shot."

"Don't you think that it was all worth it just to restore America's faith is us? You saw the ticker-tape. The crowds. Made me proud to be an..."

"We're talking about 100,000 deaths here!"

The bartender who had just poured the men a fifth drink took it back.

"If that was the price of flushing the 'Vietnam Syndrome' from America's collective conscience forever, then so be it! I'd say it was damn worth it."

A twinge of anger ignited the slow fuse that was now spreading up Fran's back. He spun around and caught the man's eye. Francis recognized him from a Pentagon brass party he had attended a year ago. The soldier's eyes riveted on the man's black Italian leather shoes. He had seen these shoes before from beneath a Pentagon bathroom stall.

"And the defense budget. If we hadn't had this victory your damn Democrats would have hacked it all to hell. And the economy! Ten percent of the American economy is built on defense contracts. More than that. Without a war every decade or so to clean out the inventories, we're bound for recession or even worse. Kind of an armory enema!" He started to laugh.

"We're talking about 100,000 Iraqi lives!"

"We're also talking American jobs..."

"100,000 human beings!"

The human volcano couldn't hold back much longer.

"100,000 lives!"

"What does America care about a bunch of dead sand niggers?"

A split second later the polished gold of a U.S. Marine Corps ring and the iron fist behind it was rapidly deployed to a mouth full of bigot teeth. Khalil dropped a $20 on the bar and nodded to the bartender. "Tell him the drink's on me... a veteran."

The Vietnam Memorial glistened as a light rain began to fall. Golden names on black granite cried silently out to be read and remembered. A small Asian man was making charcoal rubbings, undaunted by the drizzle. Fran's eyes were drawn down the familiar path to a spot on the far end at eye level. Tonight he could see his own reflection even more clearly as it slid across the wet stone to stop at his brother's name. It was a world away and a different war. He remembered how Joseph was itching to graduate West Point before the conflict ended. His older brother got his wish. His last wish.

"I thought I might find you here."

Francis spun quickly to peer into the dark green eyes of an unknown woman.

"Oh, excuse me. I..." she paused, searching his face. "I'm sorry. I thought... I thought you were someone else."

"That's all right," said the soldier. "So did I."

The woman glanced at the wall. "I've never seen this before. It's quite impressive."

Francis nodded, but didn't answer. He wanted to tell her about Joseph. He wanted to tell her about *Shobash* and Adanon and Kathryn and a baby not yet conceived. He wanted to talk of war and hell and victims and decisions made by the few and paid by the many. But he could say nothing. The words wouldn't move beyond his throat.

Unwrapping a clear plastic bundle in his hands, Francis knelt and laid his sacred offering of fresh flowers gently against the stone altar. The phrase "Everyone is a victim," rolled over and over in his mind. He couldn't remember where he had heard it or seen it written, but it stuck.

A few moments passed before Francis could bring himself to speak. He looked up, but the woman was already gone. "Only 10 seconds," he thought out loud. The woman had passed by all those names in 10 seconds. Each was a heartache. Each a tragedy. Each was somebody's son, someone's father, brother, lover. But the whole sorry lot of them got only 10 seconds from this woman. That's all the war was worth. That was all their lives were worth.

Francis read the names and in one mystic moment felt the senseless pain of the entire wall reaching out to him. A voice spoke: "These did not ask to be here. They did not choose to be here. Someone else made that decision for them." It was *Shobash* , or his ghost, whispering in the Marine's ear. "Who is the victim? Who is the slayer? Speak." He was now quoting Sophocles. "We are simply pawns in their game; disposables to be used and discarded when no longer needed. Yes, we are all hostages, my friend. The ones who kill and the ones who are killed - all victims. I am. And so are you."

"It's not resolved!" Francis screamed to the silent night and its sacred wall.

"Resolved? Resolved?" The *jinna's* laugh now echoed through the emptiness within. "You think in war anything is resolved?" He laughed again. "What is it that you seek?"

Fran looked up. This time *Shobash* was not alone. An old Bedouin stood by his side. "What do you..."

"I do not know!"

"What do you seek?"

"I told you, I don't know. Peace." Francis was as surprised by his own words as he was of the ghost's.

"You wish peace? Join me, my friend. Join me, Lui Chi."

"Peace." Lui Chi was the name this *jinna* philosopher of lonliness called himself. The sinister voice now betrayed its intent and transformed *Shobash* and his old friend into two black smudges swirling up against the colors behind Fran's closed eyes. He couldn't listen. He wouldn't listen. Not tonight. "Go. Leave me alone."

"Alone? Ah, alone. As you wish. But know this: I wait for you. Like a pair of blinding headlights in the driving rain, I wait. I wait. And you will one day join me. One day, Lui Chi, alone with your beating heart."

The heady scent of cherry blossoms and a familiar dampness ate into his bones and called the soldier from a trance. He glanced at his watch, surprised that 20 minutes had passed in an instant. He must have fallen asleep. Standing to shake the cold stiffness out of his swollen leg, Francis retrieved the crutch and hobbled off.

He thought of taking the train to Arlington. Those rows of white stone always seemed to calm him and clear his head. He thought of going back to Kathryn. But he didn't know if he could. There was so much to say that Fran could never say. And how do you go back to a place you've never been? No, he couldn't go back. Not yet.

He thought of calling the major. The Old Man was one who would listen, even if he wouldn't understand. Fran pondered and wandered, and finally turned instead to the home of another friendly old mentor.

Mr. Lincoln spoke with him often as he read the walls. The wartime president always seemed to have the right words to say to his young friend. This night it was a line from the Gettysburg Address: *"We cannot dedicate, we cannot consecrate, we cannot hallow this ground. The brave men, the living and the dead... the living and the dead..."*

A gray trail of jet exhaust turned to indigo, then to black as the last traces of sunlight melted into the western horizon. The phantom line in the sky cut a perpendicular course across the Washington Monument. If you stretched your imagination, you could almost make out the figure of a man on the fading crimson clouds behind the cross. Francis sat on the steps of the Lincoln Memorial watching the receding pageant, trying to make sense of it all. He sighed.

"Everyone is a hostage, my friend," whispered *Shobash*. "Everyone..."

And for possibly the last time in his life, a young Marine cried.

Chapter 54: Cleveland
A Washington, D.C. Classroom
March 11, 1991

Kathryn asked the little girl in the front row to answer the knock at the classroom door. The third grader walked past a green chalkboard with its ABCs and construction paper Easter Bunnies smiling to the world. She didn't bother to look up until the young messenger had returned and placed the envelope on her desk. She opened it without removing eyes from her reading. A pair of airline passes fell out.

The knock came a second time. The girl returned from the door with another small envelope. On the top left corner, scrawled in red pen, were the words: "V. Kalinov. Hope you enjoy!" Kathryn tore the folder open and found herself holding two tickets to the Russian ballet. She began to tremble.

A third knock pounded through the room and into her soul. The child was held in place with a single motion of her teacher's hand. Kathryn took two steps and stopped. Both breath and blood froze in her chest as the door slid open. On the other side, silhouetted in the dark hall light, was the figure of a man leaning on a crutch. It was a soldier. Her soldier. His face was battered but his eyes were still magic.

"You... you want to..."

"Yes."

"... want to go watch a bunch of communists jump around in tights?"

"Yes."

"With me?"

"Yes." She bit her quivering lip.

"In Cleveland?"

Kathryn nodded and wiped a tear from her eye.

"And maybe make a baby?"

The crutch fell away. In three steps the answer was in his arms.

EPILOGUE: Victory's Crown
The Last Day of the Gulf War
November 4, 1992

"Did you bring him his paper?"
"Yes."
"And what did he say?"
"He said 'thank you.'"
"And his coffee and pastries?"
"Yes."
"And what did he do?"
"He said 'that will be all.' No. No, he said, 'thank you, that will be all.'"
"And then?"
"He read the headline and put the paper down."
"That's all?"
"Yes."
"And now? What is he doing now? Can you see?"
"I can't tell."
"Is he moving?"
"No."
"Is he happy? Angry?"
"I don't know."
"Did you..."
"Wait! He's picking up the paper again."
The aide squinted cautiously into the darkness of the silent space as a small shaft of light crept through a crack in the curtain and settled like victory's crown upon the leader's wrinkled forehead.
"And what? What is he doing now?"

"Smiling. Simply smiling."